JANE TOOMBS

◆

DEAD SILENT

Complete and Unabridged

ULVERSCROFT
Leicester

First published in the
United States of America

First Large Print Edition
published 2005

British Library CIP Data

Toombs, Jane
    Dead silent.—Large print ed.—
    Ulverscroft large print series: mystery
    1. Detective and mystery stories
    2. Large type books
    I. Title
    813.5′4 [F]

    ISBN 1–84395–815–5

Published by
F. A. Thorpe (Publishing)
Anstey, Leicestershire

Set by Words & Graphics Ltd.
Anstey, Leicestershire
Printed and bound in Great Britain by
T. J. International Ltd., Padstow, Cornwall

This book is printed on acid-free paper

Jane Toombs was born in California, raised in Michigan's Upper Peninsula and now lives in the Hudson River Highlands of New York. In addition to historical romances, she writes gothics. Her father was an author, as is her husband.

When not writing, Jane runs the Cornwall Friends of the Library Attic Bookstore, reads, knits, solves acrostic puzzles, plays bridge and tries to avoid housework.

DEAD SILENT

Driving with her young daughter to El Doblez, California, Dr. Helena Moore was looking forward to starting her new job, working with her stepsister Fran at Harper Hills Hospital. But when she arrived at Fran's home, she found her lifeless body ... The police ruled it an accidental death, but Helena was convinced that Fran had been murdered. Ignoring warnings not to make any waves, she began turning over the long-undisturbed stones at Harper Hills, never realizing that the venomous secrets she would unearth could prove deadly — because in the shadows of the hospital's too-quiet corridors a murderer was now waiting patiently for Helena ...

Books by Jane Toombs
Published by The House of Ulverscroft:

HARTE'S GOLD
NIGHTINGALE MAN
AND THEN CAME THE DARKNESS

1

Helena Moore licked her cracked lips as she angled the wind-wing of the old squareback VW so the desert wind no longer rushed past her face. Just her luck to have to drive the last two hundred miles with a Santa Ana blowing. She could blame her discomfort on Roger — he was the one who wound up with the air-conditioned Porsche — but that was too easy. After all, she could have fought for the Porsche.

Glancing at Laura in the back seat, she saw the child was sleeping. Or was she? With Laura you were never quite certain. Roger had been willing enough to give *her* up. Permanently. Helena had full custody of their daughter.

Her mother had never taken to Roger. 'There's nothing terribly *wrong* with him, dear,' she'd said when Helena had first told her they planned to marry. 'The problem is that I sense he's not your other half. We all do *have* another half somewhere on this earth, you know.'

Helena had never accepted any of her mother's peculiar beliefs and, even if she'd put any credence in the 'other half' business, her mother's record of three failed marriages would be enough to convince her that other halves were mighty hard to find. In a way, though, her mother had been right. Roger had proved to be a lousy choice.

To Helena's right the sun inched toward the Pacific. Even the blue-green water didn't look cool. El Doblez, she read, next three exits. She shifted to the right lane and slowed, watching for Seasand exit, saw it, and turned off the freeway. The streets were clogged with going-home traffic so she crept along, feeling sweat trickle between her breasts as she searched for Plumeria Drive.

As soon as the car slowed, Laura began a high-pitched croon. In the rear-view mirror, Helena saw her daughter had turned over to face the back, her dark hair blowing in the breeze from the open front windows. One of Laura's hands stroked the plastic seat back. Back and forth, back and forth.

Does she feel the heat like I do, Helena wondered. What does she feel? How can my own four-year-old daughter be such a stranger?

The setting sun gleamed off a large white pyramid-shaped building on a hill ahead. A sign thrusting above the peak of the pyramid proclaimed XENARA in glittering blue letters. What can that be, Helena wondered. A restaurant? A health club? It looked more like a temple than anything else.

Her speculations ended when a red Corvette cut in front of her to the left-turn lane. She swerved, almost grazing the Honda next to her, and missed the turn onto Plumeria. Now she'd have to circle the block and go back. All because of that damn pyramid. If she believed in omens — and she didn't — seeing the pyramid would be chalked up as a bad one.

She finally parked the VW in front of a salmon-pink, two-story, quasi-Spanish building with immaculate landscaping. A sign saying DE LA MAR decorated the wrought iron entrance gate. How could Fran afford to live in such an expensive apartment complex on her nurse's salary? Helena doubted she'd be able to manage anything like this on what Harper Hills Hospital had agreed to pay her as a pediatric resident. Even with the professional discount, Laura's fees at Sea Mist Manor would be astronomical. And she had no choice but to put Laura in Sea Mist.

Helena opened the car door, unstuck herself from the plastic seat, and got out. She reached into the back for Laura and set her on her feet on the sidewalk, hoping for the best.

'We're at Aunt Fran's, Laura,' she said, expecting no response. Her daughter rarely said anything and it was often impossible to tell whether or not she even understood.

Sometimes Laura would walk and sometimes not. Helena sighed with relief when, despite the long, hot ride from Bakersfield, Laura stayed upright instead of crumpling limply onto the ground. She gripped her daughter's arm — the girl refused to hold anyone's hand — and led her toward the entrance.

Apartment 22 was up an outer stairway and to the left. Passing by windows with ornamental protective grills, Helena rang the bell, waited, rang again. Peering through the broad leaves and snake-like orange and purple blossom heads of a giant bird-of-paradise, she caught a glimpse of the ocean. Could her sister have gone out? Helena banged on the door.

Damn it, Fran knew I was coming, she thought. Fran begged me to stay here with her — so where the hell is she?

Helena shook the knob in frustration. To her surprise it turned and the door opened. Cool air tinged with a hint of honeysuckle greeted her like a blessing. As she stepped into the apartment, she heard water running. Not very bright of Fran to take a shower with

4

the door unlocked.

Leading Laura across the carpeting, she sat her down on the floor with a wall on one side and the blue plush velvet couch on the other. Laura hated to sit on furniture and she was afraid to be in the middle of the room with nothing to touch. She'd like the feel of the velvet under her fingers.

'I'm here, Fran!' Helena called down the short hall leading off the living room.

She glanced at Laura. Her daughter seemed content; she might as well unload the car while she was still sticky from the drive and shower when she got through.

Helena made three trips to the car, carefully closing the apartment door each time so Laura wouldn't take it in her head to wander off. On her final trip she passed a red-haired youth coming down the steps. He ducked his head away from her and she half-smiled, remembering how she hated to look at strangers when she was his age.

She pushed open the door to bring in the last suitcase, automatically checking for Laura as she did. Panic flared in her chest when she saw her daughter wasn't where she'd left her. Where had she gone? Had Laura somehow managed to open the door? She sighed in relief when she realized the water was no longer running. Of course. Fran had come out of the shower, seen the mound of luggage, and found Laura.

'Fran?' she called, looking around the apartment. They weren't anywhere in sight. Fran had probably brought Laura into the bedroom while she dressed.

'I've finally got all our junk up those steps,' Helena said as she walked along the short hallway. 'Where do you want it stowed, Fran?'

No one answered. Helena looked in through the first open door and saw a bedroom decorated in shades of blue, with a few stuffed animals on the bed. She decided this was the guest bedroom she and Laura would share — it was far too neat to be Fran's. She passed a bathroom, complete with tub, and at the end of the hall came to another bedroom — this one done in pink and white — with more of her sister's stuffed animals scattered on the bed and a strong smell of Fran's favorite honeysuckle scent. A door inside the room stood slightly ajar and Helena could see it led to a second bathroom.

'Fran?' she called, louder. 'Where are you?'

Still no answer.

A high-pitched croon reached her ears. Laura. Unlike Fran to put her on the potty but maybe Laura had gotten up and walked into the bathroom on her own. She did that sometimes when she had to use the toilet.

Fran might have remembered that if no one helped Laura she was likely to stand beside the toilet and wet herself.

Helena pushed open the bathroom door and looked in. She saw Laura first, sitting on the floor, crooning her meaningless song while her hand stroked back and forth.

Helena stopped breathing, grasping the door for support as she realized what Laura was doing. 'Oh my God!' she cried, unable to move for unmeasurable moments.

Fran lay naked on the floor beside the child, her pale blue eyes open in the fixed, glassy stare of death. Blood glistened wetly on the tiles, matting Fran's brown hair — hair that Laura's tiny fingers constantly stroked.

2

Harris Maklin took a deep breath and let it out slowly. She's upset, he reminded himself. With reason. Headquarters was checking on whether Ms. Helena Moore — correction, Dr. Moore — had actually driven down from Bakersfield today as she claimed but he had little doubt her story was true.

Helena's eyes flared with anger as she looked up at him. 'Why don't you do something instead of just standing there scowling?' she demanded. 'I pointed out the burnt matches in the living room and told you my sister doesn't smoke, I mentioned the red-haired man on the stairs — but you don't seem at all interested. Fran's fall didn't kill her, she was murdered!' Helena's voice broke on the last word.

'Sergeant Smith and Lieutenant Garcia don't need instructions from me,' he said carefully, 'and it's homicide's policy to draw no conclusions about the cause of death until all the facts are in. A post mortem will be done and, as you know, doctor' — he stressed the word slightly — 'the results of the post should tell us what we need to know. Until

8

then . . . ' He shrugged.

What color are her eyes, Mak asked himself as he watched her clench and unclench her fists. Stan Smith must have put blue on the report but they weren't really, they were the color of the ocean, not quite blue, not quite green. Black hair, twenty-eight years old, five feet two inches, weight around one hundred pounds — the description was accurate enough but it didn't add up to the woman in front of him.

He wouldn't call her pretty — her mouth was a touch too wide, her cheekbones too high. But attractive, yes, he found her damned attractive with her small breasts under her tee shirt thrusting belligerently at him and her worn jeans emphasizing the curve of her hips. She sure as hell didn't look like any doctor he knew.

He's got to be one of the homeliest men I've ever seen, Helena thought, glaring at him. A real Abe Lincoln clone — except for those cold blue eyes. He probably grew the beard to play up the resemblance to Honest Abe. Her upper lip curved scornfully.

'Aren't you going to investigate while you wait for the post?' she asked, thrusting away the knowledge that it was Fran she was talking about, Fran's body they'd be cutting open. She couldn't afford to go to pieces.

'Dr. Moore,' he said, 'you saw the technicians in here earlier. Deaths from no known cause are always investigated, as I'm sure Lieutenant Garcia has told you. He's the one handling the case.'

She brushed the lieutenant away with a flick of her fingers. She'd heard the others call him Captain Maklin, but she'd have known he was the head honcho without that clue. Anyone with a single brain cell working could see this Abe Lincoln replica was born to command. So why did he persist in letting the others do everything? He hadn't given a single order since he arrived.

'I don't need the post to tell me Fran didn't die from a fall,' she said firmly, surprised that her voice wasn't as quivery as her stomach felt. 'The blood was from a superficial scalp laceration but she didn't bleed long — she must have been dying when she fell. What about the place I showed you — *and* Lieutenant Garcia — on her thigh? I'm positive she was given an injection there. Where's the syringe and needle? You didn't find it in the apartment. Someone took it away; the person who killed Fran. Captain Maklin, can't you understand?'

'Mak,' he muttered. 'Just plain Mak.'

Why on earth would a policeman expect her to call him Mak?

10

'And you shouldn't have touched the body, doctor,' he added.

'I *found* clues for you.' Helena's voice rose. 'Why won't you listen? Why won't you *do* something? Don't you believe me?'

Mak spread his hands. 'It's not a question of belief. The police go by the reports of their own doctors. You'll have to admit that's a reasonable precaution.'

She ignored that, intent on forcing him to pay attention to what she'd found. 'What about that pyramid of burnt matches on the coffee table in the living room? Fran wasn't given to playing with matches and I told you she wasn't a smoker. Laura couldn't have done it — she's afraid of fire. How about the water in the shower being shut off? Who did that?'

'You admitted it isn't beyond your daughter's abilities to turn off the shower.'

'Not beyond her ability, that's right, but beyond probability. I know Laura didn't touch that tap. What about fingerprints? Won't they show she didn't? You certainly can't believe Fran shut off the water — she was dead before I ever got to El Doblez, much less into the apartment.'

'I'm not deciding anything,' Mak said. 'Lieutenant Garcia — '

'I'm talking to *you*, not the lieutenant!'

He touched her shoulder gently but she jerked away, not wanting comfort from him.

Mak knew Phil Garcia suspected the deceased had probably accidentally ODed on heroin. Relatives usually were the last to know when someone was on the hard stuff. He might be figuring the same as Phil if it hadn't been for what he knew about Franchon York. Suicide couldn't be ruled out. Nor murder.

Too bad the kid had to be the one to find her aunt like that. Enough to give the kid nightmares for weeks, even if she was odd. Cute little thing — had the same cloud of dark hair and the same sea-colored eyes as her mother.

Seeing that Phil and Stan were getting ready to call it quits, Mak laid a firm hand on Helena's shoulder.

'Make sure the door's locked after we leave,' he ordered.

Her blue-green eyes flashed at him. 'You don't have to tell me to be careful. I *know* Fran was murdered.'

★　★　★

After they'd gone, Helena persuaded Laura to eat a banana — the girl refused anything else — and put her to bed in the blue room.

12

Up until then Helena had been able to hold back her grief by concentrating on immediate tasks.

Standing in the doorway of the blue room, she looked down the hall toward the room that had been Fran's, knowing she couldn't face going inside it again, not tonight, maybe not ever. The faint but pervasive scent of Fran's honeysuckle cologne brought tears to her eyes. They'd never been really close, she and her half-sister. Yet, in a way, they understood one another better than anybody else every could. Possibly because they'd been forced to band together as children against a mother who constantly bombarded them with her frightening psychic insights.

Fran was the only person who truly accepted Laura and loved the child for herself. Fran's calls during the bad time of Helena's divorce from Roger, even though she hadn't said much more than 'Hang in there,' helped more than Helena had ever told her.

And now it was too late ever to tell Fran anything again.

I can't let myself cry, Helena thought. I'll break down completely if I do and that's no good. Laura needs me to be calm and coping — I'm all she's got. Besides, I need to stay alert. After all, I'm staying in Fran's apartment and Fran was murdered.

The thought of murder made the hair on her neck prickle. She glanced around involuntarily, then shook her head in annoyance. She would *not* allow herself to be frightened.

★ ★ ★

Two days later, as Helena drove through El Doblez to the hospital, she decided the town was typical of the beach communities between LA and San Diego with the haves in mansions nestled in the hills and the have-nots in sub-standard housing in the older, going-to-seed downtown section. Then there's the rest of us, she thought wryly, the sort-ofs, living in between.

She pulled into the doctors' parking area at Harper Hills Hospital, got out, and stood for a moment staring up at it; she noted what must be a new addition, a glass and concrete outcropping rising five stories into a cloudless sky. The building looked functional enough, though the addition seemed haphazardly attached to the Spanish-tiled older unit, also five stories, that sprawled picturesquely over neatly landscaped grounds. The new unit rather reminded her of a random tumor growth.

As she walked toward the main entrance, Helena recalled from the brochure they'd sent her that the new unit had expanded the original 275 beds to 350. Harper Hills, she'd seen from their map, resembled the layout of most hospitals with the business offices, the emergency room, the cafeteria, and the auxiliary services such as labs, pharmacy, and X-ray on the first floor in the old building. The fancier diagnostic equipment such as the CAT scanner and MRI were on the ground floor of the new unit. The patient beds, as well as the operating room, occupied the other four floors of both units.

When she'd phoned the Chief of Staff. Dr. Tyrone Rand, he'd been courteous but curt. She knew Dr. Rand was a neurosurgeon and he sounded typical of the breed, saying he was sorry to hear about her sister, telling her she needn't report in as scheduled if she didn't feel up to it, the unspoken message coming through clearly: *I expect you here, doctor. On time. Ready and able to work.*

Helena took a deep breath. She'd made the arrangements for the cremation to be done whenever the police saw fit to release Fran's body. Her mother and stepfather hadn't yet arrived in Peru and, though she'd left a message at the Lima Hilton, she had no idea when they'd reach the hotel.

Her mother was touring the Peruvian ruins to absorb color for her next beings-from-outer-space-have-visited-us-in-the-past book. Helena exhaled with a snort. How could intelligent people believe such ridiculous nonsense?

Neither her mother nor her stepfather would hear about Fran's death for at least a week, possibly longer if they didn't call the hotel for messages. Whatever she arranged for Fran in the meantime wouldn't suit her mother; it seemed nothing Helena did had ever suited her mother. Their most recent argument had been about putting Laura in Sea Mist Manor.

What else could she do? Laura tried the patience of all the caretakers Helena had ever hired — not one had stayed longer than a week. Sea Mist was a well-run facility for disturbed and retarded children. Roger had recommended it. No matter how disinterested he was in Laura, he'd hardly place his daughter in some shoddy vegetable bin.

When she'd left Laura at Sea Mist that morning, Helena had been favorably impressed by the cleanliness of the children and the facility. In any case, there was no choice. She had to work and Laura needed constant care, but it bothered her to turn her daughter over to strangers. She wished with all her heart she could find a way to be with Laura but, unfortunately, there was no such immediate possibility.

Helena shook her head, shifted her grip on her black medical bag, and started toward the entrance to Harper Hills.

'Dr. George Wittenburg, please,' she said to the receptionist in the lobby.

'Dr. Wittenburg's office is on the third floor in the new wing,' the woman told her. 'That's Three North, the pediatric unit. Follow the yellow arrows to the elevators.'

Helena breathed in the familiar hospital odor, a blending of antiseptics and food, slightly tinged with something she had never quite put a name to. The elusive scent of illness? The smell made her relax a little as the elevator doors closed her in with two pink-coated volunteers and a green-garbed scrub nurse.

As she got off on the third floor, she ran a quick hand over the dark hair curling casually onto her shoulders and wondered briefly if she should have pulled her hair atop her head into a knot. First impressions, after all . . .

No, damn it, she'd discarded pretense during her last year in med school at the same time she'd pruned away a number of misconceptions Roger had grafted onto her mind. Why drag rejects back in? She was

Helena Moore, M.D. — take her or leave her.

Checking the signs, she saw that a blue arrow indicated Three North. She remembered Fran telling her on the phone that the newborn nursery where she'd worked was on Three West — in the old building. Maybe she'd have a chance later today to go over there and talk to the nurses who worked with Fran. Did they know anything? Would they tell her even if they did?

Helena had been stunned when Dr. Rand told her Fran had left Harper Hills at his request well over a month ago. Fran hadn't said a word about being fired when they'd last talked, the day before Helena drove down from Bakersfield. Why hadn't she?

So many questions with no answers. Helena sighed, touched her hair again, and turned to follow the blue arrow to Three North. This was no time to dwell on Fran — she had to keep her wits about her to survive her first day on pediatrics. Dr. George Wittenburg, she'd heard, might be a fine clinician but he was also a hard taskmaster.

Ready or not, she thought, here I come, doctor.

Dr. Wittenburg was not in his office. The peds charge nurse, Idalia Davin, an attractive black woman about Helena's age, led the way along a corridor and into a four-crib room where a fortyish stocky blond man in a white coat stood holding a solemn infant.

'Hey there, tiger,' he was saying to the child, 'you're about ready to go back home to Mama.'

'Doctor,' Idalia said, 'this is Dr. Moore.'

He turned his head and Helena looked into friendly but appraising brown eyes. He held the child out to Helena and she set down her bag and took the baby into her arms.

'This little girl gave us a bad time for a while there,' George Wittenburg said. 'She was a fussy, colicky baby who kept Mama and Daddy awake all night, so the old family GP gave Mama a prescription for Nembutal elixir to quiet their little tiger.'

Helena waited but he said no more, watching her, and she realized he was testing her. 'What happened?' she asked. 'Did the mother give her an overdose?'

'No. Mama was meticulously careful with the dropper. But tiger, here, developed respiratory paralysis and was rushed to the ER damn near dead.'

Again there was silence. Helena glanced from Dr. Wittenburg to Idalia Davin. Ms. Davin was smiling faintly as she watched the doctor. Helena turned her gaze to the child. The little girl's wide blue eyes stared back at her. How old was she — six months? Helena frowned. A bit old for colic.

How can I make a diagnosis on such a skimpy history? Helena asked herself frantically. He can't expect me to come up with anything intelligent! At the same time she automatically totted up what she could observe about the baby: fair skin, very blond, a female. Allergic to barbiturates? Allergy must be the clue.

Respiratory failure wasn't the usual symptom of barbiturate intolerance if there was no question of an overdose. Something nagged her about barbiturates — what was it? Quickly, she reviewed all the information he'd given her: A fussy, colicky six-month-old girl. Fair-haired and blue-eyed.

What diseases shouldn't you prescribe a barbiturate for? Anything affecting the liver, metabolic disorders like porphyria. A rare one, porphyria. Barbiturates can trigger very severe symptoms in that disease and one of the symptoms is abdominal pain — colic. Who gets porphyria? Hereditary in Swedes and white South Africans.

He hadn't said anything about skin blisters, though, and in this climate the mother would certainly have taken the baby outside in the sun a few times. What about photosensitivity, the inability to tolerate sunlight common in porphyria victims? Not all of them, though, not in all types of the disease. George Wittenburg was trying to trick her with a rare one, she was sure of it.

Helena smiled tentatively. 'I'd be interested to know what the lab results were on her stools,' she said. 'I'm thinking specifically of fecal coporphrin III levels.'

Dr. Wittenburg's mouth twitched but he controlled the smile. 'Very high,' he said.

'With normal blood porphyrins?'

He nodded.

'Wow!' Helena exclaimed. 'I don't think I've ever heard of an actual case of hereditary coporphyria, much less ever seen one.' She looked down at the baby before staring triumphantly at the doctor.

He grinned back at her. 'That's exactly what tiger, here, has.'

'She's a lucky little girl to have you diagnose it so early,' Helena told him admiringly. 'You not only saved her life, you've given her the chance to have a normal life span.'

'Maybe a damned uncomfortable one at times,' he said, taking the child back and depositing her in the crib. The minute he put her down the baby began to cry.

'You've spoiled that little girl, doctor,' Idalia Davin said.

Helena noted the nurse spoke gently, even

fondly. So the chief of peds was well-liked by at least one of the staff — a good sign.

'Ah well, Mama will be taking her cub home tomorrow,' he said. 'Tiger'll forget me in no time — just like all women do.' He smiled at Idalia, then put a hand on Helena's shoulder and walked her into the corridor. 'Welcome to peds, Dr. Moore. I'm George but I'm afraid I've forgotten your first name. I'm terrible with names.'

'Helena,' she said. 'I'll wear my name pin from now on.'

Helena turned and saw a massive dark-haired, dark-eyed man heading toward them. He was younger than George.

'This is Jeff Hillyer,' George said as the man joined them, walking beside Helena. 'He's our neurosurgical resident but spends half his time on peds. Maybe if we both work on him we can convince him he's in the wrong specialty. But you have to watch Jeff or he'll convert you to mysticism when you're not looking. He's also our resident shaman.'

Was she imagining it or was there a tinge of annoyance in George's voice? Helena blinked, not certain of what to say, finally murmuring, 'Hello, Jeff.'

'Since Xenara built that godawful pyramid,' George went on, 'El Doblez attracts every kook in the country.'

'I noticed a pyramid coming into town,' she admitted.

'You sure as hell can't miss it.' George stopped outside his office and glanced at his watch.

'Why don't you take Helena for a cup of coffee, Jeff? I'm late for a medical ethics meeting.' George turned to Helena. 'Leave your bag in my office. I'll meet you here at eleven and we can fill out your ten thousand and one forms before I show you around.'

When they sat at a table over coffee in the doctors' dining room off the cafeteria, Jeff didn't speak and Helena once more lapsed into stewing over Fran's death. Captain Maklin said he'd be by the apartment at five to see her and she didn't mean to omit one single detail that might give him a lead as to why Fran died. That redhead she'd seen on the steps, for example. He must have been eighteen or so, certainly old enough to have noticed anything suspicious.

If 'Red' lived at De La Mar, maybe he'd seen someone visiting Fran. If he didn't live there, he still might have seen something. Or even be the one who . . .

'You can learn a lot from George.' Jeff's voice jolted Helena from her speculations. 'Has he done his riddle number on you yet?'

'I passed, I think.'

Jeff nodded. 'He likes women — though not necessarily in medicine. What he doesn't take kindly to is having his beliefs tampered with. I unsettle him. Like Xenara does.'

'What *is* Xenara?'

'It's the name of an ancient goddess of healing. Psi-healing's what Xenara's all about.'

'Holistic?'

'Yes, if your definition of holistic means considering the spirit along with the mind and the body. George doesn't believe patients — or any of us for that matter — have spirits.'

Helena frowned. 'You're saying you do?'

Jeff's eyebrows rose. 'It's self-evident.'

'Not to me.'

For the first time Jeff smiled. 'I'll work on you. Me and Vada Rogers. Wait until you meet her — she's really impressive. Vada has psi power you wouldn't believe.'

He was right, Helena thought. She wouldn't. Nothing she'd ever seen, read, or heard had ever convinced her parapsychology was anything but a lot of mumbo-jumbo. She no more believed in mysterious powers than she believed beings from outer space had landed on Earth.

'You look skeptical,' Jeff told her.

'I'm simply not interested.' She was trying

her best to be polite but she was losing her patience.

'A good doctor keeps an open mind.'

'Open, yes: credulous, no.'

'If you define 'credulous' as believing despite uncertain evidence, then you ought to try being credulous. You have to remember the paranormal *is* uncertain. How can it be otherwise when no one knows the rules? Any experimental science — '

'What you're talking about is not a science,' she broke in heatedly. 'I'm sorry, you're wasting your time trying to convert me.'

'It's possible your complete dismissal of the paranormal hides a secret fear, that you're really afraid of what you might find if you investigated without prejudice.'

Helena tamped down her irritation, remembering that her upset over Fran's death and the concurrent lack of sleep was making her testier than usual. Jeff might be a tad peculiar but what turned him on was his business. She could and would get along with him as long as he didn't persist in trying to force his beliefs on her.

Looking directly into his eyes, she smiled and changed the subject. 'I'll need to know the on-call schedule as soon as possible. Do you happen to know where George — '

'If you have a family I'd be glad to help out

when I can,' Jeff offered.

'Just a four-year-old daughter who's at Sea Mist. I shouldn't have any trouble handling my call.'

'Sea Mist.' Jeff echoed the word, frowning.

Helena's eyes widened in alarm. 'Is there something wrong with the place? Roger — Laura's father — told me Sea Mist has an excellent reputation.'

'Why is your daughter there?'

'Laura's been diagnosed as autistic, though she's not completely typical.'

'There's nothing wrong with Sea Mist, not really. I happen to disagree with the way they use operant conditioning.'

Helena's stomach lurched. She hadn't done an in-depth evaluation of Sea Mist, trusting to Roger's judgment. She should have known better than to trust him. Roger always took the easy way out; why had she forgotten that? Did Jeff mean they might *hurt* Laura? Use pain to condition her?

She closed her eyes to shut out such an unacceptable possibility and when she opened them she found herself staring at a young man with red hair standing in the doorway of the doctors' dining room. Helena tensed. Was it Red from Fran's apartment complex? She wasn't sure.

He glanced around as though searching for

someone. When his eyes met hers she saw sudden recognition in them and knew he *was* Red. Before she could rise or call to him, he jerked back and disappeared.

'Wait!' Helena shouted, leaping to her feet and running to the door.

She was too late. There was no sign of Red in the cafeteria's main dining room. Helena retraced her steps. Maybe Jeff could tell her Red's name.

'Did you see him?' she demanded. 'Did you see that redhead?'

'Sorry,' Jeff told her, 'I wasn't looking. Why, what's the matter?'

Helena, near tears, sat down and rested her elbows on the table, propping her chin on her hands while she stared at nothing. 'My sister was killed two days ago,' she said, fighting to keep her voice even. 'I think she was murdered but the police won't listen to me. Maybe you knew her. Her name was Fran, Fran York. She was a nurse in the newborn nursery.'

'That explains it,' he said. 'I sensed a dark aura around you from the moment we met.'

Helena raised her head to gaze at him in disbelief. Dark aura? What the hell was he talking about? 'I asked if you knew Fran,' she said coldly.

He shook his head. 'The nursery's outside

my territory. But I am sorry about your sister.' He touched her hand. 'Really sorry.'

Helena blinked back tears. She didn't want to sit here soliciting sympathy from a stranger but she couldn't help herself. She had no one to share her grief with. Or her guilt.

She hadn't wanted to come to El Doblez in the first place. She'd been forced into it, dragging her feet all the way. If she'd only arrived a day sooner, Fran would be alive. If only . . .

Jeff's hands covered hers, a stranger's hand maybe, but warm and comforting. He might be as odd as they came but she appreciated his concern. There was nothing as helpful as the touch of a fellow human at a time like this.

'If I'm not interrupting, Dr. Moore,' a man's voice said, 'I'd appreciate a few minutes of your time.'

She recognized the voice and noted the sardonic tone. Captain Maklin. Mak.

Helena jerked her hand away from Jeff's and sat back in her chair, feeling like a naughty child and annoyed because she did. She turned to scowl up at him.

'I thought we were to meet at five o'clock,' she said.

'We are.' He stood over her, making no attempt to sit down.

Because she felt forced to, Helena introduced the two men.

'Captain Maklin,' Jeff repeated.

'Just Mak, please.'

Jeff nodded at him and rose. 'I've got to show for rounds on the neuro unit or Zel Markowicz'll have my ass. See you around, Helena.'

'Known him long?' Mak asked, seating himself in Jeff's vacated chair.

What possible business is that of his, she wondered, tossing him a sharp, 'No.'

'Captain's a courtesy title,' he said. 'I don't use it. If we're going to be working together you might as well start calling me Mak.'

'Are we working together?'

'We're hardly at cross purposes when we're both interested in solving the riddle of your sister's death.'

'Riddle?' she cried. 'Is that all it is to you — a riddle?' To her horror she burst into tears.

Mak pulled her to her feet and, his arm around her, led her from the room. She followed blindly, dimly aware they'd gone through a door to the outside. He halted, pulled her into his arms and she clung to him, unable to control her weeping. He stroked her back, murmuring soothingly.

She hadn't cried when she found Fran's

dead body, hadn't cried when she washed Fran's blood from Laura's hands, nor when her sister was slid into a body bag and taken away. She hadn't slept much the last two days but she hadn't cried, not even last night, alone in the apartment. Now she couldn't stop.

Held in the arms of a man who looked like a reincarnation of Abe Lincoln, a man she didn't even like, she sobbed her heart out.

3

As Mak did his best to comfort Helena, he admitted to himself she felt every bit as good in his arms as he'd known she would. He also knew he couldn't afford to let her distract him.

He'd bet this was the first time she'd cried over her sister's death and he thought it might very well be the last. She struck him as a tough and stubborn lady who hated to give way to tears. He admired both traits — his own toughness and stubbornness were the only reason he was still alive.

Too mean to die was the way Doc Lewis had put it.

So, okay, tough and stubborn was classy as far as he was concerned but the reason he enjoyed holding Helena was more basic. He wanted her. Not for always, he'd given up that route permanently. For just a day, though, or maybe a week — that had a lot of appeal. After he finished his investigation.

He wondered how much Helena knew about her sister. He couldn't count on her sharing her knowledge with him. Because Fran had died, he'd have to change direction.

He hated being proven wrong — in his line of work it was dangerous, even fatal, to be wrong.

Helena's long, shuddering sobs eased. He stopped patting her and made no effort to stop her when he felt her begin to pull away. She stepped back and pulled a tissue from a pocket to wipe her eyes.

'Sorry,' she said.

'I'm glad I was here.' He savored telling the plain unvarnished truth — he seldom had the chance.

He'd come along just in time. Better she cried on his shoulder than on that doctor's who'd been holding her hand a while ago.

'She was so alive. Fran, I mean. Brimming over with energy, always on the go.' Helena crumpled the damp tissue in her hand. 'It's hard to believe I'll never see her again.' She took a deep breath. 'I swear I'll find whoever killed her. And when I do . . . '

'Better leave the investigating to the police. They know what they're doing.'

'You don't even believe Fran *was* killed.'

'She might well have been.'

Helena's eyes widened. 'Don't tell me you've had a change of heart.'

Mak shrugged. 'I never did say I excluded murder.'

He glanced around to make certain they

were alone. Birds flitted from shrub to shrub in the planters surrounding the small patio off the dining room and bees hummed in the red bottlebrush blossoms on the bush beside him. He pulled a white metal chair away from one of the glass-topped tables and gestured to it.

'If you have a minute more, I need to talk to you,' he told her.

Helena glanced at her watch before she sat down. He seated himself in the chair across the table from her and tipped it back. 'The preliminary results of the post came in and I knew you'd want to hear.' He kept his tone level, his voice without inflection. Though Helena was a doctor, it was never easy to discuss autopsy findings with the relatives of victims.

She leaned forward, intent on his words.

'Did you happen to know your sister was pregnant?' he asked.

Her expression showed her surprise but she recovered quickly. 'How far along?'

'Six weeks. Any idea who the father might be?'

She shook her head. 'Fran didn't confide in me. I didn't even know she'd lost her job here. What else did the post show?'

'As you surmised, the head injury didn't kill her. Until all the results are in, no one can be sure what did. Preliminary testing found no heroin, no cocaine, no barbiturates. And she hadn't been raped.'

'So whoever it was killed Fran on purpose.' Helena spoke as much to herself as to him.

'Looks that way.'

Her gaze caught his. 'Why don't you come right out and admit it was murder?'

He half-smiled. 'Cops, like doctors, tend to hedge until there's proof.' Seeing her check her watch again, Mak rose. 'I won't keep you.'

'Do you still want to meet me at five?' she asked as she got up.

'Yes. I'd like to talk to you about your sister at some length. Okay?'

'You'd better give me a number to reach you in case I get held up.'

He jotted the number on the memo pad he always carried, tore off the sheet, and handed it to her.

'This isn't the police station number?' she asked.

'No.' He didn't elaborate. 'It could take a while. I thought we might go out and have something to eat while we talk.'

When she hesitated he found himself holding his breath. Why should it be so important to him for her to say yes? Because if he took her to dinner he'd get to spend more time with her?

'If you like,' she said finally, looking around the patio. 'I'm not quite sure where I am.'

'Al fresco dining,' Mak said, touching her arm to guide her to the door to the dining room. 'For physicians only.'

'Do you think we don't deserve it?'

'Merely an observation. But if you want an opinion, some do, some don't.'

She smiled. 'Hedging again.'

At last he'd gotten a genuine smile from her, Mak thought as they went inside. If he played his cards right, he hoped eventually there'd be more than smiles. He definitely wanted more from Helena Moore.

For a man whose looks were enough to break mirrors, he did all right with women. Not that he hadn't made mistakes — Mima had been the worst. He scowled, remembering. When he messed up, he did it in spades.

'When I made mean faces like that as a child,' Helena said, 'my mother used to warn me that my expression would freeze that way.'

He blinked, glancing at her in confusion.

'Not perfect,' she said, scrutinizing his expression, 'but an improvement. At least you won't scare little kids on the street now.' With a wave of her hand, she left him.

Mak watched her stride away. Trim. Compact. He liked the easy way she moved. When he dropped in to see Ty, he'd find out the name of the beefy doctor she'd been with. It didn't pay to underestimate the competition.

★ ★ ★

I can't believe I agreed to have dinner with Mak, Helena told herself as she entered the elevator. Talking to him as part of the investigation into Fran's death is one thing but dinner is something else. Practically a date.

Dating was *not* on her agenda at the moment. The breakup with Roger had been enough grief, she wasn't yet ready to be more than casually friendly with a man. God knows she didn't trust any of them.

Though he'd proved surprisingly understanding there on the patio, it was best to be exceedingly wary of a man like Mak. He wasn't conventionally handsome, like Roger, but there was something about that craggy face that intrigued her. And that was a clear warning to tread very carefully.

I'll think of it as a business dinner, she decided, a necessary evil.

Checking her watch when she emerged on the third floor, Helena saw it was fifteen minutes of eleven and so she decided to walk around the peds unit to get the feel of the

36

place until it was time to meet with Dr. Wittenburg in his office. If she saw Idalia Davin she'd ask about Fran. Idalia might have known her and, given the usual hospital grapevine, was bound to have heard why Fran lost her job.

Idalia wasn't at the nurses' station, nor in any of the rooms Helena glanced into. At the far end of Three North, she pushed through double red doors marked ISOLATION: NO ADMITTANCE.

The communicable disease unit was small, only four rooms, all private, with a desk at the end of the corridor. The doors were closed. Peering through the small window in the center of the first, Helena saw the bed was unoccupied but there were several patients' charts resting on top of the covers. Charts were normally never brought into a CD room. Curious, she eased the door open to take a look inside and caught her breath.

A man and a woman so engrossed in each other they were oblivious to the open door stood in the space between the bed and the near wall. She recognized both of them. George Wittenburg held Idalia Davin in a fervent embrace. Gathering her wits, Helena began a silent, embarrassed retreat, hoping she could close the door and escape without alerting them.

Stepping back into the hall, she bumped into someone. Helena managed to swallow her startled exclamation but lost her grip on the door. It swung shut with a loud thump. She turned.

A tall brown-haired woman wearing the pink smock of a volunteer stared at her. 'Carin Wittenburg,' the name tag on the smock read. Good God! George's wife? Helena hoped Carin hadn't seen what she had. This was none of her affair but she had to do something.

'I'm sorry, I didn't know you were behind me,' Helena said, advancing toward her, forcing Carin to move away. She held out her hand. 'I'm Helena Moore, the new peds resident.'

As Carin eyed her, the door opened and George came out of the room.

'Carin!' he exclaimed. 'You know volunteers aren't allowed on the CD unit.'

'Oh, they don't bother about me,' Carin said. 'They know I won't contaminate anything. I've been looking for you.'

'Well, you've found me.' Taking his wife's arm, he led her to the red doors and pushed through them.

Helena decided she ought to follow suit but before she had the chance, Idalia, carrying the charts, appeared in the doorway to the room.

'I guess you saw,' Idalia said.

There was no point in lying. Helena nodded.

'Did *she?*' Idalia asked.

'I don't know.'

Idalia bit her lip. Without another word, she walked past Helena and disappeared through the red doors.

Without really being acquainted with any of the three and without knowing the circumstances, Helena sympathized with Carin. When they were married, Roger had betrayed her in similar situations at least twice she knew of; she remembered the anguish and pain all too well.

Later, during Helena's meeting with George, he behaved as though the episode on CD had never occurred. Since she wasn't about to bring up the subject, nothing was said. Which suited Helena just fine. The last thing she wanted was to be caught in the middle — she had enough troubles of her own.

'I just heard you were Fran York's sister,' he said when they finished the forms. 'You didn't have to come in today.'

'I prefer to keep busy,' she said.

'A shame, a real shame Fran had to die so senselessly. El Doblez is getting as bad as LA these days. You're sure you wouldn't like to leave early?'

'I'd like to get away by five, no earlier.'

He nodded. 'Work's an antidote of sorts.'

'Did you know Fran?' she asked.

'Only from working with her in the newborn nursery. If you'll let us know when the funeral is — '

'No services, no burial. Fran once told me she wanted her ashes scattered over the ocean so I'm having that done.'

He nodded again. 'Sensible.' He lifted a chart from his desk and rose. 'We've time before lunch for me to show you an interesting case I admitted this morning.'

Helena followed him from the office, relieved to get to work. Involvement with patients was the only way she could banish her anger and grief at Fran's death at least for a few hours.

Making rounds with George, meeting Dr. Tyrone Rand, the Chief of Staff, getting oriented to the peds unit and to the hospital in general, made the rest of the day zip past. Helena left a few minutes before five, parked in front of the apartment, and found Mak leaning against the wrought iron entrance gate.

'Any objection to letting me look around the living room of the apartment before we go to dinner?' he asked.

She shook her head. The lack of sleep had

caught up with her and all she really wanted to do was crawl into bed. Alone. If this was an ordinary date she'd cancel the dinner but under the circumstances, she didn't have that choice. Not if she wanted to help find Fran's killer.

Mak followed her up the stairs and into the apartment. She left him in the living room and entered the blue and white guest bedroom where she'd been sleeping. Or trying to. She'd put Fran's stuffed animals on top of the dresser, all except a bright green alligator. Laura had taken a fancy to the alligator, so Helena had sent it to Sea Mist with her.

After Jeff had told her about the operant conditioning, Helena called Dr. Flanagan, Sea Mist's medical director, and he'd agreed to consult with her before beginning any system of punishment to try to improve Laura's behavior. Flanagan had reassured her to some extent but since he obviously believed in what he called his 'aversive therapy' she planned to investigate other possibilities for Laura in the area. She'd never allow Laura to be deliberately hurt. Never.

Wearily she slid open the closet and surveyed her wardrobe. She hadn't thought to ask Mak what kind of dinner he had in mind but she decided her black cotton velveteen pants with a turquoise shirt would fit in anywhere. Luckily the apartment had a second bathroom — she hadn't yet been able to bring herself to go into the one where she'd found Fran dead. Despite the fact she'd thoroughly aired the apartment, she still caught a faint whiff of honeysuckle now and then, reminding her that Fran had lived in these rooms.

After she'd bathed and dressed, Helena rejoined Mak. He was standing by a small bookcase studying a pamphlet.

'Did you find something?' she asked.

He offered her the pamphlet and, as she took it, she saw 'Xenara' written in blue script across the top of the cover. Below the word was a drawing of the white pyramid and superimposed over the pyramid was a blue caduceus.

'Snakes twining around a winged staff, the symbol of medicine,' Mak said. 'Mercury's rod originally, wasn't it?'

She nodded absently, staring at the blue and white cover. 'Where did you find this?'

'In the bookcase. Did your sister ever mention Xenara to you?'

'No.'

'Is this something she'd be interested in?'

About to deny it, Helena paused. Neither of them believed in the paranormal but while she had absolutely no use for so-called healing cults, her sister had once mentioned taking a laying-on-of-hands course at UCSD. Perhaps Fran wasn't as adamant as she was.

'I'm not sure,' she said finally.

'I understand Xenara teaches psi-healing.'

Helena grimaced. 'I'm afraid my opinion of psi-healing is as negative as Dr. Wittenburg's. I don't understand how intelligent people can be attracted to fakery.'

'Some people swear by psi-healing.'

'Not me. I don't believe in it. Or in the paranormal power of pyramids. Or table-rapping spirits. Or ouija boards. Or ghosts and goblins. Or astrology. Or — '

He held up a hand and smiled, distracting her. It was astonishing how a smile warmed his somber face. 'I have a feeling your disbelief list might take all night. I don't know about you, but I'm hungry.'

★ ★ ★

Helena's eyebrows raised as Mak handed her into a sleek black Jaguar. 'You didn't buy this car on a policeman's salary,' she said.

'I — inherited a few bucks.' He closed her door and walked around to the driver's side. When he'd settled himself behind the wheel and fastened his seat belt, he said, 'I hope seafood isn't one of your negatives because my favorite restaurant doesn't have anything else on the menu.'

'I'm a firm believer in seafood,' she assured him.

The Chez Mer was in a cluster of buildings — restaurants and stores — in a new beach development called Sea Fair. After they'd been seated and had ordered drinks, Helena turned from a spectacular view of a salmon pink and mauve sunset over the Pacific to look at Mak.

'The ambience is great, the music unobtrusive, and I'm sure the food will be delicious,' she said. 'But this is still strictly a business dinner.'

'What else?' he asked.

'So what do you want to know?'

He started to tip his chair back, then, apparently remembering that wasn't acceptable behavior in a restaurant, sat up straight. 'Tell me about your sister,' he said.

'Anything specific?'

'I want to know what she was like — from your point of view.'

'Actually, Fran is — was — my half sister, five years younger than I. We have the same mother.'

'Your mother's now married to Fran's father?'

Helena half-smiled. 'My mother doesn't stay married to *any* man very long. She's divorce prone. Her current husband is her fourth and no relation to either Fran or me.'

'Will your mother and stepfather be coming to El Doblez?'

'Not soon. They're somewhere in Peru so I don't know if they have the message about Fran yet or not. Do you have any idea when — when Fran's body will be released?'

'Sorry, I don't.'

The waiter arrived with the drinks; Helena picked up her vodka and tonic and took a long swallow. 'Her death just doesn't seem real to me.' Her voice quivered and she wrapped both hands around the glass and stared into it.

'Was Fran depressed lately?'

She glanced up quickly. 'No!'

He raised his eyebrows at her vehemence but made no other comment.

Helena sighed. 'I suppose I'll have to qualify that. She wasn't depressed but something was bothering her. She urged me to come to El Doblez a week before I did — though she wouldn't say why. Fran was always secretive, even as a child. We were close in some ways but she was a private person.

'I know she didn't kill herself, if that's what

45

you're leading up to. Even if I believed she was the type, the evidence I found in her bathroom is against suicide.' She fixed him with a defiant gaze. 'Admit it!'

'Supposing you didn't dispose of the syringe and needle, I admit it doesn't look like suicide.'

Helena's eyes widened. 'You can't think I'd do such a thing!'

He shrugged. 'People often hide or destroy evidence to hide a truth they think is harmful. Why not you?'

'I wouldn't. I couldn't.'

Again he started to tip back his chair and caught himself. 'To avoid argument I'll accept your word. For the moment.'

She started to protest, stopped and shook her head. 'Do they teach cynicism in police school?'

He half-smiled. 'We're forced to learn it on our own.' He took a long swallow of his Scotch and water. 'Have you any idea why your sister was upset?'

'I don't think the pregnancy would faze Fran — she'd be well aware of her alternatives. She *had* lost her job and she must have had bills to pay. The apartment rent alone . . . ' Helena paused, feeling vaguely guilty, as though she'd somehow be betraying Fran if she speculated out loud on how Fran could afford an expensive apartment on a nurse's salary.

'. . . was more than a nurse could afford,' Mak finished. 'She might have stopped working at Harper Hills but her bank deposit slips showed regular and sizeable cash amounts during the last eight months. The manager says she's been in the apartment four months. Could the money have come from your parents?'

'No way. Not with my tightwad stepfather handling the family finances. I have no idea where the money came from.'

'From what I understand, this is your second year of a pediatric residency. You spent the first year at Kern County Medical Center in Bakersfield. Why did you decide to come to Harper Hills?'

Helena hesitated for a long moment before replying. 'Their chief of peds, Dr. Wittenburg, has an excellent reputation — he's one of the leading experts on encephalitis. I wanted to work with him.'

Mak said nothing, his cool blue gaze watchful.

She sipped her drink.

'So your decision had nothing to do with your sister,' he said finally.

Helena didn't want to answer, didn't want to stir the embers of the frustration and anger that had simmered inside her over the past few months while she tried to cope with Laura, the divorce, and her mother's pleading and prodding:

I just know Fran's up to something. You're the only one she ever did listen to. She's your sister, it's your responsibility to find out what's going on and to help her.

Telling her mother Fran was an adult who could take care of herself and was well able to ask for help if she needed it hadn't made a dent in her mother's conviction that Fran was in trouble:

Helena, I can tell by her voice Fran's afraid. Why won't you go to El Doblez? Don't you care what happens to your poor little sister?

In the end, her mother's nagging, combined with an increasing need to get father away from Roger, led Helena to check out the peds residency possibilities in Southern California. Harper Hills Hospital had the only one available.

'I did come here partly because of Fran,' she admitted to Mak. 'Our mother believes she has psychic flashes and she claimed one showed her Fran was in trouble. Frankly, I don't believe in second sight or precognition or true dreaming and so I ignored mother's premonition. If you knew how many times she's claimed to 'know' something would happen and the almost equal number of times nothing did happen, you'd understand my reluctance.

'But she wore me down. Besides, I had personal reasons for wanting to leave the Central Valley.' Helena shook her head. 'For once Mother was right. I wish I'd come earlier. Fran would be alive if I had.'

'You can't know that.' This time he did tip the chair onto its back legs. The waiter's arrival to ask if they cared to order brought the chair back down in a hurry.

'I'm not very hungry,' she said.

'I'll order for both of us, then.' Without waiting for her to agree or disagree, Mak went ahead.

Well, it was his money. If he could afford the Jag, he could afford to pay for her uneaten meal. Come to think of it, that jacket he wore wasn't exactly a Sears special, either. Woven silk, if she wasn't mistaken. He must have inherited a pile.

If he'd inherited it. Hadn't he hesitated for a second or two before saying that's where the money came from? Was he lying? Was it dishonestly earned from bribes and pay-offs? It was hard to believe a man who looked so much like Lincoln could be bought off but what did she really know about Mak?

'If I didn't know better, I'd think you were a cop and I was a suspect,' he told her. 'That's a third-degree look if I ever saw one.'

Helena blinked. 'I was only admiring your sports jacket. Custom made?'

'I'm hard to fit.' He shifted his shoulders. 'Did your sister give you any hint why she wanted you to come sooner than scheduled?'

'No.'

'What did you think might have been her reason?'

'It crossed my mind she might want me staying with her to help with the rent. Fran wasn't a saver — she spent what she earned.'

'The question is, how did she earn the extra money and why was it paid in cash instead of by check?'

'You think it has something to do with why she was murdered, don't you?'

He shrugged. 'I'm looking for anything that might give some clue — the pregnancy, the cash deposits, the people she knew . . . '

Remembering the blue and white pamphlet he'd taken from Fran's bookcase, Helena said, 'Xenara?'

Mak frowned, as though finding the word distasteful.

'There *is* that redhead I saw on the stairs,' she added. 'I almost forgot to tell you I saw him again in the hospital cafeteria. He took off as soon as he noticed me so I couldn't confront him. Don't you think that's suspicious?'

'Did you get his name from anyone?'

'Jeff — Dr. Hillyer — didn't see him. But couldn't you ask around the apartment complex? Maybe he lives there.'

'I'll tell Lieutenant Garcia and I'm sure he'll check it out. If I'm not mistaken you already gave him a description of the man.' Mak picked up a bread stick and bit off the end, crunching it between even white teeth. For some reason Helena was reminded of Laura's alligator.

As if tuning in on her thoughts, Mak asked, 'What did you do with your daughter?'

'Laura's in a residential facility for disturbed children.' Why did she feel so guilty saying the words? She'd had no choice.

'Cute little thing. I hope what happened won't affect her.'

Helena sighed. 'No one knows what affects Laura and what doesn't. I'm sure she didn't realize her Aunt Fran was dead.'

The waiter set clam chowder in front of them. Mak picked up his soup spoon. 'End of discussion,' he said. 'I never mix business with the pleasure of eating.'

Mak mentioned liking a movie he'd recently seen, a movie she'd hated. She became so engrossed in defending her position that before she knew it she'd finished the cup of soup and was halfway through the salad. The more she ate, the hungrier she realized she was and she managed to do justice to the entree as well.

'We're right on the beach,' Mak said as they left the restaurant. 'Let's take a walk.'

When Helena pulled off her heeled sandals to walk barefoot in the sand, he removed his shoes and socks.

'Somehow I never picture Lincoln barefoot,' she said. 'You must know you resemble him — otherwise why the beard?'

'It makes people trust me. Without it I've been told I look too intimidating.' A wave caught him unaware, washing over his feet and ankles and he smiled. 'What we both should do is take a day off and spend it at the beach. You could bring Laura.'

Like a normal, happy family, she thought, instead of one sardonic Lincoln clone, one frazzled doctor, and one disturbed little girl. She sighed.

He stopped and turned her toward him, hands on her shoulders, surprising her. Before she could react, his lips touched hers, his beard brushing her face in a gentle caress. The kiss was over almost as soon as it began. She'd sound foolish if she protested because it was obviously meant to be a comforting kiss rather than a violation of her privacy.

And yet it upset her because she'd felt the damn kiss along every nerve in her body, setting Mak up as a threat to her determination to keep free of involvement.

She didn't need any more complications in her life and she wasn't going to accept any. Certainly not a bearded cop she barely knew and didn't entirely trust.

4

The effect of the kiss on the beach had dissipated by the time Mak brought Helena home shortly before midnight and she decided she'd merely overreacted to a friendly gesture. It wasn't like her and it wouldn't happen again.

When he walked her to her door, Helena watched him warily but, somewhat to her surprise, he didn't assume he'd be invited in. Perhaps Mak was more sensitive than she'd thought. On the other hand, maybe the truth was she didn't have much appeal for him.

Though she hadn't meant to, for a long, tension-charged moment she gazed into his eyes, then he touched her upper lip lightly with his forefinger.

'See you,' he said, turning away.

'Good night,' she called after him, oddly shaken by his slight caress.

It's probably part of a technique he's perfected, she warned herself cynically as she let herself in and locked the door behind her. The laid-back approach. Guaranteed to ultimately conquer by underwhelming.

Though she was tired, at first sleep eluded

her and, when she finally did doze off, the jangle of the phone jerked her awake. She fumbled it from the bedside stand.

'Dr. Moore,' she mumbled sleepily.

No answer. After she repeated her name, Helena heard a faint sound of breathing, telling her someone was on the other end.

'Who are you calling?' she demanded to know, suddenly very much awake.

Breathing, nothing more. Someone breathing and waiting. Waiting for what?

Helena slammed down the phone, her heart pounding. Sitting up in bed, she flicked on the lamp. Though she'd heard of 'breather' phone calls, she'd never been a victim and she hadn't realized how upsetting such calls could be.

The phone number hadn't been changed — was it possible the breather meant to phone Fran? Didn't he know Fran was dead? The sudden thought she might have listened to Fran's killer chilled Helena. But her killer would certainly know Fran was dead — why would he call? And, come to that, how could she be sure it was a man? Breathing sounds don't reveal sex.

She waited apprehensively for the breather to try again, reluctant to unplug the phone in case there might be an incoming emergency call. When it occurred to her that the call might have been to see if she was in the apartment, she got up and checked the windows near the stairs to make certain they were locked. Even with their protective grillwork, she didn't feel safe.

She finally fell back to sleep near dawn and had to force herself out of bed when the alarm rang. It wouldn't do to be late for rounds on Three North. Hastily swallowing a glass of orange juice, Helena ate a slice of oat bread covered with peanut butter as she drove to Harper Hills.

She'd barely gotten off the elevator on peds when Idalia Davin hurried up to her.

'Dr. Wittenburg was just paged to the ER to consult on a two-year-old with a fever and vomiting,' Idalia said. 'He wants you to join him there.'

When Helena found the doctor in a curtained-off examining cubicle of the ER, he was endeavoring, without success, to flex the patient's neck forward. The little boy, face flushed, whimpered in protest, evidently too sick to struggle.

'Stiff neck,' Helena observed. That symptom, she knew, was diagnostic of meningitis, an inflammation of the brain and spinal cord covering, and also of encephalitis, an inflammation of the brain itself.

'We'll be doing a spinal tap,' George

Wittenburg said, confirming her suspicions. 'His father's a horse trainer,' he added, glancing at Helena expectantly.

Though fairly sure what George was thinking, she leaned closer to the boy, checking for telltale bites, and nodded when she saw red welts on his tiny arms. The virus causing Western Equine Encephalitis, WEE, was carried by horses and transmitted to humans by mosquitos.

'WEE?' she asked.

'The odds are ten to one. Once we tap him, I hope the CSF, cerebro-spinal fluid, will give us a firm diagnosis. We'll draw some blood for testing, too. I imagine you saw quite a bit of WEE in the San Joaquin Valley — lots of horses up there.'

'Lots of mosquitos, too. I treated enough cases so I always put it down as a possible when I find a stiff neck on exam. I had one death in a ten-month-old; he kept convulsing and we just couldn't stabilize him.'

'Luckily tiger here isn't that sick. We'll admit him and watch him for the next few days.'

Since there were no antibiotics effective against the arbovirus causing the different equine encephalopathies, Helena knew keeping a close eye on the boy and treating his symptoms was all they could do.

'Jeff's interested in encephalitis — I'll let him take a look,' George said. 'He's got some crazy ideas but he's good with kids and he knows his medicine. If you need help sometime and I'm not around, by all means give Jeff a ring.'

After she and George finished making rounds on Three North, Helena sat down at the nurses' station to familiarize herself with the patients' charts. She'd been there for some time when Idalia came to answer the phone while the ward clerk went on a break.

Seeing they were alone at the station, Helena decided this was the time to ask Idalia about Fran. Though they hadn't worked on the same unit, Helena knew from experience how efficient hospital grapevines were.

'Did you know my sister, Fran York, personally?' she asked.

Idalia's glance was wary. 'You could say I knew who Fran was by sight, that's about it.'

'Did she go out with any of the doctors?' Helena persisted. 'Or anyone from the hospital?'

After a moment's hesitation, Idalia said, 'I heard Fran dated Reed Addison a couple of times after his wife left him — he's the head pharmacist.'

Helena filed Reed's name away. 'Dr. Rand told me Fran was asked to leave Harper

Hills,' she went on. 'Do you have any idea why?'

Idalia shook her head, glancing down at the desk instead of directly at Helena. 'I really don't know what goes on in the newborn nursery.'

Though she had no basis on which to challenge Idalia, Helena wondered how true that was. Grapevines usually sprouted rumors, at the very least.

'I'm sorry about your sister's death,' Idalia said, 'but I didn't know her well enough to be able to tell you anything.' The phone rang and she picked it up.

Can't or won't? Helena asked herself, turning back to the charts.

After lunch with Jeff Hillyer, she detoured to the pharmacy before returning to peds. Glancing through the open counter, she froze when she saw a man with red hair. Then he turned slowly and she relaxed. He was too old to be the teenager she'd seen at Fran's and too young to have a red-haired son that age.

'Reed Addison?' she asked, noting not only that he was tall and thin but that his blue eyes appeared dazed. Either he was on drugs or something was bothering him a great deal.

'I'm Reed,' he announced after a moment. 'I understand you knew my sister, Fran

York,' Helena said after introducing herself. 'Could we go somewhere for a few minutes and talk?'

His expression told her he'd like to refuse but either he couldn't summon up the energy or he had second thoughts. Moments later they were cooped up together in his minuscule office, the desk piled high with forms and pharmaceutical samples.

'Fran and I went out together a couple of times,' he said. 'We had a few laughs, you know what I mean?'

He didn't act like he remembered how to laugh, Helena thought. She decided to be blunt. 'Why was Fran fired from the nursery?'

Reed blinked. 'She never said. Actually, we were barely acquainted. Fran came to see me when she heard about Sally leaving.' Pain clouded the blue of his eyes. 'Sally's my wife. We had a baby who died of crib death — Kim was only four months old — and Sally, well, she couldn't stand living in the apartment afterwards. And she couldn't stand me.'

SIDS, Sudden Infant Death Syndrome, was a terrible tragedy for parents. Feeling more sympathetic toward Reed, Helena murmured that she was sorry.

'All the docs were sorry,' Reed said. 'It doesn't bring Kim back. Anyway, Fran brought me some material to read about

SIDS, there's a support group and all. She meant to be helpful but I just wanted to be left alone. So then she persuaded me to go out with her.' He smiled slightly. 'I've got to admit Fran could take your mind off everything except her when she tried. Good as she was, though, I could tell she wasn't really interested — not in me. It was like she felt she had to cheer me up one way or another. Not that I wasn't grateful but . . . ' His words trailed off and he shrugged.

Helena struggled to assimilate this new view of Fran. If she interpreted it right, Reed felt Fran had sex with him to assuage his grief over losing the baby and his wife. That seemed uncharacteristically noble of Fran, especially since Reed was not particularly attractive. Except, of course, Fran had always brought home hurt animals and fussed over them. Maybe Reed fit into that category.

'When did you go out with Fran last?' she asked.

'We stopped seeing each other after she latched onto that new guy. Maybe you ought to be talking to him instead of me.'

'Fran was dating another man?'

'Yeah. He showed up around here about a month or two ago, give or take a week. Don't know what the hell his business is, he never said. I forget the name but you can't miss him

— he looks like Abe Lincoln, beard and all.'

Helena's eyes widened in shock. He could only mean Mak! 'Fran was dating this man?' she queried intently.

Reed nodded. 'Ask anyone. Cozy as two ships in a bottle.'

Fran and Mak? Why hadn't he told her? Mak had a lot of explaining to do!

Anger gripped Helena and she struggled to keep it from showing. 'Thank you for your help,' she managed to say before hurrying from the pharmacy.

When she left Harper Hills at six-thirty, Petey, the boy with encephalitis, was stable, his prognosis favorable. She planned to come by around ten for another look at him before going to bed. Though she was on call, she didn't anticipate any crises on the peds ward or in the newborn nursery.

Because Harper Hills' patients had private physicians, 'on call' meant she'd handle any of George Wittenburg's hospital patients who needed care or any pediatric patient coming into the ER with no doctor listed who proved too much of a problem for the ER doc. She might even get a full night's sleep — something she'd never managed as an intern on call.

As soon as she reached the apartment, Helena unearthed the card with Mak's phone number and punched the numbers in.

Nobody answered. You'd think a cop would have to have an answering machine but apparently he didn't. She looked up the El Doblez Police number and shook her head. No, she didn't want to catch him on the job so he could weasel out of explaining with the excuse of being too busy. If he'd been seeing Fran, he owed her a few answers, damn it.

She tried the phone number again but failed to reach Mak so she drove back to the hospital to check on Petey. The evening charge nurse, Joe Morton, told her she'd just missed George Wittenburg.

'He took a quick look at Petey,' Joe said, 'before he was paged to go to maternity to catch a Caesarean preemie.'

Hospital rules called for a pediatrician to stand by during Caesareans in case the newborn required special care. After examining Petey and deciding his condition was stable, Helena thought about seeing what was going on in the maternity delivery room but decided against it.

She'd be superfluous there and, at the moment, she needed sleep more than anything else. Passing George's office, she noticed the door was open and the light on. Carin Wittenburg, wearing her pink volunteer's jacket, sat at her husband's desk. She glanced up, saw Helena and beckoned to her.

Reluctantly, Helena entered the office. She fervently hoped Carin didn't intend to question her about what had happened in the CD unit the previous day. If George was having an affair with Idalia that was none of Helena's business and she was damned if she'd get mixed up in it — even if her own unhappy experiences did lead her to side with Carin.

'I'd call this volunteer work above and beyond the call of duty,' Helena said lightly.

Carin smiled. 'I often come with George on his evening rounds and, since not everyone on the evening shift knows me, I wear my pink jacket to make me legitimate.' She gestured to the chair beside the desk. 'Please sit down for a moment. I know you're either busy or longing to go home and fall into bed but if I don't grasp this chance we may never find the time to become acquainted.'

She nodded at the pediatric journals spread on the desk in front of her. 'I try to help George by abstracting the meat from the articles so he can decide if any are worth reading in full. No doctor can possibly keep up with all that's printed these days — not and take care of patients, too.'

Not wanting to come right out and ask what Carin's medical background was,

64

Helena said, 'He's lucky you know enough medicine to be able to assist him.'

'I was a pharmacist's assistant when George and I got married,' Carin told her. 'And, from the day we met, George always shared his work with me.' She laughed a little, tapping the pen she held against the desk top in quick, nervous spasms. 'I had to learn medical terminology to survive.'

Looking at Carin's round, pleasant face, Helena wondered if she knew what her husband was sharing with Idalia. She hoped not. As she'd learned, discovering your husband's not the faithful, loving man you thought you'd married was a bitter pill to swallow.

'I work at Harper Hills almost every day as a volunteer,' Carin went on. 'The cafeteria food isn't the greatest but perhaps we could have lunch together sometime. Always supposing George doesn't keep you too busy to eat. He expects everyone to match his pace, no matter what.'

Helena smiled. 'I haven't gone hungry so far. I'd enjoy having lunch with you.'

'Good!'

Deciding it wouldn't hurt to ask Carin, Helena said, 'Did you know my sister, Fran York?'

Carin looked dismayed. 'Oh, my, George

did tell me she was your sister and I completely forgot to offer my condolences. I *am* sorry. What happened to her was a shame.' Carin shook her head. 'A shame.'

Helena gave a slight nod in acknowledgement of Carin's sympathy. 'Were you acquainted with Fran?'

'Not really. We volunteers eventually meet all the day shift hospital personnel so I did know who she was and possibly I spoke to her once or twice.'

So far no one she'd asked had 'really known' Fran. Of course, she hadn't tried the nursery nurses who had actually worked with her but she was beginning to suspect none of them would admit to being Fran's friend either. If she were a bit more paranoid, she might begin to think that there was some kind of a cover-up going on at Harper Hills.

'It's too bad about that little boy with encephalitis, isn't it?' Carin asked.

'Too bad? In what way?'

'I was reading an article here — ' she tapped the pen on a journal — 'about the aftermath of brain inflammation in children.' Carin shook her head. 'They suffer both mental and physical deficits. Such a tragedy.'

'Some children do get well and are perfectly normal,' Helena pointed out.

'But how could anyone be sure they'd *be*

normal? The article says some of the problems show up years later.'

'Whoever wrote it sounds like a real pessimist.' Privately, Helena thought Carin didn't have enough medical background to interpret what she read with any degree of accuracy. Standing up, she said, 'I've got to be on my way.'

'I'm so glad we had this little chat,' Carin said. 'Good night, now.'

★ ★ ★

The phone was ringing when Helena let herself into the apartment. Muttering that it always happened this way — no sooner did you leave the hospital than in came an emergency — she rushed to the living room phone.

'Dr. Moore.'

There was the sound of breathing.

'Are you calling Dr. Moore?' she snapped.

No answer, just the breathing.

Holding back a variety of scathing expletives, she slammed the phone down. Getting any kind of attention was what these crazies wanted!

'That does it!' she announced, aware that she couldn't pull the plug, not when she was on call. 'Tomorrow the phone company gives me a new number.'

Though it was getting on toward midnight, she punched in Mak's number, feeling in the mood to yell at someone — God knows he had it coming for not telling her he'd dated Fran.

His phone rang and rang with no answer or pick-up recording. Again she slammed the phone down.

Despite her fatigue, she was too agitated to go to bed, so she flicked on the TV with the remote. Nothing she saw on any channel appealed to her. Noticing Fran's VCR, she rummaged through the cassettes. None had a label except the last. 'Xenara,' it said in blue letters on white.

Helena slid this cassette into the VCR and adjusted the remote buttons.

The white pyramid-shaped building she'd seen coming into town flashed onto the screen. The camera zoomed in for a close-up, focusing on the entrance, where Egyptian columns flanked double blue doors. The doors swung open to frame a blonde thirtyish woman.

'My name is Vada,' she said, in a low, throaty voice. 'I am the soul of Xenara.'

Vada's high cheekbones and slightly slanted green eyes gave her an exotic cast. Though slender, she was exceedingly well endowed, a feature her long white gown with its silver sash did little to hide. Not only was she striking physically but, even on tape, her green eyes had a mesmerizing quality — somehow the viewer couldn't look away. The original Xenara may have been an ancient goddess of healing but Vada could pass for a present-day sex goddess.

What she talked about wasn't new to Helena — meditation, bio-feedback, trance states — though Vada didn't use those terms. 'Spiritual health through etheric pathways,' was the gist of her pitch. Pathways lit by the 'blue flame of life,' whatever that was, to 'spaces on another plane' where 'spirit guides' existed to help the seeker.

Essentially, Helena believed not a word of it but she listened intently until the woman in white finished her spiel. Vada's charisma was considerable; it was obvious she had the power to entice the gullible into this spiritual health cult of hers. Helena's question was — had Fran been suckered into joining? And, if so, did Xenara play any part in what had happened to Fran?

The phone rang, cutting off her musing. Helena grimaced and got to her feet. After midnight. It was that weirdo breather again, an emergency call, or her mother had finally gotten her message about Fran's death. She didn't feel up to coping with any of the three.

'Dr. Moore.'

'This is Harper Hills, doctor, Ms. Peterson on Three North.' The nurse's voice was ominously tense and Helena braced herself. 'Your patient, Peter Kirk, has coded. They're working on him now.'

'I'll be right there.' Helena hung up, rammed her feet into her shoes, grabbed her bag, and rushed from the apartment.

Why had Petey suddenly gone sour, she asked herself as she drove to the hospital. When she'd seen him a little more than two hours ago, his fever was down a degree and there were no symptoms of impending shock. Equine encephalitis could be fatal, she knew, but in the previous cases she'd seen there'd been ample warning that the patients weren't doing well.

Nothing in Petey's history or physical indicated a particular weakness — he didn't have any observable congenital anomalies, he wasn't anemic or malnourished. What had she missed?

By the time she dashed into Petey's room on Three North it was all over. Dr. Choi from the emergency room was detaching the equipment and the nurses were retrieving used syringes and returning other paraphernalia to the crash cart.

'We tried but we couldn't get anything going,' Dr. Choi told Helena. 'I'd say he was flatlining before we ever got the cart in the room.'

Flatlining. Seeing that sign — a flat line — on a heart monitor meant the heart had ceased to beat, meant it was too late.

Helena leaned over the lowered crib rail and touched Petey's already cooling cheek, holding back any feelings, as she learned to do in order to survive. Why hadn't she hooked him up to a monitor earlier, so the nurses could have spotted the impending heart failure?

She knew the answer: because she hadn't thought Petey was that sick on admission — because at her final check around ten he'd appeared to be improving, not getting worse.

George Wittenburg hadn't thought a monitor necessary either, she reminded herself, and George was a hell of a lot more experienced in pediatric medicine than she was. Encephalitis was his speciality.

So what had they missed on Petey? She didn't know and, as she walked to the nurses' station to call George, she fervently hoped he'd be able to come up with an answer.

'That boy shouldn't have died,' he told her when she reached him. 'Wait for me, I'm coming over.'

George hung up and for a long moment Helena held the receiver to her ear, wondering if he blamed her for Petey's death. Did he intend to take it out on her? She took a deep breath, not entirely certain he wouldn't be right.

A nearby whispering caught her attention, distracting her, and she glanced to her right where a nurse assistant huddled with the night charge nurse.

'Say what you want,' the assistant muttered, 'this kid's death makes another one.'

'You better watch who you talk to like that,' the nurse warned. She glanced around and, when she noticed Helena in the act of hanging up the phone, she stiffened.

Helena's gaze shifted to the assistant who was edging away. She read the name tag and called her by name.

'Ms. Olivera.'

The assistant halted, looking everywhere but directly at Helena.

'I wasn't trying to listen but I couldn't help overhearing what you said,' Helena told her. 'Were you referring to Petey Kirk?'

'I didn't mean nothing.' The assistant's voice was sullen.

'Was it Petey?' Helena persisted.

Ms. Olivera nodded reluctantly.

'What did you mean his death made 'another one'?'

'I don't know, I was just sort of talking.'

Helena stepped closer, positioning herself between the assistant and the night charge nurse. 'Have there been other sudden deaths on peds?' she asked, shifting her gaze from one to the other.

'The last one wasn't on peds,' the assistant muttered.

The last one! Last sudden death? Before now no one had said a word about sudden deaths. Was something odd going on at Harper Hills?

'It's just talk,' the charge nurse put in. 'You know how rumors fly.'

Ignoring her for the moment, Helena concentrated on the assistant. 'Where was the last one?' she demanded to know.

The assistant moved her shoulders uneasily. 'In the newborn nursery.' She spread her hands, meeting Helena's gaze for the first time. 'Look, I don't know nothing about it, not really.'

'That's for sure.' The charge nurse's tone was emphatic. 'None of us know anything. Like I said — it's a rumor.'

Realizing they'd told her as much as they were going to and, perhaps, most of what they actually knew, Helena nodded. But she didn't mean to let them go without stating her position. 'Petey was my patient,' she said.

'He shouldn't have died. I mean to find out why he did.' She picked up Petey's chart and sat down.

Staring unseeingly at the papers, she replayed the nurse assistant's words in her mind, making uncomfortable connections. Petey wasn't the first sudden death. She had no idea how many there'd been recently but the last one had been in the newborn nursery. Where Fran worked. No one wanted to talk to her about Fran, or why her sister had been fired.

Helena filed the information away for the moment. One thing at a time. Right now she was faced with Petey's death and the need to find the reason why his heart had failed so suddenly. She focused on his chart, reviewing the history and physical, then reading the nursing notes.

The evening shift notes indicated Petey's temperature was only a degree above normal, his pulse fast but regular, and that he'd seemed to be sleeping normally when the charge nurse, Joe Morton, went off duty at 11:30 P.M.

The night charge nurse found nothing to alarm her when she checked Petey during her first rounds at a few minutes past midnight, though Helena noticed her recording of his pulse rate showed it had slowed quite a bit.

74

Still, that wouldn't be unusual in a sleeping child. When the nurse looked in on him one hour later, he wasn't breathing and, unable to detect a heartbeat, she called a code.

'Helena.' George's voice startled her.

She closed the chart and stood up. 'I don't find any reason in here.' She tapped the chart cover with her fingers. 'I don't know why Petey died.'

'We may have to wait for the post to find the reason,' he said.

Sometimes the pathologist's post mortem exam was the only way to determine why a patient had died.

'Did the posts on the other sudden deaths show the reasons?' she asked.

George blinked. 'What deaths?'

'The last one was in the newborn nursery, I understand.'

'You know better than to believe what comes off the grapevine,' he chided. 'That baby was congenitally defective. If she'd lived she'd have been a vegetable.'

'Her deformities were incompatible with life?' Helena wasn't sure why she persisted but she felt she had to. For Fran's sake.

George scowled, obviously annoyed with the question. He hadn't chewed her out, blaming her for Petey's death. She'd better stop pushing her luck.

'Her heart was normal on autopsy,' George said crisply. 'The other problems evidently caused the heart to fail.' He stared at her disapprovingly. 'I suggest you tend to business and stop listening to troublemakers.'

Helena backed off, unwilling to brave George's displeasure by asking if there'd been any other inexplicable sudden deaths. For all she knew, he could be right; the two most recent deaths might be a mere coincidence. Yet he'd indicated the newborn died of heart failure, as Petey had. Ultimately, of course, every death was because the heart failed. Even Fran's.

Still, she wasn't satisfied that the nurse assistant's remark had been pure smoke with no fire behind it.

After all, there was her sister to consider. Fran might not have been a patient at Harper Hills, but she sure as hell had died suddenly.

5

On Sunday, Helena's first day off duty, she rose early and made quick hospital rounds, then jumped into the VW and drove back to the apartment to change. The rest of the day was Laura's — they'd spend the morning on the beach and then she'd decide what to do next. It all depended on Laura. If it was one of her daughter's bad days, they might simply stay in the apartment until it was time to take Laura back to Sea Mist Manor.

Helena scanned the sidewalk as she got out of the car. At Harper Hills as well as at the De La Mar apartments, she'd been keeping an eye out for the red-haired teenager she'd passed on the stairs the day she'd arrived — the day Fran had been killed. She hadn't seen him again at either place. From the guarded questions she'd asked other tenants, she decided the youth probably didn't live at De La Mar. So what had he been doing there? If she couldn't force the police to do it for her, sooner or later she'd locate him and find out.

Once she'd changed into her maillot, jeans, and a tee shirt, Helena paused and glanced at her watch. Not quite nine. The card with Mak's number lay beside the phone. Call him before she left? She nodded grimly. With luck she'd get him out of bed and it would serve him right.

'Mak.' His voice was clipped.

'Helena Moore. You've got some explaining to do. Why didn't you — ?'

He cut across her words. 'I never explain anything over the phone. If you want answers, it'll be in person or not at all.'

'That's ridiculous!' she snapped.

'Not in my business, doctor. Take it or leave it.'

'I'm spending the day with my daughter and I can't be bothered finding time to — '

He interrupted again. 'You called me, I didn't call you. You want to talk, we meet.'

Helena held the phone away from her and glowered at it. She was tempted to slam it down but . . . no, she damn well was going to get her explanation.

'We'll be on the beach — look for us,' she said tersely, hanging up before he could get another word in.

She fumed and fretted all the way to Sea Mist. Why had she given in and invited Mak to the beach? Laura usually didn't take to strangers and it was doubtful she'd remember Mak from the night Fran died. His joining them might upset her daughter. On the other hand, if he didn't appear, he'd sure as hell upset *her*. Either way, she lost.

Laura didn't smile when she saw Helena but, when her mother knelt to talk to her, Laura unexpectedly hugged her, clinging for a long precious moment before reverting to her usual aloof manner. Laura's brief embrace almost undid Helena and she fought to keep from crying.

Though she once had known, Laura had forgotten how to respond to love. Quantitative impairment in reciprocal social interaction, the books said. Autistic Disorder, the psychiatrists labeled it.

At first Helena had fought the diagnosis. Laura had been such a sweet and responsive baby. But, as Roger had pointed out, time and again, quite often autistic children were normal infants before they changed into stiff little strangers. Ages ago, people had another word for children like Laura — changelings.

Long ago superstitious people had believed changelings, inhuman creatures who could never be taught to love, were put in the place of human children the elves and fairies took to be their own.

Helena certainly didn't believe old myths but sometimes, when she was tired and discouraged, it almost seemed to her that in some frightful, inexplicable way, Laura's spirit had been exchanged for something alien. But she loved her distant four-year-old just as much as she had her responsive baby.

Looking at her daughter now, Helena thought Laura seemed paler than usual, with dark circles under her eyes. Was she sick? Apparently not — her skin was cool, not feverish, and there was no evidence of illness.

I'll give her a thorough exam before I bring her back to Sea Mist, Helena promised herself.

She rose and grasped Laura's wrist gently, knowing the girl wouldn't take her hand. 'We're going to the beach,' she said. 'You'll like the ocean.'

She hoped her words would prove to be true. Laura generally did take to water — she liked swimming pools and gushing hoses and baths and showers. Oh my God, showers. Helena grimaced, unpleasantly reminded of Laura crouched beside Fran's dead body.

Firmly she thrust the image from her mind. She couldn't forget Fran's death any more than she could forget Fran but she must put it aside for the moment in order to share as pleasant a day as possible with her daughter.

El Doblez's public beach wasn't too crowded this early. Helena rented an umbrella and, choosing a spot near the water, spread an old quilt under its shade. Stripping down to her suit, she peeled off Laura's shorts and shirt and persuaded the girl into her swimsuit. After slathering sunscreen over both of them, she took Laura's wrist and led her across the sand to the water's edge. She stopped there, watching Laura's toes curl as the cool salt water lapped over their feet.

Laura sat down abruptly and dug her fingers into the wet sand, staring intently as it squished up between them. If left alone, she might keep doing this for hours, Helena knew. Kneeling beside her daughter, she mounded damp sand into the beginnings of a castle.

After a time a shadow fell across her and she looked up. Mak, wearing brief, bright blue trunks, stood over her. Helena drew in her breath when she saw the scars crisscrossing his tanned and muscular torso. Scars healed not all that long ago. Two years, maybe three.

He smiled briefly before crouching down near Laura. Cupping water in his palm, he trickled it over her knees, once, twice, then again and again until finally she looked at him.

'Hi, Laura,' he said. 'Remember me? I'm Mak.'

Her hand lifted until she touched his beard

with her wet, sandy fingers.

'Want me to take you into the water?' he asked.

Without waiting for a reply — not that Laura would have answered him — he lifted her into his arms, stood, and began wading into the surf. Helena tensed, uncertain how Laura would react. To her relief the girl neither screamed nor fought to free herself.

Helena rose and followed them, wincing at the water's chill. When she'd waded out far enough, she plunged into an oncoming wave, feeling an enjoyable shock as the water sluiced over her. When she surfaced she looked at Mak and Laura. He held one of Laura's wrists loosely, encouraging her to splash with her hand.

How the hell was she supposed to stay angry at a man who took her difficult daughter so matter-of-factly, who did his best to entertain Laura?

She wondered how he'd come by the scars. Obviously he'd had a near brush with death in the not-too-distant past. Danger might be par for policemen but whatever had happened to Mak must have been particularly violent.

When the three of them tired of the water and were sprawled peacefully on the quilt under the umbrella, Helena decided to defer her questions. Laura, now twisting a string around her fingers, had been so good that Helena hated to disturb the status quo. She wanted answers and she meant to get them but it could wait until later.

'Alligator,' Laura said suddenly, still intent on the string.

Mak raised an eyebrow. 'Where's the alligator?' he asked.

As Helena had expected, Laura didn't reply.

'Laura has a green stuffed alligator,' Helena explained. 'For some reason she thought of it.'

He nodded and rolled over onto his stomach, resting his head on his folded arms. 'We could have lunch together,' he suggested without looking at her.

Helena hesitated. It was always risky to eat out with Laura. She could invite Mak to the apartment but, since she hadn't planned on feeding him, she didn't have much to work with. Unless he was as fond of peanut butter as Laura was.

'If you'd rather eat at home,' he said, as though reading her mind, 'I'll spring for the pizza and milk.'

'Milk?' she asked in surprise.

He turned his head and opened one eye to look at her. 'Don't tell me Laura prefers beer?'

She poked his leg with her toe. 'Very funny.

As a matter of fact, she doesn't like anything that fizzes.'

'Okay, no beer then.' He shut the eye. 'What topping?'

'Cheese and sausage. She won't chew pepperoni and I loathe anchovies.'

'Gotcha.'

Pretty exciting company you've got here, Moore, she told herself ruefully. She glanced from Laura, silently involved with her piece of string, to Mak, who as far as she could tell was falling asleep.

She continued to look at him, at his tanned, scarred skin covering what appeared to be solid muscle. Not an ounce of excess fat anywhere. If she were writing up a history and physical she'd note that he was a well-developed, well-nourished male in his late thirties. Black hair, blue eyes, 6-foot-plus, weight about 220 pounds.

But that didn't capture his essence. Nor did it explain why she was sitting here fighting an impulse to push a strand of that dark hair off his forehead at the same time she was mentally condemning him for withholding facts.

'Six-two-and-a-half,' he said without opening his eyes, '221 pounds.'

'I've a good mind to pour sand in your ear,' she told him.

His eyes popped open. 'I can't believe a doctor would do anything so despicable.'

'You're right. But only because I'd wind up syringing the sand out so you wouldn't sue me. It's not worth the trouble.'

'I've never yet sued a doctor. Why should I make a lawyer wealthy?'

Helena smiled at him. 'A man after my own heart.'

He sat up, grinning. 'So you admit it. Good. I was beginning to think this affair was too damn one-sided.'

Despite his broad grin, Helena didn't miss the underlying seriousness in his voice. Affair? They weren't having an affair and they wouldn't *be* having an affair. Ever. Not that she meant to say so because it would give him an opening to discuss their relationship. She was searching for a flippant response when her daughter took her off the hook.

'Alligator,' Laura said, offering her piece of string to Mak.

Helena, making the connection, burst into laughter. 'It's your teeth,' she told him, when she could speak. 'Her toy alligator has lots of sharp white teeth.'

Mak, holding the string, raised his eyebrows at Helena. 'I file mine every night,' he said, 'so watch out. You never know what an alligator might do.'

Turning to Laura, he tied the string around his middle finger. 'That's so I'll remember to get the pizza,' he told her.

He was charmingly disarming, no doubt about that, Helena thought. But after lunch, if Laura napped as she usually did, there'd be a confrontation time. Mak was going to need more than charm to convince her he wasn't hiding from her what he knew about Fran. As well as what he and Fran had been to one another. Though the idea set her teeth on edge, how did she know he wasn't the father of Fran's baby?

★　★　★

Mak climbed the stairs to Helena's apartment, balancing the giant pizza carton in one hand while he carried the bag with the milk, grapes, ice cream, and hot fudge topping in the other.

Alligator. He smiled, remembering what Laura had called him. According to Helena she rarely paid any attention to people and never spoke to a stranger. He liked kids and he'd taken quite a fancy to Laura, odd little thing that she was — maybe she sensed that.

He'd taken quite a fancy to her mother, too, rotten timing though it might be. Have to watch himself with her or, considering his

86

involvement with this case, he'd wind up in deep shit.

Mima had taught him, the hard way, never to trust a woman. Ironically, the last laugh had been on her. She'd expected him to wind up a cripple but he'd fooled both her and the doctors. He hadn't expected to have all that money fall into his lap — Mima sure as hell would have stayed around if *she'd* known. But by that time their divorce was final — signed, sealed, and delivered. She didn't get a cent.

As he pushed Helena's doorbell with his elbow, he tried to decide how little he could get away with telling her when she began to ask her questions. Unfortunately, doctors had a way of probing until they found what they were looking for but she'd be dealing with a world class evader.

She opened the door and stepped aside to let him in. He'd savored the way she looked in her blue maillot but now, in the long pink tee shirt that hid the shorts she must be wearing underneath, with her dark hair still damp from the shower, she looked so fresh and desirable that everything went out of his mind except his need for her. He stood there with the food in his hand, staring at her like an idiot.

'Since Laura decided she was willing to sit

on a stool,' Helena said, 'we'll eat at the kitchen counter instead of the dinette table.'

Her words jerked him back to reality — and reality was knowing enough to keep his hands off her.

Though the sticky cheese on her slice of pizza seemed to fascinate Laura, she ate nothing but a few grapes and a small dish of ice cream before Helena took her away to wash her face and hands.

'She's half asleep so I put her on my bed,' Helena said when she returned alone. 'All that sun and sea air got to her, I guess.'

Mak slid off the stool, smiling wryly. 'So now it's my turn to be got to?'

'I was going to let you finish your coffee first.'

He waved the coffee aside and sauntered into the living room, standing by the window so he could lean on the top of the book case. 'I've always hated third degrees — let's get it over with.'

'If you're trying to put me on the defensive, you've failed, Captain Maklin.' She marched up to confront him. 'Why didn't you tell me you'd dated Fran?'

'Because I didn't. Who said I dated her?'

'Reed Addison, the head pharmacist told me you were Fran's 'new interest'. That certainly implies dating.'

'I interviewed her several times. For my own reasons I didn't want to talk to her at Harper Hills and, for her own reasons, she didn't invite me to her apartment. We had coffee together in a beach cafe during one interview and, for another, we met in a bar. Her choice.'

Helena stared at him. 'Interview Fran? Whatever for?'

'I can't tell you, it's privileged information. Like between patient and doctor.'

Her eyes narrowed and he could see she was trying to make up her mind whether to believe him or not.

'Police business?' she demanded.

He hesitated. God knows he'd given her enough hints that he was no longer a cop: he might as well come right out and admit it. 'Not exactly. I'm not a member of any police force.'

'But — but you came here with the El Doblez Police when I called them about Fran. They acted as though you were one of them.'

He shrugged. 'I used to be a cop in LA — they know it. Cops are like any other professionals — we tend to stick together. They knew I was on a case and they also knew I'd talked to Fran. I happened to be at the station when your call came in so they let me tag along out of courtesy.'

She folded her arms across her breasts and glared at him. 'If you're no longer a cop, just what in hell are you?'

'Private investigator. The business attracts a lot of excops.' Actually he didn't have to work at all if he didn't want to, but he wasn't going to tell her that. 'Questioning your sister was part of the case I'm on. My questions and her answers belong to my client and to no one else.'

'You won't tell me what you're investigating?'

'I can't.'

'Does it have something to do with Harper Hills Hospital?'

He shrugged. 'I can't tell you that either.'

She exhaled with a short, angry sound. 'I think I deserve to know if Fran's death was a result of something she was involved in, something you questioned her about.'

He considered a moment. 'The truth is I don't know. Not yet.'

The phone rang, giving him a break he was glad to take.

Helena picked it up. A moment later she slammed the phone down.

'Wrong number?' he asked.

'He's a breather, that's all I know.' Her voice was gritty with anger. 'This wasn't his first call. I asked the phone company to change my number but they haven't gotten around to it yet.'

'I'll make sure they do first thing tomorrow,' he said grimly.

'Thanks.' Her brief smile looked forced. 'He never says a word — I don't know why it upsets me so much.' The smile grew more genuine. 'At least I know *you're* not the caller. Not that I ever seriously suspected you.'

'I sure as hell hope not!'

'It's just not your style.'

The tone of her voice told him she'd decided to forgive him for not letting her know he was acquainted with her sister. Mak relaxed a little. 'What *is* my style?' he asked.

'Laid-back. Sort of all-good-things-come-to-he-who-watches-and-waits.'

'Seems like most good things would be more likely to pass by a watcher and waiter on their way somewhere else.'

She shook her head. 'I don't believe for one minute that you underestimate your style. Or yourself.'

Was she right? All he knew was he'd damned near died three years ago because he'd overestimated his abilities. Thought he was God, or the next thing to it. Mighty Mak. Invincible. He'd learned he was wrong — the hard way. Pushing those dark memories back where they belonged, he moved closer to where she was perched on the arm of the couch.

'I'll accept the diagnosis, doctor,' he said. 'It's not often I get one for free. But the truth is I don't feel particularly laid-back at the moment.' He was near enough to smell the faint, flowery fragrance of the soap she used. 'Must be the company I keep.'

The pupils of her blue-green eyes dilated slightly, responding to his closeness. He'd read somewhere that meant a woman was attracted to a man. It sure as hell was mutual, unwise though it might be. For both of them.

'Watching's okay but I don't really want to wait,' he told her.

Her hand moved a little, as though to ward him off. 'I'm not available.' Her voice was breathless, telling him she was lying — to herself, maybe, as much as to him.

The El Doblez Police had run a routine check on her so he knew she was divorced from Laura's father — she was available in that sense. He held back his impulse to touch her. One touch wouldn't be enough for him, and with Laura asleep in the bedroom, this wasn't the time or place for anything more.

'A man?' he asked.

She shook her head. 'Just plain not available.'

So there wasn't anyone else. Mak smiled to himself. Eventually the right time and place would present itself and then he'd test that nonavailability.

'I'm bothered about a case at Harper Hills,' she said, obviously switching to what she considered a safer topic. 'Ordinarily I wouldn't mention it to anyone on the outside but, though you won't — or can't — tell me, I suspect your investigation has something to do with the hospital. It's too much of a coincidence that Fran worked there, was fired for some reason nobody will explain, and you interviewed her twice. So I'm going to break a rule. If you'll stop looming over me and sit down.'

Mak ambled away, lowered himself onto a chair, and looked at her expectantly.

Helena slid down onto the couch until she was curled in one corner. 'I had a little boy die unexpectedly the other night. Soon afterward I overheard a nurse attendant on peds telling the night charge that my patient's death 'made another one'. When I asked what she meant, no one wanted to tell me anything more but I managed to learn there'd been at least one other unexpected death of a child recently. In the newborn nursery — where Fran worked. I couldn't help but put the pieces together. Do you know if that's why Fran was fired?'

Mak hesitated. She was bound to find out about Fran sooner or later, so he might as well tell her that much.

'I know a baby died in the nursery,' he said carefully. 'Fran told me she made a fuss about the baby's death because she thought she'd seen someone slip from the nursery earlier that night. Her supervisor decided Fran was trying to cover up her own negligence and said so to the Director of Nursing. I gather Fran had been calling in sick a lot in the past few months and was often late in getting to work when she did show up — that didn't help her case. The DSN recommended she be let go for 'unsatisfactory performance of professional duties'.'

Helena bit her lip. 'That was over a month ago. Why didn't she tell me?'

Mak shrugged. 'Pride?'

'I guess I didn't know Fran as well as I thought.' Helena's forlorn expression tempted Mak to get up and put his arms around her. He forced himself to stay seated.

Visibly pulling herself together, Helena sat straighter. 'How about Xenara? You asked me about Fran and Xenara but I'll bet she told you everything there is to know about any involvement she had with that cult.'

'You're wrong. Fran was fairly open about Harper Hills but close-mouthed about

Xenara. I know she went a lot to the temple or pyramid or whatever they call it, but what she did there is as much of a mystery to me as Xenara's real purpose.'

'Real purpose? Isn't it spiritual healing, whatever that may be?'

'So they say. I'd like to know the mechanics of this so-called healing.'

'There's a cassette here . . . ' she began.

He waved it away. 'I've seen the cassette —Vada Rogers in a slinky white dress reciting a bunch of gibberish, making nonsense sound like the truth of the ages.'

'I thought Vada was very attractive. Do you know her?' Her tone held a slight edge he'd like to think might be jealousy.

'I've met her.'

'Does that mean you've been to Xenara?'

He nodded. 'Sat in on a couple of sessions. Never been so bored in my life — and that includes stakeouts, the acme of boredom.'

Helena sat forward. 'Our mother, Fran's and mine, has been into the supernormal ever since I can remember and she did her best to brainwash both Fran and me from the cradle on up. Maybe that's why we gravitated to science — to compensate. Anyway, once we grew up neither of us could tolerate even a suggestion of the paranormal. We just plain didn't believe in any of it. Feeling that way, it's hard for me to understand how Fran could become a convert overnight. But why else would she get involved in something like Xenara?'

The hair on Mak's nape prickled. Helena's words convinced him he'd missed something when he'd investigated Fran's connection to Xenara. If he'd known Fran was unlikely to be a believer, he'd have dug deeper. Fran had been the only link he'd found between Xenara and Harper Hills and he'd all but dismissed the connection as a coincidence. He had some checking to do.

'Did Fran ever get breather calls?' Helena asked suddenly.

He frowned. 'Not that she ever told me. And I think she would have.'

'So the calls are for me.'

'Come on, Helena, some weirdo dials a number at random, hears a woman's voice, and so keeps the number in mind. That's the most likely explanation.'

'But is it the right one? My sister's dead and suddenly I'm getting breather calls. I told you he never says anything. There really isn't any suggestion of the obscene in his breathing pattern, either. It's not like he's getting it on or anything, he just — breathes. Or maybe she. How can I tell?'

'It's almost always a man.' Mak spoke

absently, her words triggering alarm bells in his mind. Damn it, the calls *could* be related to Fran's death. He leaped to his feet, strode into the kitchen, and grabbed the phone.

Helena tagged after him. 'What're you doing?' she asked.

'What I should have done the moment you mentioned the calls. What you should have done instead of putting up with them. I'm notifying the El Doblez Police.'

He turned to look at her before punching in the number. 'I can't prove it and neither can they but my gut feeling tells me your sister's death was murder one.'

6

At noon on Thursday, Helena was about to set her lunch tray on an empty table in the doctor's dining room when Jeff Hillyer hailed her from one of the outdoor tables. She joined him.

She was taking her dishes off the tray when a handsome silver-haired man of about forty carrying a cup of coffee approached.

'Mind if I sit down for a minute?' Since he'd already placed his coffee on the table, Jeff's shrug was superfluous.

'Helena, this arrogant shrink is Peter Herron,' Jeff said. 'And I warn you, he didn't choose this table because of his fondness for me.'

'Don't pay any attention to him, Helena,' Peter Herron said with a smile. 'Jeff's a classic paranoid when he's with a woman — always thinking someone's trying to muscle in on him.'

'Not someone — you. Not think — know.' Jeff's tone held an edge of belligerence.

Since there was no romantic involvement between her and Jeff, Helena realized Jeff's antagonism came from some other time and some other woman.

'Actually I just wanted to meet George's paragon,' Peter said. 'I can't recall when I last heard him admit a woman doctor had any expertise whatsoever. Helena, he claims, 'might turn into a halfway decent pediatrician.' For George, that's high praise.' Peter's smile focused on her.

With his wavy silver hair, gray eyes, and even features, the psychiatrist was as handsome in his way as Mak was homely in his. And, unless she'd lost her touch at reading signals, he was interested in her.

Helena raised an eyebrow at Peter. 'You're sure you didn't leave off a qualifying word or two of George's? Like — 'though it'll take her at least twenty years'?'

Jeff stood up abruptly. 'See you later,' he said to Helena. With a curt nod to Peter, he strode off.

'Have you got something going with Jeff?' Peter asked.

Somewhat surprised at the blunt question — weren't shrinks supposed to be subtle? — Helena tried to decide whether Peter was invading her privacy or not. Possibly he simply wanted the decks cleared and she could understand that.

'No,' she said.

There was a moment's silence. 'Interesting

you didn't add 'we're just friends',' Peter observed. 'Most women would have.'

She took a sip of her coffee. 'My rule is never to give a psychiatrist any advantage.'

'Is that a warning?'

She shrugged. 'Nothing personal. I just feel you guys tot us up with every word we say.'

'Aha, prejudice. We'll discuss that problem at greater length over dinner Saturday night. You're not on call — I asked George.'

Was he actually assuming she had no choice but to go out with him? She was beginning to understand why Jeff labeled him an 'arrogant shrink.'

Before she could come up with an answer, Peter leaned toward her and added, 'Please don't refuse. I really do want to get to know you. It's not often Harper Hills acquires someone as unusual as you.'

She felt his charm surround her like a force field. Rather than resist it, she asked herself what she had to lose by dining with him. Peter might irritate her but so far he hadn't bored her. Besides, going out with him might break up her increasing absorption with Mak. She was afraid to think about what might have happened between them last Sunday if Laura hadn't been in the apartment.

She was becoming far too attracted to Mak and this was the time to stop it — before they passed the point of no return. Peter might be the antidote she needed.

'I'll dine with you on Saturday evening, Dr. Herron,' she said formally, 'but if there is a next time I'd prefer the option of saying yes or no before you make any assumptions. Otherwise my refusal will be automatic.'

He smiled. 'Well said. I look forward to an interesting meal — I always enjoy a worthy opponent.' He rose. 'I'll call for you at eight.'

Helena watched him walk away, pondering his words and wondering what she was letting herself in for. A doctor wasn't basically any different from the next man when it came to moving in on a woman — but surely a psychiatrist ought to pick up cues that would tell him she wasn't about to leap into bed with him. Or with any other man, for that matter. Not in the near — or even in the foreseeable — future.

She finished her tomato and alfalfa-sprout on wheat sandwich and settled back to nurse the remainder of her coffee while going over what she'd learned the past few days. Not much. Confronted with what Helena had picked up from Mak, Idalia Davin had admitted hospital gossip linked Fran's firing to a nursery death but she'd refused to discuss that or any other sudden deaths on peds, claiming she knew absolutely nothing.

Why, though, had Idalia been so nervous while they talked?

As for the breather — Helena hadn't heard from him since her phone number had been changed. She supposed she had Mak to thank for the telephone company's prompt response.

Laura remained a worry. The physical she'd done on her daughter hadn't shown any gross abnormalities, though she wasn't satisfied about the neurological exam — a failure since Laura wouldn't cooperate. Perhaps she could bring Laura to Harper Hills sometime soon for George to look her over. And, as long as she'd accepted a dinner date with Peter Herron, she might as well take the opportunity to get a psychiatrist's opinion of the Sea Mist staff and their approach to autism.

From Laura's problems, her thoughts drifted toward another child with potential problems — the three-pound premature baby she'd helped George with earlier today. The incredibly tiny girl had seemed unusually vigorous for so small a baby but immature lungs, kidneys, liver, and immune and nervous systems could lead to all sorts of life-threatening problems in a preemie.

Sepsis and meningitis were four times greater than in a normal gestation infant so she'd have to be on the alert for infection. The baby was being monitored carefully

— the hospital was exceptionally lucky to have a nursery nurse as well-qualified as Clovis Reilly — but a preemie could go sour between one heartbeat and the next. The last thing they needed was another sudden death.

She succeeded in raising her anxiety level so high that she decided to run over to the nursery and check the preemie's condition before she returned to peds.

'Little Kristle's doing okay, doctor,' Clovis assured her as they gazed down into the incubator where tubes and wires crisscrossed the little body. 'Don't forget, she's a girl — that gives her an extra chance.'

Clovis's reminder was right. More female newborns than males survived — including preemies. Feeling moderately reassured, at least for the moment. Helena smiled at Clovis.

As she was leaving, Helena paused. 'I realize no one in Harper Hills wants to talk about my sister,' she said, 'but you worked with Fran and you must have gotten to know her. I've been told why she was fired. Do you think that baby died because of her?'

Clovis looked at her for a long moment before answering. 'I knew Fran,' she said finally. 'She wasn't a bad nurse — I don't think she'd willfully neglect a patient. But — ' she hesitated — 'something happened to her in the last couple of months she worked here. She was on the night shift; I work days but I'm the nursery supervisor for all three shifts so I know she began calling in sick a lot and when she did show up she'd be late more often than not. That kind of behavior runs up a red flag in the DNS's office. Mrs. Morrin, the Director, got on my case and I had to confront Fran.

'She admitted she had a problem but assured me she was close to solving it. I gave her another chance.' Clovis sighed. 'Then the baby died and there were no more chances left for Fran.'

In more ways than one. Helena blinked back tears and forced herself to go on. 'Fran claimed she saw someone slip out of the nursery that night.'

'As far as I know, she wasn't a liar,' Clovis said slowly, 'but . . . ' Her words trailed off and she shrugged.

'Thanks for being so frank,' Helena said, her voice husky with the tears she held back. 'I appreciate it.'

If only Fran had told her what was happening, had shared her problems, maybe her sister would still be alive. Unfortunately, it was Fran's nature to be secretive.

That night Helena slept poorly, jerking awake at intervals and sitting up, listening, thinking someone had called her name. When she woke near three in the morning, a faint scratching sound from the living room made her sit bolt upright.

Someone was trying to get into the apartment! Had she remembered to lock the windows facing onto the walkway? Though the grill might prevent entry, it wouldn't keep someone from opening an unlocked window. Terrified, she flicked on the bedside lamp, grabbed the bedside phone, and called Mak.

He arrived within minutes, giving his name when he knocked on the door. By then Helena had regained some control and, as she let him in, she apologized for disturbing him.

'I really got hyper,' she said. 'I did hear something but I guess I should have called the police instead of bothering you.'

'I'm here, I'll take care of it,' he said shortly. After a quick check of her apartment to make certain all the windows were locked, he went back outside. Moments later, he summoned her to join him.

'Look at this,' he said.

His flashlight illuminated a pyre of burnt matches on the cement walkway outside one of the living room windows.

Helena gasped, clutching his arm. 'It's a pyramid!' she cried. 'Like the one I found in

Fran's ashtray the day she was killed. The very same.'

He urged her back inside, locking the door behind them.

'Fran's killer was out there!' she exclaimed in horror. 'Mak, I'm scared.'

He pulled her into his arms, holding her close and she clung to him, comforted by his solid warmth, feeling safe and secure in his embrace.

'I'm glad your first thought was to call me,' he murmured into her ear, his breath a warm tingle, his beard brushing softly against her skin. 'I won't let anything happen to you. Ever.'

She didn't want to let him go — she needed Mak's arms around her. His lips touched her ear, traveling across her neck, then her cheek to her mouth in what he might have meant to be a reassuring kiss. She'd never know for sure because when their lips met it was like being in a major earthquake — at least 6.5 on the Richter scale.

Nothing like it had ever happened to her before. Shaken beyond thought, all she could do was cling to him, responding to the deepening kiss with every cell in her body.

Desire flared inside her as she savored his rich dark flavor, his masculine scent, the hard strength of his body. What with her disillusionment over Roger's betrayal, the struggle to study for and pass her licensure boards, the never-ending hours of the internship plus trying to be a mother to Laura, she hadn't had the time, energy, or inclination for sex.

Or possibly she just hadn't met the right man. This particular one. Mak. Because she wanted him more than she could ever recall wanting anyone else — including Roger.

When he rocked her against him, showing her that his need for her was equally urgent, a thrill sliced through her. She murmured in pleasure when his hand slipped under her sleepshirt to caress her bare skin. She longed to feel that touch everywhere.

'If you want to stop,' he whispered against her lips, 'say so now or it'll be too late.'

She wanted his love-making to go on forever, yet his whisper coiled in her mind like a snake, chilling her.

What did she know about Mak? Damn little. Caution filtered through the erotic haze fuzzing her senses and she pulled back a little. As though he'd been anticipating a negative signal, he immediately released her, his blue eyes almost as dark as night as they looked into hers.

'I swore to myself I wouldn't touch you,' he

said, his voice raspy, 'but, damn it, I had to. It's all I can do to keep from reaching for you right now.'

Could he see how difficult it was for her to keep from falling into his arms again?

He smiled one-sidedly. 'Hell of a powerful current running between us. Much more and we'd be electrocuted.'

She nodded, swallowing, unable to look away or move.

'You want to take more time, right?'

'I — I don't know.' She spoke the truth. 'You confuse me.'

He relaxed a little and his smile broadened. 'I don't have AIDS, doctor. Honest. Or any other STD.'

'It didn't even cross my mind,' she admitted, aware it should have, shocked that she hadn't even wondered if he might have any one of the many sexually transmitted diseases. 'But, as long as you've brought it up, I don't either.' She ran her fingers through her hair. 'What a conversation to be having at two in the morning!'

'Yeah. Romantic as hell, isn't it?'

She began to giggle and heard him chuckle. Their laughter broke the spell for Helena so she was able to turn away, still smiling, and walk toward the kitchen.

'Want some coffee?' she asked over her shoulder.

'Nope. But, if you like, I'll sleep on your couch for the rest of the night.'

She knew if he left she wouldn't sleep; she dreaded being alone to wonder if someone waited and watched outside her windows. 'I'm not usually a scaredy-cat,' she told him, 'but, yes, I'd like you to stay. You could use the other bedroom.'

'Your sister's?'

She nodded.

'The couch is comfortable enough, thanks.'

'Well, then, good night.'

He caught her wrist as she made a move to leave. 'What's between us isn't polite enough to quietly tiptoe away. You'll have to make up your mind sooner or later.'

'But not tonight,' she said.

'How about dinner Saturday night?'

'I'm — that is, I have another engagement.'

He scowled. 'With Jeff?'

Helena's eyes widened. Mak looked like a thunderstorm. What business was it of his who she went out with?

'No, not Jeff.' She had no intention of telling him anything more — he didn't even deserve that much. Did he think one kiss meant he owned her?

If he was going to behave unreasonably, it

would be better if she didn't see Mak again, if she cut the relationship off before it grew any more intense. The last thing she needed in her life was a jealous man.

Once in bed, she tossed restlessly. Not because she feared the prowler had returned but because she was all too aware of Mak on the living room couch and couldn't help vividly recalling how wonderfully exciting it was to be in his arms. If she hadn't made up her mind to stop seeing him, the temptation to join him might well have overcome her.

Near dawn she fell into such a profound sleep that when the alarm rang, jerking her into awareness, for a moment she couldn't remember where she was or why she smelled coffee.

Fran's apartment, she told herself dazedly. The guest bedroom. Mak slept in the living room. He's made coffee.

But, when she'd made herself presentable enough to appear, she found he wasn't in the apartment. He'd fixed coffee, had drank a mugful, and left her the rest. Mak was gone and there was no note.

Good, she told herself, trying to ignore her disappointment. Maybe he realizes there's no future in this for either of us.

★ ★ ★

Friday night she was on call and, when the ER doc phoned her around midnight about a kid with a stiff neck, she was dozing on the couch, having put off going to bed.

Dr. Kim, a policeman, and two nurses were trying to cope with a screaming cocaine OD when she walked in so she was on her own. By glancing behind each examining cubicle curtain, she located the pediatric case, an eighteen-month-old boy.

'I'm Dr. Moore,' she told the dark-skinned mother. 'Can you tell me how long Hodey has been sick?'

'We was down south the last couple weeks, you know? He pukes in the car going down and he look kinda puny afterwards so I takes him to this clinic they got down there.'

'Down where?' Helena put in as she bent over the lethargic Hodey, peering in his eyes with her ophththal-moscope.

'San Ysidro. This doctor, he give Hodey a shot and he say come back but I tell him we ain't gonna be there, we going to Escondido, so he give me some medicine, he say make Hodey swallow it down.'

'How long did you give Hodey the medicine?'

When the mother didn't answer, Helena turned to look at her and the woman, her face sullen said, 'Hodey, he don't like no

111

medicine, he done spit it out.'

'That does happen,' Helena said. 'A going-on-two-year-old can be pretty stubborn.'

The woman's face lightened. 'That sure be the truth.'

Turning back to Hodey, Helena said, 'Did you happen to bring the medicine along with you?'

'I sure did, doctor, 'cause I knows you be wanting to see it.'

When Helena finished listening to Hodey's heart and lungs with her stethoscope, she took the bottle the woman offered her. Almost full of the ampicillin prescribed by Paul Salvador, M.D.

Helena set the bottle on the stand near the little boy's gurney. 'Did Hodey get any better after the shot?' she asked.

'Seem like he did, only then he gets worse.'

Helena nodded, trying to bend Hodey's neck forward. Stiff as a board. 'Can you remember anything Dr. Salvador told you about Hodey?'

'After he poke my poor baby in the back with this great big needle, he say something-itis, I don't recollect them long doctor words so good.'

So Dr. Salvador had done a spinal tap and

come to the conclusion Hodey had meningitis. Since he couldn't be certain without waiting for a C&S, a culture and sensitivity test, he'd given an antibiotic, ampicillin, that would kill most of the bacteria that caused meningitis.

With luck Dr. Salvador *had* done a C&S and by now the organism would have grown in the media. A phone call to San Ysidro would give her the results. Meanwhile, she didn't dare leave Hodey untreated until she found out what organism was causing his meningitis so she'd give him another shot of ampicillin right now and then admit him to the CD unit where she'd do another spinal tap. To do the procedure here would delay admission and further upset the mother. Besides, the ER personnel were otherwise occupied.

She was convinced Hodey did have meningitis — inadequately treated, through no fault of Dr. Salvador.

'I'd like to keep Hodey in the hospital for a couple of days,' Helena told the mother. 'He needs to have some more shots to get rid of his infection.'

The woman's hands clenched in her lap. 'He be that sick, doctor?'

'I think you know he's pretty sick,' Helena said as gently as she could. 'We've got to get the medicine into him so he'll get better. Shots are the quickest way.'

'You gonna take care of him?'

Helena nodded. 'I'll be his doctor. Along with Dr. Wittenburg. He's a specialist in meningitis and I'm pretty sure that's what Hodey has.'

'Long's you gonna be there.'

'I promise. You can come up to the unit with us so you'll know what room he's in and all. And, if you want to stay — '

'Wish I could, doctor, I surely do, but I can't. Hodey ain't my only child, I got four more.'

'They're all well?'

'Bright and fine, they be.'

'Good. If any of them gets sick, you be sure to call and tell me, okay? I'll write my name and number down for you.' Helena folded an admittance form and scribbled her name and number.

The woman's eyes widened. 'You mean what Hodey's got's catching?'

'Not necessarily. Not like chicken pox. But just in case, you take this.' She handed over the paper.

By the time Hodey was settled in a crib in CD and the spinal tap was done, it was close to three o'clock. The thought of going home and climbing the stairs alone to her apartment sent a shiver of dread along Helena's spine.

'Where can I catch a few hours sleep?' she asked Ms. Peterson, the night charge nurse.

'Only two of the CD rooms are occupied,' Ms. Peterson pointed out. 'You could use one of the empty ones.'

'Thanks. If nothing else comes up, wake me about six, would you please?'

The nurse woke her at five. 'Hodey's mother is on the phone. Something about a sick baby. She insists you said to call her.'

Helena sat up groggily. Swinging her legs off the bed, she nodded. 'I'll take the call.'

As Helena picked up the desk phone, she heard sirens approaching the hospital. The ER must be having one of those nightmare nights. 'Dr. Moore here,' she said.

'Kezia, she my niece, her ma's my sister. She sort of shaking all over. You say call you, so I does.'

Helena tried to clear her mind enough to sort this out. 'How old is Kezia?'

'She be 'bout six months.'

'Has she been around Hodey?'

'They done drive down south with us. My kids, they all fine. Kezia, she don't be so good.'

'Can you or your sister bring her to the Emergency Room?'

'Soon's we find a ride. You gonna be there?'

'If I'm not in the ER, I'll be here in the hospital. You tell the ER receptionist that I said to page Dr. Moore, okay? I want to examine Kezia myself.'

Helena looked in on Hodey and, after satisfying herself he was stable, brushed her hair and washed her face in the peds nurses' lounge. She thought about running home for a shower and a change of clothes but decided instead to go down to the ER. If they were busy she might be able to help while she waited for Kezia.

In the ER she found barely controlled chaos. Dr. Kim and two nurses had the crash cart in one cubicle, trying to revive a coronary infarct. Two ambulances had just unloaded the victims of a one-car crash, both with multiple injuries. The woman, an intravenous line in place, was in obvious shock and Helena hurriedly evaluated her while the receptionist paged any doctors in the house.

'Call a neurosurgeon immediately — stat!' Helena ordered after lifting the woman's eyelids and seeing the pupil of her left eye was grossly dilated, with the right one normal-sized. A brain injury, for sure.

The paramedics had strapped the man's right leg into a splint. He had several superficial lacerations of his right arm and a nasty-looking deep one across his shoulder. All during her examination he groaned, clutching his abdomen and complaining of pain there. The skin of the abdomen was intact. Ruptured organ from blunt trauma? She couldn't be sure.

Trauma cases had never been her forte, so when she heard Jeff Hillyer's deep voice behind her, she sighed in relief.

'Got an OR case at seven,' he said. 'I just walked in the door when I heard the page. What've we got here?'

She told him what she'd found so far. By the time she finished, Dr. Kim came hurrying up. At the same moment, the receptionist called, 'I got a baby convulsing here!'

Helena ran into the waiting area and plucked the infant from the arms of a thin black woman. 'Follow me,' she said over her shoulder as she carried the twitching baby into the examining area.

'Kezia?' she asked as she lay the infant down and pulled off the blanket. The child's normally dark skin was gray from cyanosis, the eyes rolled up, the body rigid in a tonic seizure.

'Yeah,' the woman whispered.

'I'm Dr. Moore,' Helena told her. Raising her voice she shouted for a nurse to bring an ampule of phenobarbital stat. Grabbing an infant's mask from an emergency pack, she hooked it to oxygen and clapped it over the baby's nose and mouth, turning the child onto one side to reduce the chances of her choking if she vomited.

'How long has she been sick?' Helena asked as she waited impatiently for the phenobarb.

'She had like a cold for a couple days. Then she starts in to jerking sometimes. I done bring her over to my sister for her to see and she calls you up right away quick. By the time I got me a taxi — ' the woman's voice broke — 'Kezia's eyes roll up in her head and she stiffen out like she already dead.'

A nurse hurried up with the ampule and Helena injected an appropriate dosage intramuscularly. Considering the rush in the ER, she decided, a spinal puncture could wait until Kezia was admitted.

'Like Hodey, Kezia may have meningitis,' she said. 'She needs to stay in the hospital, okay?'

Kezia's mother nodded. 'She gonna be all right?'

Helena believed in being honest. Meningitis in babies under a year of age was often fatal. 'I hope so. We'll do our best — but she's very sick.'

The woman swallowed, her eyes filling with tears. 'She the onliest one I got. She all I got.'

Helena wanted to put a comforting hand on her shoulder but Kezia required her full attention. 'I have a little girl, too,' she said, offering what she could, knowing it wasn't enough. Sometimes she felt that whatever doctors offered was never enough.

7

When George Wittenburg arrived at the CD unit shortly after eight Helena was still hovering over Kezia even though the baby had stopped convulsing.

'I have this notion that if I turn my back, she'll go sour and I'll lose her,' Helena said as she watched George examine Kezia.

'You're heading for ulcer country,' he warned her. 'This little tiger's stable enough for you to eat breakfast. Let the nurses keep an eye on her — that's what they're here for.'

George joined Helena for coffee in the cafeteria. While she ate, she filled him in on the history of the cousins, Hodey and Kezia.

'Paul Salvador used to practice at Harper Hills,' George said. 'He's sure to have done a C&S — I'll put a call in to him.'

'Hodey's definitely improved after two shots of ampicillin,' she said. 'He never did convulse.'

George nodded. 'So we're probably looking at bacterial meningitis. With luck, Paul will have already identified the organism for us.'

'I did spinal taps on both of them and sent C&S's to our lab,' she put in.

'Confirmation's always welcome.'

He spoke casually but she knew if she'd failed to do the spinals he'd be letting her have it right about now. 'What do you think of Kezia's chances?' she asked.

Before George answered, his wife, Carin, strolled up to the table with coffee and took a chair. 'Don't pay any attention to me,' she said. 'I'm just a fly on the wall.'

'Got a couple of admissions to CD last night,' George told his wife. 'Meningitis.' He turned to Helena. 'If Kezia makes it, she may be left with some residual deficit,' he said. 'I didn't do a complete neurological on her but she has a couple of abnormal reflexes, as you probably noticed. Let's entice Jeff down here and see what he thinks.'

'He's scrubbing on a case this morning,' Helena said.

'We'll catch him before lunch,' George said, rising. Helena started to get up, too, but he waved her back down. 'Take your time — I've got an ethics committee meeting that'll run a half-hour, anyway. We'll make rounds after the meeting.'

'George hates meetings,' Carin observed as her husband left the cafeteria. 'He's not a political person.'

Helena smiled, reflecting on the fact that she wasn't political either, a fact Roger had lamented. Her exhusband's view was that apple-polishing paid off. He claimed he wouldn't go so far as to kiss ass but Helena wasn't so sure.

She supposed she ought to welcome this chance to ingratiate herself with George's wife. She didn't dislike Carin but she was too tired and too worried about Kezia to relax and make idle conversation. Even at her best she wasn't good at small talk.

'You look beat,' Carin said. 'Up all night?'

'Some of it, anyway,' Helena confessed.

'I suppose it was the meningitis cases. Are either of them on the critical list?'

Helena hesitated. Carin had mentioned that George discussed patients with her — that was his privilege and his decision. But she wasn't George. And she'd never made it a practice to talk about her cases to anyone other than the doctors she worked with. On the other hand, she didn't want to antagonize Carin needlessly.

'Meningitis is always serious,' she said finally. 'Which reminds me that I'd better run up and have another look at my patients before rounds.' Helena rose. 'Nice to talk to you, Carin.'

'Sometime when you're not on call we'll have a *real* talk,' Carin promised.

Helena nodded, smiling, but as she walked

away she wondered what Carin meant by *real*. Was it only a pleasant and probably meaningless courtesy like 'we'll have lunch sometime' or did Carin plan to try to use her to probe the George/Idalia relationship?

Of course it was possible Carin suspected nothing about her husband and the peds charge nurse. Helena grimaced. Carin wouldn't be the first wife to wear blinders — maybe even on purpose.

Jeff stopped by CD just before noon to take a look at Kezia. Helena, helping him do the neurological exam, noted with dismay a definite abnormality in the reflexes on the baby's right side.

'You can't be sure of permanent brain damage in infants,' Jeff said when he finished and was washing his hands. 'They sometimes bounce back and test out relatively normal later on.'

'But she's not testing normal now.'

'No. If she doesn't improve, it could be she'll have some residual hemiparesis on the right.'

'What about intellectual deficit?'

He shrugged. 'Too early to tell. We'll have to wait and see.' Jeff stepped behind her, put his hands on her shoulders, thumbs touching her nape, and began massaging her muscles. 'Relax,' he advised. 'Your shoulder girdle's all knotted up. Hasn't anyone ever told you that uptight doctors don't cure any more patients than laid-back ones?'

'That feels wonderful,' she told him, her tension dissipating as her muscles relaxed under his expert touch.

'Ever do meditation?'

'I never seem to have time.'

He sighed. 'The point is to *take* time. Why don't you visit Xenara for a few sessions? It'll do you more good than harm.'

More good than harm. What a strange way to put it, she thought.

'I'm not into holistic,' she said firmly. 'I believe in the idea but everyone seems to have a different notion of how to put the concept into practice. And, frankly, I have no patience with most of the methods I've heard touted.'

'There are many paths to the light,' he said. 'Keep looking and you'll find yours.'

Jeff's remark was a perfect example of the vagueness Helena disliked and mistrusted when holistic healing was discussed.

'What light?' she said crossly, jerking away from his massaging fingers and turning to face him.

He shrugged. 'You'll know when you reach it. Even if you don't believe.'

'Jeff — ' she began, her exasperation growing.

He held up his hand. 'End of lecture. Where's the other case you wanted me to look at?'

Hodey was sitting up in his crib fitting removable toy people into a wooden bus. Jeff looked at him intently.

'I'd bet this boy has no deficit even before I do the exam,' he said.

He won the bet with himself.

Later, as they pushed through the double doors to return to peds, Jeff asked, 'You going out with the Silver Shrink?'

Helena had no trouble identifying who he meant — Peter Herron. Though the nickname amused her, she didn't smile. 'None of your business,' she said.

'Granted. But are you?'

'I don't want another lecture. What do you have against psychiatrists anyway?'

'Nothing. And no lecture, except to tell you the name my grandfather, a world class judge of people, would have given Herron: Bad Heart. So don't say you weren't warned.'

Before she could respond, Jeff turned into the nurses' station, picked up Kezia's chart, and began flipping through it, his back to Helena. Since the ward clerk and an LVN were at the desk, any personal conversation with Jeff was out. Just as well, since she didn't really want to discuss the matter.

By four o'clock she was so tired her chin was all but dragging on the floor.

George, who'd dropped in to check on Kezia, ordered Helena to go home. 'Get some sleep before you fall on your face,' he advised.

She didn't argue — and fell into bed when she reached the apartment, not waking up until Saturday morning. At the hospital, she found Kezia was more alert but couldn't move her right arm or leg.

Kezia's mother, sitting beside the crib, looked beseechingly at Helena and asked, 'Is she ever gonna be right again?'

Helena would have liked to pass the question on to George, as the authority, but she was there and George wasn't and the woman deserved an immediate answer.

'I don't know,' she admitted. 'Sometimes the paralysis improves — it's too early to tell about Kezia.'

'She got a chance then, that what you be saying?'

'We'll have to wait and see,' Helena said, echoing Jeff's comment and wishing she could offer more hope to this anxious mother.

She returned to the apartment near noon, through for the day. And the evening and night as well, since she was off call. As she fixed a peanut butter and banana sandwich, she pushed away her worry about Kezia.

She'd learned in her internship not to carry patient problems into her personal life. The interns who couldn't master this compartmentalization wound up with *no* personal life — and often other unpleasant problems, both mental and physical.

It was time to concentrate on what she was going to wear to dinner. Obviously, the Silver Shrink wouldn't expect to find her in jeans and a tee shirt when he called for her at eight. Helena shook her head when she realized she'd thought of him by Jeff's nickname. That wouldn't do — not at all.

The man's name is Peter, she told herself firmly. Forget you ever heard him called anything else.

Was she looking forward to the date or not? It *was* a date, after all — the first real one she'd had since the divorce. Though she'd gone to dinner with Mak, that had been because they needed to talk. A business dinner, so to speak.

And the kiss on the beach — was that business, too?

Helena shook her head. She wasn't going to think about Mak, wasn't going to remember how he'd held her or the zinging thrill of his kiss sizzling along her synapses. Mak was a complication she could do without. If she wanted involvement with a man it would have to be on *her* terms, with Helena Moore setting the rules and the limits.

That let Mak out. When he kissed her she could hardly remember who she was, much less recall any rules. As for limits, once in his arms, she forgot the meaning of the word.

Peter Herron, smooth and polished though he was, didn't affect her the way Mak did. She was sure she'd be in complete control of herself with Peter — which meant she could handle any situation. And that was how she wanted it.

Helena, half the sandwich in her hand, wandered into her bedroom and peered into the closet, studying her clothes. Not exactly a fashion show there. She took a bite and savored the nutty flavor while she eyed one garment after another.

The white skirt and black jersey top? No, she'd forgotten the skirt needed to go to the cleaners. The yellow cotton print? No, the dress was getting limp from too many washings. Eventually she eliminated everything she owned. Swallowing the last bite of sandwich, she licked peanut butter off her fingers and frowned. Damn it, she was not going to rush out and buy a new dress; she was going to find something and wear it.

At home, in the old days, she and Fran

used to borrow tops and accessories from one another. Helena sighed. She hadn't had the heart to go through Fran's clothes yet. Even if she did, she knew she couldn't bear to wear anything that had been her sister's. Not after what had happened. Perhaps she ought to leave everything for her mother to go through. Any day now her mother and stepfather would reach the hotel in Lima and find her message about Fran's death.

Whatever she did with Fran's clothes in the meantime would be the wrong thing, as far as her mother was concerned. By the time they were teenagers, she and Fran had been able to laugh at their mother's propensity for finding fault — sharing the problem made it amusing rather than hurtful.

Oh, God, Fran, I miss you, she thought.

Blinking back tears, Helena wiped her sticky hands on a tissue and reached into the closet for the nearest dress — a deep pink, rather frothy vee-necked shift. She'd bought it in a hurry for Kathy O'Hara's wedding two years ago and she doubted if she'd worn the dress since — it was a bit too fussy for her taste.

Fussy or not, she'd wear the shift tonight. With the varicolored heeled sandals she'd bought at the same time. Maybe she'd even put her hair up with those antique ivory combs her mother had sent her from India a few years back. She'd be transforming herself into someone she wasn't but maybe when dating a psychiatrist it was safest to hide behind a few veils. At least until she discovered what he had on his agenda.

Was curiosity over the new doctor, the new-girl-in-town syndrome, the only reason Peter had asked her to dinner? She was realistic about her looks — though far from a dog, she was no raving beauty. And the fact that George thought she was competent surely couldn't have been all that intriguing to Peter. Did he have some hidden reason?

Stop it! she warned herself. A man asks you for a date and you immediately start suspecting him of all sorts of deviousness. With his looks and charm, the probability is he's bedded all the local girls and you present a new challenge. That's something you can certainly handle.

By eight, Helena was ready. Long years of medical training and being on call had honed her ability to dress rapidly so that she hurried even when she had time. As she stared at the stranger in pink with artful wisps of hair framing her face, the living room mirror confirmed her feeling she wasn't Helena Moore. In fact, though her coloring and the shape of her face was different, for the first time she detected a fleeting resemblance to her half-sister.

What had Fran done that made her so menacing to someone that murder was the only solution? Getting pregnant could hardly be the reason — not with so many alternatives available. Helena still didn't understand why Fran had been so careless — unless it had been deliberate. But why?

Surely not to trap a man into marriage — not in today's world. Because she wanted a child? But Fran had been well under thirty, still young, with many years ahead of her to decide about having a child. Anyway, Fran hadn't been particularly maternal.

Who'd killed her? And why? What was the significance of the burned matches arranged in a pyramid? Did it have anything to do with Xenara?

Helena turned away from the mirror. Damn it, I'll take Jeff up on his offer, she decided. I'll visit Xenara and find out for myself what goes on there and, if I can, how Fran was involved.

The doorbell rang, startling her. Thinking about Fran, she'd all but forgotten she had a date. Peter, she noted, was exactly ten minutes late. A deliberate ploy?

He wore a silver-gray linen suit with a darker gray shirt and a maroon tie — the ensemble setting off his silver hair. He really was movie star-handsome. Stepping inside, he glanced quickly around the living room.

Feeling unaccountably defensive about the décor, Helena said, 'This was my sister's apartment.' Annoyed at herself for the implicit apology, she asked bluntly, 'did you know her — Fran York?'

'Yes, I did. Slightly.'

He answered readily enough — had she only imagined the flash of wariness in his gray eyes?

'I was sorry to hear about her death,' Peter added. 'It must have been a shock to you.'

Helena nodded. 'I've been asking myself who'd want to kill her.'

Peter blinked. 'Kill? I understood from the paper it was an accidental death.'

'Fran was murdered. The police can't prove it but she was.'

'I see.' His tone was neutral, noncommittal. She could imagine him using that exact tone with a patient.

Stay cool, she advised herself. There's no point in getting annoyed with Peter over the tone of his voice. You're overreacting — he doesn't necessarily mean he thinks you're a flake.

After several moments of silence, Peter asked, 'Do you have a wrap?'

Without comment, Helena picked a crocheted cotton shawl from the back of the couch and allowed him to usher her from the apartment.

'We can discuss Fran's death further in the car, if you like,' he said as they walked down the stairs. 'I thought we should get started since I made reservations for eight-thirty.'

Helena shook her head, uncertain whether he was merely being polite of offering therapy. 'Not unless you know something about Fran you haven't told me,' she said, still a bit irritated with him despite her resolve not to be.

'You think I know something about Fran?' He sounded no more than mildly inquisitive.

When she recognized the echo technique, a basic psychiatric tool, she blurted, 'I am *not* one of your patients. Dr. Herron!'

Peter grimaced. 'Sorry. I sometimes slip into the wrong mode — it's a bad habit, I know. Shall we go back and start over on the right foot?' Without waiting for an answer, he said, 'Dr. Moore, you look charming in pink. I can't remember when I've seen a lovelier woman.'

Helena turned to him, deliberately widening her eyes. 'Oh, I'll bet you say that to all your patients.'

Peter chuckled. 'I assure you I've never

invited a patient to dinner so you're off that hook.'

'Just as long as you don't try to put me back on it.'

'Warning heeded.' He stopped beside a silver Rolls and opened the passenger door.

As she slid into the seat, Jeff's nickname for Peter flicked into her mind and she smiled. Silver Shrink, indeed. His practice must be going *very* well. But why not? For all she knew, he might be an excellent psychiatrist, entirely worthy of his hire.

They had dinner at The Apex, a restaurant seemingly precariously balanced on the edge of a cliff overlooking the Pacific. Gazing from her seat by a window at the lights and the dark sea below, Helena felt as though she was suspended in midair and said so.

'Actually it's cleverly cantilevered for just that effect,' Peter said. 'I live on a cliff, too, and the same architect designed my house.'

What response did he expect to that statement, she wondered. Would *Wow!* do? Or *How interesting?* Maybe he was angling for *I'd love to see it.*

She finally said, 'Do you ever find it unnerving? Considering this is earthquake country.'

'San Onofre's on the same fault line. If a nuclear reactor can be designed to withstand a quake, why not my house?'

'But if the cliff goes?'

He shrugged. 'No one lives forever. I thought we might have an after-dinner drink at the house. Unless you have a premonition a quake is due.'

'I don't have premonitions. In fact, I don't believe in them.'

'I thought every — ' he paused long enough for her to ask herself if he meant to say 'woman,' before he finished smoothly — 'everyone did at one time or another.'

'*I* don't. I mistrust the so-called paranormal. And I don't need a psychiatrist to tell me the reason is probably because my mother lectures and writes on the subject and has tried all my life to program me. Whatever the cause, I have difficulty accepting what can't be proved.'

'What would you say if I told you I know a woman who does have premonitions that come true?'

'I'd say you're entitled to your beliefs.' As she spoke, Helena wondered if the woman could possibly be Vada Rogers. Acting on impulse, she asked, 'Is she connected with Xenara, by any chance?'

'Yes. Have you met Vada?'

'Only on the VCR. She's a striking woman.'

'I'll have to introduce you to her sometime.

If anyone could change your mind, Vada's that person.'

Helena didn't agree. After all, when her own mother had tried for twenty-eight years without success, what chance did a stranger have? She was more interested in whether Vada had been the woman Peter and Jeff had clashed over but she could hardly ask. So she changed the subject.

'Do you happen to know anything about Sea Mist Manor?' she asked.

Peter put down his coffee cup and motioned to the waiter. 'I'm acquainted with Josh Flanagan, the medical director. Why do you ask?'

'My four-year-old daughter's there. Laura's been diagnosed as autistic. Jeff Hillyer told me Sea Mist favors operant conditioning for autism and I'm not sure I agree with that treatment as far as Laura's concerned.'

'Sea Mist has a good reputation. So does Flanagan. I'm sure you realize operant conditioning can be of value.'

'Maybe. But I don't want it used on my daughter. Dr. Flanagan agreed to hold off but I don't think he'll agree to keep her there if I don't change my mind.'

'I've got some articles on aversives you ought to read before you decide once and for all.'

'If it were your child what would you do?'

Peter's expression changed, his face grew bleak and cold. Before he spoke, the waiter materialized at his elbow and laid the check on the table. Peter pulled out a case, extracted a credit card, and by the time the waiter bore both check and card off, the bleak look was gone.

'You haven't said no,' he told her, smiling, 'so we'll run up to the house and have that drink.'

Helena wasn't sure she wanted to go to Peter's house. The evening had been fine so far but who knew what he might have in mind once they reached his place? Not that she couldn't handle him but she hated a hassle. Still, he seemed far too suave for any crude moves.

The problem was she didn't want to go home and be alone. Since she didn't intend to invite him into her apartment, going to his house was the alternative. She'd have to get over her fear of being alone at night in the apartment, she knew, or move. At the moment, though, she preferred company.

To be honest, what she really wanted was to go home and find Mak there — but that was impossible.

'I'm looking forward to seeing your place,' she told Peter.

He drove the Rolls up a twisting, winding road where lights shimmering behind shrubbery hinted of expensive homes tucked into the hillsides.

'You must be king of the hill,' she joked as he kept climbing.

'I always promised myself that one day I'd build a home on top of the world,' he told her. 'This is as close as I could come.'

When she stepped from the car, the sweet, heavy scent of night-blooming jasmine surrounded her, following her up the stone walk to an entry that was peaked with a flare like a Japanese temple.

Inside was glass and brass, black and white with bold accent colors of varying shades of magenta and blue. You could, she thought, lose a golf ball in the thick plush of the off-white carpeting. The décor was stunning but completely overwhelmed by the view from floor-to-cathedral-ceiling windows. The house not only overlooked the ocean but El Doblez as well.

Helena had never been overly impressed with glamor or the trappings of wealth but she had to admit the place was magnificent. 'I'm speechless,' she told Peter.

Smiling, he led her to a seat by the window. 'I'll have Lamas bring us a drink,' he said.

Though she hadn't seen him do it, he must

have pushed a button because a slender man dressed in black appeared in the archway and Peter told him what he wanted.

Servants, yet, she thought. I could get used to living in luxury.

Lamas left and returned pushing a small glass and chrome bar cart. After he maneuvered it next to the black leather couch, Peter waved him away, saying, 'We'll serve ourselves.'

Discovering she had her choice of more liqueurs than she'd ever heard of, Helena settled for Amaretto on the rocks. While she sipped hers, Peter poured himself a B&B and sat down on the couch.

Helena leaned back in the oddly shaped but very comfortable white leather chair, her gaze roving about the room. Her attention was caught by a portrait of a young boy hanging on a paneled divider. The artist had caught a touching vulnerability in the child's fox-red hair and pointed face — a longing in his red-brown eyes that tugged at the heart.

Peter, following her gaze, said, 'My son, Quinn, when he was eight.'

'It's a wonderful portrait of the boy — he looks positively huggable. How old is Quinn now?'

Peter grimaced. 'I'm afraid he's turned into a not-so-huggable teenager.'

Recalling the bleak look on Peter's face in the restaurant when she asked what he'd do if he had a child like Laura, Helena decided the teenaged Quinn must have a serious problem of some kind — drugs maybe — and Peter would rather not discuss him.

As she was searching for a way to shift to another subject without being too abrupt, Peter set down his drink and leaned toward her.

'I understand better than you think what you're feeling about Fran's death,' he said. 'When Peter's mother died eight years ago the official ruling was an accident. I didn't argue even though in my heart I knew it wasn't.'

Helena stared at him. 'You mean someone killed her?'

He sighed. 'Renata killed herself. I was a long time facing that because my guilt made me believe I might have driven her to do what she did.'

Peter's gaze probed her face. 'I don't usually talk about what happened, but because of your sister, I feel you should know.'

Helena wasn't certain she wanted to hear but she had no chance to say no.

'You see,' he went on, running a hand through his silver waves, 'Renata was

140

threatening to leave me and take Quinn with her. Disturbed as she was — she'd been on Valium — she was in no condition to look after Quinn. So, to make sure he'd be safe, I secretly sent him to a cousin of mine in Montana. I wasn't home when Renata discovered Quinn was gone. Since it was summer, she decided he was at a camp on Catalina he'd attended before and she started off alone in our cabin cruiser.

'How she made it to Catalina Island, I'll never know. But once she discovered Quinn wasn't at the camp, she evidently decided to kill herself. The Coast Guard found the cruiser drifting off the island with Renata inside the cabin, dead. She'd ODed on six or seven different drugs — none prescribed by me. I worked through my guilt feelings but I'm not sure Quinn doesn't blame me to this day for what happened to his mother.'

'That's a shame,' she said. 'Is he in therapy?'

'He has been. And I've tried to talk to him. He listens but he shuts out what he doesn't want to hear. Quinn aside, though, what I'm trying to tell you is that if I, a board-certified psychiatrist, couldn't pick up on Renata's danger signals, how can you be sure what was on your sister's mind? How do you know she wasn't suicidal?'

Like Quinn, Helena didn't care to hear what Peter was saying. Unfortunately, she wasn't adept at shutting him out. Suicide. Was it possible?

No, she couldn't accept it. Besides, she wasn't alone in her belief Fran had been murdered — Mak thought so, too. Plus there'd been the breather calls and the pyramid of burnt matches in the apartment the day Fran was killed and then, just a couple nights ago, under the window.

Even if he hadn't succeeded in making her believe her sister's death was suicide, it was kind of Peter to let her know she wasn't alone in her grief by sharing his own anguish. Her glance was drawn once more to Quinn's portrait and her heart twisted. That poor, sweet little red-haired boy.

She sat up straight, jolted by her own observation. Red-haired! And Quinn was now a teenager.

8

Helena stared unseeingly at her drink. Was it possible the redhead she'd met on the apartment steps the day Fran died was Quinn Herron? If he was, that might explain why she'd seen him again in the hospital cafeteria.

She glanced at Peter, wondering how to approach the subject. 'Does Quinn live here?'

Peter nodded.

'Is he home now?' she persisted.

Something flashed in his gray eyes and was gone before she could identify it.

'He's spending the summer in Catalina. The island has a morbid fascination for him and he insisted on going. Maybe I shouldn't have given in but — ' Peter shrugged.

If she believed Peter — and she had no reason to doubt him — Quinn couldn't have been the one she saw at Fran's apartment. Still, Catalina was only a few miles off the coast, with daily boat and air service to the mainland. It wasn't impossible for Quinn to come over to El Doblez without telling his father.

Deciding that more questions wouldn't help, Helena sipped her drink, inhaling the fragrance of almonds along with the sweet and nutty taste of the liqueur. Far below, the lights of El Doblez beckoned while the Pacific was only a vast darkness. Somewhere in that darkness, too far away to see any lights, was Santa Catalina Island. Was Quinn Herron on that island? Or was he hiding somewhere among the lights of El Doblez?

Peter either couldn't or wouldn't tell her but she must find out — if only to eliminate Quinn as the redhead she'd seen. Suspecting him while she sat in his father's house made her feel guilty and uncomfortable.

'I should be getting home,' she said, setting her glass on the table and rising. 'I've enjoyed the evening, Peter.'

He stood up and moved to put a hand on her arm. 'I hate to see it end. If I've weighed you down with gloom and doom, I'm sorry.'

'I appreciate what you shared,' she told him, wishing she dared confess her suspicions of his son. But they were too tenuous and there was no reason to upset Peter unnecessarily.

'This is only the beginning,' he said, smiling. 'Providing you'll trust me with your phone number.'

The beginning of what, she wondered. Sharing? Seeing each other? Did she want to go on with Peter? At the moment she thought she might. How far was a question she couldn't answer now. What if the redhead *was* Quinn?

'You don't trust me?' he asked, one eyebrow arched.

Belatedly realizing he'd asked for her phone number, she rattled it off, watching him scribble it, along with her name, in a small notebook he took from a cabinet drawer. 'You've turned solemn,' he said.

Helena forced a smile. 'I have a meningitis case in the CD unit I'm concerned about.' It wasn't a lie — Kezia's condition did trouble her. In fact, she'd like to stop by and see the little girl on her way home.

'Don't tell me you're a victim of the they'll-never-recover-without-me syndrome.'

'George warned me I'd have ulcers if I didn't learn to let go,' she admitted. 'The thing is — I thought I *had* learned until I lost a patient the other night. I still don't know exactly why he died — the post was inconclusive. And my meningitis case is a lot sicker than the boy I lost.'

'I'd take you by Harper Hills now but it's not a good idea,' he said, as though reading her mind. 'If any of the staff gets a whiff of alcohol on a doctor's breath, the next day's grapevine labels that doctor a hopeless drunk.'

She nodded ruefully, aware that he was right.

'But if you're really concerned, call peds,' he added, lifting a black modular phone from the cabinet behind him and handing it to her.

The night relief charge nurse, Mrs. Alvarez, didn't seem to know who she was.

'I'm sorry, but I can't tell you anything about Dr. Wittenburg's patient,' Mrs. Alvarez said. 'Please wait a moment.'

Helena tapped her foot impatiently until the nurse came back on. 'Dr. Hillyer will speak to you, Dr. Moore,' she said.

'Helena?' Jeff asked.

'Jeff!' she exclaimed. 'What's going on? Why are you on peds at this hour?'

'When I stopped by on my way down from seeing my post-op case on the surg unit, the peds nurse was about to pick up the phone to call George and tell him Kezia had flatlined.'

Helena sucked in her breath and closed her eyes for a moment. 'Damn.'

'Kezia was long gone by the time I got to the room,' Jeff went on. 'George had seen her about two hours earlier and his note on the chart reads, 'Stable'. She must've gone sour fast.'

'What does George think happened?'

'I didn't call him — why wake him up? Even George's expertise can't reanimate the

146

dead. Morning's soon enough to let him know.'

'Why do *you* think she died?'

'Because her heart stopped. I'll wait for the post to tell me why.'

Jeff's comment about the cause of death being the heart stopping was a hoary standard from med school days. Cardiac failure was *always* the ultimate cause of death.

'Have you notified Kezia's mother?' she asked.

'I was about to call her. You want to take over?'

Helena didn't. At the same time she knew she had to. She was the doctor Kezia's mother knew. And trusted. To no avail — the little girl had died anyway.

She hated to make death calls. It was always hell to tell parents their child was dead but, when she had a choice, she preferred doing it face to face. That way she could offer a consoling touch or even a hug. She often found a minim of needed comfort for herself in the contact because, though her grief could never be as strong nor as deep as theirs, she also had lost the child.

'Give me the number,' she told Jeff reluctantly.

After she finished talking to Kezia's

147

mother, Helena covered her eyes with her hand, unable for the moment to move or speak. The arm coming across her shoulders startled her. Dropping her hand, she looked into Peter's gray eyes.

'It's never easy,' he said softly, pulling her closer.

Grateful for his understanding, she leaned against him and both his arms wrapped around her. She gave herself up to the comfort of being held until she belatedly realized he was becoming aroused. Before she could pull away, he kissed her.

Helena didn't resist. She didn't respond, either, and he didn't prolong the embrace, letting her go.

'My timing's off,' he said lightly and smiled.

On the surface he was offhandedly casual. Why, then, did she have the feeling her lack of enthusiasm had annoyed him — considerably. Was the Silver Shrink egotistical enough to believe every woman should immediately succumb to his charms or was she being unfair?

Though the kiss hadn't been unpleasant it hadn't speeded her pulse, either. He was suave, he was handsome, he was rich, and he was available. And his timing wasn't off. As a psychiatrist he well knew that confronting death gave the living a need to reaffirm life and making love was as reaffirmative as you could get.

If he'd been Mak she'd have melted like snow in the sun. A case of the right time but the wrong man. Peter certainly wouldn't like hearing that!

'It's time I went home,' she said.

Once they reached her door he said, 'I'll call you Wednesday evening,' then bent his head and kissed her lightly. 'Good night.'

Moments later she was alone in the apartment with the door locked behind her. After checking to make certain the windows were also locked, she got ready for bed, leaving the living room lights on.

When she woke to the alarm, Helena was surprised. She hadn't expected to fall asleep easily nor to sleep through until nine. She stretched and considered the day. Stop by the hospital, then pick up Laura and find a playground. Laura usually enjoyed the swings. Focus on Laura. Don't think about Harper Hills or last night or whether Quinn Herron might have something to do with Fran's death. And don't wish Mak had asked to come along today.

Later, leading Laura toward the VW, Helena noticed the tip of Xenara's white pyramid was visible from Sea Mist. Strange how Xenara seemed to be important to so many people she knew. Jeff. Peter. And Fran. Even Mak. Recalling Jeff's invitation to take her there, she promised herself she'd take him up on it first thing Monday.

Laura seemed listless, though with her it was always difficult to tell. She enjoyed the swings but didn't eat much all day. Since she often didn't eat well, that might mean nothing. Before taking her daughter back to Sea Mist that evening, Helena examined her and again found nothing unusual. Yet she wasn't satisfied and wished she could keep Laura with her and observe her for a few days to be sure she was really all right.

'How has Laura been?' she asked the evening attendant, a plump middle-aged woman whose name tag read 'Pauline.'

'Laura kept holding her head yesterday,' Pauline said. 'The day shift thought she might have a headache so the doctor ordered Tylenol for her. She went right to sleep last night, though, so the medicine must have taken care of the trouble.'

'Any fever?' Helena asked.

'Her temperature was taken three times — all normal.'

'I'd like to be notified if Laura holds her head again. Or in any way acts as though something's bothering her. Will you make a note of that?'

Pauline nodded.

Laura made no fuss about being left — but then she rarely did. Helena, though, sat in the parking lot for a time without starting the VW. Why was she haunted by the suspicion that something besides autism was wrong with her daughter? Was it because of the guilt she felt over putting Laura in Sea Mist? Finally, after deciding she'd call Dr. Flanagan tomorrow, she drove home.

The phone was ringing when she walked into the apartment. She hurried to pick it up.

'Dr. Moore.'

Through the crackle of static, she heard her step-father's voice. 'Helena, is that you?'

'Charles, where are you?' she demanded. 'Where's Mother? Did you get my message?'

'I'm in Lima and yes, I got the message you left at the hotel. Your mother's still on that damn mountain in the middle of nowhere — no way to reach her.'

'Oh God, then she doesn't know about Fran!'

'Helena, I think she does. On the mountain last week she had a trance vision. She told me Fran appeared, draped in snakes, and said she'd been poisoned. Your mother thought

151

she meant by a snake bite. Is that how Fran died?'

Helena was so taken aback, so stunned and upset by what he'd told her, that she couldn't think what to say for a moment. 'No snakes,' she said at last. 'The police aren't sure what caused Fran's death. She may have been murdered.'

'The snakes must mean something or your mother wouldn't have seen them.'

'Damn it, Charles, don't give me that crap — Fran's dead!' She burst into tears.

'I'm sorry about her death, of course.'

Helena spoke through her sobs. 'Why isn't Mother with you?'

'She wasn't ready to leave the mountain because the UFO manifestations were still occurring. I had to come to Lima and find a doctor — caught a bad case of dysentery. I'm having trouble with it yet.'

Neither a vision of her daughter's death nor her husband's illness was enough to pull her mother away from whatever the manifestations might be, Helena thought bitterly, her tears drying. As for Charles, she couldn't expect him to care about Fran being dead when he hadn't given a damn about her when she was alive.

'Without your mother here I can't give you any idea of when we'll be along, so you'd best go ahead and make whatever arrangements are needed for Fran,' Charles added.

'Thanks,' she said sourly.

Ignoring or missing the bitterness, Charles said, 'As your mother says, you've always been the efficient one. I know you'll handle everything properly.'

It was no use to waste her anger on Charles. He'd never be any different. Yet she couldn't resist one last tart remark.

'Yes,' she said, 'I'll take care of all the gory details.'

After hanging up, Helena hugged herself, shivering from a chill that seemed to penetrate to her bone marrow, certain she'd never be warm again. She'd never felt so alone in her life. She had nobody she could count on, no one at all. Right from the beginning Roger had fled from any suggestion of emotional intimacy — she should have had better sense than to marry him. The only person she'd ever been able to share any of her feelings with was her half-sister. And now Fran was gone forever.

When she was able to move, Helena ran the bathtub full of hot water and immersed herself until the skin of her fingertips began to pucker.

While she was toweling herself dry, she gave herself a lecture. Neither Charles nor her mother was truly heartless; they were merely self-focused. Knowing this, she shouldn't have expected support from them. Fran remained her responsibility in death as she'd always been in life.

Helena Moore *was* efficient — she'd damn well had to be to survive. She'd learned to be self-sufficient as well. And she'd find Fran's murderer if it took the rest of her life.

Near midnight she lay sprawled on her bed in her nightshirt trying to read a peds journal but her thoughts kept slithering back to Charles's words: . . . *a vision . . . poisoned . . . snakes . . .*

Helena moved her shoulders uneasily. No, she didn't believe in visions, didn't believe in the paranormal. And yet — what had her mother experienced on that damn Peruvian mountain? Because, though Charles could be a son of a bitch, he wasn't a liar — her mother had at least thought she'd seen Fran.

I can't accept that, Helena told herself. Mother had a dream, that's all.

But what a coincidence, with Fran dead at the time.

Helena shook her head and focused determinedly on the journal article but the words refused to make sense and she tossed the magazine to the floor. What she needed was a good night's sleep. She must at least attempt to rest.

Sleep proved elusive and she tossed and turned. She must have barely dozed off when the phone rang because she bolted up, her heart thudding in panic. The lamp she'd left on in the living room provided enough light so she could locate the phone. As she lifted it, her throat felt as clogged as her mind. Her mother? The hospital?

'Dr. Moore,' she croaked.

No response. But the caller remained on the line.

The breather!

Her grip on the phone tightened. 'Who the hell are you?' she demanded, fear edging the words.

No answer, just the faint sound of breathing.

She broke the connection and, without stopping to think, punched in Mak's number, not even aware she'd memorized it. Counting the rings, she muttered under her breath, 'Answer, damn it, answer!'

After twenty rings she gave up. By then her heart had stopped racing and she could think straight. She flicked on the bedside lamp and padded into the living room, reaching to activate the answering machine she'd connected to the other phone. Once she'd gotten the new number she hadn't expected to hear from the breather again.

Back in bed, she propped herself up with pillows and asked herself who had her new number. The hospital switchboard and peds, of course — but they wouldn't give it to just anyone. Mak knew the number. So did George. And Peter Herron.

She knew Mak wasn't the breather and she couldn't imagine George or Peter doing such a thing — neither seemed kinky enough. But they both had people related to them. Carin. Quinn — if he wasn't on Catalina. Of course, any person connected with the hospital could find the number on the doctors' Rolodex at the peds nursing station without much trouble.

So, okay, the breather almost had to be someone who either worked at Harper Hills or was related to George or Peter. She thought it likely he was also involved somehow with Fran's death. She longed to discuss it with Mak.

She reached for the phone and punched in his number again. Still no answer. At two in the morning. Where was he?

Helena sighed. Mak could be anywhere. With anyone. What did she know about him, after all? He'd refused to tell her what he was investigating in El Doblez. She didn't even know where he lived. LA? He'd been a cop there. If he didn't live in El Doblez, where was he staying while here — in a motel? Or was he renting an apartment?

He wasn't her private property, so why should she expect him to be instantly available when she needed him? Though he'd given her the impression he wasn't involved, he might be married. Have a family. Commitments she wasn't aware of. And it was damned selfish to be calling him at two in the morning when it wasn't an emergency. If he'd been at home asleep he'd probably be furious with her.

And yet she wished he'd answered.

Resigned to staying awake herself, Helena leaned down and retrieved the peds journal. It fell open in her lap to an article entitled, 'Treatment of Pit Viper Envenomation in Children Under Five.'

Snakes. Helena shuddered.

Whatever her mother had dreamed, Fran had *not* been bitten by a snake and died from its venom. A human, not a serpent, had injected an unknown substance into Fran and killed her. The official autopsy hadn't uncovered what the substance was but how exhaustive had the tests been? Still, even if every test had been done, there were certain drugs that metabolized so rapidly they couldn't be found in the body after death.

She eased the journal shut and, leaving the bedside lamp on, slid lower in the bed and closed her eyes. She couldn't solve Fran's murder without more information and there was no way to find anything out at two in the morning. Let the answering machine deal with the breather, she'd give sleep another try.

The last thing she remembered before she finally succumbed was wondering where Mak was and if he slept alone.

* * *

At noon on Monday, Mak ambled into the Harper Hills cafeteria, picked up a ham and cheese sandwich, and found a strategic table in the doctor's dining room where he could keep an eye on the door while he ate. After he'd downed the sandwich he refilled his coffee cup, propped back his chair, and yawned as he watched doctors come and go, occasionally nodding to one he'd met.

God knows he was tired — sports cars weren't designed for resting. He'd never liked stakeouts anyway.

He was on his second refill when Helena finally came into the dining room with her tray, Jeff Hillyer trailing behind her. Mak scowled. Not because he was jealous of Hillyer — he knew better now, knew the woman Hillyer was hung up on wasn't Helena. But he'd hoped for the chance to talk to her alone.

She spotted him immediately so he rose and gestured to a chair at his table. Helena hesitated for a moment, then walked toward him. Mak found himself not only wishing Hillyer wasn't tagging along but that this place wasn't so goddamned public — having her within reach made him want to pull her into his arms.

Hillyer followed her to the table and Mak managed to greet him amiably.

'What did you think of the session the other night, Mak?' Hillyer asked after he sat down.

'Vada Rogers is damn convincing,' Mak admitted.

Helena glanced from one to the other, fixed on him, and asked, 'Xenara?'

He nodded.

'Jeff's taking me there Wednesday evening,' she said.

Mak scowled. He hadn't lied; if anyone could get him to believe in that esoteric crap, Vada was the woman. But when he'd circulated during the break in the session, eavesdropping shamelessly, he'd overheard from other attendees that the up-front sessions, like this one, were only a part of what went on at Xenara. Not everyone was 'chosen' to be guided along the 'blue-lit path,' whatever the hell that was.

Hillyer had been damn close-mouthed when he'd dropped a casual question about it to him, rousing Mak's suspicions. In his experience, cults with secret rites were trouble. And more times than not, the trouble involved sex. Sooner or later the law got called in and he'd seen some unsavory cases in his time. It made him wonder if Fran could have been mixed up in something messy behind the scenes, become disillusioned, and threatened to blow the whistle, thus signing her death warrant.

He didn't want Helena anywhere near Xenara, not until he knew for sure the cult had nothing to do with her sister's death.

'I thought you didn't believe in the supranormal,' he said to her.

She threw him a tight smile. 'I'm trying to keep an open mind. Didn't you say yourself that Vada Rogers was worth listening to?'

'She has a real gift,' Hillyer put in. 'She's a true seer.'

Granted, the woman was as charmismatic as they come. And it was obvious Hillyer was hot for Vada.

Mak didn't hold with getting that fixated on any woman. He'd once hoped for a stable marriage and children — he'd always wanted kids — but his experience with Mima had cured him. Mima had put off getting pregnant until he finally realized she never had meant to and never would. She'd lied to him from the beginning. It'd be a long time — if ever — before he trusted another woman.

Wanting one was another bowl of *menudo*, as Phil Garcia would say. He wanted Helena — what the hell, that was normal enough; she was smart, sassy, and good-looking.

Belatedly aware that he was staring at her, he tried to cover himself by saying, 'You look tired.'

She frowned, opened her mouth to speak, glanced at Hillyer, and shut it again.

Hillyer, catching the look, stood up holding his coffee cup. 'Anyone else want a refill?'

Watching him walk away, Mak nodded slightly. Nice guy. 'So,' he said to Helena, 'want to tell me why you're so tired?'

She leaned toward him and spoke in a low tone. 'The breather knows my new number — he called me at two this morning.'

The hair bristled on Mak's nape. 'Why didn't you let me know?'

'You weren't home!'

'Who could get hold of your new number?'

She told him. Mak jerked his head toward Hillyer, coming back with his coffee. 'You suspect him?'

'No, not really. But I didn't want to talk about the breather in front of Jeff.'

'We need to talk. Tonight.'

'I'm on call — it'll have to be at the hospital.'

Hillyer, though taking his time, was almost at the table so Mak nodded rather than arguing, though he knew damn well she could and did take calls from home. She was afraid to be alone with him in her apartment and he supposed she had a point there — he couldn't trust himself where she was concerned.

Since he had no choice, he relaxed and half-listened to her and Hillyer discuss a meningitis case, coming to attention when he discovered the baby had died, if not completely unexpectedly, at least abruptly.

'Mrs. Alvarez's last nursing note a half-hour before the death showed Kezia's heartbeat had slowed significantly,' Helena said.

'I asked her about that,' Hillyer said. 'She told me she thought it was because Kezia had fallen asleep and so she let it go. After all, George had been in not long before and told the evening nurse the baby was stable.'

Helena bit her lip. 'Why would the heartbeat slow so dramatically?'

Hillyer shrugged. 'Further brain damage maybe. I'm curious to see what the post shows.'

Mak took mental note of the name. Kezia. She wasn't on his list.

When Helena and Hillyer got up to leave, Mak rose, too, putting a restraining hand on Hillyer's arm. Helena glanced at him curiously but didn't wait around. He watched her walk away, thinking the long white coat she wore hid far too much.

'What about this guy Herron?' he asked Hillyer.

'The Silver Shrink?' Hillyer's tone was caustic. 'I sure as hell can't give you a non-biased account.'

'Personal or professional dislike?'

Hillyer's eyebrows rose as he answered shortly, 'Mostly personal.'

Ten to one it's a woman, Mak decided. The most likely candidate was Vada Rogers but he figured he'd gotten everything he was going to get from Hillyer on the subject of Dr. Herron.

'Thanks.'

After Hillyer turned and strode off, Mak sat down again and stared into the dregs of his coffee. *Mostly* personal, Hillyer had said.

That meant there must be something in Herron's practice that could stand looking into. He hadn't been hired to investigate Herron and, because he was busy with the job they were paying him for, it might take him a while to uncover just how and where the doctor had erred. Sooner or later, though, he'd ferret it out.

Smiling wolfishly, Mak muttered, 'The Silver Shrink's going to be damn sorry he trespassed on *my* territory.'

9

Mak made a few calls and visited the pathologist, Dr. Urdah, before he took the elevator to Three North. He found Helena sitting at the nurses' station looking at a patient's chart.

Waiting until she looked up and saw him, he asked, 'Got a few minutes?'

She glanced at her watch, closed the chart, stood up, came around to his side of the counter and stopped, looking at him. 'A few minutes,' she echoed.

He glanced around. 'In private.'

Apparently she'd already decided on where they'd talk because, without hesitating, she led him through red double doors into the communicable disease unit. They walked along a short, deserted corridor past closed, windowed doors to a small desk at the end of the corridor. Helena picked up the phone and said, 'Dr. Moore. I'm on CD if you need me.' Then she turned and faced him.

Mak looked around. 'Something like a jail.'

'A jail!' She sounded indignant. 'We try to keep contagious cases isolated as much as possible but we certainly don't lock patients in cells.'

'I need the key to your apartment,' he told her.

Helena, obviously taken aback at his abrupt change of subject, stared at him. 'Why?'

'Because you may not be able to get home and the telephone people are putting in a special Caller ID unit for you at five-thirty tonight. It flashes the caller's number on a screen beside the phone immediately after the first ring. The next call the breather makes to you may be his last. Even if he's using a pay phone, we'll get a fix on his area of operation and Garcia will know where to send men to watch for him.'

'Mak, that's wonderful! I can't thank you enough.'

'The lieutenant's the one to thank. He okayed the special order.'

'I'm grateful to Lieutenant Garcia but I know you're the one who talked him into it.'

Mak shrugged. 'He's as uneasy about your sister's death as I am and hopes the breather will provide a few answers — once we catch him. He asked me to tell you Fran's body will be released tomorrow.'

Helena looked so stricken he put his hand on her shoulder momentarily, afraid if he pulled her into his arms he'd immediately forget it was for consolation. 'Want me to make the arrangements?'

She took a deep breath. 'No, she's my sister. Oh God, poor Fran.'

He nodded, wishing Fran had been more up front with him. It might have saved her life.

'About Xenara,' he said. 'Don't get involved.'

She stiffened. 'Since when do you give me orders, Captain Maklin?'

Damn, he'd gotten her back up. 'What I mean is, keep away for now. I don't like the feel of the place.' What he really meant was he didn't want anything to happen to her but he had a hunch she wouldn't accept that either.

'One session won't hurt. And I'm *not* going alone.'

'Jeff Hillyer's so hung up on Vada Rogers he's no help.'

'Do you suspect *her* of being involved in Fran's death?'

'I have no reason to. Yet. What I do suspect is that things at Xenara are not what they seem on the surface. And whatever's going on, Vada has to know.' He smiled wryly. 'After all, she's supposed to be psychic.' He risked touching her arm. 'Do me a favor, give Xenara a pass. For now.'

As though she hadn't heard his last few

words, she said, 'My mother believes *she's* psychic and Charles — my stepfather — never doubts a word she says. He called me from Peru last night. Supposedly last week my mother had a vision of Fran covered with snakes and feared it foretold Fran's death.'

Helena's eyes filled with tears. 'Mother's not with Charles in the Lima hotel, she's off on a damn mountaintop somewhere having visions and there's no easy way to reach her to tell her Fran really is dead.'

Enough was enough. Mak pulled Helena into his arms, buried his face in her hair, and drew her close. She smelled right, she felt right, everything about her was right for him. Though he was beginning to doubt he'd ever have enough of touching this woman, he did his best to do no more than soothe her, murmuring comforting words.

All too soon, she edged away and wiped her eyes with a tissue. 'The apartment key's in my bag on peds,' she said. 'I'll get it for you.'

'You won't be home at all this evening?'

She hesitated before saying, 'Actually, I probably will. It's pretty quiet. Of course, all hell could break loose — you never know.'

'Good. I'll have dinner waiting.'

She frowned. 'Mak, I don't — '

'If you don't make it, I'll eat the whole works myself, okay?'

Helena's smile was reluctant but it *was* a smile. When she said, 'I didn't realize cops could cook,' he knew she'd given in.

'Try to make it by six, doctor,' he told her. 'Cops who cook tend to be temperamental.'

It was six-thirty before she arrived. By then the telephone guys had come and gone and their gadget — a bit larger than a TV remote control, sat next to the bedside phone.

'Smells good,' she said as she came into the apartment.

'I guarantee a taste treat you'll never forget,' he assured her.

By the time she'd washed and changed into jeans and tee shirt the food was on the table.

'Stew!' she exclaimed delightedly. 'I haven't had stew in years. It takes too long to prepare.'

'Ragout,' he corrected. 'Using the micro-wave cuts down on the time but not the flavor.'

'Mmm,' she agreed after the first bite.

After they ate, he insisted on loading the dishwasher without her help before joining her in the living room.

'I talked to the Harper Hills pathologist today,' he said as he sank into a chair next to her. 'Dr. Urdah's cagey as hell but I got the impression he's not satisfied about the cause of Kezia's death.'

Helena looked at him blankly. '*You* talked to Dr. Urdah? About Kezia? Why?'

'Neither you nor Jeff seemed too sure exactly why she'd died. I found out the doctor who's supposed to have all the answers wasn't certain either.'

'Medicine isn't an exact science. But that's not the point — why are *you* getting involved in Kezia's death?'

'In a way I was already involved. And don't ask me any more about it.' He slid down onto his spine. 'Damn chair's too short to get comfortable.'

She shot him an exasperated look. 'Maybe you should try sitting in one like a normal human being.' But he knew what really annoyed her was his refusal to explain why he'd been asking Dr. Urdah questions.

'The problem is I'm not one hundred percent normal,' he told her. 'If I was I wouldn't be sitting here looking at you when we could be making love.' Like he'd sat outside her apartment in the damn car every night watching to make sure the match-burning prowler didn't come back when it would have been a hell of a lot more comfortable in her bed.

But he'd been scorched once by Mima and

he wasn't about to be burned again. What smoldered between him and Helena was beyond his previous experience and he wasn't ready to risk lighting a fire that might consume him completely.

'Making love on call's not a good idea,' she said calmly.

As if to underscore the point, her phone rang. Mak reached her bedroom before she did, intent on the numbers flashing on the Identifier's tiny screen. 'Harper Hills,' he muttered in disappointment as she picked up the phone.

He waited until he heard her tell the caller she'd be right there, then hang up. 'Don't give me an argument,' he told her. 'I'm staying here until you return from the hospital so if the breather calls, I'll be around.'

She stared to nod, then frowned. 'You told me this gadget records the numbers, dates, and times of calls up to twenty-five,' she said. 'So why do you have to stay?'

'You're a tough lady to slide anything past. The truth is I'm staying so there'll be someone — me — in the apartment when you come home from Harper Hills late, okay?'

She opened her mouth to say something, hesitated, then reached up, cupped his face,

171

and kissed him lightly. 'You can be a real sweet guy sometimes,' she said, stepping away quickly.

Mak insisted on escorting her to her old squareback VW. 'A wonder this keeps running,' he said.

'Don't you know a classic when you see it?'

'No, but I do recognize a junker and you're driving one. Odds are she'll break down on you at the most inconvenient time and place.'

She stuck out her tongue at him and slid behind the wheel. 'If you've jinxed her I'll never forgive you,' she threatened as she started the VW.

Mak fell asleep the moment he reached the couch and didn't rouse until he heard a key in the door. Coming instantly alert, he automatically reached for his gun, forgetting he didn't routinely wear a holster any more.

'Helena?' he called.

'Yo,' she answered, opening the door.

He relaxed, yawning, and glanced at his watch. Three in the morning. He thought of spending the rest of the night in his car and groaned. 'Mind if I sack out here until it gets light?'

She shot him an evaluating look.

He grinned at her. 'I swear I'm too tired to have so much as a lascivious thought.'

'That makes two of us. Stay if you like.' She

walked on toward her bedroom and disappeared.

He tried not to imagine her undressing and failed, picturing garment after garment being discarded. The last would be her panties: she'd pull them down, step out of them and stand naked. He ached to stride down the hall and slip into her bedroom before she reached for the long tee shirt he knew she wore to sleep in.

'So, okay, I lied,' he muttered to himself as he shifted position on the couch, trying to get as comfortable as his rampaging hormones would allow.

★ ★ ★

When Helena's alarm woke her at seven, her first thought was of Mak. Was he still asleep on the couch? Grabbing a robe, she eased into the hall and tiptoed to take a look. To her disappointment, he was nowhere in the apartment — apparently he'd kept his word and left at dawn. Much as she hated to admit it, she'd looked forward to having breakfast with him.

I wish I'd told him to sleep in Fran's bedroom, she thought. He'd have been more comfortable and maybe Mak's use of the room and the adjoining bath would have

173

helped to exorcise the haunting memory of Fran lying dead.

Not that she should have let him stay to begin with. But knowing he was in the apartment erased her fear that she might encounter the match-burning prowler when she came home from the hospital after midnight.

Reminded of the reason she'd been called to the ER, Helena sighed. A six-month-old boy in convulsions brought on by inhaling too much crack smoke because his mother used the stuff while she fed him his bottle. A baby ODing on cocaine at the age of six months — it was getting to be a damn frightening world. She'd managed to save the boy and, since the mother hadn't gotten hooked on crack until after he was born, the baby might even have a chance to be normal — providing he remained in foster care.

Babies born to mothers addicted to crack during their pregnancies didn't have the same option. Those who survived were more often than not permanently damaged.

When she reached the peds unit, she checked on the boy and found he'd improved. Before rounds with George, Helena stopped by the nursery to see Kristle, the preemie.

She found a lanky, sandy-haired man

sitting in the nursery rocker feeding one of the newborns. He looked up and smiled before concentrating on burping the infant.

'New nurse?' Helena asked Clovis once they were outside the glassed-in nursery proper.

Clovis smiled. 'That's Phil Vance. He's our guitar-playing, folk-singing psychiatrist.'

'What's he doing — getting an early start on sharing in the care of his baby?'

Clovis shook her head. 'Phil isn't married. And he doesn't have any children.'

Helena looked surprised. 'Don't tell me he's treating that baby for birth trauma!'

'Phil just likes babies. This started a couple years ago when Harper Hills had a nurses' strike and I was trying to handle the nursery alone for all three shifts. I conscripted Phil to help me feed the babies at night and it turned out he's a natural. That one he's burping now is up for adoption. I keep telling him that's what he ought to do — adopt. I mean, he wouldn't have to get married or anything.' Clovis's tone was wistful.

Watching the yearning in Clovis's face as she looked at Dr. Vance, Helena decided the nurse was in love with him.

The phone rang, Clovis picked it up, said she'd be right there, hung up, and hurried away.

As Helena finished making a notation on Kristle's chart, Phil Vance left the enclosed nursery and walked up to the desk.

'You must be Dr. Moore,' he said, offering his hand. 'I'm Phil Vance.'

'Helena,' she told him, shaking his hand.

'George will have to bring you to our next get-together. How are you at folk-singing?'

'Out of practice,' she admitted. 'Though I used to be able to sing all the verses of Tom Lehrer's parody of an old Irish ballad — the one about the girl who did her entire family in.'

'One of my favorites. I'm partial to ballads in general. Do you know the one about Mighty Quinn?'

'I've heard it.' Helena spoke absently, the name Quinn echoing in her mind. Surely Phil knew Peter — was there a way to ask Phil about Peter's son without sounding nosy?

'Isn't Peter Herron's son named Quinn?' she ventured finally.

Phil nodded. 'You know the boy?'

'I may have seen him. Rather thin, with red hair. In the cafeteria, as a matter of fact. Does he come to the hospital often?'

'He used to. Haven't seen him around lately.' Phil's gaze sharpened as he studied her.

Damn. Her questions had triggered his

curiosity. She needed to defuse it. 'Did you ever get a look at that portrait of Quinn when he was eight?' she asked. 'I never saw such vulnerability captured in a painting.'

'The world's one hell of a place for the vulnerable.'

'I know. I have a four-year-old autistic daughter.' Much as she hated to drag Laura in, she didn't want Phil to continue wondering why she was so curious about Quinn.

'Is your daughter left-handed?'

Helena blinked. 'No. Why?'

'There are recent studies suggesting the left-handed are more prone than the right-handed to certain diseases and mental problems, including autism.'

'I haven't heard of this study.'

'It's in the preliminary research stage. Maybe more will come of it, maybe not. I find it interesting.' He picked up the phone — with his right hand, she noticed, using his left to punch in the numbers. When he saw her watching him, he said, 'Quinn Herron's left-handed, too.' Then his party answered and he gave his attention to the call.

Helena returned to peds, feeling that Phil knew damn well her questions about Quinn didn't come from simple curiosity. She ought to know better than to try to outwit a shrink, even a genial, folk-singing one.

At noon she and Idalia happened to ride down on the same elevator, then they stood next to each other in the cafeteria line. Rather than go into the doctor's dining room, Helena sat at a table with the peds charge nurse.

Helena told her about meeting Phil Vance in the nursery. 'I got the impression Clovis is quite fond of him,' she added.

Idalia gave a ladylike snort. 'He's no use to her.'

'Why?'

'Don't get me wrong, I don't have anything against the man but Dr. Vance swings the other way.'

'Poor Clovis. Does she know?'

Idalia nodded. 'It's like sometimes a gal can't help who she wants, even when she knows better.' She raised her chin a little and looked directly at Helena.

Like you and George, I suppose, Helena thought unhappily. Not wanting to dwell on that, she switched back to Phil, mentioned Clovis's comment about him adopting a baby.

'Do you have any children?'

Idalia smiled. 'Kyesha. She's five.'

Helena told her about Laura and they talked about their daughters for the remainder of their lunch, Idalia confiding that

Kyesha had mild sickle cell anemia.

As she finished the last of her coffee, Helena said, 'I've never asked George if he had children. Does he?'

To her surprise, Idalia glanced quickly around as though checking for eavesdroppers. Assured no one was within earshot, she leaned closer to Helena and said, 'Terry Wittenburg's eight and he's got Down's Syndrome. He's in a place for retarded kids up near Anaheim. Terry's the reason George is so anti-Xenara.'

'What happened?'

'Carin couldn't accept the mongoloid diagnosis. A couple of years ago, she took Terry, without George's knowledge, to Vada Rogers. This was when they were building Xenara and Vada still operated out of a tiny place down by the beach. I'm not sure of the details but I think Vada must have told Carin she couldn't help Terry.

'So then, still without George catching on, Carin brought Terry to a faith healer in San Diego. This guy also dealt in herbal medicine. Whatever he gave Terry almost killed him. That's when George found out what she'd been doing and blew a fuse. After Terry recovered, they sent him to Anaheim. And, though it really wasn't her fault, George blames Vada Rogers to this day.'

'Is this common knowledge?'

Idalia's smile was cynical. 'Nothing, but *nothing* stays secret at Harper Hills. Everyone knows exactly why George froths at the mouth when spirit healing or Xenara is mentioned.' She sighed. 'And they probably know everything else there is to know about him, too.'

Helena took that to mean his affair with Idalia. The more she saw of the peds charge nurse, the better she liked her. She still felt that Carin was getting a rotten deal but she couldn't blame Idalia for the affair.

'If I could do different, I would,' Idalia added, as though reading her mind.

Would it change the effect Mak has on me if I discovered he was married, Helena asked herself. She had to admit that, though she'd sure as hell struggle against ever giving in to the way she felt, she'd probably still be rocked by seismic waves whenever he kissed her.

'No one promised life was fair,' she said finally, aware that Idalia was waiting for a response.

'Amen.'

The rest of the day was routine and, since she'd been on call the night before, she left before four. On the way home, the VW suddenly began to jerk alarmingly, something in the innards gave a clattering clank, and the car stopped dead.

'Damn!' she muttered as she tried without success to restart it. Now what was she supposed to do?

Luckily she was in the right-hand lane, and even more fortunately, the car behind her agreed to push her into a gas station a block away. From there she called the auto club.

By the time their tow truck arrived, the station attendant had already given his opinion free of charge. 'She threw a rod,' he said. 'Needs a new block for sure.' He told her where the nearest VW garage was.

Damn you, Mak, she said to herself. If you hadn't called a curse down on the poor old gal she'd still be running. This is all your fault.

She rode to the garage in the tow truck and arranged for the car to be diagnosed by a VW specialist. Treatment, she suspected, would be more than she wanted to pay. They agreed to rent her a loaner until her VW was functional again and she drove it home.

It was almost six when she unlocked the door to the apartment. Once inside she noticed the answering machine's red light was on, indicating a message.

Peter had called and left his number. After jotting it down, she returned his call.

'I'm having a few people over Friday night for a barbeque,' he said. 'Bring your swimsuit.'

'I haven't said I'm coming,' she protested. 'What happened to your agreement to ask me instead of telling me?'

'The party was planned weeks ago. Since then I've met you and I'd like you to get acquainted with some of my friends. The party won't be a success for me unless you're there.'

'That's blackmail.'

'I didn't promise to play fair — but I apologize. Please accept my humble invitation.' He sounded anything but humble.

She wondered if by any chance Quinn would be there. She couldn't ask as Peter would think it strange. Even if Quinn wasn't, she was inclined to go. It'd be interesting to see Peter among his friends and, face it, she loved his house.

'This is absolutely the last time you'll get away with telling me what I'm going to do instead of asking me,' she warned.

There were no other messages on the machine. She took a deep breath and made the call she'd put off all day — to the Nature's End Company to ask them to pick up Fran's body at the city morgue. The woman who answered went over the arrangements Helena had made earlier — cremation, a scattering of the ashes at sea — and when Helena hung up, she was shaking with grief and misery.

After a long, hot shower, she changed into jeans. Before leaving the bedroom, she glanced at the ID gadget. Peter's number would be registered on its tape, she supposed. She certainly hoped the Identifier would have no other calls to tape — she couldn't cope with the breather tonight.

Luck was on her side — he didn't bother her.

★ ★ ★

On Wednesday evening, she met Jeff in the parking lot at Xenara. Up close, the pyramid was more formidable than garish — it towered above her, as tall as a five-story building. Lit by spotlights, the glaring white of its slanting sides all but blinded her and the Xenara sign's blue neon spiraled up, continuously wave after wave, reminding her unpleasantly of perpetually coiling snakes. Recalling Mak's warning to stay away, she raised her chin.

'This place must have cost a pretty penny to build,' she observed, determined not to let herself be intimidated or impressed.

183

'Power works best in the round,' Jeff said, 'as any Indian medicine man could tell you. Corners dissipate the energy.'

'A pyramid isn't exactly round,' she pointed out.

'The inside is. Vada saw to that.'

'I'm looking forward to meeting her.'

'She's not like anyone you've ever met before. Vada's unique. One of a kind.' Jeff's eyes gleamed with enthusiasm. 'She's beautiful, of course, but that's only a part of her. I can't begin to describe all that Vada is.'

Jeff was certainly besotted. Helena wondered if Peter's admiration of Vada was as acute. She doubted it. Somehow she couldn't see Peter losing his head over any woman.

The blue double entrance doors swung apart as they approached and two white-clad women fastened the doors open. 'Good timing,' she said lightly. When Jeff frowned without replying she decided he didn't take anything about Xenara lightly.

He led her through a spacious entry into a large domed room that appeared to rise almost all the way to the top of the building. Helena craned her neck to make sure but the darkness overhead defeated her. Though it was spacious, she realized the room didn't take up the entire building and she wondered what else the pyramid contained. Mak had muttered about a blue-lit path — was this an actual corridor or just a figurative phrase denoting some kind of higher spiritual plane a Xenara believer might aspire to?

Unlike the white entry, everything in the round room was in shades of blue from the deep midnight of the carpeting to the pale pastel of the curved walls. Nothing hung on the walls except behind the dais. The chairs, wooden with a simple modern design, were a uniform delft blue. Before she seated herself next to Jeff, Helena saw at least half the chairs were already taken — apparently many people came early. Others trickled into the room until every chair was taken and then the doors swung shut.

'What about latecomers?' she asked Jeff.

'Not admitted.'

This surprised her. Turning away potential customers — or would they be clients or students? — was turning away money. Was Xenara above the mundane concept of profit? She doubted it.

Blue velvet curtains shielded the wall behind the dais, curving to follow its concave surface to the floor. Suddenly the drapes fell away from the wall to hang straight from their rods. A hand appeared and pushed them apart as a golden-haired woman dressed in a long white gown with a silver sash appeared between the folds of blue velvet. For a long moment she stood framed there, then she glided to the front of the dais, her gown floating behind her.

Helena, as caught up in the theatrical entrance as the rest, recognized Vada Rogers. Since Jeff had secured second-row seats, she got a good look. Jeff was right — even the woman's bone structure was beautiful. And, as she'd noted when she watched the cassette of Xenara, the white gown, though modest enough, enhanced Vada's lush curves.

Vada stood silent for a time, her green gaze flicking over the people in the room, one at a time. Her glance fell on Helena and she paused for a fraction of a second, a tiny frown crossing her white forehead.

Because I'm sitting next to Jeff, Helena wondered as Vada's glance moved on. She can't know who I am — it isn't that.

When she'd finished looking at everyone, Vada raised her head until she was staring into the darkness overhead. Slowly she raised her arms, her fingers extended, reaching, reaching. She began to hum, unintelligible but somehow hair-prickling words buried in the hum. When Helena thought she couldn't bear to listen one more second, Vada's hum stopped and she appeared to pull something invisible from the air over her head and toss it toward the audience.

People drew in their breath. Someone moaned.

Though Vada's tossing gesture had startled Helena, she told herself *she* hadn't seen or felt a thing and she was damned if she'd let Vada hypnotize her into thinking she had. She glanced at Jeff. His eyes were closed, his hands rested, palms upward on his thighs. From his expression he was perfectly relaxed.

'Use the energy,' Vada told the group, her voice low and intense, slightly husky. 'Gather the healing Ch'i power to you so that it flows through you into the earth.'

Helena saw that most of the people around her had assumed Jeff's position of meditation.

'Close your eyes, quiet your mind, and feel with your spirit,' Vada intoned.

What the hell, Helena thought. Since I'm here to experience what Xenara is, I might as well go whole hog.

Closing her eyes, she uncrossed her arms and let her hands come to rest, palms up on her thighs. With both feet flat on the floor — in this type of meditation, Helena knew, nothing could be crossed — she tried to empty her mind. Here was where she'd always come up against it when she tried to meditate. Her mind stubbornly refused to quiet itself.

She tried to focus on the word 'Om' and failed because, just when she thought she had it, something extraneous would flash across her mind. Like how ridiculous they must look, a bunch of adults sitting here in identical positions searching for something that didn't exist. No, that wasn't right — energy did exist and certain kinds of energy could be harnessed.

What *was* Ch'i power? The Chinese had believed in this energy for centuries so there must be something to it. Okay, maybe, but she didn't feel anything. And she doubted that any of the others around her did, either — though they might believe they did because they wanted to.

'Those of you who feel the power flowing and who have mastered the technique, rise and begin the laying on of hands,' Vada ordered.

Chairs creaked and clothes rustled. Helena didn't move except to open her eyes. Next to her, Jeff was on his feet. He eased in back of her and she tensed as she felt his hands come to rest on the top of her head.

'Relax,' he told her quietly.

Why not, she asked herself, closing her eyes and trying once more to empty her mind. Jeff's hands felt warm and solid on her head. Fran had once told Helena about a university extension class she had taken featuring the laying on of hands, so Helena knew something about this so-called method of energy transfer. His right hand would be lying at a 30-to-45-degree angle over his left and it didn't matter whether one or both or neither felt the flow of Ch'i energy from him to her — it would happen anyway. Or so the proponents of the method believed.

Relaxed, doing her best not to think, she drifted in a pleasant near-doze until she suddenly realized Jeff's hands were gone. She smelled smoke.

Her eyes popped open just as, from the dais, Vada cried 'Fire!'

10

Was Xenara on fire? Alarmed by Vada's cry, Helena jumped to her feet and scanned the room. There was no sign of fire and she no longer smelled smoke. On the dais, Vada writhed frantically as though to escape from invisible coils.

'Oh, the flames, the dreadful flames!' she wailed in an unfamiliar thin and reedy voice, totally unlike the low and husky tones she'd used earlier.

Helena looked for Jeff and saw him rushing toward the dais along with the two white-robed attendants. He reached Vada first and, arms outstretched, caught her as she collapsed.

Helena pushed through the alarmed onlookers to his side. Seeing her, he said, 'I'm taking her back there.' He nodded toward the curtained wall behind the dais.

'This way, Dr. Hillyer,' one of the women in white said, holding the velvet draperies aside to reveal a blue door. She opened it.

As Helena trailed after Jeff, she heard the other attendant begin speaking to the crowd, reassuring them there was no fire and that what Vada had experienced was a vision of the future.

'These visions come on unexpectedly,' the woman said, 'and the trance state is so spiritually draining that she faints afterwards. With rest she'll recover quickly. As I'm sure you understand, we must cancel the rest of tonight's session. Please leave your name at the door so you can be admitted to another session at a future date.'

Following Jeff, Helena stepped into a dressing room, complete with lighted mirror and bottles, boxes, and tubes of makeup on the table underneath. Jeff laid Vada on a blue velvet *chaise longue*, her feet at the raised end, and dropped to one knee beside her, feeling her wrist for a radial pulse.

Noting that the attendant who'd opened the door had closed it behind them without coming into the room, Helena felt free to ask Jeff the question troubling her.

'You expected her to collapse,' she said, 'so this must have happened before. Was it syncope or does she have some type of petit mal epilepsy?'

Jeff shot her a glare. 'She doesn't have epilepsy.'

'Then what was all that writhing about?'

'Vada says she feels trapped when she enters a trance and so she tries to escape. I think the struggle might be what brings on the collapse — but I'm a novice in this field.'

Helena leaned against the makeup table. 'Yeah. I don't expect 'paranormal physician' to become a board certified specialty in *my* lifetime.'

'Don't sneer at what you don't understand.' Jeff spoke without looking at her, his attention focused on Vada.

Slightly ashamed of herself, Helena edged around to the other side of the chaise. Making her own check of Vada's pulse, she found it rapid and weak — typical of syncope, or fainting, after the first few moments. But then, whatever she might think of the rest of the performance, she hadn't really believed Vada faked her collapse.

'Sorry, Jeff,' she said. 'My upbringing left me with a bias against the paranormal.' As she spoke it occurred to her she'd smelled smoke *before* Vada had cried, 'Fire!'

Could it be because someone in the wings had deliberately burned something to enhance the drama of the supposed vision?

'Did you smell smoke earlier?' she asked Jeff, certain he'd say yes.

He glanced at her. 'Smoke? No, why would I? There wasn't an actual fire at Xenara — only in Vada's vision.'

Helena stared at him. Obviously he was

telling the truth. He must not have noticed, she told herself. That's the only possible explanation.

Vada's eyelids fluttered and she moaned. Jeff leaned close to her and said softly, 'It's over, you're in your dressing room. I'm here, Vada, it's all right.'

Without sound, Vada's lips formed Jeff's name. She opened her eyes, turning her head toward him. 'I tried not to,' she said weakly, her voice low and throaty once again. 'I did my best to go on with the session but once I saw her — ' Her words trailed off.

'Saw who?' Jeff asked.

Vada's eyes widened. 'Don't you know her? She was sitting next to you.'

Involuntarily, Jeff shifted his eyes to Helena. Vada followed his gaze, saw Helena and gasped, shrinking against Jeff. Taken aback, Helena tried to edge away but was too close to the wall to move.

'I — I'm Helena Moore,' she managed to say. 'I didn't mean to distress you.'

'She's a doctor at Harper Hills,' Jeff put in, his arm around Vada.

Vada shifted, trying to sit up. Jeff helped her into the proper position on the chaise. Once she was comfortably settled, her gaze drifted to Helena. 'It's not your fault,' she said. 'You can't help it.'

Helena licked lips that had gone inexplicably dry. 'What upsets you about me?' she asked.

'Nothing. Not now. Earlier, though — ' Again Vada paused, then took a deep breath and went on. 'I saw that you will destroy Xenara.'

'By fire, you mean?' Helena asked, astounded.

Vada shook her head. 'The flames came to me later. And not from you, though you were somehow connected.' Distress clouded her green eyes and she tightened her grip on Jeff's hand.

'Believe me, I mean Xenara no harm,' Helena said earnestly. 'I may not be able to swallow what goes on here but I — '

Vada waved a languid hand, cutting her off. 'You speak the truth as far as you know, but what will be, will be. You can't change it, nor can I.'

Vada's words disturbed some deep, primitive center inside Helena — goosebumps rose along her arms and her nape prickled with dread. Damn it, she *hated* this sort of stuff. She needed to get out of here.

'I'm sorry to have caused any trouble,' she told Vada. Easing her way between the chaise and the wall, she made for the door. When she had her hand on the knob she looked back at Jeff. 'See you tomorrow,' she told him. She couldn't manage to thank him for her introduction to Xenara.

'You must come back again!' Vada's voice froze Helena in her tracks. Before she could speak, Vada went on. 'Please say you'll return to at least one more session and stay to talk to me afterward. For my own peace of mind I must see you when I'm not energy-depleted.'

As a refusal rose to her tongue, Helena hesitated. She'd come here not for herself but to discover what Fran's connection to Xenara might be. She hadn't unearthed one single clue. While she couldn't ask questions about Fran at the moment — especially with Jeff hovering protectively over Vada — the need for answers was still urgent. Vada, for her own purposes, had invited her to a *tête-à-tête* after another session and she must take advantage of the offer or her questions might never be answered.

'Thank you,' Helena said, though the words all but choked her. 'I'll do that.'

An attendant, one of the few people lingering in the round room beyond the velvet drapes, hurried up to ask how Vada was. On hearing Vada was awake and talking, she smiled in relief and insisted on taking Helena's name.

'For a return session,' she said. 'Free of charge.'

Helena complied. Though the last thing she wished was ever to enter those blue doors again, gratis or any other way, she knew she must.

★ ★ ★

Over the next two days uneasiness over what had happened at Xenara clouded her mind. Even during her trip in the Nature's End boat to sprinkle Fran's ashes over the ocean — easily the most depressing journey she'd ever made. This final goodbye brought it home to her that Fran was gone beyond recall, gone forever. Into the void. And she was no closer to knowing why her sister had died and who had killed her.

Discovering the new engine block for the VW would cost over three thousand dollars did nothing to raise her spirits. And not once had Mak called. Everything combined to make her greet Friday evening and its prospect of a party with more enthusiasm than she'd felt when she accepted the invitation. She badly needed to be among smiling faces and hear laughter — even if it happened to be alcohol-induced.

Deciding that Peter's definition of casual

might not be hers, she rejected jeans and a tee shirt in favor of white shorts and a black embroidered slip-on blouse from the Philippines, another gift from her mother. She carried her maillot and cover-up in a brightly-decorated straw bag she had bought in Tijuana and never used.

Lamas, impeccable in white, met her at the front door and directed her through a gate to the side of the house where shouts and splashing told her the pool was in use.

Peter, who wore tailored Bermuda shorts and a matching gray shirt, took both her hands in greeting and pulled her to him for a brief hug. 'How charming you look,' he said warmly. Glancing at the straw bag, he added, 'I see you've brought your suit. Introducing you can wait if you'd like to swim first.'

'I'd enjoy a dip in the pool.'

He gestured toward three round structures built to resemble South Sea huts. 'You can change there, if you like. Or, if you'd prefer to use the house — '

'The cabanas are fine,' she assured him.

When she emerged in her blue maillot, she looked around. This entire side of the house was devoted to the pool area and landscaped with tropical plantings. The scarlet of flame trees blended with blooming hibiscus bushes in every shade of red and pink. Tall oleanders with white flowers screened the area from the drive while at the far end of the enclosure two palms rose picturesquely to tower over the deep green and white of gardenia bushes in bloom, their heavy perfume blending with the more prosaic smell of chlorine from the pool.

The sunset had left a red glow in the evening sky and, as she walked toward the pool, the air, summer-warm, caressed her bare skin. A perfect evening in a perfect setting.

'Pretty lady,' a voice tinged with a Spanish accent said as she passed. 'Pretty lady.' Strangely, it seemed to come from over her head.

Helena glanced up and saw, suspended from a branch of a gnarled bottle-brush tree, a gaudily-feathered parrot in a silver cage. One beady eye watched her go by, then the parrow squawked indignantly, apparently expecting a tidbit for his compliment.

Five people shared a large bubbling hot tub to the side of the pool. In the pool itself a couple drifted on a plastic raft shaped like a giant teardrop, while others splashed and swam around them. Helena, who had begun to think she didn't know a soul here except Peter, was pleased to recognize a man pulling himself from the pool practically at her feet.

'Hello, Phil,' she said, noting that, though

thin, he had a well-developed musculature. 'How's the water?'

He smiled. 'Helena. Good to see you. The water's a bit warm for my taste but acceptable. I can't imagine Peter owning anything that wasn't perfectly acceptable.' The even tone of his voice and his smile robbed the words of any real sting, yet after a moment Helena realized Phil had not only captured Peter's essence in that phrase but somehow diminished him. Perfectly acceptable.

Phil's slight smile told her he'd caught her reaction and she suspected he knew exactly what was going through her mind. A very astute man, Dr. Vance. Sharp as a scalpel.

'I hope you and I are never enemies,' she blurted unthinkingly.

To the sound of his pleased laughter, she dove into the pool and immediately realized Phil was right again — the water was a tad warm.

After six laps she stopped counting. Winded, she climbed from the pool and helped herself to one of the thick black towels stacked strategically about. After drying off, she slipped on her blue net coverup and accepted a crab puff from a waiter circulating with an appetizer tray.

Phil seemed to have disappeared — not

that she was sure she wanted to talk to him again — and there wasn't a familiar face in sight. Deciding to dry her hair, she ducked into the cabana where she'd left her belongings. The round huts were partitioned into two cubicles each and, as she seated herself before the mirror and picked up the hand dryer, she heard footsteps entering the other cubicle. Two women, from the sound of their voices.

' . . . a real shame,' one of them said. 'The boy's never been the same since Renata died.'

Remembering Renata had been Peter's wife, Helena delayed turning on the dryer and listened.

'Well, yes,' the second woman said, her voice louder. 'I did hear about the fire, but it was all hushed up. Are you sure — ?'

'My dear, ask anyone. And it wasn't the first time. My husband claims sexual frustration is at the bottom of fire-setting.' She giggled. 'Do you know what I told him?'

Listening to the sexually explicit conversation that followed, Helena towel-dried her hair. Interesting as it might be, she hoped they'd return to 'the boy' because she suspected they meant Quinn. But when they left the cabana they were still occupied with the sexual inadequacies of the men they'd married. Turning on the hair dryer, Helena

200

sifted through the few bits of information they'd dropped.

Fire-setting. Was Quinn a pyromaniac? In the light of Vada's so-called vision Wednesday night, the thought sent a chill along her spine. She wished she could be sure the women were speaking of Quinn. If they were, the pyre of matches left in Fran's apartment and, later, outside under a window, took on a new and sinister meaning.

Dressed, her hair dry and brushed into shape, Helena emerged from the cabana into the hum, chatter, and shifting movement of the crowd. A waiter stopped and offered her a stemmed glass from a tray he carried, murmuring, 'Champagne.'

She accepted the glass and sipped, looking around for Peter, though she knew he was the one person she didn't dare question. If Quinn *had* set fires, she couldn't trust Peter to be honest with her — even if she had the gall to ask him bluntly if his son was being treated for pyromania.

Phil Vance, if he knew, wasn't likely to tell her either. Shrinks, like all doctors, regardless of whether they disagreed with or disliked one another, formed a solid front against outsiders — sticking together like glue.

She wished she could find a picture of Quinn as he looked today and compare it to her mental image of the teenager on the apartment stairs. As the thought occurred to her, she glanced at the house. Why hadn't she accepted Peter's offer to change inside? Too late now, she'd have to conjure up another reason.

Quite possibly there wasn't anyone inside except servants. But if she went in to look around for a photo, what would be her excuse? The cabanas had fully equipped bathrooms, so that was out. A phone? No doubt if she searched she'd find one somewhere in the pool area but she couldn't be expected to know that.

One last sweep of the crowd failed to find Peter, so Helena began to drift unobtrusively closer to the brick walk that led to a flagstone patio where sliding doors opened into the house. Bird of paradise plants lined the walk, their orange and blue crested flowers reminiscent of snake heads. Helena left her glass on a wrought iron table and slid aside a screen to step inside.

Pausing a moment to consider what she was doing, she glanced around. The room was a veritable jungle of greenery with plants everywhere — hanging and in planters and pots of every size and description.

A conservatory? It was clear she'd find no photos here — she'd have to go on. Since she had come this far, she might as well.

After walking through the room she found it was really the ell of a larger recreation room containing a pool table, a forties juke box, what looked like an old wind-up phonograph, a bar, and scattered wicker chairs and divans. She glanced quickly around but saw no family photographs. Nor a phone. So her excuse for the intrusion was still intact. She was about to go through the door at the far end of the room and explore further when something about the papered wall behind the bar caught her attention. She retraced her steps.

What she'd thought at first was cartoon wallpaper was, instead, caricature drawings cleverly put together so they covered the recess completely. The one she'd noticed was of Dr. Rand, Harper Hills' chief of staff, capturing his you're-dirt-beneath-my-feet manner perfectly. The artist was clever and talented.

Among many she didn't recognize, she picked out Peter, Phil, and Clovis and then her breath caught. Fran! Though he'd exaggerated her high cheekbones and slanted her eyes more than their actual slight degree, there was no mistaking her sister's face. What was a caricature of Fran doing in Peter's house? And who was the artist? She slid behind the bar to look closely at the drawings. There was no written signature but in the left hand corner of each was what appeared to be a tiny wide-brimmed, peaked hat with a pigtail below the brim — a hat and a braid like Chinese field workers wore in the old days.

What could that mean? A Chinese man's braid was a queue. Q. Quinn? Helena's heart began to beat faster. If Quinn was the artist, then he'd known Fran.

The soft scrape of the screen sliding open alerted her. Heart thudding, she slipped from behind the bar and got as far as the juke box before Peter appeared at the end of the room.

'There you are,' he said.

'I was looking for a phone,' she said, amazed at the calmness of her voice.

He pointed to the wall near where she stood. She looked and saw an old-fashioned black phone with a separate receiver fastened to a polished oak box hanging at eye level.

She hadn't noticed it before. 'Does it actually work?'

'Of course.'

'The juke box, too?'

He smiled. 'Everything I have works. After you make your call I'll put in a nickel and show you.' He crossed to the phone. 'The number buttons for the phone are in the wood to the left. The mouthpiece is a bit high for you — come closer and I'll adjust it as best I can.'

She hadn't thought about actually making a call, especially with Peter standing over her. Flustered, she edged closer, lifted the receiver off its hook and punched in the first number that came to her.

Two rings and it was picked up on the other end. 'Mak,' he said.

Oh, God, now what? Why hadn't she called the hospital? 'Uh, wrong number,' she muttered and hung up. She made sure to call Harper Hills on the next try, got the nursery, and asked about Kristle.

'Remember what I said about the 'indispensable' syndrome,' Peter commented after she hung up. 'Nobody is, not even you. Now I insist you wipe your mind clear of Harper Hills and concentrate on having fun.' Without waiting for a response, he walked to the juke box, lifted a black cube from a shelf above it, and waited for her to join him. When she came up to him he said, 'Hold out your hand.'

She extended her palm and he shook a coin from the cube into her hand. She stared down at it. A buffalo nickel! Her Grandfather Moore had given her a buffalo nickel once when she was little and she'd saved it for years until it got lost during one of her moves. Indian head on the front, buffalo on the back. She hadn't seen one since then.

'I open the machine every so often and recycle the nickels,' Peter said. He gestured toward the juke box, its front swirling with shifting colors. 'Make your selection.'

The few song titles she recognized went with the buffalo nickel — older than golden oldies. She dropped the nickel in the slot, pushed the number 10 button for 'Tennessee Waltz,' and shoved the lever in, watching as the 78 RPM record slid free of the stack and onto the turntable. The needle arm came down and the music began.

'Good choice,' Peter approved. 'We'll dance.' He held out his hand.

Helena shook her head and put her hands behind her back, saying primly. 'I'm certain your mother taught you better manners.'

'You do stick to your guns,' he told her. Making an exaggerated bow, he asked, 'May I have the pleasure of this waltz?'

She allowed him to take her in his arms and they swept across the floor and around the pool table. He moved gracefully and guided her so expertly he made her feel that she was a wonderful dancer. She knew better but it was fun to pretend. Until he pulled her closer, fitting her body against his.

She wasn't ready to become this intimate with Peter but rather than making an issue of it, she submitted, hoping the record would soon end. When it did, she pulled away, planning to rejoin the pool party rather than remain alone with Peter.

'As long as we're inside,' he said, 'would you like the grand tour? I didn't have a chance to show you everything the other night.'

Every instinct said no. But a house tour would offer her the chance to see a current photo of Quinn, so how could she refuse? Still, she didn't want him to misunderstand if she accepted.

'A tour would be interesting,' she said, easing her hand free, 'but I believe you said you'd invited me to meet some of your friends and I haven't yet.'

Peter waved a hand. 'The night's young — they'll be around for hours. First things first.'

After he led her through a library-study and a music room on the same floor as the recreation room, they climbed a short staircase onto a second level, where she'd been on Friday night — to the living room, another study, and a dining room. She found something to admire in every room — whoever had designed and decorated the house was talented.

Peter waved a hand toward a short corridor, saying, 'The kitchen and the servants' quarters are back there,' then ushered her up spiral steps to the five bedrooms.

Since she hadn't seen family photographs anywhere else, she was hoping to find them on this level. The first door, though, was closed. Peter passed it by.

'Quinn's,' he said. 'I don't trespass.'

Helena stopped, reluctant to miss Quinn's bedroom. Even if Quinn didn't have a photo of himself he was sure to own school yearbooks with his picture inside and she could casually pick one up and leaf through it.

'If your son's on Catalina we wouldn't be disturbing him,' she said. 'Would he really mind me having a look?'

'I'm afraid so.' Peter spoke tersely. 'He's a very private person.'

Helena had no choice but to go on. She saw nothing relating to the family in the three unused bedrooms — each with its own bath — and, as they approached the master bedroom, she tensed. Quinn's photo would be here or nowhere.

Just inside the room, she stopped short, staring. She knew black satin bedspreads existed but she'd never actually seen one on

208

the bed of anybody she knew. The spread on Peter's king-sized bed was beautifully quilted but she still found the color depressing.

Never mind the damn spread, she reminded herself, or the mirrored dressing room or the hot tub. Look for pictures.

She saw no photos on the bedside stands or the chest of drawers, then Peter distracted her by taking her arm and leading her to the wall of windows overlooking the darkening ocean and the lights of El Doblez. God, what a view!

'I'd never get tired of looking at this,' she murmured, hypnotized.

'I find looking at you more exciting,' he told her.

Helena came alert too late. At the same time she started to move away, he reached for her. 'Peter, no,' she said as his arms went around her. 'Please, don't.'

Though he didn't release her, he did refrain from kissing her, gazing intently into her face. 'You're acting like a skittish schoolgirl,' he said softly. 'Why not give this a try?'

'I — can't,' she said.

'Can't? That's a strange answer. Unless there's someone else, or you have an STD.'

'I do not have a sexually transmitted disease,' she snapped, wishing he'd let her go.

His arousal pressing hard against her made her wonder if he found her refusal sexually stimulating. 'Nor am I involved with another person. I find nothing odd in not wanting to go to bed with someone I don't know well.'

'I'd diagnose that as inhibited. And who said we were going to leap into bed immediately?'

'In view of the fact that we're in your bedroom and you're definitely aroused, I didn't think it needed saying.' His 'inhibited' diagnosis didn't hold water. With Mak she sure as hell hadn't been. And she didn't know him any better than she did Peter.

She'd come right out and tell Peter he just didn't turn her on if she hadn't learned that men tended to take that as a challenge. Peter seemed too urbane to try force — but a woman never could be sure.

He bent his head and she knew he meant to kiss her. She remained passive in his embrace, the pine woods scent of his after-shave surrounding her, neither resisting nor responding. She kept her mouth firmly closed when his lips pressed against hers.

After a long moment when she wondered what he meant to do, Peter released her. 'You've made your point,' he said coolly.

In her relief, she turned from him without looking where she was going and her shoulder hit against a whatnot shelf fastened to the wall, knocking it askew and tumbling its contents to the plush gray rug. Upset by her clumsiness, she dropped to her knees and gathered up the spill — an exquisite black-glazed Japanese bowl that had held crystal roses with silver stems and leaves.

'Thank God I didn't break anything,' she said as much to herself as to Peter as she reinserted the roses into the bowl. She'd begun to rise to her feet when she saw, under the dresser, a white rectangle of a photograph. Thinking it had come off the whatnot shelf, she stretched and retrieved it. On her feet, she glanced at the picture.

She stared down at a gangly red-haired teenager standing by a motorcycle and gasped. Still clutching the bowl, she handed the photo to Peter.

'Is this your son?' she asked, holding her breath as she waited for his answer — because it was the same boy she'd seen on the apartment stairs, the one who had run from her in the cafeteria.

He nodded and tossed the picture onto the dresser. Releasing her breath slowly, Helena set the vase on the shelf, lingering to rearrange the crystal roses while she fought for composure. What was she to make of Fran's caricature in Peter's house and Peter's son on Fran's apartment stairs the day her sister was killed?

'My advice is to loosen up,' Peter said.

Helena started, then realized he was still talking about her rejection of his lovemaking. To hell with that!

She whirled to face him. 'How about Fran?' she demanded. 'Did you tell her to loosen up, too? Damn it, did you take my sister to bed?'

11

Though he hadn't a hair out of place, Peter slid a hand over his silver waves. It was the first nervous gesture Helena had ever seen him make.

'What my relationship with your sister might or might not have been is none of your business.' The coolness of his voice conflicted with the uneasy gesture.

'If Fran was still alive I'd agree with you,' Helena said, her voice quivering with building fury. 'She's dead. And someone killed her. You told me you scarcely knew her. How can I believe that when her caricature, drawn by your son, is on your wall downstairs?'

'We'll leave Quinn out of this!'

Helena struggled to keep her anger under control. 'Why? He must have known Fran to be able to draw such a clever sketch.'

Rage sparked in Peter's gray eyes. 'I will not allow you to drag my son into this — this paranoid ideation of yours.'

Helena's lips drew back over her teeth in a smile that had nothing to do with humor or friendliness. 'As any third-year medical student knows, doctor, a patient suffering from paranoia isn't easily convinced by a psychiatrist that his beliefs aren't perfectly sound so, if I *were* paranoid, your threat would be useless. But I'm not paranoid. Nor am I your patient. I know very well you're deliberately concealing things but don't think that will stop me from finding out why my sister died. Or who killed her.'

She turned away and strode toward the bedroom door only to be stopped short when he gripped her arm so tightly she winced.

'I'll repeat it one more time.' His words were taut with suppressed rage. 'You will *not* bring Quinn into this.'

'You're hurting my arm. What's the next step, breaking my neck?' She spoke with bravado while quaking inwardly. His icy fury was frightening.

'Peter!' a man's voice called. 'Where are you? What's a folk song without our mellow tenor?'

Peter let her go abruptly and, rubbing her arm, she marched from the room. Phil Vance, guitar under one arm, stood at the head of the spiral staircase and she hurried toward him, eager to leave the house and Peter Herron.

As she started to push past Phil he said quietly, 'It's not wise to cross a vengeful type, Helena.'

She threw a quick look behind her but Peter wasn't in sight. 'Your advice comes a bit too late,' she muttered.

'Then keep your guard up,' he said as she edged past him and on down the stairs.

As she retrieved her belongings from the cabana, she refused to dwell on what might have happened if Phil hadn't come to call Peter when he did — all she wanted was to get out of this house and never come back.

The loaner VW didn't start on her first two tries and she bit her lip as she tried to calm herself. Finally the motor caught and she screeched from the parking area and drove down the winding hill as fast as she dared.

Peter Herron had lied to her. Now that she knew he had, she didn't believe Quinn was on Catalina. Or at least he hadn't been when Fran was killed. Had Peter sent him to the island because he knew his son was somehow involved in Fran's death and wanted Quinn out of the way?

Damn the man! She didn't appreciate being mauled — or scared. She hadn't needed Phil's advice to realize she'd need to be very, very careful in the future where either of the Herrons was concerned.

Interesting that Phil *had* warned her, though. Why had he? Because Peter had taken revenge on others in ways Phil didn't approve of? She moved her shoulders uneasily.

I'll get Phil in a corner as soon as I can, she vowed, and insist on knowing if what he told me about Peter's vengefulness had anything to do with my sister's death.

She pulled into her De La Mar parking slot, locked the car, and strode around to the stairs leading to her apartment. As she reached them, she caught sight of a dark figure lounging against the wall and halted, her heart thudding.

'Why in hell did you tell me you had a wrong number and hang up on me?' Mak demanded, pushing away from the wall.

'You gave me the scare of my life just now!' she cried.

'Sorry. I wasn't thinking.' He reached for her hand, removed the keys she held and pulled her with him. 'Come on, I'll take you upstairs and make you a cup of coffee in reparation.'

'It's my apartment and my coffee,' she protested — in vain.

After he'd unlocked the door and followed her inside, she turned on him. 'Did anyone ever tell you — ?'

'Often, starting with my mother,' he interrupted. 'I'm unimprovable.'

Giving up, she dropped her straw bag on the floor, walked into the living room, and flung herself onto the couch. 'So, okay, where's the coffee?' she asked.

He ambled into the kitchen and she heard him open the refrigerator. 'Looks like Mother Hubbard stocked this,' he complained. 'Don't you ever buy real food?'

Helena, suddenly realizing she was hungry, bounced off the couch and joined him in the kitchen. 'My food doesn't happen to be in the refrigerator,' she told him, opening a cupboard and removing a jar. 'See — here's peanut butter.'

'Kid stuff.'

'The hell it is. I'll have you know this is full of protein *and* it's cholesterol free. Do you prefer your sandwich with or without bananas?'

'Bananas and peanut butter? Doctor, I swear you've flipped.'

'Bananas happen to be loaded with — '

'Yeah, I know — potassium. And I don't want any. If I'm stuck with peanut butter I hope you've got some jelly.'

'Sorry. Will honey do?'

He sighed. 'I'll give it a try.'

When the coffee was made, he insisted on loading everything onto a tray and carrying it into the living room. Helena polished off her peanut butter and banana sandwich and reached for a half of the two she'd made for Mak with honey.

'The Silver Shrink doesn't feed the people he invites to his parties?' Mak asked.

Helena's hand stopped in midair. She turned to Mak indignantly.

'Hey,' he protested, 'don't go telling me it's none of my business. If you remember, I didn't call you, you called me.'

She opened her mouth and closed it again, finding it impossible to explain the circumstances of that call without telling him everything that had gone on. She wasn't sure she wanted to until she had more time to think.

'How did you know I was at Peter Herron's?'

'Simple. I fell in love with your Identifier so I got myself one. I called the number back and some flunky answered, 'Herron residence'. I'd heard via the hospital grapevine he was throwing a party tonight. Now it's your turn. Why did you call me?'

She'd give him part of the truth. 'I meant to dial the hospital number to ask about a patient and I punched in yours by mistake. When I heard your voice I was too embarrassed to admit what I'd done.'

'Didn't you know I'd recognize yours?'

It *had* occurred to her and that's why she had mumbled. Evidently Mak had an acute ear for voices. 'I'm sorry if I caused a problem,' she said.

Mak ignored the apology. 'I think you punched in my number for a reason you won't tell me. I thought we were on the same side — am I wrong?'

'If you must know, using the phone was an excuse I made to cover up something I was doing that I didn't want revealed.'

Mak scowled. 'Something involving your sister's death?'

She nodded.

'That's exactly what I figured. Damn it, Helena, I know you've got brains — use them. You wouldn't turn *me* loose in an operating room with a scalpel and expect the patient to survive, would you? So leave the investigating to professionals. Me. Garcia and his men. Otherwise *you* might not survive.'

She matched him glare for glare. 'Why should I leave it to you and the police? None of you seem to be getting anywhere. And, anyway, you told me yourself Fran's death isn't your primary concern. But it *is* mine — why shouldn't I do what I can to find her killer?'

'Because killers are dangerous. Even for cops, sometimes. And for someone like you, who doesn't know zilch — ' He stopped and shook his head. 'Why do I get the feeling you're not listening to word one?'

Taking a deep breath, he sighed deeply. 'Okay, consider yourself warned. Now it's sharing time. What did you uncover during your sneaky maneuvering inside the Silver Shrink's mansion?'

Why not tell Mak, she thought. Some of it, anyway. After all, they really were on the same side.

'Peter said he barely knew Fran but I found a caricature of her on his wall.'

'If you'd asked me I could have told you Fran had been at his house. More than once.'

Helena stared at him. 'Did she tell you that?'

'No. Your sister never mentioned him.'

'What else do you know about her that you haven't bothered to let me in on?' she demanded bitterly.

He shrugged. 'Nothing I can think of.'

She eyed him unbelievingly. 'I've heard enough lies for one night.'

'I'm not in the same category as your shrink. I've never told you a deliberate lie. One or two by omission, maybe, but that can't be helped. My hunch is you're concealing as much or more from me than I am from you.'

Her gaze turned indignant. She hadn't hidden anything from him! The only reason she hadn't told him about Quinn was because he'd distracted her by confirming Fran's involvement with Peter. Well, maybe there was a bit more to it — she wanted to talk to Quinn herself before exposing an already-disturbed teen to police questioning. Or even to an ex-cop's.

She still didn't really know what Mak was investigating here in El Doblez — other than the fact that Harper Hills was somehow mixed up in it. Mak had unearthed practically her entire life and what had she learned about his? Talk about concealment!

'You've never even told me where you live,' she said accusingly. 'Or where you got all those scars. Or whether you've ever been married. I don't even know how old you are!'

Mak's lips twitched — whether in annoyance or humor, she couldn't be sure. 'I live in LA, Portuguese Bend, but I'm currently camping in a condo in the hills on the other side of the freeway — be glad to give you both addresses. The scars are a reminder never to underestimate an opponent again — on or off duty. I prefer to forget the grisly details but, if you insist, I'll dredge them up. I'm divorced and damn glad of it. And I'm thirty-seven.'

Nothing he'd said explained the expensive clothes and car but she could hardly ask about them. What she was actually most curious about was the woman he'd divorced.

Helena poured herself more coffee and took a sip. 'How long were you married?'

'I'm beginning to feel like I'm on a quiz show,' he protested.

'Hey, you were the guy who suggested sharing.'

'Me and my big mouth.' He stared up at the ceiling a moment or two as if calculating. 'Eight years. How about you?'

'I thought Lieutenant Garcia let you read my — what is it, dossier?'

'File. And I just got the highlights — like, he was a doctor, too.'

'I was with Roger six years,' she said. 'Like you, I'm glad it's over.' She glanced at him and found his gaze flicking over her.

'Guy's crazy,' he muttered. 'You're worth a few fights.'

'Roger found — uh, other interests.'

Mak grimaced. 'One of those. Mima's main interest turned out to be Mima. So she only bet on sure winners.'

Helena set down her cup, watching him finger the scar on his right upper arm. 'Your wife left after you got hurt,' she said with sudden insight. Judging by his startled expression, she'd scored a direct hit.

'Once the docs decided I'd live,' he said slowly, 'they hit Mima with a bunch of potential problems — like would my colostomy be permanent or temporary. She couldn't handle the possibility I'd be disabled. I'd become a loser, in her eyes.' His smile held a hint of malice. 'So I fooled her and made a miraculous recovery just to get even.'

Helena pictured his painful recuperation. Once he'd improved enough to be a good surgical risk, they'd have done a second major operation to revise the colostomy and put his bowel back together. The long convalescence must have been extremely frustrating for an active man like Mak. Plus he'd lost his wife and his livelihood.

Shaken by a surge of tenderness, she slid closer, reached out, and hugged him. Instantly his arms wrapped around her and he pulled her onto his lap and kissed her.

With Mak she had no choice of how to react. The instant his lips touched hers she wanted more and more and more. What felt wrong with Peter felt right with Mak, felt amazingly right and wonderful.

He tasted sweet as honey. As honey and peanut butter, in fact. She loved kissing him.

He lifted his head slightly, his face so close she could feel the erotic caress of his beard. 'Yes or no?' he said huskily. 'I can stop now but if we keep this up I won't be able to.'

She forced herself to pull back far enough to look at him, the glow of desire in his eyes taking her breath away. 'One night stand?' she asked when she could speak, hearing the hoarseness of passion in her voice. 'Or longer?'

'Definitely longer. But no guarantees.'

God knows she was tempted. If it had been lust, pure and simple, she'd have an easier time making up her mind. Lust was there, all right, but by now she knew it was more than that as far as she was concerned. She not only wanted Mak, she *needed* him in some deep, unspecified way she was afraid to examine.

No guarantees. That meant his investigation over, he'd go back to Portuguese Bend, maybe run down to see her once in a while. For a while.

That wasn't enough. For her, it was like the old Sinatra tune, all or nothing at all. Mak might as well hear her say it flat out. If it scared him off for good at least she wouldn't be tantalized to death by these cut-short kisses.

'Sorry, too low a bid,' she told him, easing herself from his embrace. Her effort at flippancy was a miserable failure.

Before she could get to her feet, he grasped her arm. 'What do you expect — a promise of forever?' Anger edged his words.

'I don't believe in forevers but, yes, I want some kind of promise.'

'You must know you're driving me out of my mind. Why the hell can't we — ?'

She put her fingers over his lips. 'Since you insist, I'll give it to you plain and simple. I need commitment from you because you mean something to me already. Even though we're not lovers.'

He took her hand away, holding it in his as he stared at her. 'You scare the hell out of me,' he said.

She smiled wryly. 'I know the feeling.'

'I don't seem to be able to stay away from you and when I'm with you I can't keep my hands off you. So what're we going to do?'

'Be friends?'

His snort of disgust told her what he thought of that.

'Come on, Mak, it's better than nothing.'

'Damned if it is,' he growled.

'The alternative *is* nothing.' As she spoke her heart fluttered with the realization she might lose him completely. Right now.

He pulled her against him, her head on his shoulder. 'You wouldn't like that any better than I would. Why the hell do you have to make things so complicated, doctor?'

'Blame it on medical school,' she said, taking a deep, breath of relief. 'They spend four years training us to make the simple seem complex. A patient never gets hurt, he suffers trauma. If his heart doesn't work right, it's not that the heart can't pump enough blood — no, he's got cardiac insufficiency. If — '

'You and you alone are enough to give me cardiac arrest,' he told her, resting his cheek against her head. 'To say nothing of causing a dozen other interesting, but fortunately not terminal, physiological phenomena.'

'I'm impressed — I thought they only taught you to shoot straight at cop school.'

'Police Academy, if you please.'

Oh God, how she enjoyed this man. Was she a damn fool not to take what he could offer her?

They nestled together in companionable silence for a time until finally Mak yawned and sat up straight, easing away from her.

'Okay,' he said. 'Straight from the shoulder from now on, right? So, do I spend the rest of the night on this couch or cramped behind the wheel of that damned car of mine?'

'What are you talking about?'

'I've been staked out on your street near the apartment every night. I figure the prowler's going to return sooner or later and I damn well mean to nail him.'

Helena was speechless for a moment,

assimilating what he was saying. 'Every night?' she echoed in amazement.

He nodded. 'I can't very well pick and choose.'

'But — ' She paused, remembering that Mak must have seen Peter bring her home on one of those nights. And kiss her at the door. She flushed in annoyance. 'It's like spying on me!'

He shrugged. 'At least I had the satisfaction of seeing you didn't like the way that shrink kissed you.'

'Damn it, Mak — '

He held up a hand. 'The prowler may be Fran's killer so we can't afford to take chances. I'm making sure he can't get to you at night.'

Helena bit her lip. Whether she liked the idea or not she had to admit Mak was right. She shot him a dark look. 'You know perfectly well I can't possibly condemn you to spending any more uncomfortable nights in that sports car so it'll have to be the couch.'

'Your bed would be even more comfortable. Plus the other benefits.'

She jabbed him in the ribs with her elbow. 'Don't push your luck, captain.' Then she was reminded of something else. 'There *is* another bedroom in the apartment,' she said slowly.

'Your sister's.'

'You're welcome to use the room — and it does have a private bath.'

'I remember.'

'Well, what do you think?'

'The couch tonight. Tomorrow, if you don't mind, I'll bring over a few things and start using that bedroom. I'll bet you haven't been in it since your sister died.'

'You're right.'

'So I'll take the curse off for you, okay?'

'I appreciate that but it's not a good idea for either of us to have you sleeping in the apartment every night.'

'What's the alternative? To leave you unprotected?' He shook his head. 'No way.'

She couldn't argue with his logic. Truthfully, she'd rest easier knowing that if anything happened at night he was within earshot. Having him that close, though, meant she also faced temptation every night. She trusted that he'd stay where he was supposed to — but how long could she trust herself?

She left him on the couch when she went to bed. It wasn't until she was almost asleep that she remembered she'd forgotten to mention Quinn. She couldn't be sure Peter's son was the prowler or if he'd been responsible for the pyre of matches but she did know he was the teenager she'd seen on the apartment stairs the day Fran was killed. Mak should be told. Helena started to sit up, then shook her head. Mak might be asleep. Or misconstrue her reason for rousing him. Morning would be soon enough.

When the alarm rang at seven, Helena rose, smelled coffee, and smiled. Mak was sweet. She grabbed her robe, hurried into the living room, and found him gone. Before she could dial his number, the phone rang. She was on call and they needed her stat for a pediatric problem in the Harper Hills ER.

What with one thing and another at the hospital, Helena forgot to call Mak until after lunch and then there was no answer. She decided to wait until she saw him that night.

Because she was on call, she didn't leave the hospital until close to six. When she came into the apartment, the red light of the answering machine was on and she listened to the message.

'This is Mak. I can't get to the apartment until after ten P.M. I know you're on call; if you're not home I'll come by the hospital.'

As it happened she wasn't called during the early evening and, near ten, began looking forward to Mak's arrival. When the phone rang at three minutes to ten, she groaned.

Remembering to answer in the bedroom,

she said, 'Dr. Moore,' her glance automatically flicking to the Identifier screen, even though she was sure it was the hospital.

No response. And the number flashing in green was not Harper Hills. She grabbed the pad and scribbled it down with shaky fingers before it faded from the screen, even though she knew the tape registered every number automatically. Staring at the numerals while she listening to the breathing, she decided they were familiar. Hadn't she jotted down that same number recently?

A mental picture flashed of her listening to Peter's message on the answering machine a few days ago, a message with his phone number. A number she'd written on a scrap of paper. The hair rose on her neck as she realized who this must be.

'I know you!' she shouted into the phone. 'You're Quinn Herron. And don't you dare hang up on me or I'll tell the police. You are Quinn, aren't you?' When he didn't immediately respond, she cried, 'Answer me, damn it!'

For a long moment she thought he wouldn't but finally a sullen voice muttered. 'How'd you know?'

She didn't bother to tell him. 'I saw you on the stairs the day Fran died,' she said. 'You're going to tell me why you were there.'

'Not on the phone,' he said in a shaky whisper.

'Did you kill her?'

'Oh, God, no! What do you think I am? Jesus, I'd never hurt her. I'd never hurt *anyone*.' He sounded so agonized she was tempted to believe him.

'But you were at Fran's apartment. I saw you. What were you — ?'

'Look, I'm not even supposed to be here — I can't stay any longer. And there are things I can't say on the phone.'

'You want to meet me face to face, is that it?'

'Oh, Jesus, I'm not sure. I'm really fucked up, you know?'

He sounded it.

'What, then?' she demanded. 'You want me to call the cops?'

'No, please don't. My dad'll kill me if you do. I mean, he doesn't know — ' Quinn's words trailed off. 'Look,' he said in a lower tone. 'Someone's coming, I got to split. I'll meet you in the Xenara parking lot tomorrow night about this time, okay? But you got to come alone or I won't show.'

Before she could answer, he hung up.

12

Quinn was the breather! Helena stared at the phone in her hand, hearing the buzz of the disconnection. As she replaced the phone on the night stand, she told herself she couldn't possibly meet Quinn tomorrow night — not alone.

On the other hand, he'd implied if she brought someone with her, he wouldn't show. Was he dangerous? Helena thought of the vulnerable child he'd been at eight and sighed. He must be seventeen or eighteen now — ten years would change any child.

Did Peter know Quinn was at home? Surely the servants would tell him even if Quinn slipped in while his father was at the office or the hospital.

She must talk to the boy. But how?

The doorbell chimed and she started. Mak! She'd forgotten he was spending the night in the apartment. What was she going to tell him? If he knew about Quinn, he'd never let her meet the boy in the Xenara parking lot alone. Not that she actually intended to.

The chime rang again. 'I'm coming,' she muttered.

'I had to drive up to LA to see a client,' Mak said when she let him in. 'Everything okay?'

'Yes,' she said brightly, 'everything's just fine.' Not until the words were out of her mouth did she realize she'd already decided not to tell him about Quinn. Not yet, anyway.

Mak carried an attaché case, she noticed. No doubt the belongings he planned to leave in Fran's — no, not Fran's, the other — bedroom. It occurred to her then that he'd be here on Sunday night, too. If she did decide to meet Quinn, how could she possibly get away without Mak asking where she was going?

She'd have to lie and say the hospital.

What if I told Lieutenant Garcia about Quinn, she asked herself. Would he pull him in for questioning? Always supposing he could find Quinn. She had a strong feeling the boy wasn't staying at home but only dropping by there from time to time. She doubted very much that the lieutenant would surround Xenara's parking lot tomorrow night in an effort to trap Quinn. After all, what was the boy guilty of? Nothing more than being on the apartment steps the day Fran was killed.

She might suspect Quinn knew something about Fran's death but she had no proof. Not until she talked to him. And how was she going to do that unless she met him at Xenara?

'You seem distracted,' Mak said.

'I had a couple of rough cases at the hospital,' she said quickly — the truth. 'One was an eight-year-old with severe abdominal pain — we were all sure he had a hot appendix. And he did, in a manner of speaking. When the surgeon removed the appendix, a worm crawled from the opening, grossing out the OR staff. It seems his parents fed him raw fish and he ingested a fish parasite, *anisakis simplex*.'

'Live and crawling, huh?' Mak grimaced. 'Looks like I've eaten my last sushi.'

'I never touch the stuff. Though, to be fair, good sushi chefs do know about the worms and they check their fish fillets to make sure *anisakis* isn't present.'

'How about cooked fish?'

'Cooking kills the worms, just like it does in pork and beef.'

'Beef's got worms, too? Keep on and you'll convince me to become a vegetarian. What happens to the kid now?'

'He's doing well, minus one appendix and one worm. He'll be treated for other possible parasites before we discharge him. I doubt his parents will ever feed him raw fish again. Or eat it themselves.'

'I don't think I want to hear any more, thanks just the same, or I may never eat anything again.'

Helena smiled and didn't mention the other case — a four-year-old with a fever and generalized skin rash that she strongly suspected was due to a hypersensitivity reaction to the oral penicillin he'd been getting at home for a strep throat. Though she didn't feel he was so acutely ill he needed corticosteroids, she'd admitted him for observation because drug allergies sometimes got worse fast. She planned to call Three North to check on his condition before she went to bed.

'I'll stash this in the bedroom,' he said, indicating his case.

'You know where it is.' She didn't look directly at him. Strange how guilty she felt, keeping Quinn's call to herself, but she'd never been good at hiding anything. 'Time I headed for my bedroom, too.'

'Mind if I stay for breakfast, seeing it'll be Sunday?'

'Not at all. Though I might not join you — depends on whether they call me again or not.'

'I'll hope the juvenile population of El Doblez remains healthy for the rest of the weekend.' He crooked an eyebrow at her.

'Any chance of a good night kiss?'

'Any chance it'll be merely a friendly kiss?'

'None.'

She smiled. 'That's what I figured. I think we'd better leave well enough alone.' She reached up and brushed his cheek with a quick caress of her fingers. 'Sweet dreams.'

★　★　★

The phone woke Helena at six — the relief night charge on Three North telling her the boy with the suspected drug rash had a fever of 105.

'I'll be right over,' Helena told her.

★　★　★

At the hospital, she examined the boy and found no reason for alarm other than the high temperature. A cool sponge bath and Tylenol brought it down two degrees. She started an intravenous infusion to counteract his mild dehydration.

The post-op patient who'd had the worm was sleeping, all his vital signs normal, so she didn't wake him.

By the time she finished, the day shift had taken over and Idalia was on duty.

'Don't you ever get a weekend off?' Helena

asked her. 'I thought charge nurses never worked Saturday and Sunday.'

'We rotate days off,' Idalia said. 'My relief prefers it that way and I don't mind.' She gestured toward the nurses' lounge. 'I got some fresh coffee brewing in case you'd like a cup before you go on home. And some Dunkin' Donuts.'

'Sounds good.'

Idalia joined her in the lounge and Helena decided to probe a little about Quinn.

'I overheard something about Peter Herron's son,' she said. 'This woman made him sound like a pyromaniac.'

'That Quinn's a sad case,' Idalia said. 'He set more than one fire before he got caught last year. If his papa hadn't been the Silver Shrink, you know the kid would be in juvie. I guess maybe he's better 'cause I haven't heard he was in trouble lately.'

'Do you think Quinn's dangerous?'

'I never heard anything bad about him except for the fire-setting. Seems like I read someplace that kind gets it off watching things burn.'

Helena nodded.

'Then there's another kind,' Idalia commented, 'that think they can cure every disease in the books by going to those Xenara sessions.' She cast a sly look at Helena.

237

'What'd you think of the place?'

Helena realized that, thanks to the grapevine, the entire hospital probably knew she'd gone to Xenara with Jeff.

'I went out of curiosity,' she told Idalia, 'because I found a Xenara brochure in Fran's apartment and wondered if she'd gotten involved. Vada Rogers is quite impressive — and so's the building. It must have cost a fortune.'

'That's no lie. Vada started with a bitty group in an old store down near the beach. They say she found a secret backer, a silent partner like, and that's where the money to build Xenara came from. Lots of rumors as to who the mystery man is.' Idalia shrugged. 'Could be anyone. *I* sure don't know.' She swallowed the last of her coconut donut and stood up. 'Got to get back to work.'

'Thanks for the coffee. I'll be leaving in a couple of minutes. Give me a call at home if that temp spikes again.'

'Will do.'

★ ★ ★

Mak was sitting at the dinette table in the kitchen alcove reading the Sunday paper and drinking coffee when Helena returned to the apartment. He looked up when she came in.

'I take it you're not able to bring Laura here on your weekends on call,' he said. 'I can stay around today, if you'd like to go get her. She and I did all right together, I don't think she'd be afraid if you had to go to the hospital and leave her with me.' As he spoke he poured another mug of coffee and pushed it toward her.

Helena, flabbergasted by his offer, eased herself onto the chair opposite him and cradled the mug in both hands while she searched for words. 'I don't think you know what you're letting yourself in for,' she said slowly. 'There's no predicting Laura's behavior.'

He shrugged. 'I'll survive. And so will she. Let's give it a try.'

It would be another week before she saw her daughter if she didn't accept Mak's offer, so Helena decided to take a chance. 'Thanks,' she said.

'I'll drive you over to Sea Mist Manor — that VW loaner's not in much better shape than your old squareback was.'

'As long as it keeps running until Wednesday. They promised me mine would be ready then.' She swallowed a sip of coffee and set the mug down, staring into it while she sorted out how much she wanted to tell Mak.

'Idalia Davin, the peds charge nurse, told me something interesting about Xenara,' she said finally. 'Vada Rogers has a silent partner — one with money. He built the pyramid. I wonder who it is?'

'I'm fairly close to finding out,' Mak said.

She shot him an exasperated look. 'It seems each time I offer you a choice tidbit from the grapevine you've heard it already.'

'I'd be a damn poor investigator if I didn't make it my business not only to listen to rumors but to follow up on them. Most contain at least a kernel of truth. Vada's partner went to a lot of trouble to keep his name a secret but I know he's connected with Harper Hills in some way and so it's only a matter of time before I know his name.'

'Is he part of your investigation?'

Mak shrugged. 'Who knows? Maybe, maybe not. But once a cop always a cop. Hint at a secret in front of any one of us and it goads us on like the matador's cape does a bull.'

'Will you let me in on this secret when you find out?' she asked. 'Or do cops hoard their discoveries?'

He grinned at her. 'yeah, I'm like the dragon curled around the treasure trove. But this particular pearl I'll give you as soon as it drops into my reptilian claw.'

She was keeping back information, too. Now was the time to come clean about Quinn, to share all she'd learned with Mak. Except then she couldn't drive to Xenara alone tonight. And she knew in her heart Quinn wouldn't appear unless she *was* alone.

Helena still hadn't told Mak by the time they picked up Laura at Sea Mist. Since she had her beeper along, they stopped at a park playground on the way back and Mak pushed Laura on one of the swings.

When they returned to the apartment for lunch, he waited until Laura was occupied with her peanut butter sandwich before saying in a low tone, 'She doesn't seem like the same peppy kid I took into the ocean with me a couple weeks ago. Are you sure she's okay?'

'I do an exam on her every week,' Helena said defensively, 'and I can't find anything abnormal. They drew blood for lab work at Sea Mist on Monday — it tested within normal limits.'

'I hear what you aren't saying,' Mak told her. 'You're worried about her, aren't you?'

Helena bit her lip and nodded. 'There's nothing I can point to but she's not herself. Maybe it's because she's at Sea Mist. I always kept her at home before I came to El Doblez, though it was getting almost impossible to find babysitters I could trust.'

Mak gazed at Laura thoughtfully. 'I'm no doctor but she looks kind of peaked to me. Maybe you better run her through some more tests and get that hotshot you work for to go over her.'

'I've been meaning to ask George to look at her. I'll do it this week for sure.'

When Laura settled down for an afternoon nap, Helena returned to the hospital to check on her patients, leaving Mak at the apartment. The boy with the drug rash still had a low-grade fever but looked better and the post-op appendix boy, discovering the surgeons had taken a worm from inside him, was full of questions.

'I sure wish I could take that worm to school and show the guys,' he said after listening to her answers.

'Has school started already?' she asked. The days and weeks had slipped by since her arrival but surely it wasn't September yet.

He gave her a pitying look. 'We got year-round school in El Doblez, everybody knows that. I get my free time in November.'

'Tell you what,' she said. 'I can't get the worm for you but I have a picture of *anisakis* worms in one of my journals — I'll make you a copy. Did you know an appendix looks a lot like a worm? They even call it by the latin name for worm — vermiform — so what you had was sort of like a worm inside a worm.'

'Vermiform,' he said tentatively, repeating it twice more. 'Everybody's got one of those appendixes? Girls, too?'

'Appendices is the plural. Yes, every baby is born with an appendix inside. Once in a while the appendix gets inflamed and sore so a surgeon has to remove it. Like yours. If that doesn't happen, you keep your appendix for life though not even doctors are sure what use it is to you.'

'Boy, wait'll I tell Monica she's got a vermiform appendix inside her. Is she gonna be grossed out!'

'Who's Monica — your girlfriend?'

He made a face. 'Naw, she's just a girl I know at school.'

Helena left the boy's room smiling but the smile faded as it occurred to her that Laura would never be any boy's girlfriend. Or even be able to attend an ordinary school class. She tried not to think of the other problems ahead for both her and Laura; it was all she could do to face the here and now, the daily worry of having Laura at Sea Mist Manor instead of at home.

As she passed George's office, she saw the door was open and glanced in. Carin, standing by her husband's desk sorting through medical journals, looked up and said hello.

'Is George on the unit?' Helena asked.

Carin shook her head. 'He's sailing with friends but I'm the world's worst sailor so I begged off. I've been shopping at the mall and came by to pick up the current neurology journal. There's an article Jeff recommended so I thought I'd abstract it for George.'

'I admire your enterprise on a Sunday,' Helena told her. 'If I were in your shoes I think I'd pop a dramamine and opt for the sailing.'

'Not me. I never take drugs.' Carin's tone was smug.

Her manner irritated Helena, who couldn't help thinking it was self-defeating not to take a medication that would help avoid seasickness because you prided yourself on never taking drugs. Did Carin refuse antibiotics when she had a bacterial infection?

George's wife could be somewhat off-putting, Helena decided. Had Carin always been such a busy beaver or had she changed after she'd had a retarded child? No doubt she missed the little boy and probably felt guilty because he'd been placed in an institution. Helena's heart went out to her; she wanted Carin to know she wasn't alone.

'I have a four-year-old autistic daughter,'

she told Carin, 'and I have trouble finding baby-sitters who can manage her so I've had to put her in Sea Mist Manor. I miss having Laura at home. I understand your little boy with Down's Syndrome — Terry — doesn't live at home, either. It's hard, isn't it?'

Carin froze, the journal in her hands falling onto the desk. She stared blankly at Helena for a long tension-filled moment, then rushed toward the door. Helena, stunned by Carin's reaction to what was meant to be a friendly gesture, hastily moved aside to let her pass and stood watching as Carin hurried toward the elevators.

'What got into her?' Idalia asked, coming up to Helena.

'I don't know, all I did was mention Terry and — '

Idalia rolled her eyes. 'Oh, Lord, I never thought to tell you. You don't ever say that child's name to her. Ever since George shipped the kid off to Anaheim, she sort of pretends Terry doesn't exist. Like, she never goes to see him.'

Helena sighed. In trying to do a good deed she'd done Carin a bad turn instead. The poor woman — apparently denial of Terry's existence was the only way Carin could cope with his absence.

She drove home feeling more depressed

than ever. Laura was awake and sitting on the floor by the couch with Mak next to her. He was reading aloud from a Beatrix Potter book that had belonged to Helena when she was a child.

'Flopsy, Mopsy, Cottontail, and — ' He broke off when he caught sight of Helena. 'Your mother's here,' he told Laura.

Laura, who'd been stroking the side of the couch, stopped and began to cry, making Helena feel like bursting into tears herself.

Forcing an even tone, she said to Mak, 'Laura can't tolerate having any activity interrupted. Start reading again and she'll be satisfied.'

Looking dubious, Mak picked up where he'd left off. Laura's sobbing gradually eased and soon she was quietly stroking the fabric of the couch again, not looking at Mak or the book or her mother. Helena walked to the stereo unit, found Laura's favorite tape of marches, pushed it in, and waited.

As Mak neared the end of the story, she started the tape, keeping the volume low until he read the last sentence, then she turned up the sound, hoping the music would distract Laura. Fortunately, it did.

'I forgot to warn you about reading to Laura,' Helena said as he eased up from the floor to sit on the couch. 'Once you start you can't stop without her throwing a tantrum. Sometimes she'll let you stop at the end of a story and sometimes you have to keep reading indefinitely. You can get really hoarse before she's ready to let you quit.'

'I'll remember. Otherwise we got along fine.'

Seeing that Laura was absorbed in the martial music and in stroking the soft fabric of the couch, Helena sank down on a chair. 'Did you know the Wittenburgs have a son with Down's Syndrome?' she asked Mak.

He nodded. 'Squirreled away someplace in Anaheim, I understand.'

'You *do* find out things,' she said wryly. 'Well, I made the mistake of mentioning the boy to Carin, thinking she and I had something in common — her son in Anaheim, Laura at Sea Mist. How could I know I was breaking a taboo? She got all shook and rushed from the hospital. Apparently she tried to make herself forget she even has a son. I feel so sorry for her.'

'She took him to Vada Rogers once,' Mak said. 'In the days before they built the pyramid.'

'Idalia told me. Carin also took Terry to a faith healer who gave him some concoction that almost killed him. I guess that's when George found the place in Anaheim.'

Mak shrugged. 'Could be. From what I heard, Vada tried a laying on of hands, without results. Carin wanted her to go on 'treating' Terry but Vada refused, saying she couldn't help the boy.'

So, okay, she thought to herself, Vada wasn't a complete charlatan — one point in her favor. Carin wasn't so lucky in her second choice of faith healers. Aware of how desperate the mother of an abnormal child could feel, Helena wondered whether she might have been driven to something similar if her medical training hadn't made her certain no magical potion or paranormal power could cure her daughter of autism.

'It's all so sad,' she murmured.

At that moment the tape of marches ended and Laura put her hands over her eyes and began to scream. There was no way to be certain if she was in pain or merely frustrated.

After Helena managed to calm Laura, she examined her thoroughly and found nothing unusual. Mak went out for pizza and between them they coaxed Laura to take a few bites. Afterward she seemed drowsy and Helena decided to take her back to Sea Mist before the child fell asleep.

'I know you hate having Laura at Sea Mist,' he said, 'Isn't there any way you can arrange for someone to stay with her at the apartment?'

'I wish. But good help's almost impossible to find — and extremely expensive as well. Besides, I work such weird hours, being on call. Every time I've tried to keep Laura at home, the caretaker left soon after she started — sometimes without notice.'

Mak seemed lost in thought as he drove to Sea Mist — he'd insisted on taking them in his car. On the way home, he asked if she wanted to stop by the hospital for a final check on her patients.

Jolted from her preoccupation with Laura, she shook her head. Glancing at her watch, she saw it wasn't quite seven and belatedly realized he'd offered her the excuse she'd need if she decided to meet Quinn later tonight.

'It's too early,' she said hastily. 'I'll drop in just before I go to bed — around ten. With luck, no emergencies will turn up after that.'

When they got back to the apartment, she and Mak made popcorn and watched an old western on TV, so ancient the bad guys actually did wear black hats and the good guys white ones.

'Notice how the baddies fire round after round without ever picking off the hero,' he muttered between munches. 'Never saw such lousy shots. Hard to believe all the old west outlaws were that inept.'

'Billy the Kid was a pretty good shot, by all accounts.'

'You don't believe that bit about him killing twenty-one men before he died at twenty-one, do you? I've always thought that was too neat and tidy not to be made up by some smart-ass reporter.'

'Billy *was* a killer,' she protested.

'True. And he started in his early teens. Young killers are always dangerous.' He stared so fixedly at the idiotic TV commercial that she decided he must be looking into his own past instead of seeing what was on the screen. Did it have something to do with his scars?

Why had she brought up Billy the Kid, of all people? Probably because she hadn't made up her mind whether or not to meet Quinn at Xenara. Quinn was a teenager just like Billy. But was he a killer? Or dangerous? How could she tell?

Showing up to meet him was one way, she thought mordantly. If he didn't kill her he wasn't dangerous. Of course, maybe he'd just set her on fire instead.

Get real, Moore, she admonished herself. You're not going to meet him and that's final. Since you told Mak you had to make a final check at Harper Hills, you'll make that trip but afterward you're coming straight back here. And then you're going to tell Mak all you know and suspect about Quinn Herron.

Her mind made up, Helena relaxed and finished the popcorn while she lost herself in the last half of the movie, aware of how good it felt to have Mak sitting next to her in companionable silence.

★　★　★

At ten she was on Three North where all her patients were stable and asleep. In the newborn nursery, preemie Kristle looked good — she'd gained an ounce in the last two days. The ER was fairly quiet — a possible coronary and a drunk the cops had brought in. Nothing for her. No one needed her services, so it was time to go home.

As she pulled away from the hospital it occurred to her she could easily drive by Xenara without compromising her safety. Just to see what she could see, if anything. No harm in that.

Without making a conscious decision, she found herself making the turn that would take her past the pyramid. Why not, she asked herself.

The closer she got to Xenara, the faster her

heart rate became — an acute case of tachycardia. By the time she drew even with Xenara's parking lot she was hyper-ventilating, breathing so rapidly she was practically panting. Why, in God's name? She wasn't in any danger.

It wasn't until she swerved at the last moment, tires screeching as she turned into the lot, that she realized what she meant to do — and had, subconsciously at least, intended to do all along.

Dangerous or not, she was here to meet Quinn.

13

As Helena turned the VW loaner into the parking lot, headlights flashed in her rearview mirror, startling her. Was she being followed? Heart thumping, she headed for the exit driveway, all the while watching the mirror. No other car entered the lot and she decided she must have been mistaken.

When she was almost to the exit, she braked. Should she leave now or make a sweep of the lot to see if Quinn was here? She could see no other car but if he'd ridden his motorcycle he could have it stashed among the giant oleander bushes lining the lot.

Peter used oleanders to curtain his property, too — as many people in southern California did. Helena had ceased to trust the showy plants after treating a child in Bakersfield who had almost died from nibbling on an oleander leaf. If eaten, any part of the bush was poisonous to humans and animals.

What the hell, as long as she'd gone this far, she'd cruise around the lot before she left. Lamps on four tall poles lit the area but as she slowly drove around the perimeter she saw the lamp in the farthest corner was burned out. Or had it been broken on purpose by Quinn? She was nearing that unlit corner now — was she asking for trouble?

Reflexively, Helena's foot flew to the brake but, to her horror, the motor died. Hurriedly, she tried to restart the VW but the engine refused to catch.

Stay calm, don't flood it, she advised herself, so intent on the recalcitrant car she didn't notice anything else until a reedy voice asked, 'Can't get her started?'

Helena jumped, choking back a scream as she stared at the face topped with red hair on the other side of the partly-rolled-down right front window.

Swallowing her fear as best she could, she said, 'Hello, Quinn,' pleased to get the words out without a single quaver. Though the doors were locked he could easily reach in and unlock the passenger door.

'Hi,' he said, running a hand through his hair in a nervous gesture that reminded her of his father. 'I wasn't sure you'd come.' He kept glancing around and his obvious uneasiness restored her confidence.

He was unlikely to try to get inside the car if he was concentrating on making a quick getaway in case something alarmed him.

'But since we both made it to the

rendezvous, let's not waste time. What were you doing at my sister's apartment the day she was killed?'

'Fran called me and said to come over.'

'Why?'

He shrugged. 'She said she had news that was gonna knock my socks off.'

Helena had heard her sister use that phrase dozens of times, making her inclined to believe Quinn.

'What did she tell you?'

He gulped audibly. 'Nothing. Like, I rang the bell but she didn't come to the door.'

When it seemed he wouldn't go on, Helena decided to prod him. 'I know you were inside — I found the pyramid of burnt matches. The same as the one you left outside my window later.'

As a threat, should she mention that she knew about his previous brushes with the law because of his pyromania? Helena shook her head. It could well backfire. More than likely he'd discovered one way or another the link between pyromania and sexual problems and he'd probably realize as a doctor she was well aware of the connection. He might clam up completely. Or even take off.

'I didn't mean to scare you,' he said earnestly. 'What I wanted was to, like, you know, talk to you in private only I couldn't

255

get up the nerve to ring the bell. Or even, like, talk on the phone. I figured you wouldn't believe me.'

'What about Fran? You went into the apartment that day, didn't you?'

'The door was ajar,' he admitted. 'When I got inside I heard the shower running so I, you know, sort of waited around but she never showed. I called her, like, really loud, okay? Nothing.' He hunched his shoulders. 'I figured maybe she didn't hear and waiting around makes me nervous, you know? I mean, I wasn't gonna try anything, I, like, just wanted her to know I was there.' His face contorted. 'Jesus, I never expected to find her lying there dead!'

Controlling a shudder, Helena said, 'You must have been in the apartment when I came. Right?'

He nodded. 'I didn't know what to do. I was standing there looking at Fran when I heard you calling her. I figured you'd find me for sure. But then you left.' He bit his lip. 'Before I sneaked out myself, I, like, did something dumb — I turned off the shower 'cause I couldn't stand to see it coming down on her. You know?'

Before Helena had a chance to speak, Quinn was illuminated by the bright beam of a flashlight. He cried out, his face white and sticken, whirled, and fled toward the oleanders at the dark end of the lot, the man with the flashlight in pursuit. Helena tried to start the VW again and it caught on her second attempt. She shoved the car into gear and drove after the pair.

Moments later, her headlights centered on the pursuer and she gasped. Mak! Pulling even with him, she rolled down her window and shouted, 'Stop! Don't you dare hurt him!'

He slowed to glance at her and, as he did, she caught a glimpse of Quinn plunging up the ice plant covered slope into the oleanders. As Mak picked up his pace again, she heard the roar of a motorcycle, loud and then gradually diminishing.

Mak broke stride, turned, and walked toward her. She stopped the car. 'He's gone. Must be an alley back there,' he grumbled when he reached the VW. He tried the door. 'Open this damn thing!' he growled.

She reached over and flicked the lock. Mak slid into the passenger seat. 'Want to explain meeting Quinn Herron in Xenara's parking lot?' he asked.

She glared at him. 'Damn it, if you hadn't scared him off I might have learned who killed Fran. Now he won't trust me.'

'I'd have caught him if you hadn't come

barreling after me screaming about not hurting him. Once I had my hands on him he'd have spilled his guts and we damn sure would have found out who killed your sister.'

'Quinn found Fran dead — he didn't kill her.'

'Yeah? You'd be surprised how many times I've heard that. From killers.'

Helena snorted in exasperation. 'You followed me!' she said accusingly. 'Why?'

'You lied to me,' he said, 'but you forgot to erase the tape on the Identifier. I know Herron's number when I see it and I remembered you carrying on oh-so-innocently about Quinn the pyromaniac. I've had a lot of training in putting two and two together and, though I had trouble believing you'd be such a goddamned idiot as to sneak off and meet him alone, I couldn't take the chance you might.' He shook his head. 'I know you've got brains — what'd you do, put them on hold?'

'Quinn wouldn't hurt me.'

'You want that carved on your tombstone? Listen up, doctor — when you're dealing with someone who's killed once, never forget it's easier for him to kill the second time.'

'Can't you get it through your thick head that Quinn *didn't* kill Fran? He's the breather and, yes, he was the prowler, but he's not a killer.'

Mak grasped her by the shoulders. 'Who says? Quinn?'

'I'm sure he's telling the truth.'

He gave her a shake. 'You're not listening. I'm telling you that just because Quinn's young doesn't mean — '

Helena's annoyance flared into rage. 'Take your hands off me! You act as though I'm some airhead who doesn't realize kids can kill. For your information I've dealt with a lot of very disturbed teenagers. Quinn may turn into a killer someday — who can predict? But he isn't one yet and I was in no danger from him.'

Mak released her. 'You don't know what you're talking about.' His voice throbbed with anger. 'So you've shot a few punks full of tranqs, that doesn't mean a damn thing. This punk was on the loose, not in some ER with a bunch of guards or cops holding him down for you. You're lucky you're not dead, doctor.'

'Why don't you get the hell out of my car?' she demanded furiously. 'And out of my apartment. And my life!'

'Suits me.' He slid out, slammed the door shut, and strode away without looking back.

When she got home, she marched into the bedroom Mak had been using, intending to gather up his belongings and toss then outside the apartment door. She found nothing of his anywhere. Either he'd packed up and taken his stuff with him before he followed her or he'd left the door unlocked. Or he'd had an extra key made — she wouldn't put it past him — and beat her to the apartment, cleaned out his things, and left before she got there.

Helena was already in the bedroom and, aware she'd never be able to sleep until she simmered down, she began a task she'd been dreading — sorting through her sister's belongings. As she opened the closet, a faint whiff of honeysuckle drifted from inside, making her eyes prick with tears.

I'll have to air the closet out when I finish, she told herself, unable to bear any reminder of her sister.

She found several empty suitcases and began packing clothes to take to the Salvation Army, keeping her mind from dwelling on what she was doing by nursing her anger at Mak's interference.

If he'd left them alone, she was certain Quinn would have told her everything he knew. It was obvious he wanted to confide in someone and had chosen her, perhaps because she was Fran's sister. She didn't have any idea how to contact him and she doubted he'd call her again since he was sure to believe Mak's arrival was her doing.

She flung a white robe into the larger of the two bags and then paused, staring at it. Retrieving the robe, she studied it carefully. Not a bathrobe or a negligee — no, this was exactly like the robes the Xenara attendants wore. A blue sash was stuffed into one of the pockets. Laying it aside, she continued packing, not allowing herself to be distracted by what she'd found, even though the robe revealed a direct link between her sister and Xenara. She could do nothing about it tonight and she needed to finish the packing while she had enough strength of mind.

When all of Fran's belongings had been removed from the bedroom and the adjoining bath and packed in the suitcases or in plastic bags, Helena, robe in hand, walked down the hall to her bedroom where she hung the robe in the closet. While she didn't know how to reach Quinn, she could easily find Vada Rogers and that's exactly what she planned to do. As soon as possible.

★   ★   ★

After rounds the next morning, she tracked Jeff down. 'I need to talk to Vada,' she said.

'Not on Monday,' he told her. 'Vada isn't available. There are no sessions at Xenara on Mondays, either.'

261

'All I need is her phone number.'

'I'll give it to you but she doesn't take calls on Monday — and often doesn't return them on other days.' A tinge of bitterness tinged Jeff's voice. 'You can try to call her but your best bet is to go to a session tomorrow evening and talk to her afterwards — as she asked you to. How's George, by the way?'

Helena blinked at the change of subject. George had been the same as always on this morning's rounds — or had he? Actually, he'd been unusually terse. 'Isn't he feeling well?' she asked.

'He's got the trots. My guess is he picked up a bug on his weekend sailing trip to Mexico.'

'He must be better — he didn't mention it.' The words were no sooner out of her mouth than she was paged.

'Dr. Moore, please call Three North. Dr. Moore.'

Idalia answered the phone. 'Dr. Wittenburg would like to see you in his office, stat,' she told Helena.

As soon as Helena saw the way George was hunched over his desk, she knew he was far from better.

'I'm going home,' he said. 'These cramps in my gut are giving me hell. I'd like you to take over for me today and tomorrow.'

It meant extra work but she was gratified to think he trusted her judgment. 'No problem. What do you think you've got? Salmonella?'

'Could be that or Shigella. Or a virus. I'm going to bed and load up on Lomotil until I get my GI system straightened out.'

'Good idea.'

'If you don't mind, I've told my office nurse to send any patient she thinks needs to be seen immediately to the ER for you to take a look at.'

'I'd be glad to.'

'Puts an extra strain on you after weekend call, I know. Sorry. And then there's the possibility of an after-hours emergency.'

'Don't worry about me,' she advised, 'go take care of yourself.'

George hadn't been gone five minutes before his office nurse, Kelly Ames, was on the phone.

'I'm sending Penelope Danvers to the Harper Hills ER,' Kelly told Helena. 'She's ten and she's not really a patient of Dr. Wittenburg's. The Danvers are new to the area and were recommended by the parents of one of his patients. I'd have told the mother to call another doctor but I think Penelope should be seen as soon as possible — I hope that's all right with you.'

'Fine,' Helena assured her. 'What are

Penelope's symptoms?'

'She's been lethargic with a low-grade fever for several days and this morning she woke up with a stiff neck. I know it doesn't sound like an emergency, but — '

'You made the right decision,' Helena said, thinking that George had found himself a very sharp nurse. 'In my opinion, all children with stiff necks should be evaluated by a doctor. Anything else I should know about her?'

She jotted down the few facts Kelly gave her and went to the emergency room where she told the ER clerk that she'd be seeing any patient of Dr. Wittenburg's who came in today and tomorrow. She found the ER physician, Dr. Oshiba, writing an admission order for an elderly patient with severe stasis ulcers on both legs and had a quick cup of coffee with him.

'Fine with me if you take over George's patients,' he told. 'I'm too busy as it is.'

Penelope walked in with her mother a few minutes later. Helena introduced herself and, without waiting for the nurse who was busy with another patient, ushered mother and daughter into an exam cubicle herself, noticing that the girl favored her right leg. While the mother helped Penelope undress and stretch out on the gurney, Helena asked about the onset of the illness.

'I noticed Penny started looking droopy about three days ago,' Mrs. Danvers said. 'I keep an eye on her because she's not one to complain; she'll keep going until she drops if you let her. I took her temperature but it wasn't very high — only a little over ninety-nine so I didn't pay too much attention until this morning when she couldn't move her neck. And then she said her jaw hurt when she tried to eat breakfast. She wouldn't even try to drink her orange juice.'

Mrs. Danvers's words plus the other symptoms began to add up to a diagnosis Helena hoped would be proved wrong. Before she began her exam, she told the girl what she'd be doing and finished with, 'Would you rather I called you Penelope or Penny?'

'Penny, I guess.' Noting how the girl barely opened her mouth as she spoke, an alarming possibility occurred to Helena.

'Open your mouth for me, Penny,' she said.

The girl's pupils dilated in fear. 'I can't,' she mumbled.

Bad news, thought Helena.

To calm Penny, she smiled reassuringly. 'Okay, we'll start at the other end. I'll check your feet.'

On the instep of the right foot she found a

small scabbed-over lesion with a slightly reddened perimeter. 'When did this happen?' she asked, pointing to the sore.

'Oh, Penny banged into something,' Mrs. Danvers said. 'She likes to wear those thongs, you know, and they don't protect the feet much.'

'Do you remember what you stepped on?' Helena asked Penny.

'Some old wood. Got a splinter.' Again the girl hardly opened her mouth when she spoke.

'You didn't tell me about the splinter,' Mrs. Danvers said to her daughter.

'I got it out by myself.'

'Where was this old wood, Penny?' Helena asked.

'By the ruins.'

'We live in El Doblez but my husband's family owns a few acres near Lake Elsinore,' Mrs. Danvers explained. 'There's an old adobe that's falling to pieces on the property. I'm told it was once a part of one of those old Spanish ranches.'

'Tell me about your daughter's immunizations,' Helena said as she continued with the exam, disturbed to feel the involuntary spasm of Penny's muscles when she tried to palpate the girl's abdomen. 'Did she have all her childhood shots?'

'Well — ' Mrs. Danvers hesitated, then went on. 'She had her polio vaccine — I argued and he gave in because it wasn't shots. My aunt had polio when she was little and she's been a cripple all her life. I wasn't going to let that happen to Penny.'

'Just the polio vaccine?' Helena persisted, wondering who the 'he' was — Penny's father? 'None of the other immunizations?'

'Percy, that's my husband, doesn't hold with those shots so he wouldn't let her get any. The school made a terrible fuss so we've been sending Penny to a private church school. They don't like it, either. But Percy — ' Mrs. Danvers sighed and said no more.

Helena, almost certain of the diagnosis, said, 'So Penny's never been immunized against tetanus — lockjaw. Is that right?'

'That's what I told you.' Mrs. Danvers's voice was defensive. Her expression changed from sullenness to shock as the significance of Helena's last question penetrated. 'Oh, God, no!' she cried. 'You think Penny has lockjaw?'

'I'm afraid she does.'

Mrs. Danvers sprang to her feet and clutched her daughter to her, weeping, ignoring Penny's moans. Helena laid a hand on her shoulder.

'Please sit down,' she urged, repeating the

words over and over until Mrs. Danvers finally obeyed, wiping at her eyes.

'I want to admit your daughter to the hospital immediately,' she told the woman. 'The sooner we start treatment, the better for Penny.'

Mrs. Danvers nodded, biting her lip.

'I know this will seem harsh,' Helena continued, 'but try to understand. Because of the tetanus, when you hug Penny it sends her muscles into spasm and hurts her. So don't touch her any more than is absolutely necessary.'

Helena turned to Penny. 'You must be scared about what's happening to you. What we're going to do while you're in the hospital is give you medicine to help you get better. We'll be putting you in a dark and quiet room so you can rest because resting is important. Right now I'll find someone to get you settled in a room while your mother signs some papers. Then she'll come to see you, okay?'

'Mom?' Penny whispered.

'You do what Dr. Moore says, honey,' her mother said, leaning over but carefully not touching Penny. 'I'll be there as soon as I can.'

Once Penny was on her way to the CD unit and her mother had entered the Admissions Office, Helena called Idalia. 'I need a debridement kit and 500 units of tetanus human immune globulin stat for Penny Danvers, the new patient you'll be getting in CD. She's NPO — nothing by mouth.'

As she hurried to the floor, Helena reviewed the treatment procedure for tetanus. It wasn't the tetanus organism itself, *Clostridium tetani*, that posed the danger to Penny but the toxin the bacillus released as it multiplied in the body, affecting the central nervous system and causing anything from mild muscle spasms to full-fledged tonic convulsions leading to death.

So first of all she'd given an intramuscular injection of the antitoxin in an effort to prevent any more of the toxin from reaching the CNS, the dosage to be repeated daily. Then, because the tetanus bacillus had gotten into the girl's body through the puncture wound in her right instep, the wound must be debrided to remove all dead tissue and any foreign material present. This drastic cleansing would eliminate as much of the source of the infection as possible.

Intravenous fluids with diazepam to control the spasming. Penicillin. And round-the-clock nurses to monitor Penny's condition. Unless the girl's status worsened, she might not need a tracheotomy.

At least Mrs. Danvers had called a doctor

as soon as she noticed unusual symptoms, Helena thought. I can only hope like hell we got Penny early enough to save her.

When she finished and left Penny resting quietly, Helena found Mrs. Danvers waiting beyond the red double doors, explained what had been done and why, then asked if Penny's father had been notified.

'I can't reach Percy until late this afternoon,' the woman said. 'He's going to blame himself, I just know it. You see, his six-year-old twin brother died while the two of them were getting their booster shots. Percy saw it happen and the death twisted his mind. He honestly believes he was protecting Penny by refusing to let her have immunizations. Neither of us ever thought she'd — ' Her voice broke.

Helena took her hand. 'I can't deny tetanus is a very serious illness but we'll do all we can to pull her through. And when she's better I'll talk to your husband about the importance of Penny getting properly immunized. Having tetanus once doesn't prevent a person from contracting it again — only the shots can do that.'

She walked with Mrs. Danvers to Penny's room and left her there with the nurse.

'You missed lunch,' Idalia pointed out when Helena sat down at the nurses' station to write up Penny's chart.

'I'll stop by the cafeteria and grab a bite after I finish this,' Helena replied.

She wasn't through when the ward clerk handed the phone to her. 'It's Kelly, from Dr. Wittenburg's office.'

'I've sent four more patients to the ER,' Kelly said. 'Twin boys with severe poison ivy rashes, a three-month-old with what sounds like croup, and a boy who got hit with a baseball. He's got a facial laceration that the mother claims needs stitches. Did the new patient ever show up?'

After telling her briefly about Penny, Helena started for the ER, detouring past the cafeteria to grab a cheese sandwich and a cup of coffee to take with her.

When she finished examining and treating the four patients and sent them home, it was after five. She returned to CD to look in on Penny and found a man sitting outside the room, hands between his knees, head hanging. Percy Danvers, she decided.

'I'm Dr. Moore,' she told him.

He looked up at her despondently, not rising. 'She's going to die, isn't she?' Without waiting for her answer he went on, 'When you get lockjaw, you die.'

'That's not true, Mr. Danvers. Tetanus is dangerous but people do survive.'

Looking away, he continued as though he hadn't heard her. 'I've as good as killed my little Penny.'

She forced harshness into her voice. 'I've no sympathy with guilt trips, so snap out of yours. Penny's a very sick girl and it's going to take her some time to recover. Your wife needs your help in getting through the next few weeks and so will Penny.' Without giving him time to reply, she pushed open the door and went into the room.

When she came out, Mr. Danvers was standing by the window at the end of the short corridor. He hurried up to her.

'What can I do to help?' he asked.

'Convince your wife that for Penny's sake she needs to keep up her strength — then take her somewhere and make her eat. There's no point in her getting sick, too. Penny has a nurse in her room at all times so don't worry that she'll be left alone.'

'I'll try,' he said. 'Do you really think Penny will get better?'

Helena didn't hesitate. 'She has a good chance.' She spoke more positively than she felt, God knows this man needed some ray of hope to lighten his guilt. And Penny wasn't any worse than on admission — a favorable sign.

But, damn it, tetanus was a deadly disease.

She didn't even get to her car before her beeper sounded. Dr. Wittenburg's answering service had an emergency for her.

* * *

Tuesday was even busier than Monday. Joe King, a pediatrician and one of George's friends, called her around four in the afternoon.

'You know how stubborn George can be,' he began.

'How is he?'

'He's been better. I went by his house at noon and took a look at him. Christ, the man was so dehydrated he'd screwed his ion balance to hell and gone. But would he let me call an internist? Not on your life. So I brought over some IV equipment and stuck the needle in his vein myself. I'll be keeping tabs on him but I'll tell you now he's not going to be back to work for another couple of days. He told me you were taking his emergency calls — think you can go on handling them?'

'Sure. Tell George not to worry. If there's anything else I can do, let me know.'

'Thanks,' Joe said. 'I think I've got things under control — even if old George isn't the ideal patient. I'll take a screaming baby any day.'

Helena managed to pick up the squareback from the VW garage at noon on Wednesday but any other plans she had for the rest of the week were shot. George called her late Friday and claimed to be recovering but, since Joe had already told her that he was in no shape to go back to work yet, she offered to take call over the weekend.

As it turned out, George didn't put in a full day's work until Thursday of the following week.

'You still don't look so great,' she told him on Friday morning. 'I can take call — '

'I may look like a hollow shell,' he informed her, 'but I feel better than I look. You're off call this weekend and that's an order.'

So, as Helena left the hospital Saturday at noon, she felt like a child let out of school. Her two problem patients no longer worried her — Penny's condition had improved markedly, though she still wasn't able to eat, and preemie Kristle was gaining weight so fast she'd soon be going home.

At last she could get back to her own problems — finding Quinn and arranging a meeting with Vada Rogers. She hadn't heard from or seen Mak since their argument in the Xenara parking lot and she'd been so damned busy she hadn't had time to decide if she missed him or not.

Who cares, she asked herself. He'd never be a permanent fixture.

She had meant to pick up Laura on her way home and keep her until Sunday afternoon but when she reached Sea Mist, Laura wasn't there.

'Didn't you remember this is the Big Bear camp weekend for the children?' the receptionist asked. 'You must have signed a permission slip.'

And so she had.

Helena drove home hoping her daughter would enjoy the experience. At least it meant Laura was well enough to go — that was one less to worry about. When she entered the apartment, she noticed the red light on the answering machine. Playing back the tape, she was surprised to hear Vada Rogers's voice.

'It's most important that you come to the meeting on Saturday evening,' Vada said. 'Before seven. We'll be expecting you.'

The *regal* we? Helena wondered, listening a second time to the message because a dark undertone in Vada's voice had caught her attention. Or did Vada mean the mysterious partner?

After she'd heard the tape still a third time,

Helena turned off the machine and stood looking at it. Unless she was wrong in her interpretation, Vada hadn't wanted to make that call — reluctance permeated her every word. And yet Vada was a superb showman who could damn well do just about anything with her voice.

The only possible conclusion was that Vada expected Helena to discover the hidden message. In that case the 'we' took on real significance. Who else at Xenara wanted her at tonight's meeting? And why?

14

As the two attendants ushered Helena through Xenara's double blue doors, she took a good look at their white robes. As far as she could tell, the robe she'd found in Fran's closet was exactly the same — except for the sash. The attendants' robes had white silk sashes and the sash in the pocket of Fran's robe was blue silk. Vada's, she noticed, was silver.

'Does the color of your sash have any significance?' she asked the attendant to her right.

The woman hesitated. 'Only Vada wears silver,' she said after a moment.

'How about blue?' Helena persisted.

'Blue is for the inner path. Few are chosen to wear blue.' Did the slight edge in her voice mean she was unhappy because she hadn't yet been chosen?

'May I have your name, please?' the attendant asked. When Helena told her, the woman checked a list.

Craning her neck, Helena found her name on the paper before the attendant and noted it was double-starred.

The attendant smiled at her. 'You're one of the special session people. This way, please.' Leaving the other attendant at the entrance, she led the way across the round room to a concave door at the far side that Helena hadn't noticed before — perhaps because it blended into the walls. To Helena's surprise, the woman produced a key and unlocked the door. Why was the door locked?

Helena stopped on the threshold. 'If you plan to lock it behind us, I want to know if there's another way out — one that isn't locked.'

'Xenara meets all city fire regulations,' the attendant said somewhat huffily. 'As you'll see.'

Helena found herself in a small white windowless room furnished with several chairs and a round coffee table holding stacks of pamphlets. Spider plants of all varieties dangled from the ceiling. Counting the door they had entered, the room contained four doors — two white and two blue, all closed. A sign reading EMERGENCY EXIT THIS WAY was fastened to one of the white doors.

'Please make yourself comfortable,' the attendant said, gesturing toward the chairs. 'Vada will be with you shortly.'

Helena nodded but didn't take a seat. As soon as the attendant withdrew, she crossed to the door with the sign and tried the knob. When it opened, Helena peered along a short corridor and saw what she took to be an outside door clearly labeled EMERGENCY EXIT. It had a bar across it that she assumed allowed it to be opened only from the inside. Satisfied, she retreated into the room and found the remaining white door led to a small rest room. The blue door, like the one she'd entered, was locked.

She picked up one of the pamphlets, 'Color Auras,' and leafed through it. There were seven basic colors for auras, it seemed. Violet for spiritual power, indigo for intuition, blue for energy, yellow for wisdom, orange for health, and red for life.

Black was the worst color for an aura, especially if shot with a crimson red — the most vicious combination of evil known, according to the author.

Helena smiled, conjuring up a conventional picture of the devil dressed in black with touches of red. The author was certainly traditional.

She had no quarrel with the premise that a weak electric field surrounded all living creatures — science had proved this to be true. But she found it difficult to believe that so-called psychics could see this field with the unaided eye, much less that they saw different colors for different people. She'd have little patience with Xenara's blue-lit path if it involved auras. But she hadn't come here to be immersed in the paranormal; she was here to find out about Fran.

A click warned her the blue door was opening and Helena focused her attention. Vada stood framed in the doorway, stunning in her white robe with its silver cord.

'Will you come with me, Helena?' she asked in her husky voice.

Feeling she'd learn more in the long run if she went along with the house rules, at least for now, Helena nodded and crossed to the blue door.

Vada conducted her down a short flight of steps and inside a tiny room with no furniture. A white robe hung on a hook; three other hooks were empty.

'You must undress down to the skin and put on the white robe,' Vada said.

Helena gave her a long, level look. 'Why?'

'Putting your clothes aside indicates your willingness to bare your worldly self in preparation to accepting your spiritual nature. The ideal would be to travel the blue-lit path wearing nothing at all — the robe is a gesture to modesty.'

'I'm not a believer.'

Vada smiled sadly. 'Few are, even those

who will belief to come to them. A believer or not, you've been chosen to walk the blue-lit path.'

'By you?'

'I'm not a part of the choosing,' Vada said evasively.

'Who is?'

Vada turned her hands palm upward in a gesture of helplessness. 'Xenara doesn't reveal all its secrets.'

'You promised you'd answer my questions.'

'I'm answering to the best of my ability.'

Helena swept the words aside with an abrupt wave of her hand. 'I think you know I have more important questions.'

Vada inclined her head. 'They must wait until after you put on the robe and — '

'I want to know about my sister, Fran York,' Helena insisted.

'Not now.' Vada spoke emphatically. 'I'm already late for my session upstairs.' She turned toward the door.

Putting a restraining hand on her arm, Helena said, 'I must know about Fran.'

Vada gazed into her face for a long moment, her green eyes beginning to glaze over. 'Flames,' she murmured.

'No!' Helena cried, shaking the arm she held. 'Don't go into a trance.'

Vada blinked. 'You're right, I must not.'

She looked away from Helena, then reached into a pocket of her robe. 'This is my private number. Call me tomorrow.'

'But — '

'I can tell you nothing now,' Vada said. 'Nothing.' She bit her lip. 'Do what you will about the path — I refuse to be responsible.' She freed herself from Helena's grasp and hurried from the room.

Helena rushed after Vada only to see her run down another short flight of stairs and disappear through a silver door. When Helena tried to follow her, she found the door locked. She pounded on it, a panel in the door opened, and an attendant's face appeared.

'Let me in,' Helena ordered.

'No one passes who does not wear the robe over the body's flesh,' the woman intoned, her voice as expressionless as a computer's. A sweetish, half-familiar odor floated through the open panel before she slid it shut.

Helena grimaced. If she wanted to get through that door she'd have to put on the damn robe. Correction, strip and then put on the robe — both Vada and the attendant had been specific. She wouldn't put it past that automaton of an attendant to make her open the robe to be sure she was naked underneath before she let her through.

But why bother? There undoubtedly was another way for Vada to escape upstairs and by now she'd be up there leading a session of those not chosen for the path.

If I don't go through that silver door, Helena thought, I'll have to exit through the fire door to the outside or else create a fuss to get back into the round room through the other locked door. Even if she got in, she'd have to sit through Vada's session in order to talk privately or else leave Xenara knowing not much more than when she entered.

Words echoed in her mind, Jeff's accusation on the day they'd met: *It's possible your complete dismissal of the paranormal hides a secret fear that you're really afraid of what you might find if you investigated without prejudice.*

She'd dismissed the words at the time but they haunted her now. Was there any truth to what he'd said? Was she searching for an excuse to back off? Staring at the silver door, a frisson prickled the hair on her arms and her nape.

Nonsense, she told herself firmly. There's nothing on the other side of that door but fakery — certainly nothing to fear.

Then why not go through their stupid routine and prove to yourself you're not afraid? Go ahead, Moore, give the blue-lit path a try. You're not scared of a bunch of would-be psychics and their so-called spiritual path.

Or are you?

With a final glare at the silver door, she marched back to the dressing room and shut herself inside.

Helena had never liked taking her clothes off for a physical exam and, somehow, stripping and putting on the robe reminded her of that. Especially when she discovered the robe didn't have a sash. Since she wasn't wearing a belt, she had nothing to tie around the robe to keep it closed and the best she could do was overlap the edges and hold it shut with her hands.

At least the damn thing was ankle-length and more concealing than those ridiculous paper garments in doctors' offices. When and if she went into private practice she planned to shop around for a better disposable gown than the ones she'd so far encountered. Little kids didn't need them but few people were as shy about exposing themselves to a doctor than teenagers.

She stomped back to the silver door, knocked, and when the panel slid aside, said crisply, 'I've got the robe on — do I get in now?'

The panel closed, the door opened and

Helena stepped through. 'The sash is missing,' she complained, eying the blue one the attendant wore. 'Do you have an extra?'

'Those to be initiated wear no sash,' the woman intoned, her face perfectly blank. She was tall and strongly built, reminding Helena of a wrestler. With a beckoning gesture, she preceded Helena along a corridor.

On this side of the silver door, all the lighting was indirect, blue and dim, giving the effect of walking through a haze. The sweet scent Helena had smelled earlier was now overlaid with the spicy musk of incense. She'd always loathed incense.

Doors led off the corridor — they passed three before the attendant stopped and ceremoniously opened the fourth. 'Enlightenment and fulfillment await you here,' she said in her neuter monotone.

Since she seemed to have no choice. Helena entered and the door was closed behind her, leaving her alone in a room so dimly lit she could hardly make out the only furnishing — a padded bench along the far wall. Everything was blue or the light made it seem so. With the door shut, the smell of the incense was almost overpowering. She explored the dimensions of the small room — four by six? — and finally sat on the bench.

'Lie on the bench and close your eyes,' a

soft voice murmured.

Since there was nobody in the room with her, Helena knew the voice came over an audio system though the light was too dim to pinpoint the speaker.

'Lie on the bench, close your eyes,' the voice repeated, 'and view the darkness within you.'

Helena thought it was bound to be dark with her eyes closed — what else? But she decided to play along and stretched out on her back.

'Inhale to the count of ten and hold for five, release the air slowly, slowly to the count of ten,' the voice ordered. 'Inhale through the nose, exhale through the mouth. Breathe deeply. Match the rhythm of the sitar.'

Haunting Oriental music tinkled in a minor key as, eyes closed, Helena began the breathing exercise. A common meditation technique, one part of her said while she mindlessly counted and kept breathing deeply.

She had no idea how much time passed before she began to feel slightly dizzy. Somehow the feeling didn't bother her — she was relaxed and drifting in a pleasant, timeless darkness. Warm air flowed over her bare skin caressingly and a bit of remaining awareness told her that her robe had fallen open but it didn't matter, nothing mattered but to go on drifting.

Something soft brushed her face, her breasts, the touch exquisitely comforting. *Open your eyes*, something inside her ordered. *Open!* But her lids were leaden, she couldn't summon the effort. Softly, thrillingly, the feather-gentle strokes along her skin continued.

You're not alone, a small voice deep within her mind warned and finally she summoned the energy to move her eyelids. She saw only darkness, profound and absolute, and her eyes drifted closed once more. The stroking grew more intimate, touching her abdomen, her inner thighs and she grew conscious of the scent of pine forests and another, earthier smell.

It's a man, the tiny warning voice told her. *You smell a man. A man is in the room. He's doing this without your consent. Wake up!*

Helena's eyes popped open to darkness. Though her arms felt as though they didn't belong to her, she lifted one and her fingers touched something that wasn't herself. Human skin. A man?

Vague alarm trickled through her, dissipating some of her lethargy. She struggled to rise. Arms held her down, wrapping around her; a man's naked body pressed close, his arousal hard and insistent against her thigh.

She pushed weakly at him and the adrenaline stimulated by her resistance fueled her will to fight, combating the strange lassitude gripping her, clearing her mind. The struggle remained unequal because he was stronger than she but now that she was able to think once again, she remembered something a street-smart teen in Bakersfield had once told her.

If he got you down on your back, meaning rape, what you do is jam your nails into his prick hard as you can. Fake nails, they works the best.

All she had was her own fingernails but Helena gave it a try.

The man yelped and let her go. She slid from under him and stumbled away, groping in the darkness for the door. It eluded her searching fingers and she scrambled desperately along the wall.

Finally the knob was in her hand, then she was in the hazy corridor running toward the silver door, ignoring her open robe as she fled. She flung herself through the door, ducked into the dressing room to retrieve her belongings and, with them bundled under one arm, rushed up the stairs to the blue door. Not locked from this side, thank God. There was no one in the waiting room as she rushed through on her way to the emergency exit.

She found herself at the rear of the parking lot, near where Quinn had escaped through the oleanders. The fresh air helped her mental fuzziness but it took an effort to remember to clutch the robe closed. As she hurried toward where she'd left the VW, she thought she heard a motorcycle, though none was in sight.

Quinn? She glanced behind her. Despite the milky film she seemed to be looking through, she was sure nobody was following. Where in God's name had she left her car?

She felt like she'd searched through the entire lot before she finally saw the familiar square silhouette of the VW. With a man leaning against one fender. She halted, gasping. As he straightened and strode toward her, she backed away.

'No,' she mumbled. 'No, no.'

He reached her and caught her by the shoulders. 'Damn it,' he said, 'I told you to keep away from Xenara.'

Mak! She'd never been so glad to see anyone in her entire life. Forgetting about the robe and the clothes she carried, she flung her arms around him and hugged him to her. Safe, she was safe.

All too soon he held her away, his nose

crinkling. 'What in hell have you been smoking?' His eyes widened. 'Christ, you're naked under that damn robe.'

She clutched at the sides of the robe to close it around her. 'Something's wrong with me, Mak,' she mumbled. 'I can't think straight.'

Without another word, he bundled her into his Jag, parked next to the VW, tossed her clothes and shoulderbag into her lap, slid behind the wheel, and drove to her apartment. He helped her up the stairs and onto the couch.

'Coffee,' she said.

He nodded and disappeared into the kitchen. When he returned he edged her over until there was enough space for him to sit beside her. He leaned down, sniffed at her hair, and frowned.

'Was it pot?' he asked.

She stared at him uncomprehendingly.

'The stuff you were smoking,' he growled impatiently. 'It sure as hell wasn't tobacco.'

'I didn't smoke anything,' she said.

'Then someone pickled you in the stuff. What happened?'

'It's fuzzy. My mind isn't working.'

Sometime later he brought her coffee, propped her up, and made her drink several cups. As the caffeine worked its way into her system, stimulating her, her thoughts grew clearer.

'The scent,' she said slowly. 'I did smell marijuana. I didn't place the odor at the time.' She frowned, 'But there was something else mixed with it. Maybe opium?'

Mak, sitting next to her on the couch, shrugged.

'Opium would account for the lethargy,' she said. 'Breathe deeply, that's what they told me — so I did. At a heavy enough concentration, I could have taken in enough to drug me.'

'You're telling me someone at Xenara drugged you?'

She nodded. 'With my cooperation. I thought the blue-lit path was a harmless exercise in meditation.'

He flicked the vee of the robe with a finger. 'You must have hightailed it out of there pretty fast if you didn't stop to dress.'

Helena swallowed. 'Something touched me in the dark. Someone. A man. He — I got scared.' She shuddered and grabbed his hand, holding it tightly between both of hers.

'Think you can start from the beginning?' he asked grimly.

As she haltingly began her story, she realized there were still gaps in her memory — whatever drug she'd inhaled wasn't entirely out of her system.

'In a way, Vada tried to warn me,' she said after she finished.

'Yeah, after enticing you there in the first place and setting you up.' Mak's voice bristled with hostility. 'If Vada won't talk, I'll damn well unearth that secret partner and find out what the hell's going on.'

Because the drug was still affecting her, Helena didn't feel the fury she sensed bubbling in Mak but that didn't prevent her from coming to a decision.

'Sooner or late I mean to close Xenara down,' she said calmly.

'If I don't beat you to it. Why in God's name you went there tonight — '

'Don't lecture me,' she pleaded. 'I'm so tired.' She leaned her head against him.

Mak sighed and put his arm around her, drawing her closer. 'It's getting so I'm afraid to let you out of my sight.'

She snuggled against him. 'Don't go away,' she murmured.

She heard him draw in his breath, then he shifted, lowering his head until their lips met.

★   ★   ★

As soon as he kissed her, Mak's anger melted into a passion that zoomed out of his control.

She was so warm and soft, she felt and tasted so good, and he wanted her so damn much. When his hands slid beneath the robe to caress her bare skin, he went wild with need.

Touching her was like touching fire and silk — hot and smooth at the same time. She quivered with eagerness under his fingers, increasing his desire until he thought he'd go mad.

Never had a woman offered herself to him so sweetly and so ardently. He'd be damned if he'd allow anything to prevent him from having her.

Not here, not on the couch, a hasty consummation in limited space without the joyous agony of anticipation. No, he wanted to lie next to her, be as naked as she was and prolong their lovemaking moment by delicious moment until they both were beyond thought.

Mak extricated himself and stood, lifted Helena in his arms, and carried her into her bedroom, easing her onto the bed. Her robe fell apart, exposing her to his greedy, loving gaze. He'd never have enough of looking at her beautiful body. She lay without moving, smiling up at him.

He began undressing, his fingers clumsy with eagerness. It seemed to take forever before his clothes were off. He turned toward the bed, hard and swollen with need. As he eased down beside her, he saw her eyes were closed, her lashes long and dark against her pale skin. She looked so young and fragile that an unexpected bullet of tenderness pierced him through.

Leaning over her, he gently kissed one of her eyelids, then the other. She sighed but her eyes didn't open — she didn't turn to him with open arms.

If he touched her, kissed her, caressed her, took her in his arms, he knew she'd rouse from her drug-induced sleep and respond. His need throbbed achingly and he reached for her only to stop himself.

She'd respond to him, yes, but would it be completely of her own volition? Whatever they'd made her inhale at Xenara had affected her judgment — she'd told him that. Her behavior indicated she wasn't entirely free of the drug's effects. Look at her — sound asleep. He'd be taking advantage of her if he woke her and they made love now.

It took willpower he didn't even know he possessed to rise from the bed. He picked up a quilt and carefully covered her, then gathered his clothes and quietly left the room. When he made love for the first time with Helena, he wanted her fully aware, wanted it to be her choice as well as his, a choice she made with an unclouded mind.

* ★ *

Helena woke from a disturbing dream she couldn't quite recall. To her amazement she found herself on top of the covers with a quilt over her, wearing a robe.

As she fingered the robe, everything that had happened at Xenara flooded her mind and she tensed, grimacing. She was dimly aware that Mak had found her and brought her home but she had no idea how she'd gotten on the bed.

She sat up gingerly, putting a hand to her throbbing head. Her mouth tasted foul.

The scent of coffee drifted in and she doubled over, retching. She barely made it to the bathroom in time, then tottered back to the bed, flung off the robe, kicked it away, and crawled under the covers, groaning.

'You okay?' Mak's voice asked.

She peered toward the door, mumbling. 'I feel awful.'

'Want some coffee?'

The thought of putting anything in her stomach started another wave of nausea and she closed her eyes and fought it back. When she opened them again, Mak was standing beside the bed.

'You really *are* sick,' he said.

'Bingo,' she muttered.

'Can I help?'

'Morphine and codeine make me vomit,' she said weakly. 'I'd never willingly take either no matter how severe the pain. They're both derivatives of opium. I've vomited once already and I'm still horribly nauseated so my guess is — ' Her words trailed off and she began to breathe deeply, fighting the urge to throw up again.

'I'll stay around until you feel better,' he promised.

'Thanks,' she managed to say but she really didn't want anything at the moment except for the nausea to pass. She closed her eyes and gradually drifted under again.

The next she knew, someone was sitting on the edge of the bed. 'Go away and let me die in peace, Mak,' she muttered without turning to face him.

'It's Jeff.'

Jeff? Jolted, Helena turned over.

'Mak called me. I brought over an anti-nausea suppository.' He held out his hand. 'You in any shape to put it in yourself or do you want me to?'

'I can manage,' she said.

He handed her a foil-wrapped suppository and a disposable glove and stood up. 'I'll be in the kitchen with Mak. When you feel better, let me know. We need to talk.'

About fifteen minutes after she'd inserted the suppository, Helena began to feel human once again. After twenty minutes more had passed, she decided she might even be able to get up. An hour and a shower later, dressed in jeans and tee shirt, she ambled barefoot into the kitchen where Mak and Jeff sat over the remains of a pizza. Beer cans cluttered the table.

'I'm better, thanks,' she said, 'but I don't know if I'm well enough to face that.' She leaned against the counter and nodded at the littered table.

Mak hastily gathered up the pizza carton and swiped at the table with a damp cloth while Jeff disposed of the beer cans.

Since her legs felt a bit shaky, Helena sat down.

'Want anything?' Mak asked.

'A glass of milk,' she said.

Jeff eased into the chair across from her. 'Mak gave me a rundown on what happened to you at Xenara. Was she — was Vada involved?'

Helena thought before answering. 'In getting me there, yes — though I had the impression it was against her will. Before she left me in that blue-lit underground she told me she wasn't responsible and that I didn't have to go ahead. Unfortunately, I had no idea what she meant — what I was facing — so I didn't pay attention.'

'Damn it, I knew something was wrong,' Jeff said. 'Vada's been uneasy and half-sick for months. Whatever's going on underground is all his doing, not hers.'

'Whose doing?' She and Mak spoke together.

'The son of a bitch who put up the money to build that fucking pyramid and talked her into a partnership.'

'What's his name?' Mak demanded to know.

'She never would tell me. But now — ' Jeff sprang to his feet. 'I'll find out,' he said grimly, striding toward the door.

No sooner had the door shut behind him than the phone rang. Only then did Helena remember that Vada had left her number and asked her to call today. When she picked up the phone, she half-expected to hear Vada's husky tones.

'Helena?' Quinn said, his voice quavering so markedly she could hardly make out the words. 'I've got to talk to you. Before something happens. Something bad.'

15

The phone in her hand, Helena glanced involuntarily at Mak. He met her gaze, eyebrows raised in mute inquiry. Even if she wanted to, and she was no longer sure she did, she couldn't possibly arrange to meet Quinn without Mak knowing.

'What's the matter?' Quinn echoed in her ear, apparently spooked by her long silence.

'Nothing.' She tried to make her voice as reassuring as possible. 'It's just that I was sick last night and I'm not entirely recovered. I want to talk to you, too. Will it be on the phone or can you come to the apartment?'

'Jesus,' he muttered, 'I don't know.'

'Why not the phone?' she asked, conscious that Mak was now hovering over her. She frowned at him and he scowled back.

'I can't hang on the phone here,' Quinn said. 'And, like, your place is not my favorite. How about that guy who chased me? Where's he?'

'I guarantee he won't bother you. Are you coming by right away?'

He didn't answer immediately. 'I guess I don't have a choice,' he said finally. 'Like, I gotta take a chance on *somebody*.'

After she put the phone down, she confronted Mak, certain he'd guessed who the caller was. 'You are not going to interfere.'

'If Quinn's coming here you damn well aren't getting rid of me.'

'He's afraid of you.'

'He has a right to be.'

'You can be so damned unreasonable. If you insist on being here the least you can do is hide in the bedroom.'

Mak shook his head. 'You may be a hotshot pediatrician but you don't know rule one about questioning a punk. Quinn'll tell you no more than he figures is safe but he'll spill his guts to me. Wait and see.'

Helena sighed in annoyed frustration. 'I could tell by his voice and what he said that he's near a breaking point. He doesn't need a hostile interrogator, he needs someone he can trust. He's picked me for some reason — maybe because I'm Fran's sister. I refuse to see him brutalized.'

'Brutalized?' Mak exclaimed in outrage. 'What do you think I plan to do — beat the kid with a rubber hose?'

She glared at him. 'You don't need a rubber hose to intimidate.'

Mak's lips twitched into a half-smile. 'My intimidation technique doesn't seem to work with you.' He touched her cheek lightly with the back of his hand.

The slight caress cut through the haze hiding her recollection of what happened after he'd found her in the parking lot the night before. Warmth tingled through her as memories surfaced — Mak kissing her on the couch, caressing her, carrying her. Then a blank until morning and she woke up in bed. Alone. Had they — ?

She shook her head. No. If she'd made love with Mak, she'd remember, drugged or not.

'How about a compromise?' he asked.

She had to readjust her thinking back to Quinn. 'I'm always willing to be fair.'

'Yeah? Always?'

She shrugged. 'Okay, I withdraw the always. I suggest you let me try the friendly approach with Quinn first. What's your idea?'

He thought a moment. 'Okay, I'll give a little. I'll stay out of sight till it's clear you're not getting to first base.'

Since this concession was more than she'd expected from Mak, she agreed.

'That was half my proposition,' he added. 'Here's the rest. Everything's off unless you sit down and drink that glass of milk I poured for you. And how about a big Mak peanut butter-banana sandwich?'

'Half a sandwich and hold the banana,' she

said, not really hungry but hoping a little food would banish her shakiness.

'You need the potassium,' he insisted. 'Jeff gave me a long lecture about how vomiting screws up your body chemistry.'

Helena rolled her eyes. 'Kindly leave the medical prescribing to me — captain.'

'Why? Fair's fair. You've done nothing but poach on my territory from day one — doctor.'

After he watched Helena drink the milk and eat the half-sandwich, Mak ambled down the hall, leaving her sitting tensely on the living room couch. In her bedroom, he shut the door enough to hide the straight-backed chair he pulled over to sit on. Tipping it back, he tried to relax. He couldn't. Waiting was always worse than taking action.

He reviewed what he'd discovered about Quinn Herron. Eighteen. Arrested three times for suspected arson between fourteen and sixteen. No convictions. Ejected from a military school near Elsinore two years ago, attended local high school, graduated in June. A loner with no friends. In the past year, a frequent attendee at Xenara, apparently with his father's approval. Not now living at home. Present address unknown.

Those who knew Quinn used words like

weird, nutcase, nerd, odd, withdrawn, unsociable, vulnerable, but no one described him as violent. Which didn't mean shit — and he had the scars to prove it.

He'd never forget that day if he lived to be a hundred and one . . .

'Andy wouldn't hurt a fly,' the mother had assured him when he'd arrived at the Coldwater Canyon house on a backup call from a squad car. 'Promise me you'll be gentle with him.'

'Kid's locked himself in the guest house and he's threatening to kill himself,' was the uniformed cop's report. 'When I heard who his old man was, I figured we'd better get somebody from headquarters here.'

Known in any business as covering your ass. Mak didn't blame them — the father was not only old LA money but also a state senator.

Andy was seventeen and had been seeing a shrink for several months. 'Nothing serious,' his mother insisted. 'He's just going through a phase.'

It was true the kid had no record, had apparently never been in trouble. The mother swore there were no guns on the premises and that Andy wouldn't know one end of a gun from another if there were. She scoffed at any notion of drug involvement. 'Not Andy!'

Mak noticed a kennel and fenced exercise yard on his way to the guest house at the back of the property but it didn't occur to him to ask where the dog was. Even if he had, the mother might not have known the dog was with Andy. If he *had* asked, though, he might have figured Andy had taken the dog into the cottage.

Then for sure he'd have thought it odd that the dog, a white German shepherd, never once growled or barked when he reached the small cottage and began negotiating with Andy, trying to talk him into coming out. Why hadn't he asked about the damn dog? Was it because he'd read too much fluff about himself in the papers and halfway believed 'Mighty Mak' Maklin was invulnerable?

Hadn't he captured the head honcho for the West Coast drug syndicate without a shot being fired? Wasn't he the clever detective/ negotiator who'd tracked down the freeway killer, then talked him into surrendering? True, there'd been a few rounds fired during the process — but no fatalities.

Some teenaged kid holed up in a back yard was a cinch. He'd show the squad guys just how slick and quick an operation he could pull off. He motioned the guys back before sauntering casually to the front door of the cottage. Pitching his voice to be heard through the locked door but careful not to shout, he said, 'Andy, my name's Mak. Let's talk.'

At first Andy didn't answer and Mak began to worry that the kid had already slit his throat or hung himself or whatever he meant to do. Before kicking the door in, though, he gave one more try, saying, 'I'll give you until I finish the count of ten to answer me.'

He began the count.

'No one messes with me,' a high-pitched quavering voice said from inside when he reached five. 'You try and you'll be sorry.' He sounded like a defiant seven-year-old.

'I won't hurt you. All I want you to do is unlock the door.'

'You can't make me come out.'

'How about letting me in? Just to talk.'

When he heard the snick of a bolt being drawn back, Mak half-smiled. Sometimes it took hours to convince a person to negotiate. This kid had been unbelievably easy. The smile was still on his lips when Andy exploded through the door with a hunting knife in each hand and literally dived at him.

Mak's defensive reaction wasn't fast enough to block the thrust of the long, sharp blades. If the squad guys hadn't been there to rush Andy, Mighty Mak Maklin would have been so much dead meat. Like the German shepherd they found inside, its white coat matted with blood.

So he'd wound up on the operating room table instead of a slab in the morgue. Mima took off while he was still in the hospital and the lawyer friend who handled the divorce talked Mak into a suit against the senator. The settlement had been hefty.

As for Andy, he eventually was committed to a hospital for the criminally insane.

Yes, Mak knew more than he wanted to about harmless kids.

The chime of the doorbell brought him to his feet, poised for immediate action. Quinn.

He heard the door open, and after a pause, Helena said 'Either come in or stay out. Make up your mind, Quinn.'

Evidently he entered the apartment, because she asked him to sit down.

'Okay,' she said, after another lengthy pause, 'if you won't begin, I guess it's up to me. When I left Xenara on Saturday, I heard a motorcycle. We must have just missed each other.'

Mak blinked. The entire time he'd waited in the parking lot for Helena to appear, he hadn't seen Quinn. Considering how many motorcycles were around, she could only be making a wild shot.

'You weren't at the session.' Quinn's voice

was suspicious. 'I'd have seen you.'

'So you were upstairs with Vada.'

'Yeah, for awhile. Like, that crap gets boring, you know?'

'I imagine you find what goes on downstairs more exciting.'

'I wasn't down there.' Quinn sounded defensive.

'Maybe not this time but I think you have been,' Helena insisted. 'Is that why you came to see Fran? I found her robe. And the blue sash for downstairs.'

'I don't know anything about it!' he exclaimed.

'You can tell me,' she coaxed. 'I'm on your side. You know that or you wouldn't have called me.'

'There's nothing to tell.'

'But you do trust me.' Her voice was soft, persuasive. 'You came here, didn't you?'

Her sweetness and light made for slow going, Mak decided. Too damn slow. The kid needed stepping on, not stroking. Slipping into the corridor, he eased along until he could see into the living room.

Quinn sat on a footstool beside the coffee table, fiddling with a book of matches. As Mak watched, he pulled one out, lit it, finally dropping the burnt stick into a round bronze ashtray to join others.

'You did that before when you were here,' Helena said. 'The day Fran died. Does watching the flame help?'

Quinn blew out a burning match and added it to those in the tray. 'Nothing helps,' he muttered. 'She's dead and nothing helps. Why'd they have to kill her?'

'Fran was your friend.'

Good technique, Mak admitted reluctantly. Don't question, make statements. But he didn't think it would work with this kid.

Quinn didn't reply. At the rate this was going they'd be here all night and maybe the kid wouldn't spill his guts then. Helena needed a little professional help. Mak pushed away from the wall and sauntered into the living room, making certain to keep between Quinn and the door.

'Hello,' he said as amiably as he could under the circumstances.

Quinn sprang to his feet, his gaze flicking from Mak to Helena. 'You said he wasn't here,' he accused her.

'I did not.' She spoke crisply. 'I told you he wouldn't bother you. He isn't, is he?'

'He's a cop.' Quinn was poised to run.

'Sit down,' Mak ordered. When Quinn didn't immediately obey, he took a step toward him and repeated the command, louder and nastier.

After a bitter glance at Helena, Quinn slid slowly onto the stool.

'I used to be a cop but I'm not now,' Mak said. 'All I want from you is a few answers. We'll start with Xenara. Don't bother to tell me you don't know what goes on downstairs because I know you do. Who was it with? And don't try to con me with spirit shit. Spirits don't fuck.'

Quinn flushed, his face turning almost as bright as his hair. 'It wasn't like that,' he protested.

'Then tell me what it *was* like.'

'I — it's none of your business.'

Mak's gaze bored into Quinn. 'Fran told you the truth about Xenara's blue-lit path. Is that why you killed her?' He ignored Helena's gasp. 'Answer me!'

'I didn't kill her!' Quinn cried. 'And she didn't really admit it, she just sort of hinted that she was the one who — who — ' He couldn't finish.

'Fran was your blue-lit spirit, is that what you're trying to say?'

Quinn, slouched miserably on the stool, nodded reluctantly.

'So why'd you come to the apartment the day she was killed?'

'She said she had something important to tell me, something she didn't want to say over the phone in case it upset me. Like, Fran *cared* how I felt. Nobody else does. But she never got to tell me. When I went into the bathroom and saw her on the floor I wished it'd been me lying there dead instead of her, you know?'

Looking at Quinn's tortured expression, Mak began to believe the kid hadn't killed Fran.

'You were in love with Fran,' Helena said softly.

Quinn blinked back tears, the book of matches clenched in his fist.

Watching him, Mak discarded any suspicion Quinn had been the 'spirit' Helena had encountered at Xenara. This kid had too many rough edges and not enough experience.

'Look,' Mak said, 'I didn't mean to scare you the other night. I was trying to protect Helena.'

'I wouldn't hurt her,' Quinn mumbled.

'What started you going to Xenara?' Helena asked quietly.

'My father thought it might, you know, help me. He meant the laying on of hands and all that crap. I never did tell him, like, about what went on downstairs.'

'You mean he doesn't know about the blue-lit path?' Helena demanded.

'Jesus, you think he'd have let me keep going if he did?' Quinn asked bitterly. 'Not him.' He ran a hand through his hair, his jaw clenching. 'Now Fran's dead and what's the use of Xenara? Or anything else.'

Mak began to understand why Helena called Quinn vulnerable. The kid had lost the only person he thought cared for him and he was fighting hard not to break down in front of strangers. If Herron *did* care, his son didn't believe it.

'I want you to think about the day Fran died.' Mak's voice was unusually gentle. 'Did you see anyone near the apartment? On the stairs? Any evidence of anyone else in the apartment? Anything at all unusual?'

Quinn shook his head. 'Except the door was unlocked. Like, Fran said she never left her door unlocked.' Tears welled in his eyes. 'I wish I'd come earlier. Maybe — ' His words trailed off.

'If you had, maybe you'd be dead, too,' Helena put in.

Quinn glanced at her, startled, and then shrugged as if to say it didn't matter.

'Look, are you okay?' she asked. 'Do you have a place to stay? Money?'

'I'm getting along.' He gave her a twisted smile. 'Without him.'

'Without who?' Mak asked, though he was

pretty sure Quinn meant his father.

'My old man treats me like a retard, you know?'

'I'm not a fan of your father's,' Helena said, 'but I think he's been doing his best to protect you.'

Quinn snorted in disbelief. 'He'll be glad to see the last of me. Like he was glad to get rid of my mom.'

While Mak digested that, wondering if he should pursue it but not really wanting to, Helena changed the subject.

'I saw the caricatures you drew,' she said. 'You're talented.'

Quinn flushed, ducking his head in embarrassment.

'If you won't go home, at least promise you'll call me if you need help,' she pleaded.

'Yeah, well, I'm okay right now.' Making an effort, he met her gaze. 'Thanks.'

Mak thought the kid might not be too secure financially or emotionally but if Quinn didn't get the chance to be responsible for himself he might never become whole. On the other hand, living in the streets, if that's what he was doing, was dangerous.

'If you need a place to sleep,' he said, 'there's room in my condo. No strings.'

Quinn stared at him as if unable to believe his ears. Mak scribbled his address and phone number on a card and handed it to him.

'Thanks,' Quinn mumbled, getting to his feet. 'I better shove off, okay?' He walked to the door, shoulders hunched as though to ward off any more good will offers.

Helena hopped up and saw him out. When she turned to Mak, she sighed and turned her hands palms upward.

'Yeah, he needs help,' Mak agreed.

'You still can't think he had anything to do with Fran's death.'

'Not any longer. What's your opinion of how Fran felt about Quinn?'

Helena was thoughtful. 'When we were young,' she said slowly, 'Fran used to bring home injured birds and starving animals and try to help them. I'm afraid Quinn would fall in that same category as far as she was concerned. Reed Addison as much as told me she used sex to try to comfort him after his baby died and his wife left him. But this spirit sex at Xenara — oh, God, Mak, how could she?'

'Have sex with strangers for money, you mean?'

'That's at least an honest business transaction. At Xenara it's a hoax. She contributed to deluding the men who believed in that blue-lit path nonsense. I don't understand why Fran would. And worse, I'm beginning to wonder if she even knew who she was pregnant by. She'd have breathed in that opium/marijuana mix, too — God knows the stuff alters your mind. Maybe she forgot to use any protection.' Helena shivered.

He reached for her hand and drew her toward the kitchen. 'Think you can keep down a cup of coffee?'

She nodded. 'Somebody must have recruited Fran. I wonder who.' Glancing at her watch, she added, 'I'm going to call Vada Rogers and get some straight answers.'

Leaving Mak in the kitchen preparing the coffee, Helena retreated to the bedroom to make the call.

'Vada,' the husky voice said.

'Helena Moore. Damn it, I'm mad as hell. Why didn't you make your warning more specific? I had to fight him off, whoever he was. I insist on knowing who told you to bring me to that blue-lit underground sex den — and why.'

'I have no part in the blue-lit path,' Vada said.

'You damn well set *my* feet on it.'

'It's none of my doing. My gift is to heal, it's all I've ever wanted to do.'

'Healing is all my sister, Fran York, ever wanted to do and she's dead. Who involved her in Xenara's phony spirit sex?'

'Can't you understand I have no control over what goes on downstairs?' Vada cried. 'None at all.'

'As a partner you're responsible for everything that happens at Xenara. You can't expect me to believe you don't know what does go on. If, as you claim, you have no control, then who does?'

'I can't tell you.'

'Won't tell me, you mean. I'm damned if I'll let this rest. All your so-called healing is only a cover for a sex scam. No one asked me for money but I'll bet your other clients fork over big bucks for their turn on the blue-lit path — in my book the light should be red. Your mysterious partner made a big mistake when he tried to involve me. Was he the one who recruited my sister? Who killed her? I'm a fighter, Vada, and I swear I'll uncover his identity and expose Xenara's blue-lit path.'

'Listen, you must listen.' Vada's voice changed pitch, became higher and shriller. 'Dark forces gather round you. You're in dreadful danger, you and those dear to you.'

'Is that a threat?' Helena queried.

There was no answer and a moment later there was a crash but no dial tone, as though Vada had accidentally dropped the phone.

'Vada?' Helena said. 'Vada!'

315

There was no response, not even breathing. I'm probably supposed to think she's gone into a trance, Helena told herself. On purpose or accidentally, Vada had cleverly managed to become incommunicado.

When she returned to the kitchen, Helena sputtered with anger as she sat down at the table with her coffee and related the conversation to Mak. 'So Vada disclaims all responsibility for Xenara's spirit sex hoax,' she finished, 'and won't reveal her partner's name.'

'We'll find out without her help,' he said soothingly. 'It's number one on my list for tomorrow.' He glanced at his watch. 'What're we going to do about tonight?'

'Tonight?'

'Yeah — do I sleep here or not? You kicked me out awhile back, remember?'

Helena rested her chin on her hands and looked at him across the table. How could such a devious man have the clear and innocent blue gaze of a child?

'Quinn admitted he was the prowler,' she reminded him. 'And, after all, I did survive a week without you acting as the palace guard.' A sudden suspicion gripped her. 'Unless you reverted to sleeping in the Jag?'

'A good cop never reveals his secrets,' he said solemnly. 'You'll never know.'

She sighed in exasperation. 'Go home,

Captain Maklin. We both know poor Quinn isn't going to harm anyone.' Except maybe himself, she thought with dismay, wishing she could think of some way to help.

Mak set down his mug. 'It's plain to see, as a result of Jeff's medication and my devoted care, that you've returned to your normal combative state. So I may as well go home.' He cast her a wicked look. 'It's been an interesting weekend, to say the least.'

Helena wished she could remember exactly what had happened between the time Mak carried her into the bedroom and when she woke in the morning. Luckily he didn't know she suffered the memory gap.

'Interesting from your viewpoint, maybe,' she said loftily. '*I* could do without most of what happened.'

Without warning, Mak jumped up, pulled her to her feet and into his arms. His kiss, hot and urgent, demanded a response. As usual, she found herself unable to resist, feeling desire curling through her, a deep and heavy wanting no other man had ever induced.

At the same time she felt safe and protected within his embrace, a feeling of coming home.

He lifted his lips from hers, pausing bare millimeters away to whisper, 'Tell me you can do without this and I'll prove you're a liar.'

16

As she drove to work the next morning, Helena's mind was on Mak. Though he'd gone home without protest the night before, she realized she had to make a decision about their relationship soon. Mak had been incredibly patient but how much longer would that last? They'd known each other how long — two months? A short time, maybe, but she wasn't planning to commit herself for a lifetime, after all. One failed marriage was enough. She was sure Mak felt the same.

With Mak, she'd realized the first time he kissed her that she wanted him. As their relationship progressed, they'd had disagreements but they'd become friends — something she and Roger had never been. She valued Mak's friendship so much she couldn't bear to think of losing it. Was it possible to find a lover and keep a friend in one and the same man? Did she dare take the gamble?

The only way to find out was to go for broke.

She was still shuffling pros and cons through her mind when she entered the doctors' parking lot. As she reached for the door handle, a silver Rolls pulled into the space next to her. Recognizing Peter Herron's car, anger filled Helena. Damn the man! How could he have exposed his son to Xenara, of all places?

Sliding from the VW, she waited until Peter emerged from the Rolls, facing him across the hood of her car. 'Dr. Herron,' she said crisply.

Cold gray eyes mets hers. 'Dr. Moore.'

'I spoke to Quinn last night. He told me you sent him to Xenara.'

'I see no reason to discuss my son with you.' He started toward the hospital entrance.

She caught up to him. 'Don't you turn your back on me! Do you realize what goes on in Xenara's inner circle? Under their cover of spiritual healing, Xenara's nothing but a sex cult. Quinn told me about having sex with a supposed spirit who was actually my sister Fran, hired for that purpose. What kind of treatment is that for a disturbed teenager? Or for anyone else, for that matter? I certainly hope you don't make it a practice to refer patients there.'

He halted and glared at her. 'I warned you not to try to involve my son in your sister's death. Quinn had nothing to do with — '

Helena waved a dismissive hand. 'I know he didn't kill Fran. The poor kid was in love with her. Peter, your son needs help. Badly.'

For an instant his features contracted with pain, then the cold anger was back. He thrust his face into hers, so close she could smell his after-shave, and snarled, 'My son is none of your business, now or ever.' Turning away abruptly, he strode rapidly to the entrance.

Helena stared after him, the scent of his expensive pine-scented lotion still in her nostrils, struggling to make a connection that eluded her. Where had she last encountered that scent? When Peter kissed her in his bedroom?

No, by God, at Xenara!

Slowly, she shook her head. I'm mistaken, she told herself, staggered by the implications. The smell is the same but Peter can't be the only man in the world who wears that after-shave.

If Peter had been the man who had tried to rape her, then he knew all about Xenara's blue-lit path and had deliberately set his son's feet on it. Setting fires sometimes served as a sexual substitute in young males but surely Peter wouldn't try to treat Quinn with such a bizarre and chancy method as sex with strangers masquerading as spirits.

Nor could she believe Peter would take the risk of luring her into the blue-lit under-ground chambers of Xenara. He'd disappeared into the hospital but she continued to stare at the entrance with Phil Vance's words echoing in her mind:

Peter's a vengeful type. Keep your guard up.

She grimaced. Peter would have had revenge of a kind if he'd succeeded in raping her. But if he really *had* been the man, it opened up a repulsive can of worms. Vada had been involved — didn't that suggest Peter must be her secret partner?

A respectable psychiatrist running a sex scam? True, he did have money; he could have financed the pyramid.

Much as she mistrusted and disliked Peter, despite the evidence, Helena couldn't quite bring herself to believe he was guilty. But she didn't dismiss her suspicions, either. If he *was* responsible, then he'd be the one who had recruited Fran. She knew her sister liked older men and might well have fallen hard for the suave Peter. It's possible she'd begun working at Xenara just to please him.

Damn it, I have to share this with someone, she told herself. There was only one person she could possibly confide in.

Taking a deep breath, she hurried into the hospital, stopped at a pay phone in the lobby, and called Mak.

'I'll be over as soon as I can make it,' he told her.

Glancing around, Helena decided too many people were walking past to risk being overheard. 'I'll be on Three North,' she said. 'I really do need to talk to you. Come by when you have the chance.'

On peds she found organized chaos. Two seriously ill patients had been admitted in the last fifteen minutes, one a two-month-old in congestive heart failure, the other a three-year-old in what appeared to be *status epilepticus* — a seizure that continued without stopping.

Jeff and Idalia were working on the three-year-old while George did a cut-down on the infant — the baby's veins had collapsed. This procedure involved cutting a vein and inserting a cannula so medications and fluid could be administered intravenously.

'Helena,' George said tersely. 'Good. I need a digoxin dose based on a weight of sixteen pounds.'

After mentally translating the pounds into kilograms, then calculating milligrams per kilogram, Helena drew up the proper amount, told George the dosage she'd figured, and passed the syringe to him as soon as he had the catheter anchored in the baby's vein. He injected the medication slowly. Observing the baby's cyanosis — the baby's entire body was mottled — Helena hoped the digoxin would reach the heart in time to stave off death.

In addition to the blueness of his skin, the baby gasped for breath, so Helena adjusted the oxygen mask for a tighter fit. Possible causes of the heart failure raced through her mind. An infant this young could have any of the various congenital cardiac anomalies, some operable, some not. If the heart and big vessels proved to be normally situated and functioning, then severe anemia should be considered, or an overwhelming respiratory infection.

George finished administering the digoxin, set aside the syringe, and hitched up a microdrip IV. 'Let's get tiger here into a monitored croupette.'

'Does he have a congenital defect?' Helena asked once the baby had been transferred into the croupette.

'Most likely, though it wasn't diagnosed at birth. We'll see what the EKG shows.'

The electrocardiogram, a tracing of the electrical activity of the heart, would help pinpoint not only whether the baby had a defect but where in the heart and the great vessels the abnormality was located.

Before studying the EKG, George, trailed by Helena, went to check on the other new patient. They'd almost reached the room when a woman sitting in the waiting niche by the nurses' station yelled, 'Oh my God!' and sprang to her feet. Her bag, open on her lap, fell, spewing its contents onto the floor. Looking desperately around, she paid no attention to what had happened.

Catching sight of George, she ran toward him, crying, 'Doctor! Doctor!'

He stopped. 'Mrs. St. Loran?' he asked. 'What's the matter?'

She grasped his arm. 'Oh, God, doctor, she's gone and swallowed every one of them.'

'You mean your daughter?' George queried. 'What was it she took?'

'My allergy pills. I went to take one just now and the bottle's empty. I have it right here.' Mrs. St. Loran fumbled for the bag she no longer carried.

'You dropped your bag on the floor,' Helena said. 'I'll find the container.' In a moment she'd brought back an empty over-the-counter antihistamine bottle originally containing 100 tablets and showed it to George.

'How many did you have left?' he asked.

'About ten or so,' the woman said, wringing her hands.

'You're sure your daughter took them?' George persisted.

Mrs. St. Loran nodded, beginning to cry. 'She was playing with my bag early this morning — I never thought about it until now. Oh, God, it's not too late, is it?'

'We'll take care of her,' Helena said, putting an arm around the woman and urging her toward the nurses' station. 'Come on back to the desk now.'

Hailing a passing nurse assistant, Helena asked her to help Mrs. St. Loran pick up her belongings off the floor. Telling the mother she'd be back to talk to her as soon as she could, Helena hurried to the little girl's room.

Jeff was gone. George looked up as she came in and handed her a lavage tube. 'You go ahead and wash out her stomach while I check the baby's EKG.'

One of the joys of being a resident was being given the dirty work. Actually, Helena didn't mind — George was really fair-minded as attending staff went. She glanced at Idalia. 'Did he tell you what the mother said?'

Idalia, wrapping a restraining sheet around the still-twitching child, nodded. Speaking to the girl, she said soothingly, 'There now, honey, you won't like this but we'll be as quick and easy as we can.'

The child, eyes rolled back, gave no sign of hearing her nor did she struggle against the sheet. Helena handed Idalia the padded mouth gag and inserted the stomach end of the lavage catheter into the child's mouth. The patient gagged, a good sign because it meant her gag reflex was still working.

Helena gently but quickly pushed the tube down through the esophagus into the stomach and began aspirating the stomach contents with a bulb syringe while Idalia held the patient on her side to lessen the risk of the child choking if she vomited.

When nothing more returned in the syringe, Helena rinsed it, carefully injected a syringe-full of water, then aspirated that. She continued with the lavage until the water returned clear.

'Did Jeff have to scrub on a case?' she asked Idalia as she removed the tube.

'Don't know. When Dr. Wittenburg came in Jeff asked was he needed and when George said no, Jeff took off.' Idalia unwrapped the sheet and wiped the child's face with a damp cloth.

'What's her name?' Helena asked as she lifted the girl's eyelids to check her pupils.

'Tina.'

Tina's heartbeat was abnormally rapid and her breathing ragged but her twitching had ceased. Jeff had started an IV drip of normal saline, Helena noticed. Good — she'd be able to give physostigmine intravenously for quick action. Examining the child's aspirated gastric fluid, she was encouraged to see flecks of yellow in the stomach contents — all the pills hadn't been digested.

'A good thing for Tina her mother happened to notice the empty bottle,' she said to Idalia. 'God only knows how long we'd have gone on treating the convulsions without discovering their cause.'

'You'd think people lucky enough to have healthy children would take better care of them.' Idalia's uncharacteristic bitterness caught Helena's attention.

She focused on the charge nurse. 'What's the matter, Idalia?' she asked softly.

Idalia's eyes seam with tears. 'Kyesha's sick. My sister's bringing her in later for George to examine and I'm scared shitless.'

Remembering what Idalia had told her about the five-year-old girl, Helena said, 'Are you worried she's having a sickle cell crisis?'

Idalia nodded. 'That'd mean she'd have to stay for a transfusion. No way do I want Kyesha in this hospital.'

'Just overnight isn't long.'

'For kids, *any* time in this place is dangerous.'

Helena stared at her. Dangerous? She thought of her own three patients who had died unexpectedly and a chill ran along her spine. Before she arrived at Harper Hills, there had been at least one other child whose death hadn't been expected — the baby who died while Fran was in the nursery. Did Idalia have a specific reason for believing something was odd about those deaths?

'Idalia — ' she began.

'No! Don't you go asking me questions 'cause I don't have answers: I just got this bad feeling and what does that mean?'

'Maybe you're simply upset about Kyesha.'

'I'm upset but — ' Idalia stopped and shook her head. 'George is the finest doctor, the finest man I know. I'd do anything for him. I would never let anyone else treat Kyesha. Lord knows, though, how I wish he practiced in another hospital.'

As she left the room to get the medication she needed for Tina, Helena wondered what was really bothering Idalia — it was more than Kyesha's illness. Did it have anything to do with those sudden deaths? Deciding it would be quicker to fetch the medicine from the pharmacy herself than to wait for it to be delivered, Helena stepped onto the elevator, still uneasy about Idalia.

When she stepped up to the counter at the pharmacy, the assistant pharmacist took her order. While she waited, she noticed Carin behind the counter talking to Reed Addison, the head pharmacist, and recalled that Carin used to work as a pharmacist's assistant. When Carin glanced her way Helena smiled tentatively, hoping George's wife had decided to forgive and forget her unfortunate mention of their retarded son.

Carin immediately cut short her conversation with Reed and came to the counter. 'I haven't seen you for a long time,' she said brightly. 'How are you?'

'Fine. I'm glad George has recovered.'

'It was his own fault,' Carin said. 'He doesn't pay attention.'

'Eating anything in rural Mexico is risky, all right.'

'It isn't just in Mexico he doesn't pay attention.' Carin's voice held a nuance Helena couldn't quite grasp. She almost sounded pleased.

Wondering if what was sauce for the gander might also tempt the goose, Helena glanced at red-haired Reed. Was it possible he and Carin — ?

The assistant's arrival with Helena's medication cut short her musing. 'Nice to see you,' she told Carin, relieved that she didn't seem to hold a grudge.

Mak was waiting on Three North when she returned and, knowing she'd be busy all morning, she asked him to meet her in the doctor's parking lot at noon. With all the ears around, the outdoors was the safest place to hold a private conversation.

Jeff showed up just before noon to see Tina and, as they stood over her crib, Helena told him what had caused the girl's convulsions.

'Antihistamine overdose, huh? Believe it or not, I was getting around to considering poisoning.'

She looked askance. 'Sure you were.'

'Actually, there wasn't much else left to consider.'

Watching him examine Tina, she asked, 'Did you ever talk to Vada?'

'She's not taking phone calls. At least not from me.'

Though tempted to tell him about her conversation with Vada, she kept her mouth shut.

'How're you feeling?' he asked.

'I'm back to normal, more or less. Thanks for your help and also for giving Mak a hand in bringing my car back.'

'I still haven't gotten over what happened to you.' He shook his head. 'I don't want her hurt.'

She knew he meant Vada. Frankly, she didn't care but there was no point in upsetting Jeff by saying so.

Shortly after twelve, she went to meet Mak.

Though the morning had been overcast, the sun shone warm now, tempered by a cool ocean breeze. It wasn't an inside day, she thought, spotting Mak waiting by her VW. Peter's Rolls was gone, as she'd expected given his busy practice.

'I know who the Xenara bastard is,' Mak said in lieu of a greeting. 'You'll never guess. It's — '

'Peter Herron,' she finished.

'Damn it!' he exploded. 'If you knew, why didn't you tell me?'

So she *was* right. Much as she despised Peter, the knowlege only partially satisfied her. As a doctor she hated to see a member of her profession brought low — and he would be, sooner or later. Deservedly so.

She laid a hand on Mak's arm, feeling the tenseness in his muscles. 'I wasn't keeping it from you — I didn't suspect him before this morning. Peter parked next to me here and when I tried to warn him that Quinn needed help I smelled his after-shave. Then I knew — ' She shuddered involuntarily.

'I have a few plans for that son of a bitch.' Mak's voice shook with fury, his fists clenching and unclenching.

'Why bother? He's destroying himself.'

'That's what you think. Slick bastards with money slide out from under more often than not. He won't be anywhere near the fan when the shit hits — Vada'll be the one, you wait and see. Does he know you fingered him?'

She shook her head. 'I couldn't believe it at first myself.'

'Don't run around broadcasting the news,' he said. 'I prefer you alive.'

'You don't think he'd — ?' She stopped, her eyes widening. 'Oh, God, is he the one who killed Fran?'

'If she was going to expose him, he sure as hell had a motive. You got time to go for a short ride?'

She shook her head. 'We've got a couple of touchy cases on peds. I have to get back.'

'The baby with heart failure and the kid who swallowed her mother's allergy pills?'

She stared at him in surprise. 'Since when are you so interested in pediatric patients?'

'I got bored waiting for you earlier and so I eaves-dropped. You can learn a lot, just listening. Provided the talkers don't realize you're tuning in. Am I right about the two cases?'

She nodded.

He cupped her face in his hands. 'Be careful.' Leaning down, he brushed her lips with his before letting her go. 'I'll see you tonight.'

Watching him stride away, she wished she

could go with him. Not merely for a short ride but for the afternoon, enjoying the perfect southern California weather. How wonderful it would be to relax on the beach with Mak, no worries, no cares — just the two of them beside the ocean, sharing the sun.

Helena sighed. That wasn't likely to happen any day soon. Especially the part about the no worries or cares. *Be careful*, he'd warned. That was a hell of a lot different from 'take care,' a phrase as meaningless as 'have a good day.' Mak meant what he'd said.

As she returned to the hospital, she wondered how dangerous Peter Herron actually was. Those cold gray eyes could easily belong to a killer. Still, though she could picture him as a dictator ordering death for all who dared oppose him, she had difficulty imagining him killing with his own hands.

When she went home that evening, the girl with antihistamine poisoning was improving and the baby with CHF was holding his own — barely. She and George would both be stopping by later to check on him.

Mak was waiting on the steps of her apartment.

'Why sit here when we both know you had an extra key made?' she asked. 'Are all cops as sneaky as you?'

'It comes with the ID,' he said, following her up the stairs. 'I'd like to keep the key until Fran's murder is solved, okay? In case I need to get in your place in a hurry. I'll try not to abuse the privilege.' He produced his key with a flourish and let her in. 'You like Mexican food?' he asked as they entered the apartment.

'Does that mean you're inviting me to dinner?'

'You got it.'

'I love Mexican food.' She examined his clothes, noting he wore chinos and an open-necked shirt. 'Not too fancy a place, I take it.'

'Jeans and a tee shirt would fit right in.'

She was happy to hear it, given the way she felt, and disappeared into her bedroom to shower and change. She didn't notice the new deadbolt on the inside of the door until they were ready to leave. Pointing to it, she cast a puzzled glance at Mak.

'It was either that,' he said, 'or me taking up permanent residence in your other bedroom. And since you vetoed me last night — ' His gaze held hers as he let the words trail off.

What she saw in his eyes told her if he ever spent the night again, it wouldn't be in the 'other' bedroom.

Mak drove her to the hospital after their dinner at a family-style Mexican restaurant in the hills on the other side of the freeway.

'The chili rellenos were the best I've ever eaten,' she told him, 'but I'll have to brush up on my Spanish if we eat there often. Mine's mostly limited to asking where it hurts.'

'I'll be happy to tell you exactly where.' He proceeded to rattle off a string of Spanish words so rapidly that the only words she caught were *corazon*, heart, and one that she was pretty sure was a slang term for the male genital organ.

'I recommend ice-packs to the areas in question,' she said.

'You doctors are sadists.'

'Only with patients we know and love.' The words were out before she realized what she'd said.

He glanced at her and she thought he was going to comment but he finally looked back at the road without saying anything.

She breathed easier. It was too soon for any talk of love, even in fun. The word had slipped past her guard. A Freudian slip?

'How did you become so fluent in Spanish?' she asked.

'If you grew up in the Lincoln Heights area

of LA, like I did, you needed to know Spanish to survive.'

She looked at him curiously. 'You hardly ever talk about yourself. Do your parents still live there?'

'My dad was a cop — he was killed in a shootout when I was twelve. My mother's living in Seattle with her sister, my Aunt Mag.'

'You were an only child?'

'My older brother died in a motorcycle accident the year after my father was shot. He was stealing the bike at the time. He was sixteen.' Mak didn't so much as glance her way.

No wonder he didn't speak of his childhood, she thought as she tried to come up with something to say.

'How about this baby with the heart condition you're going to check?' Mak asked, obviously changing the subject. 'Is he going to make it?'

Ordinarily, she didn't discuss patients with friends unless they were doctors but she saw no harm in answering this question.

'He has a chance,' she said, without adding how slim the chance actually was.

Tests had showed that the baby, instead of having a heart divided into four chambers, two upper and two lower, had only one lower chamber, or ventricle. Unless the condition was corrected, the baby had no chance to survive. Surgical correction *was* possible but, unfortunately, the morbidity and mortality rates were high. Still, some patients survived and, if they could stabilize this baby so he could tolerate surgery, he might be one of the lucky ones.

Mak said no more until they pulled into the hospital parking lot. After she directed him to a slot near the ER entrance, the easiest way to go in at night, he parked and announced, 'I'll go in with you.'

She nodded absently, her mind still on her patient. Since Harper Hills didn't have a pediatric heart surgeon on its staff, as soon as the baby's condition permitted they'd have to fly him to the nearest center that did — probably San Francisco.

She recognized one of the ER nurses and greeted her in passing. Mak followed her through the ER and all the way to Three North.

'I'm perfectly safe in the hospital,' she protested as they got off the elevator.

'Probably. But I've had my fill of lurking in cars.'

He settled into one of the chairs in the waiting niche by the nurses' station while she located the baby's chart — his name was

Edmund Flannery. Baby Eddie. After glancing at the nursing notes, she went into Eddie's room. George apparently hadn't dropped in to see the baby yet because he'd made no note on the progress sheet.

The child was about the same as when she'd gone off duty — his skin fairly pink and his heart rate down a bit closer to normal. 'Eddie, it looks like you might make it to the OR,' she murmured as she bent over the croupette.

When she returned to the nurses' station, Mak was leaning on the counter and none of the nurses was in sight. He handed her a piece of paper, a memo message.

'The ER wants me to look at a girl with a rash,' she said after she'd glanced at the note.

'I know, I read it.'

She frowned. 'How did you come to have the memo anyway?'

'I told the nurse who took the call that I was with you and she gave it to me. Since she didn't seal the memo in an envelope, naturally I read it. Why not?'

'Is nothing sacred?' she asked, only half-joking.

'Not to a cop.'

As usual in the ER, everyone was busy. Mak sat in the waiting room while Helena searched for the girl with the rash, found her alone in Cubicle 4, and introduced herself.

Mary Lou, thirteen, had a fine, red, non-itchy rash over her chest and abdomen. Though the rash was scarlatiniform, it wasn't typical of scarlet fever. Nor did Helena think this was a drug rash, despite the fact Mary Lou had been on oral penicillin for a week.

'Do you hurt anywhere?' she asked the girl.

'My throat's sort of scratchy and I don't feel good all over.'

'How long has this been going on?'

'A week. My mom called the doctor and he ordered penicillin. I took it like he said but it didn't help.'

Helena saw in the history taken by the ER doctor that, according to the mother, Mary Lou had been running a low-grade fever for a week. On examination she found the girl's throat slightly red and her neck glands enlarged. With the clues she'd amassed, she made a tentative diagnosis.

When she gently palpated Mary Lou's abdomen, she wasn't surprised to find a slightly enlarged spleen and was happy to note the liver was normal-sized. The girl's case was mild. The ER doctor had already drawn blood for testing, so she merely added a request on the lab slip to check for heterophil antibodies. She expected it to come back positive.

'Probable infectious mononucleosis,' she wrote on the consult sheet. Though the rash was an uncommon finding in infectious mono, the other symptoms were characteristic. She recommended that the penicillin be discontinued and the patient be treated at home.

After bringing the mother into the cubicle, Helena discussed the viral disease and its treatment with the two of them. 'Remember, recovery is slow,' she finished.

Later, as she climbed into Mak's Jag, Helena saw George's car in the lot and knew he was checking on Eddie. She leaned back, closing her eyes as Mak pulled out of the lot.

'Tired?' he asked.

She nodded.

At the apartment, he walked her to the door. As he reached to insert the key, she caught sight of something white taped to the door.

'What's that?' she asked, reaching for it.

He blocked her. 'Someone's left a note on your door. Must have figured I'd be with you 'cause this one's in an envelope.' Still keeping her back, he carefully grasped the envelope by a corner and pulled it free.

'Oh, great,' she said in annoyance. 'Even though it's sealed, I don't get to read it first?'

He pressed the envelope gently with his

palms. 'Nothing but paper inside,' he said and unlocked the door.

'What did you expect, a bomb?' she asked as she went in and flipped on a light.

Seeing the expression on his face, she realized with a start that that's exactly what Mak had suspected.

He locked the door before handing her the envelope. There was no writing on the outside. All of a sudden she didn't want to open it. 'It must be from Quinn,' she said. 'Who else would stick a note on my door?'

He took a jackknife from his pocket, pulled a blade free, and handed it to her. 'When you get the envelope open, hold the paper by the corners,' he said. 'There may be fingerprints.'

'Quinn's?'

He shook his head. 'I'm willing to bet it's not from Quinn.'

Helena swallowed nervously. Inserting the knife blade, she slit the envelope open, gingerly removing the paper and unfolding it. Large black letters, as crudely printed as a young child's, staggered across the white sheet. She deciphered the words with disbelief and mounting fear. Her hand shook as she offered the note to Mak. He read it aloud.

'Leave Xenara alone or you'll be sorry.'

There was no signature.

341

17

While watching Mak thrust the threatening note back in its envelope and slide it into his shirt pocket, Helena sorted her feelings. Anger vied with a sickening dread — she was torn between resentment and fear that she'd acquired a dangerous and mysterious enemy.

'I'll have the local guys dust for prints,' Mak said. 'I figure they won't find the Silver Shrink — but I'll bet he's behind this.'

Peter? Helena shook her head. He wasn't the type to leave a printed note taped to her door.

'Don't shake your head at me,' Mak told her. 'I don't mean he wrote the note or stuck it on your door. But I'll lay big odds he sends his patients to Xenara for 'spirit' sex therapy like he did his son — why not? That way he gets to charge them twice, right? Once for the office visit where he prescribes Xenara and again before they set foot on the blue-lit path. So he has the knowledge to pull the right string to panic some dumb bastard into doing his dirty work for him.'

Helena thought it over and concluded that Mak had a point. 'But don't forget Vada,' she reminded him. 'She has good reason not to want me to expose Xenara. But I'm damned if I'll be pressured by threatening letters, no matter how many I get.'

Mak eyed her levelly but before he had a chance to speak, the phone rang.

'Bedroom,' he reminded her as she started for the living room phone.

He followed her, both of them staring at the Identifier as she picked up the phone. She recognized the flashing number as Harper Hills.

'Dr. Moore.'

'Helena, this is George Wittenburg. I'm sorry if I woke you but I see by the Flannery baby's chart you took a look at him earlier tonight. How was he then?'

Helena repeated what she'd written on the progress report: 'His heart rate wasn't as rapid, he looked fairly pink — I thought he might be stabilizing. Why?'

'We lost him.'

'Damn! When?'

'I was in to see him less than an hour after you. Carin and I were just walking in the door at home when the phone rang — Mrs. Alvarez telling me the baby had flatlined.'

'How did he seem when you examined him?'

'My note's even a bit more optimistic than

yours. I could have sworn the kid might make it. He went sour so fast I wondered if you'd picked up on some symptom I missed.'

'I didn't,' Helena said. 'But even if he had survived long enough to have surgery, the mortality rates on the corrective procedure are really depressingly bad.'

'Exactly what I told Carin. Still, I thought he'd get that chance, however slim.' George sighed. 'We can't save them all. See you in the morning.'

Helena turned to Mak, feeling really depressed. 'We lost the baby with the heart problem.'

'I thought you said he had a chance.'

'I did. George thought so, too.'

'So the kid shouldn't have died.'

Mak's persistence made her look at him closely. 'What's your interest in this?'

He studied her for a long moment, then said, 'You got any left of that six-pack Jeff brought over? Mexican food always makes me thirsty.'

'If I give you a beer, will you answer my question?'

He nodded.

She settled for a ginger ale and sat at the kitchen table across from Mak and his beer.

'What I'm doing's supposed to be a secret,' he told her after taking a long swallow and tipping back in his chair. 'I've been hanging around the hospital asking questions for going on four months now and I'm sure the grapevine has come up with all kinds of reasons why I'm there. The truth is I'm investigating unexpected and suspicious deaths of infants and children while they were patients at Harper Hills. Since the hospital isn't my employer, it's an unofficial investigation that I've been ordered to keep low-key.'

Helena stared at him, speechless. She'd questioned why two of her patients had died but, in the absence of suspicious findings on autopsy, hadn't pursued the matter.

'I've had two — no, three deaths I didn't expect,' she said finally.

'Your sister was fired because one of her patients shouldn't have died,' he said. 'That was my interest in Fran. Since January, there've been five other deaths my employer believes belong in the same category. Altogether nine children died unexpectedly, with no obvious findings on the posts. I've been searching for a common factor linking the nine but so far no luck.' He took another swallow and set down the can. 'You might be able to help me.'

She leaned forward eagerly. 'I'll do anything I can.'

'I can't get an official release on the medical records of the deaths, nor am I allowed to copy them. I did get permission to look at the records with the medical librarian hovering at my shoulder but I'm not a doctor. You have the training to spot something I'd miss. And besides, you can go through those records without official permission.'

'Give me a list of the names and I'll see if I can come up with anything. I haven't been the only one to question unexpected deaths — some of the nurses are hyper about it. But I don't think they really *know* anything.'

'If they do, they're not telling anyone,' Mak said. 'No one wants to talk about the deaths. Scared they'll be blamed, maybe, I don't know. But if those nine deaths weren't natural and they weren't accidents, somebody's deliberately killing these kids. If I had a motive, I'd be closer to finding who the bastard is.'

'I read somewhere,' Helena said, 'that convicted nurses who gave fatal doses of medication to adult patients on purpose were on power trips — playing God. Some truly believed in euthanasia for the terminally ill and others just became addicted to killing. But who'd murder children?'

'I wish to hell I knew. It could be a nurse, a doctor, anyone in the hospital. Maybe once

346

you've scanned the nine case records, you'll come up with something.' He reached for his wallet and pulled out a slip of paper. 'Here's the list. Add the heart baby's name.' He drained his beer and rose. 'I'd better get going, you look beat. Unless you'd rather I stayed — in view of that damn note.'

'I'll be all right behind the deadbolt.' She smiled at him. 'It's the most practical gift I ever received — as well as the most thoughtful. You sure know the way to a girl's heart.'

'Yeah? You could've fooled me. I thought I was way off course.'

She blew him a kiss. 'Good night, Mak.'

'Just don't forget to use that deadbolt, okay?'

★ ★ ★

When Helena arrived on Three North the next morning, she found the relief charge nurse on duty and Idalia sitting in one of the rooms with her daughter.

'I delayed Kyesha's transfusion until now so I could take two days off,' Idalia said. 'I'm not leaving this child alone for one minute.'

Helena smiled at Kyesha who stared big-eyed from the bed, her hair neatly corn-rowed. 'You're as pretty as your mama,' she said.

'You a nurse like my mama?' Kyesha asked.

'No, I'm a doctor.'

'You got any little girls?'

'One. Her name is Laura. She's four.'

'I'm *five*,' Kyesha said with an air of importance. 'I go to school. Only I missed today 'cause my stomach hurts and Dr. George said I had to come here.' Her lower lip quivered. 'He's gonna stick me with a needle.'

'And after that you'll feel better and be able to go back to school,' Helena put in quickly. 'Until then, you've got your mama right here to take care of you.'

Kyesha reached for Idalia's hand as if to make sure she wouldn't leave. A lump formed in Helena's throat as she watched. True, Kyesha had a problem with her sickle cell trait but a transfusion would return her blood to normal — at least for the time being. Nothing would ever make Laura normal, even for a day.

What good came of feeling sorry for herself? Absolutely none. Rather than make herself miserable, she'd try to be glad for Idalia and Kyesha instead.

Recalling Fran's many stuffed animals piled in the closet, Helena said, 'What's your favorite animal, Kyesha?'

'Elephants!' Kyesha announced. 'They got

bi-i-g long trunks.'

Knowing there was a pink elephant in the collection, Helena did her best to look mysterous. 'I'll bet there's going to be a bi-i-g surprise for you after lunch, you just wait and see.'

As she left the room, Helena wished she'd had the chance to talk to Idalia alone. In view of Mak's investigation, Idalia's refusal to leave Kyesha alone in the hospital 'even for a minute' took on sinister undertones. Idalia wasn't worried that Kyesha might be afraid or neglected: she feared her daughter might be killed. Did Idalia know more than she was telling? When the nurse came back on duty, Helena meant to try and find out — though Idalia had resisted talking about it before. In the meantime, she had the medical records of the nine victims to look up when she had the chance.

When she went in to see Tina, the three-year-old was standing up in her crib, crying.

'Tina wants to go home,' the nursing assistant in the room said. 'Nothing else will make her happy.'

'She looks ready to be discharged,' Helena agreed. After a quick examination of the struggling child, she started for the nurses' station to write the order, saw Mrs. St. Loran getting off the elevator, and told her the good news.

'I swear I don't know how that child got the top off the bottle,' Mrs. St. Loran said after thanking Helena for what she'd done for Tina. '*I* even have trouble with those tops. Maybe she's going to be an engineer like her dad.'

At least we had one good result, Helena thought as she scribbled the discharge order on Tina's chart. And George would soon be releasing Penny, the girl who was recovering from tetanus, making at least one more upbeat resolution on Three North, thank heaven. Checking her watch, she saw it was time for rounds.

At noon, after checking the lab reports — that heterophil on Mary Lou had been positive, just as she'd suspected — Helena dashed home to get the pink elephant for Kyesha and grab a hasty sandwich. Although the rest of the day wasn't unusually busy, Helena never did find time to get to the basement where the medical records were stored.

★ ★ ★

When she arrived on Three North the next morning, Idalia was helping Kyesha dress to go home.

'She says she's going to be a doctor,' Idalia told Helena. 'I don't know if it's because of you or because she'll get to stick needles in people.'

'It's 'cause Dr. George said I was smart enough to be a doctor,' Kyesha put in.

Idalia rolled her eyes. 'Too smart, sometimes. Say goodbye to Dr. Moore and thank her for the elephant.'

''Bye,' Kyesha said, suddenly shy. She looked at Helena from under long lashes. 'Thank you.'

'I hear Alvarado Hospital in San Diego is transferring a patient to us this morning — a seven-year-old boy with a brain stem tumor,' Idalia said. 'The mother lives in El Doblez, the father in San Diego. Sounds like a problem case all the way round.'

Tumors of the brain stem were usually malignant gliomas and, because of the location, inaccessible to surgery — operating on the brain stem would kill the patient. Irradiation was the treatment of choice and the prognosis was not good. Cancer in children always seemed unfair to her; they were too young to suffer so horrendously. But they were usually the most courageous of patients — inspiring and heart-breaking at the same time.

The boy, Randy, was admitted shortly after

Idalia and Kyesha left. George called Dr. Markowicz, chief of the neurological service, for a consultation on the case and Jeff showed up with Zel Markowicz shortly after she arrived on Three North.

Randy, his brown eyes enormous in a thin, abnormally pale face topped by a mostly bald head from the radiation therapy, gazed dubiously at the parade of doctors coming toward him. George sat on the bed.

'I'm Dr. Wittenburg,' he told the boy. 'If you want to call me Dr. George, that's okay.' He introduced Helena to Randy next, then Zel and Jeff. 'When you need something you can ask any one of us for it.'

Randy's puzzled gaze shifted from Helena to Zel and back to Helena again. 'My mom said a lady was gonna come see me.'

Zel smiled at him. 'But you didn't expect two lady doctors?'

Before Randy could answer, the ward clerk entered. 'Dr. Wittenburg,' she said, 'Dr. King's on the phone.'

'Excuse me,' George said, rising from the bed and leaving the room.

'It wasn't a lady doctor my mom meant,' Randy said. 'She told me this lady didn't use needles and x-rays and like that. She said this lady's gonna teach me how to use my mind to get rid of the bad stuff in my head. That's why my mom brought me to this hospital, so I could learn.'

Helena glanced at Jeff. Could Randy mean Vada?

'Anything that helps get rid of the bad stuff is all right with me,' Zel told Randy. 'Right now, though, I'd like to examine you.'

'I suppose you got to,' he said resignedly.

As Zel bent over Randy, Jeff edged closer to Helena. 'Call me if Vada comes to see him,' he whispered, nodding toward the boy. Then he moved to the opposite side of the bed to observe Zel's neurological exam.

Helena stood by seething. Vada treating one of Three North's patients? Jeff certainly thought that's who Randy was talking about.

I must talk to Randy's mother as soon as possible, Helena decided. And yet what could she tell her? That all Vada Rogers stood for was sham and delusion? No, she couldn't do that, couldn't take away what little hope the mother might have for her son's recovery.

In Helena's opinion, one of the worst sins a doctor could commit was to offer a no-hope prognosis. Depriving Randy's mother of hope would fall into that dismal category. So, okay, she might have to keep quiet but that didn't mean she couldn't keep a damn close watch on Vada if the woman did show up on Three North.

* ★ ★

On Friday morning, shortly after rounds, Helena was coming out of George's office when she saw Vada getting off the elevator with Randy's mother. Helena immediately called neurology, discovered Jeff was in the OR scrubbing in on a case, and wound up leaving a message with the OR supervisor that 'she' was visiting Randy.

The other patient in Randy's room was Aaron, a ten-year-old whose diabetes had suddenly zoomed out of control. He'd been admitted to get his insulin dosage stabilized. He was an avid football fan and, in his enthusiasm, could go on indefinitely about the Chargers and the Rams, pinpointing player's strengths and weaknesses. Although he wasn't George's patient, Helena had talked with him several times.

She walked into the room, smiled at Randy, and passed by to go on to Aaron's bedside. Randy's mother, leaning over to hug her son, didn't notice her and Vada didn't look at her.

'Hi, Aaron,' she said. 'What do you think of the Chargers' chances in the game this weekend?'

'They're outclassed,' he told her. Instead of going on, as he usually did, Aaron motioned her to come closer. When she bent over him, he pointed toward Randy's bed, whispering, 'I saw her on TV — she's the lady from Xenara.' His awed gaze was fastened on Vada.

Evidently Vada was more famous than Helena realized.

'Close your eyes, Randy,' Vada said in her husky voice. She spoke softly but the words carried. 'I want you to breathe slowly and deeply and while you're breathing, think of your favorite color. Keep your mind on that color, imagine you're surrounded by that color, floating in it.

'You see this beautiful color all around you and feel it inside as well as outside — it's a wonderful, healthy color. There's only one place inside you this magic healing color can't reach, one dark and colorless spot.'

Vada's soothing voice went on and on, repeating over and over in various ways how enjoyable it was for Randy to float in his favorite color until Helena found herself visualizing blue, *her* favorite color, coiling mist-like around her. Giving herself a mental shake, she glanced at Aaron. His eyes were closed. She resisted the impulse to rouse him — so far nothing Vada had said or done was harmful.

After a minute or two, Vada changed direction. 'You have found the dark spot inside you, Randy. Now you will find magic crayons of your favorite color. You are going to pick up one of those crayons and use it to color the part of you that is dark. You will color all of the spot that you can and then you will rest.

'The crayons are magic and even if you use them all now doing your coloring, tomorrow you will find more crayons to color with. Every day you will color the dark place in the same way, you will make it the same beautiful color that surrounds you, your favorite color.'

Vada repeated the message several times, adding, 'How easy it is to take a crayon and color. The coloring is so easy that after this you won't need me here to tell you what to do — you'll be able to do it by yourself. Every time you feel like it, you'll be able to use the magic crayons.'

Helena couldn't see past Randy's mother to notice what Randy did when Vada stopped talking but she did note that Aaron's eyes opened and focused on her, dreamily at first, then with recognition.

'I found my dark spot,' he told her, putting his hand on his abdomen just over where his pancreas would be. 'And I tried, but it's hard to color that place. It wants to stay dark.'

Helena couldn't find words for a long moment. It was possible his doctor had shown Aaron where the pancreas was located, explaining to him how that organ produced insulin and that his pancreas didn't work right and that was why he had diabetes mellitus. Then it wouldn't be unusual for him to find his 'dark spot.' She could ask Aaron and discover how much his doctor had told him. But, wary of upsetting him, she didn't. Better not to comment one way or another. After all, what he'd overheard from Vada and tried to do wouldn't actually hurt him.

Or Randy, either. Not that she believed it would help except, perhaps, to raise his spirits. Still, she'd keep her mouth shut.

She managed a smile for Aaron and was searching for something to say about football before leaving when the door swung open and George marched into the room. He stopped in front of Vada and glared at her.

'What are you doing here?'

'Why, doctor, I asked her — ' Randy's mother began.

George cut her off with a curt wave of his hand. 'Ms. Rogers, please step outside.'

Vada gave Randy a reassuring smile before walking past George and on into the hall ahead of George. Helena trailed after them. Once in the corridor, she found that Vada hadn't stopped but was walking toward the elevator. George cut her off by stepping in front of her.

'Just a moment, Ms. Rogers,' he said. 'I have something to say to you.'

'As I recall, you said everything there was to say to me some time ago.' Vada's tone was cool.

'I warned you then never to cross me again.' George's tone was ominously flat, presaging, Helena knew, a blowup. He glanced at Helena.

'Did you know about this?'

'No,' she said more or less truthfully. Actually she *hadn't* known Vada was coming to Three North today.

Reassured that he didn't have a traitor in the ranks, he returned his full attention to Vada. 'If I ever see you on Three North again, I'll have you arrested for practicing medicine without a license. Do you understand?'

'I don't practice medicine,' she said. 'I — '

'Don't give me any of your double talk. If I call the police, they'll come. And I'll damn well fight to make the charge stick. You are not to come near any of my patients. Ever.'

'Dr. Wittenburg, I've done no harm. All I — '

'No harm?' George's voice shook with furry. 'Damn you, you prey on the gullible, you milk the credulous, you and your

358

'hell-spawned fakery.' He took a step toward her and raised his arm.

My God, I can't let him hit Vada! Helena told herself. As she hurried toward Vada and George, she heard Carin calling George's name.

A moment later Carin threw her arms around him, crying, 'No, don't!'

Helena quickly grabbed Vada's arm and steered her toward the elevator. Just as they reached it, the doors opened and Jeff started to get off.

'Hold it, we're coming in,' Helena told him. Luckily no one else was on the elevator. As the doors closed, she heard Carin screaming at George.

'You're the one I blame for everything! You know it's all your fault!'

Poor Carin, Helena thought.

'Dangerous,' Vada said.

Despite what she'd just seen, Helena couldn't believe George would actually have struck Vada.

'Yes,' Jeff told Vada, 'dangerous for you if you show up at Harper Hills again. I warned you about George. You and spiritual healing are two subjects he can't be rational about.'

'I go where I'm asked to help,' Vada said. 'I bring hope to light the darkness.'

'If you were the one who sent me that

threatening letter about leaving Xenara alone,' Helena said, 'I don't call that trying to help.'

Vada turned her green gaze on Helena as the elevator reached the ground floor. As soon as they exited, she paused and touched Helena's arm. 'Believe me, I didn't know you received any such letter.'

Oddly enough, Helena believed her. She'd struck out at Vada about the letter more in reaction than anything else. But, since she'd started, she might as well finish. 'I know who he is,' she told Vada.

'Are you crazy?' Jeff muttered crossly. 'We can't talk here.'

Suddenly conscious of others around them, Helena lowered her voice, determined to have her say whether she was overheard or not. 'A thousand threatening letters won't change my mind,' she told Vada. 'I'm damned if I'll let him go on with what he's doing at Xenara.' Glancing at Jeff, she said, 'Your grandfather would have made the right diagnosis — the man's a thorough Bad Heart and, if he has an aura, it sure as hell would be black shot with red. In case you haven't figured it out, her silent partner is Peter Herron.'

Jeff grasped Vada's shoulders, staring into her eyes for a charged instant. Without a word, he let her go abruptly and strode toward the lobby.

'He mustn't go to Peter!' Vada cried and ran after him.

Left alone, Helena hesitated, then shook her head. If Vada couldn't stop Jeff, then neither could she. In any case, she wasn't too sure she wanted to. If the result wouldn't be his arrest for murder, Jeff could kill Peter as far as she was concerned.

There are patients waiting for you, she reminded herself, and got back on the elevator.

It took her some time to calm Randy's mother.

'It never occurred to me to ask Dr. Wittenburg if he approved of alternative therapy,' she told Helena. 'I took it for granted everyone did these days.'

'Dr. Wittenburg's a fine doctor,' Helena assured her.

'But I especially want Randy to work with Vada Rogers. You don't realize how much she's helped me. I had to fight six months to get my ex-husband to allow Randy to come here. My son doesn't have much time left and I refuse to allow Dr. Wittenburg to prevent me from pursuing every possible chance. You don't believe Vada could do any harm to Randy, do you?'

Helena told the truth. 'From what I've seen I don't see how she can hurt him but I'm not convinced she can help. I only hope all the furor hasn't upset Randy.'

'I don't think so, he was talking about the coloring to the boy in the next bed when I left him.' She grasped Helena's hand impulsively. 'Oh, Dr. Moore, Vada's already helped him, I just know it. You'll talk to Dr. Wittenburg for me, won't you?'

Helena found herself promising to try to find a compromise everyone could accept and Randy's mother seemed more content when she left. For the rest of the afternoon, Helena worried in her spare time over what she could possibly come up with that George would accept and the answer was always the same — nothing, not if it involved Vada Rogers.

The call from Clovis inviting her to a going-home party in the nursery for preemie Kristle was a pleasant surprise and, after the cake and coffee, Helena left the hospital at five feeling more up than she'd been in days. Kristle was one of the pluses, one of the successes that eased the pain of the failures. Kristle reminded her of why she'd chosen to become a pediatrician and made her happy she'd learned the skills to save a premature baby.

At home, she found a message from Mak

on her answering machine telling her he'd be back from LA around nine or ten and would drop by. Her joy at the thought of seeing him was immediately squelched by her guilt over not getting to those medical records. It seemed one thing after another had prevented her. She'd grab a bite to eat and go back tonight. If she didn't finish before nine, she was on call Saturday night and Sunday and could get back to them then.

She was tossing a salad when the phone rang and she trotted into the bedroom to answer it, automatically noting the flashing number on the Identifier. It was unfamiliar and she jotted it down.

'Dr. Moore.'

'Why didn't you tell me?' Quinn cried. 'You must have known, you and Mak both. Everyone in the entire fucking world probably knew except me.'

'Quinn, take it easy,' she pleaded. 'What —?'

'Him. My goddamned father, that's what. He built it, didn't he? He runs Vada just like he runs everyone else. Everything else. He sent me there, knowing — ' Quinn's words trailed off into sobs.

As she tried to soothe him, Helena realized what had happened. He'd discovered his father owned Xenara. She wondered if that was what her sister meant to tell Quinn the day she was killed.

'Even Fran,' Quinn sobbed. 'He — he paid her to — to do it with me. The whole fucking world's a lie! I'll get even, you wait and see!'

18

After Quinn slammed down the phone, Helena immediately called the number back, counting the rings and hoping against hope he'd answer. She was about to give up after the sixteenth ring when a man's voice said, 'Hello?'

'Is Quinn there?'

'Lady, this is a pay phone and I ain't Quinn. I don't even know any Quinns.'

'Please listen — can you see a red-haired teenager anywhere nearby?'

A slight pause. 'Nope.'

'Would you tell me where the pay phone is located?'

He obliged, she thanked him and hung up. After a moment's thought, she punched in Peter's number. Lamas answered and informed her Dr. Herron wasn't available.

'It's about his son,' she said. 'About Quinn. I must speak to Peter.'

'I'm sorry, Dr. Moore. If you care to leave a message I'll make certain Dr. Herron receives it.'

Peter might or might not be home but it was obvious she wasn't getting past Lamas.

'Tell him Quinn's extremely upset,' she said, 'and that I believe his emotional condition is critical. I don't know where Quinn is but it's essential he be found as soon as possible.'

'Are the police involved?'

Helena's surprise at the question ebbed when she realized Lamas must know of Quinn's previous arrests for fire-setting.

'Not yet, Lamas, but I'm afraid for Quinn. Tell Peter I'm worried enough to start searching myself.'

She couldn't call Mak — he was in LA. Still not completely familiar with the layout of El Doblez, she found her city map and looked up the location of the pay phone — near the beach. She grabbed her shoulder bag and started for the door, then paused. Who knew how long this might take? She really ought to leave a message for Mak.

Hurrying to the phone she quickly inserted a new message on the answering tape: 'Mak, am looking for 'Q'.'

★ ★ ★

Despite being near the ocean, the pay phone Quinn had used was in a down-at-the-heels part of town that made Helena reluctant to leave her car. She drove around a several-block radius but there was no sign of Quinn and no sign of any motorcycles, either. Deciding it was futile to remain in the area — Quinn might well have chosen the phone at random — she left.

Feeling her hands shake on the steering wheel, she was reminded she'd skipped lunch and hadn't eaten anything since morning except the cake and coffee at the nursery party. Her blood sugar could use a good junk food fix, she rationalized. Stopping at McDonald's, she ordered a cheeseburger and chocolate shake to go.

Now what, she asked herself as she munched the burger. Where was Quinn likely to be?

Xenara?

It was Friday night so Vada would be having her session upstairs. Quinn probably wouldn't bother Vada. But how about downstairs, how about the blue-lit path? As Helena pondered, she automatically made the turns that would lead to the pyramid. When she reached Xenara, darkness was invading the blue of evening. She was startled to find the parking lot empty. Surely a few people should be here by now.

Getting out of the car, she hurried to the blue doors where a posted sign said, without explanation, that sessions were cancelled until further notice. She went back to the car and finished her food, wondering if her confrontations with Vada and Peter had anything to do with it. While she was eating, several cars pulled into the lot but left as soon as their occupants read the notice.

Because she couldn't think of any place else to go, Helena remained where she was until it occurred to her that if Quinn did show up here he might recognize her car and zoom off. Or perhaps he'd already been by, seen the notice, and left.

Still, her gut feeling told her Quinn would come. Or was here already, hiding, waiting for her to leave. Making up her mind, she started the VW and left Xenara, finding a less obvious parking place along a side street a few blocks away.

Walking back, flashlight in hand, she searched for the alley that Mak had told her ran behind the row of oleanders lining Xenara's parking lot. Quinn would be likely to hide his motorcycle and the alley was the logical place. She found the alley but no motorcycle. Either it wasn't there or Quinn was a better hider than she was a finder. Switching off the light and easing herself between two of the tall oleander bushes, where she had a view of the lot and the pyramid's front door, Helena settled in to wait.

As time passed, fewer and fewer cars drove in and then out of the parking lot. She stared at the white building, trying to banish her memory of smelling smoke at the session where Vada claimed a trance was filled with fire and flames. She didn't believe in precognition. Even if Quinn came here he wouldn't necessarily try to burn down the pyramid.

Or would he?

Xenara was sure to be his focus. He'd found pleasure and then betrayal there. In his mind, the pyramid must represent his troubled relationship with his father. Given Quinn's penchant for setting fires, he might very well try to ease his anguish by destroying Xenara. And she'd bet he'd managed to get his hands on a key to unlock the pyramid's door.

She meant to stop him — not to save Xenara but to save Quinn!

Hidden among the oleanders, she couldn't see the night sky but she thought the moon had risen because the darkness, rather than deepening, had lessened slightly. In the distance a dog barked occasionally and a car passed now and then on the street alongside the parking lot, often with its radio blaring.

Was she wasting her time? Helena was half-convinced she'd figured Quinn all wrong when she smelled smoke. At first she thought it might be in her mind but the smell persisted and she tensed. Where was it coming from? The night was southern-California cool but certainly far from cold, making it unlikely someone would light fireplace logs.

Yet she'd heard no motorcycle noise, and no one had approached Xenara's double front doors since the last disappointed seeker had read the posted sign. Xenara's fire door — the one she'd escaped through — didn't have an outside handle, so there'd be no way to enter that way. If Quinn was inside, how had he gotten there?

Leaving her hiding place, Helena trotted across the parking lot toward the building, sniffing the air. Was the scent stronger? She couldn't be sure. She tried the double doors and found them locked. Circling the building, she discovered three fire doors, all impossible to enter. But now the smell of smoke was definitely heavier. Though she had no evidence to back her belief, she was positive Quinn was inside.

Should she call the fire department? She could be wrong about the fire but a false alarm wouldn't bother her. It was the thought of Quinn that held her back. What if he was caught on the scene of another fire? He was older now — he'd be jailed. She didn't want that to happen. But if she couldn't get inside Xenara herself, what else could she do?

Suddenly it occurred to her that Peter, since he'd tried to keep his connection with Xenara a secret, wouldn't have wanted to be seen going to or from the pyramid. Was it possible he'd had a secret underground passage-way built when the building was under construction? If so, where would the entrance be?

She turned and scanned the parking lot, noting that the faulty light hadn't been fixed. Was that end of the lot kept in shadow deliberately? It was worth a look.

In the dark far corner, the beam of her flashlight swept over the paved lot, then along the low bank leading to the oleanders. Her heart leaped when she saw a framed cement door, painted green to blend in with the ice plant covering the bank, and slanted to fit the slope. If she'd noticed it before, she might have assumed the door led into a storage room for garden tools — as perhaps it did. Holding her breath, she turned the green knob. The door opened.

There was no need for her flashlight — dim bulbs in wall sconces revealed cement steps going down and turning at almost a right angle toward Xenara. She stood hesitating at the top. Should she risk entering? But if she didn't — who'd save Quinn? Fran had died because she delayed coming to her sister's aid — she mustn't delay again and be too late to rescue Quinn.

Helena took a deep breath and descended the stairs, finding herself in a tunnel. Rather than a smoky smell, the passageway exuded a moldy dankness. Though she hurried, it seemed to take twice as long to cover the distance across the parking lot as when she was above ground.

Eventually the tunnel ended at a blue door. When she opened it, tendrils of smoke curled into the passageway. Fearing she might have to come back this way, she stepped into the lower level of the pyramid and closed the door behind her to keep the tunnel free of smoke.

'Damn blue lights,' she muttered. Between them and the smoke she could hardly see. 'Quinn!' she shouted. 'Quinn!'

He didn't answer but somewhere overhead a door slammed. Quinn? She advanced further into the blue-lit corridor, calling his name, until she approached the silver door the attendant had guarded. It was open, smoke drifting through to form haloes around the blue lights.

'Quinn, it's Helena,' she cried. 'Please answer me.'

There was no response. She drew in her breath to call again and doubled over in a spasm of smoke-induced coughing. Before she regained her breath, the silver door began to swing shut. Helena sprang forward. Too late. The lock clicked as she grasped the knob. She opened the tiny panel set into the door and, through a pall of smoke, caught a glimpse of Quinn's red hair before he disappeared from view.

Abandoning all hope of reaching him, she turned and fled back to the underground passage. As she raced through the tunnel, she assured herself that Quinn was safe — he'd have time to escape through the same fire door she'd used the week before.

Without warning the lights went off, leaving her in complete darkness. Before she could stop, she tripped and sprawled on the floor, the flashlight flying from her grasp. Getting to her knees, she felt frantically around for the flashlight but couldn't find it. Deciding she didn't dare waste time groping about, she rose and, with one hand against the wall for guidance, stumbled on as rapidly as she could.

The fire cut off the electricity, she told

herself. The lights weren't deliberately turned off, so nobody's waiting in the darkness ahead. Certainly not Quinn — he hasn't had time to reach the underground entrance.

But it wasn't Quinn she feared. Who knew about the secret entrance besides Quinn? His father. Helena shivered. She wouldn't like to meet Peter in the darkness of this tunnel. Or the anonymous letter-writer, either. Despite knowing she must escape quickly, her steps slowed and she paused to listen for the slightest noise ahead.

She heard an unmistakable sound — the scrape of a shoe on cement — and her breath caught. She couldn't retreat when the only escape lay ahead!

The darkness, while frightening, was in her favor — whoever approached couldn't see her any more than she could see him. But almost certainly he'd heard her fall and knew someone was in the passageway. Since she hadn't left the VW in the lot, he couldn't know who she was — why didn't he call and ask who was there? She didn't dare demand to know who he was — it might be dangerous to reveal her identity.

No matter what, she had to get out of this tunnel. Cautiously she edged forward, trying to make as little noise as possible.

A roar seared her ears, jerking her to a halt.

Had something in the pyramid exploded? A blast of hot air and smoke rushed along the tunnel, enveloping her. She screamed in fright, certain the passageway was ready to collapse around her! Intent on nothing but escape, she plunged ahead through the darkness, her heart pounding in terror.

'Helena!' Mak shouted from somewhere in front of her. The beam of his flashlight blinded her, then shifted to light her way.

Mak had come to her rescue! She all but collapsed in relief.

He rushed to her side and together they hurried from the tunnel. When Helena stepped into the open air, she found it almost as smoky as the inside of the tunnel. Sirens howled, heralding the arrival of fire equipment. As Mak urged her into his Jag, she saw flames leaping from the top of Xenara's pyramid.

'Quinn?' she asked. 'Did you see him? Did he escape?'

'I don't know. No one came out of that damn tunnel except you.'

That didn't mean Quinn wasn't safe, she assured herself.

When Mak pulled away from the parking lot, a policeman jumped from a squad car and waved him down. Mak showed him a card from his wallet, saying, 'I'm trying to get my car out of the way, okay?'

The policeman studied the card, glanced at Mak's other credentials, then said, 'You can park a couple blocks down the street for now — I'll talk to you in a few minutes,' and stood aside to let him pass.

It was hours — and scores of questions — later before they reached Helena's apartment, driving separate cars. Mak waited for her by the steps. She climbed them, entered, and sank onto the couch in a daze.

'At least you left me a message this time,' he said, sitting beside her and putting an arm around her. 'Vague as your message was, I figured Xenara was the best bet to find Quinn — and you.'

She leaned her head on his shoulder. 'Quinn was trapped inside, wasn't he?'

Mak sighed. 'After the cops found his hidden motorcycle, I lost hope. But we won't know for sure until the firemen have the chance to go through the ruins.'

'He stopped me from reaching him — he didn't want to be saved.' Her voice broke on the last word and tears blurred her eyes.

'He took the ultimate revenge on his old man — suicide.'

'Quinn was too young to die,' she sobbed.

Mak cuddled her against him, soothing her, until her weeping diminished. 'Have you any idea how you look?' he asked.

A glance at her soot-and grime-streaked hands told her the rest of her must be equally dirty. 'I need a shower,' she murmured.

'Good idea. So do I.' He rose and pulled her to her feet. 'Do we make it separate, or — ?'

There was no question in her mind, no hesitation. Mak was her rock, her safe harbor. But he was more than that — she needed Mak in every way a woman needed a man and she needed him *now*. Why waste time?

''Or' sounds pretty good to me,' she told him, taking his hand and leading him to her bedroom.

Once actually in the bedroom, though, she turned strangely shy and escaped into the bathroom where she shut the door to undress in private.

Mak stared at the closed door for a long moment. He'd swear she'd given him an unequivocal yes — was this a game? He hadn't pegged Helena as a game-player. Shrugging, he shucked off his clothes, strode to the door, knocked, and announced firmly, 'Coming in.'

The door wasn't locked. Water was running and Helena, he saw through the frosted glass, was already in the shower. Sliding the door open, he stepped in, too. The shower in the other bathroom was more spacious, while this one, because it was in a bathtub, really wasn't roomy enough for both of them — unless showering was all they had in mind. As far as he was concerned, it sure as hell wasn't.

'You're hogging the soap,' he announced.

'I'm dirtier than you are.'

'Then you need help. Allow me.' He eased the bar from her grasp and pulled her against him, his front to her back. He slathered soap over her breasts and on down, savoring the feel of her under his hands.

Setting the bar in its niche, he caressed her slippery breasts, feeling the nipples rise under his fingers. He pulled her closer, pressing himself against the lush curve of her bottom while his hands traveled down to the apex of her thighs to touch the sweet softness there.

'Umm,' she murmured and turned in his arms to face him.

Water sluiced down on them as he kissed her, her lips wet and pliant under his, her mouth hot and seductive. She felt so soft and warm and he'd waited so long to hold her like this that he realized if he didn't stop, they'd wind up making love in the damn bathtub! He'd want her anywhere but a bathtub wasn't his choice for their first time.

He raised his head. 'If you're not clean enough by now,' he said huskily, 'I can always lick the rest of the dirt off.'

Desire flared deep in her blue-green eyes, setting off a chain reaction inside him that he feared for a moment would be his undoing. Pulling away from her, he shut off the water and slid open the door. 'Time to dry off,' he announced. 'And no fair hiding.'

He watched her openly as she toweled herself, recalling the first time he'd seen her, with those small and perfect, uptilted breasts covered by a tee shirt, the luscious curve of her hips molded by jeans. The brief surge of lust he'd felt then was nothing compared to the driving need consuming him now.

'You're beautiful,' he told her, watching her blush. For all her anatomical knowledge and sophisticated veneer, she was shy in front of him and this pleased and aroused him at the same time.

Since it was impossible to hide his arousal, he made no effort to and her sidelong glances amused him. Shy or not, she was checking him over thoroughly.

'See anything you like?' he asked.

She raised her chin. 'I don't know yet.'

He had to touch her — he couldn't wait any longer. 'Let's find out,' he drawled, hearing the rasp of passion in his voice as he scooped her up into his arms.

Striding into the bedroom, he yanked down the covers, eased her onto the bed and stretched out next to her. He wanted so many things at the same time — to touch her, to kiss her everywhere, to feel her come alive under his caresses, to experience the velvety warmth of her around him as he thrust inside her. He yearned to make love to her slowly and languorously but he knew his need was too great for him to manage prolonged lovemaking, not this first time.

He reached for her, pulling her close, his kiss deep and urgent.

Helena molded herself to Mak's body, the feel of his arousal pressing against her, hot and demanding, triggering an answering rush of throbbing heat within her. She wanted to confess her need to him but when his lips trailed to her breast all she could do was moan in pleasure and bury her hands in his hair to hold him to her.

'You taste good,' he murmured. 'You taste like more.'

'Mak,' she whispered. 'I want more. Now.' Slipping her hand between them she touched him.

He groaned and shuddered, lifting her hand away and turning her onto her back. He eased his knee between her thighs and she opened to him. Rising above her, he thrust into her, transfixing her with such acute pleasure she cried out, writhing against him, unleashing passion she didn't know she possessed.

He matched her rhythm — wild, fast, and passionate — until they plunged into the magic burst of release together.

He held her afterwards in the temporary peacefulness of satiation. 'You don't know what you do to me,' he said into her ear. 'I even forgot to ask if you were protected.'

'No need to ask,' she murmured. Her fingers traced one of the scars crisscrossing his abdomen. 'Ever going to tell me every gory detail about these?'

'Ugly, aren't they?'

'Everything about you turns me on,' she confessed. 'Scars and all.'

'Is that some kind of fetish peculiar to doctors?'

She bit him on the neck and they mock-wrestled for a few moments until she wound up lying on top of him.

'If you think you're getting rid of me tonight,' he murmured, 'you're badly mistaken. We've got a lot of loving to catch up on.'

'Oh?'

'In fact, one night won't do it. God knows how long it'll take. Maybe years.'

Her heart leaped with joy with the assurance that Mak felt as she did and wanted a long-term commitment. Not marriage. She wasn't ready to marry again and she suspected he wasn't either.

'No sense fooling around,' he added, 'we may as well get started right away.'

She lifted her head off his chest to kiss him in agreement when the phone rang.

Mak cursed and held onto her when she tried to roll away to answer it. 'Forget the phone,' he muttered.

'I'd like to but I can't.'

He sighed and let her go.

'Dr. Moore.'

'This is Mrs. Lipswitz at Sea Mist Manor,' a woman's voice said. 'Dr. Flanagan asked me to call you and ask you to come over right away.'

'Laura!' Helena cried, a chill seeping through her. 'What's the matter with her?'

'Doctor's with her now — he thinks she should be transferred to an acute hospital.'

'I'll be right there.'

By the time she slid from the bed and grabbed her clothes, Mak was on his feet and half-dressed. 'I'm going with you,' he said. 'What's wrong with Laura?'

She told him all she knew and didn't object when he insisted on taking the Jag. Her concern for her daughter had left her so shaken she wondered if she *could* drive. What had happened to Laura? She felt swamped with guilt. She hadn't even called to see how Laura was doing since her daughter's trip to camp.

When they arrived at Sea Mist, she and Mak followed Mrs. Lipswitz to a small room near the front entrance. 'This is where we isolate our sick children,' she said as they went in.

Isolate? Helena wondered if Laura had something contagious.

Dr. Flanagan was bending over the bed when Helena entered. Hurrying to his side, she gazed down at a Laura she hardly recognized. Her daughter's eyes were rolled up and she jerked and twitched, caught in the throes of a grand mal seizure.

'She's quieted down some,' Dr. Flanagan said, 'but I'm sure you'll agree she needs to be in an acute unit. We don't have the facilities to treat her here.'

Helena asked what medication he'd given Laura to control the convulsions. He told her and went on to describe how her daughter's illness began.

'She began convulsing about forty-five minutes ago, as far as we know. Bed checks are done every hour. When Mrs. Lipswitz came into Laura's room, she found her having a seizure and called me immediately because she knew Laura wasn't an epileptic. By the time I arrived the seizure was over, but when I started to examine Laura, she had this second episode — now about over, I'd say.'

Watching her daughter anxiously, Helena saw the jerking diminish and realized thankfully that he was right. What could be causing the convulsions? Possibilities crowded into her mind, all of them frightening.

'I'll call an ambulance, if you like,' he said. 'You'll be taking her to Harper Hills?'

She nodded. 'Please.'

Helena insisted on riding in the back of the ambulance with her daughter, pulling her rank as a doctor to get her way. Mak followed them in the Jag and was waiting in the ER when they rolled Laura in on the gurney.

'Would you call George Wittenburg for me?' Helena asked Mak as she passed. 'The ER nurse will get the number for you. Tell him what's happened and say I'd like him to see Laura as soon as possible.'

To Helena, as she waited for Laura to be placed in an exam cubicle, everything seemed to happen in slow motion. Her world had been reduced to her daughter's wan face and thin, fragile body.

I *knew* something was wrong with her, she

thought unhappily. Even Mak noticed she wasn't herself. Why couldn't I find the trouble? Why didn't I look harder? Do more tests? Spend more time with her?

By the time George arrived, Helena had pulled herself together enough to examine her daughter and do a spinal tap.

'Laura's spinal fluid pressure's elevated,' she told him. 'I sent a specimen to the lab for testing and a culture and sensitivity. I sent a blood specimen, too. Her temperature's only slightly elevated. She hasn't convulsed again but her neck's stiff. My tentative diagnosis is meningitis.'

George subjected her to a probing gaze. 'You look ready to fall over,' he told her. 'Find this Maklin who called me and have him get you some coffee. Then sit down and drink it while I examine Laura. That's an order.'

Helena left Laura's side reluctantly. She huddled on a plastic couch beside Mak in the waiting room, taking sips of her coffee only when he insisted.

'My own daughter,' she said to him. 'I've neglected her.'

'Nonsense! You're wallowing in guilt, that's all. I know how you've worried over Laura and how you've tried to be with her as much as possible so don't talk to me about neglect.

Whatever's wrong with her obviously didn't come to a head until now so how could you discover what it was? Come on, drink your coffee. It's going to be a long night.'

'I should have tried harder.'

'You did what you could — that's all any human being can do.'

She looked at him, tears welling in her eyes. 'I didn't save Quinn, either. There must have been some way to reach him. Why didn't I — ?'

'Helena, shut up,' Mak ordered. 'As a doctor, you must know people bent on suicide can't be stopped. And Laura has a good chance to get well. You've told me often enough that Wittenburg is the best pediatrician in the state.'

'But I should have — '

He stopped her by leaning over and kissing her, his lips gentle but firm — and infinitely comforting. She sighed and leaned against him, temporarily allowing herself to relax.

'You're not alone in this,' he murmured. 'I'm here whenever you need me.'

By the time George came to get her, Mak had coaxed her to down the entire cup of coffee. As the three of them walked back to Laura's cubicle, Helena, though still apprehensive, had rid herself of the heavy weight of depression and guilt. She couldn't afford to waste energy on bemoaning 'what should have been' when she needed all her strength to deal with what was ahead.

'I'm admitting Laura to peds,' George said. 'Temporarily it'll be the CD unit because, as you diagnosed, she has meningitis.' He glanced from Helena to Mak and back. 'Subacute, from all I can determine.' He paused again and took a deep breath. 'I'm calling Zel Markowicz for a neuro consult.' He laid a hand on Helena's shoulder. 'I suspect the cause of the meningitis is a cranial neoplasm.'

'A neoplasm?' Mak echoed, obviously not understanding.

'A tumor,' George told him. 'A brain tumor.'

19

George arranged with Admitting to put Laura in a two-bed room in CD. Helena spent what was left of the night dozing uneasily on the unoccupied bed, getting up often to make certain Laura wasn't convulsing.

Mak arrived before seven with a change of clothes for her and her toiletries. He glanced at Laura and asked in a low voice, 'Any change?'

Helena shook her head. Laura's eyes remained closed — she was either in a drug-induced sleep from the anti-convulsive medication or she'd slipped into a coma.

'She'll be going down for a CAT scan to locate the tumor as soon as the technicians get here,' Helena said. 'It's Saturday, but they're coming over as a favor to George.' She felt as though a stranger were talking — not Laura's mother, not even Dr. Moore — a total stranger, emotionally removed from the room and from the pale child lying so still in a bed too big for her.

'He's positive she does have a tumor, then.'

'After seeing the results of the test of the spinal fluid, yes.'

Mak put his arm around her. 'I'll stay with her while you go get some breakfast.'

'I couldn't eat.'

'You have to and you know it. What good will you be to Laura if you collapse from — if I've got the words right — low blood sugar?'

'Maybe toast and coffee,' she said reluctantly. 'But not now.'

'I'll bring it to you,' he insisted.

The door had scarcely swung shut behind Mak when Idalia pushed it open.

'Oh, Lord, I'm sorry about Laura,' she said, coming to the bedside. 'But why did you bring her to Harper Hills?'

Helena stared at her. 'Where else would I take her?'

'Just don't leave her alone, you hear? Or with anyone else, unless it's me. I can't be much help while I'm working but I'll run home after I get off duty and come back around seven or so to spell you for a couple hours, okay?'

'I can't ask you to — '

'You didn't ask, I offered.' She put an arm around Helena's shoulders and gave her a quick hug. 'So don't argue. Right now I have to listen to report but I'll come in again as soon as I get the chance.'

After Idalia left, Helena's tired mind struggled with what the nurse had said about not bringing Laura to Harper Hills. Idalia had been reluctant to have Kyesha admitted here. Because of the sudden deaths? Probably. She ought to corner Idalia and force her to tell her everything she knew. Most likely, though, Idalia's source would be the grapevine and the information nothing but rumors. In any case, with Laura's grave diagnosis confronting her, nothing else seemed to matter.

The day passed in a blur of faces — Zel Markowicz, George, Carin, Idalia, other nurses, various paramedical technicians, and Mak, always Mak. Late in the afternoon Tyrone Rand, Chief of Staff and a neurosurgeon of note, came in. She knew Zel had contacted Dr. Rand by ship-to-shore phone — he'd been deep-sea fishing off a private yacht. As he talked to her, he shed his God-on-the-mountain image, sounding surprisingly human.

'I've seen the CAT scan and the MRI printout on Laura,' he said, 'and I agree with George and Zel. Your daughter needs immediate surgery to remove the tumor before she develops irreversible symptoms. As you know, paralysis is often permanent once the nerve fibers are destroyed.'

Helena nodded.

'You want me to go ahead, then?' he asked.

'Please. I'm grateful you've made yourself available.'

'Zel will scrub with me.' He smiled at her. 'Zel and I make a pretty fair team, Helena, and we'll do our best with Laura.'

She knew she couldn't find a more talented pair of neurosurgeons in the state — perhaps the entire West Coast. She wanted to say so but all that came out was, 'Thank you.'

Before he left, Dr. Rand spent some minutes talking in a low tone to Mak at the door but Helena was too tired and spent to wonder why.

Two hours later, Laura was wheeled to the OR. Knowing she couldn't bear to watch the operation, Helena remained on Three North. Mak urged her to come with him to the cafeteria but she shook her head.

'I can't face that food.'

'Then how about me going out and getting you one of those horribly healthy salads you're so fond of — you know, loaded with alfalfa sprouts?'

She wasn't hungry but to make him feel better she agreed she might try something like that. 'While you're out,' she said, 'would you mind stopping at Sea Mist and picking up Laura's alligator. I want her to have something familiar when she wakes up.'

'No problem.'

Left alone, her anxiety mounted until she decided she had to find something to occupy her until Laura's operation was over or she'd be a basket case. But what? Then she remembered she'd never gotten around to looking at those nine charts Mak had asked her to review. Medical records would be locked but doctors had access to the key — why not go and look at those charts now?

'There was a man here asking for you,' the relief evening charge nurse told her as she passed the nurses' station. 'I told him you couldn't be disturbed. He seemed sort of upset.'

Helena paused. 'Did he leave a name?'

The nurse shook her head.

As she left the unit, Helena thought about who he might be but, unable to come up with a possibility by the time the elevator reached the basement of the old unit, shrugged and dismissed it.

Why they had to put medical records on the same floor with the morgue, she'd never understood. This wasn't the first hospital she'd worked in arranged that way and it probably wouldn't be the last. For convenience, old records of patients currently in Harper Hills were stored on the first floor but not charts of discharged and deceased patients.

Once she'd let herself into the records department, the door shut and automatically locked behind her. Helena dug into her bag for Mak's list. She noticed the case numbers were written by the names, saving her the trouble of looking them up because the charts were filed numerically.

She searched for and pulled them one by one, stacking the folders on a work table — eight in all because Baby Eddie's hadn't filtered down yet. Because she had to begin somewhere, she decided to start with diagnoses and the patients' status at the time of death. As she opened the top chart, her fatigue seemed to vanish.

Number one, two months old at the time of death, had a septic meningitis caused by an exposed *spina bifida*, a defective closure of the vertebral column. If the infant had lived, he'd have had permanent paraplegia, paralysis of both legs.

Number two, ten years old when he died, was in a coma from cerebral trauma following an auto accident. If he'd come out of the coma, as he'd shown signs of doing, he'd have had residual brain damage.

Number three, a newborn with *osteogenesis imperfecta congenita*, abnormal fragility of bone, had died suddenly the night before she was to go home. Though she'd had several fractured bones from the delivery, she'd done fairly well otherwise. If she'd lived, she'd have had to cope with numerous broken bones all her life — even changing her diaper could cause a fracture — and would probably have become dwarfed and deformed.

Number four, a three-year-old with measles encephalitis, had been in critical condition for much of his hospital stay. He'd suffered numerous convulsions and, though he'd survived and was improving at the time of his death, a mental deficit seemed likely because of the severity of brain inflammation.

Number five, a two-year-old admitted for evaluation for surgery, was a lye poisoning case whose esophagus had been literally destroyed by the caustic and whose lips and tongue were also severely damaged. George had noted that she'd been a very pretty little girl before this happened. The surgeons, while agreeing their repairs would help, hadn't expected to return the child to normal appearance or normal ability to take in food. She'd died the night before surgery.

Number six, Fran's patient, a newborn infant with a genetic defect called Cat-Eye Syndrome or Partial Trisomy 22, must have been a pitiful sight with all her facial peculiarities. Though it wouldn't be obvious until she was older, she was also profoundly mentally retarded. Nevertheless, she'd done well and her death was unexpected.

Number seven was Petey, the two-year-old with Western Equine Encephalitis who should have recovered — perhaps with no serious aftereffects. No one could predict with any certainty the long-term effects of severe encephalitis.

Number eight was Kezia, the six-month-old who'd died suddenly just as Helena had felt she was beginning to recover from her severe case of meningitis. Would her partial paralysis have cleared up if she'd recovered? Perhaps not. Would she have had a mental deficit? Maybe.

And number nine would be Baby Eddie, the two-month-old with the congenital heart problem whose eventual prognosis — if he'd lived — was not sunny.

Helena stared at her scribbled notes. What did these nine children have in common, if anything? She pondered for long moments before glancing at her watch. Over an hour had passed. Her stomach tightened. Was Laura's operation over yet?

Hurriedly she stacked the charts in the to-be-filed box and hurried to the door, releasing the lock. As she opened the door, she switched off the light. She was half-way through the opening when hands grasped her shoulders and shoved hard. She fell backwards into the record room, her bag flying from her grip. Her attacker pushed in after her.

He flung himself on top of her before she could scramble away and the door swung shut, leaving the room in darkness except for the square of light slanting through the high window in the door.

'You bitch!' he snarled. 'You're gonna get yours.'

His weight on her legs prevented her from kneeing him. When she tried to claw at his face, he cursed and grasped her wrists, holding them trapped in one hand while he tore at her clothes with his other.

He means to rape me, she thought in horror as she struggled unsuccessfully. With no weapon at hand and no way to reach one if it was, she was helpless. Gathering her breath she screamed, loud and long.

He struck her hard across the face, snapping her head to one side. 'Shut up, bitch! You're gonna get what you deserve and if you yell again I'll hurt you good.'

The door was closed, locked so no one could get in from the outside even if they did hear her calling for help. Screaming again wasn't smart. That didn't mean she had to give up.

It wasn't true she didn't have any weapon — she had her teeth. Raising her head, she found her face against his ear. Opening her mouth she bit him as hard as she could, feeling her teeth come together through the cartilage of his ear.

He screamed and reared back, letting her go. She tore free, scrambling to her feet, pulling down her skirt, and diving behind the desk.

'Damn you, I'm gonna kill you!' he howled, lunging after her.

Now what? He was between her and the door. Did he have a knife? A gun? She couldn't die — who'd take care of Laura? As she tried desperately to think of a way to escape, light suddenly filled the room as the door opened. Then the overhead light clicked on.

'Freeze, you bastard, or you're dead meat,' Mak snarled.

★　★　★

Later, sitting on the second bed in Laura's room on Three West — Laura was still in the OR — Mak stood over her while she picked at the immense salad he'd brought, her fingers trembling on the fork.

'When you finish half I'll tell you all the nasty details,' he promised.

'Half? This could feed three people and still have some left over. Besides, I'm still too shaky.'

'Want me to feed you?'

She scowled. 'You're supposed to coddle victims, not nag.'

'You're only a near-victim. Eat. Then I'll coddle.'

Helena stabbed into a green chunk and looked at it suspiciously. 'Avocado? Full of cholesterol.'

'You like avocado. Forget the cholesterol.'

After she downed a few bites, she found to her amazement that she was starved and finished the entire salad plus the two small slices of seven-grain bread that went with it.

Mak swung the overbed table away and sat next to her, putting his arm around her shoulders. 'This is my in-public coddle,' he said, pulling her closer.

She sighed and leaned against him, some of the tension ebbing away.

'The guy is a real nutcase,' Mak said. 'I mean *real*. He's one of the Silver Shrink's patients — or so he claims — and a fervent believer in Xenara. He told the cops he came after you because you destroyed Xenara.'

' 'The spirits told me she was evil and I warned her to stop but she wouldn't listen', he said, so I figure he's our threatening-letter writer. He's been searching for you ever since the fire gutted Xenara, discovered you were at the hospital, and has been waiting his chance. If I was sure by 'spirits' he meant Herron, I'd go after the bastard and pound the truth out of him.'

Helena shuddered. 'The evening nurse told me a man asked about me.'

'He must have followed you down to medical records.'

'He couldn't get in because the door locks automatically,' she added. 'He had to wait until I left. Come to think of it — how did you get in?'

'You must have dropped your bag — the strap caught in the door so it didn't close all the way and lock. I got tired of waiting for you to come back so I went looking for you. By chance, one of the nurses noticed you took the elevator to the basement. I was getting off there when I heard you scream.' He pressed his lips to her temple. 'Promise me you won't go anywhere again without telling me. I couldn't — ' his words trailed off.

'When I saw you standing in the doorway with a gun, I thought I must be dreaming,' she said. 'I didn't know you carried a gun.'

'On a case like the one I'm working on, I don't. But I didn't care for the tone of that threatening letter so when I was in LA yesterday I dropped by the house and picked up my trusty thirty-eight. I had locked it in the glove compartment of the Jag but I don't like to leave a gun in the car overnight, so I shifted it to my pocket when I came in with your salad — a damn lucky thing. That bastard carried a knife.'

Helena shuddered. Wanting to banish the memory of being trapped in the record room, she changed the subject.

'What about Quinn? Have you heard anything?'

Mak sighed. 'They found what was left of him.'

'Oh, Mak, everything looks so dark.'

'Laura's going to pull through,' he assured her. 'As for Quinn — he refused to let us help him. We did what we could.' After a moment, he said, 'I blame myself for asking you to look up those medical records. But I never figured you'd do it on a Saturday evening when the damn basement is deserted.'

Helena, reminded of what she'd found in the nine charts, eased away from him, slid off the bed, retrieved her notes from her bag, and scanned them.

'I think there's one tenuous link among the deaths,' she said finally, looking up to see Mak stretched full length on the bed, propped up on one elbow.

'Come here and tell me,' he suggested.

She sat on the bed, propping herself against him, using him for a back rest. 'The dead children were all either abnormal from birth or might have become abnormal as a result of an illness or injury.'

'Define 'abnormal'.'

'Retarded or deficient in some way, physical or mental or both.' Using the notes, she listed what those ways were, case by case.

'You've found the link, all right,' Mak said when she finished. 'Euthanasia. Someone playing God by finishing off what he or she considers defective. Any clues how it was done?'

A yawn caught Helena by surprise as she shook her head.

'You need sleep,' he said, getting off the bed. 'Now.'

'Laura — '

'I'll wake you, I promise, as soon as you're needed.'

Helena, unable to recall ever feeling so exhausted, didn't argue. Easing herself down on the bed, she closed her eyes.

The next she knew, Idalia was bending over

her. 'They're wheeling Laura back in,' she said.

Helena sat up, her head whirling. As she blinked to clear her vision, she saw two Recovery Room techs rolling Laura's bed into the room.

'I stayed with her in the Recovery Room,' Idalia said, 'so you could catnap. She's doing fine.'

Glancing at her watch as she got up, Helena saw it was almost midnight. 'Thanks, but don't you have to work tomorrow?'

Idalia smiled. 'I've come to work with less sleep than I'll get tonight.' She gave Helena a hug. 'I'm going now — remember what I said, okay?'

Helena nodded, still feeling dazed from insufficient sleep. 'You're a wonderful friend,' she told Idalia. 'Say hello to Kyesha for me.'

'She named that pink elephant after you.'

'Helena?'

Idalia shook her head. 'No, its name is Dr.Moore. She says it takes care of her other stuffed animals so they don't get sick. Wouldn't it be something if she really did go to medical school?'

'Why shouldn't she?'

'No reason, I guess.' Idalia smiled. 'Well, I guess I ought to be getting back to the future Dr.Kyesha Davin. Good night, Helena.' As she left, Idalia stopped to look down at Laura for a moment and her smile faded. Biting her lip, she eased through the door.

Alone with her daughter, Helena put down the side rail and leaned over her, touching Laura's cheek lightly. Bandages covered her head and Helena knew that underneath the dark hair was cropped short and shaved completely over the operative area.

'I love you,' she murmured. 'Mama's here and she loves you, no matter what.'

Laura's eyelids fluttered but remained closed.

The door swung open and Mak came in. Joining her at the bedside he looked down at Laura. 'She okay?' he whispered. At Helena's nod, he took her arm and led her over by the window.

'I've been in the lobby talking to Vada Rogers,' he said in a low tone.

Helena stared at him. 'Vada!'

He put a finger to his lips, glancing over his shoulder at Laura's bed. 'Vada left a message with the night operator that she absolutely had to get in touch with you and so the operator called Three North and that's how I got involved. Oddly enough, this has nothing to do with Quinn or Xenara.'

'I don't care to talk to her,' Helena said.

'Too bad, because I brought her with me.

She's waiting outside. She may be a fruitcake but in view of the problem at Harper Hills, I think you ought to hear what she has to say. I'll stay with Laura and call you if she so much as blinks.'

Helena hesitated.

'Go on,' Mak urged. 'You have nothing to lose.'

Reluctantly, feeling Vada was close to the last person she ever wanted to see again, Helena walked to the door.

Vada stood at the end of the corridor by the window, gazing out, her back to Helena. Begrudging each step, Helena joined her.

Without turning, Vada said, 'Mak told me what happened to you. I hope you'll believe I knew nothing about this man who attacked you. He was never one of *my* people. And I want to tell you I've dissolved my partnership with Peter Herron. I was aware it was wrong from the beginning but I couldn't resist him. Sometimes one's flesh is weaker than one's inner knowledge. If Peter deserves punishment, he's been hideously punished. If I deserve punishment, mine is yet to come.'

'Is this why you're here?' Helena asked coolly. 'to try to explain?'

'No. A vision brought me.' Vada turned and faced Helena, her green eyes shadowed. 'Try to open your mind, try to believe, because only you can interpret and understand what I saw. I am only the recorder, I merely report.' She took a deep breath. 'I saw nine babies lying in cribs in Harper Hills Hospital. This hospital. While I watched, snakes slithered into the cribs, crawling over the nine babies, coiling around them. Killing them. Then your face appeared and I knew the vision was a message for you. So I came to find you.'

Helena was jolted. *Nine*. The number had to be a coincidence. As well as the babies. The recurrent snake motif was unsettling. Far off in Peru, her mother had dreamed of snakes, and this was the second time Vada had mentioned them. She hated to attach any meaning to so-called visions but what Vada had said shook her to the marrow. Why would the woman make up such a preposterous story if she hadn't actually dreamed it.

'Thanks for letting me know,' she told Vada finally. 'I think you mean well.'

'I see truth,' Vada said sadly, 'but I can't control or choose what I see. It's more of a curse than a gift. Please take heed. I may not fully understand the meaning of my vision but I do know babies shouldn't die.' She thrust a card at Helena. 'In case you need to call me.'

Helena returned to Laura's room, troubled and uncertain. Was it possible she'd been wrong all these years and her mother right? Hard to believe. Or was it just that it was hard to admit she might have been mistaken?

She was over by the window telling Mak about Vada's disturbing vision when the door edged open and Carin Wittenburg's face appeared.

'All right to come in?' she asked in a hushed tone.

Surprise that George's wife would be here so late on a Saturday night kept Helena from responding but Carin slipped in anyway.

Telling Helena he'd be right back, Mak stepped out of the room.

'I came as soon as I heard,' Carin said, joining Helena by the window. 'How is your daughter?'

'She's stable,' Helena said. 'I haven't talked to either of the neurosurgeons yet to hear a prognosis.'

'How about her autism — will removing the tumor help that?'

Helena sighed. 'I'm afraid that problem predates the tumor. In any case, autism isn't caused by brain tumors.'

'What a shame for her to have to go through all this and still not be — ' the words trailed off. 'If there's anything I can do for you, just ask.' Carin's voice held genuine concern. 'If you need to get away for a few minutes, I'd be glad to sit with your daughter.'

How kind people were, Helena thought — the other doctors, Idalia, Carin and, above all, Mak.

'That's thoughtful of you, Carin,' she said, 'and I'll remember your offer. Tonight, though, I don't want to leave her.'

George pushed open the door. 'There you are,' he said when he saw Carin. 'I wondered where you'd gone to.' He stepped aside to let Mak come in and then walked over to gaze down at Laura. Mak, balancing two cups of coffee, set them on the overbed table at the foot of the second bed. George followed him.

'At this point Laura's prognosis looks good,' George said, glancing at Helena. 'Ty and Zel both think they got it all. No one's completely positive yet, but there's a distinct possibility the tumor wasn't malignant.'

Not malignant? Such intense joy flooded through Helena she thought her knees would give way and she had to hold to the side rail for support. She looked at Mak, feeling her face stretch into an idiotic grin.

'George, thank you. Thank you for — ' Helena's voice broke and she couldn't go on. Mak moved to put an arm around her shoulders.

George nodded at her. 'Time for us to go

home to bed,' he told his wife.

After they left, Helena turned to Mak, burying her face in his chest as he wrapped his arms around her. At the moment she couldn't even regret, as Carin had, that the tumor's removal wouldn't magically change Laura into a completely normal child. Her daughter would live and that was more than enough to be grateful for.

When she recovered enough to attend to Laura again, she saw that Mak had placed the green alligator on a pillow at the foot of the bed so Laura would be able to see it as soon as she opened her eyes.

'You ought to go home and get some sleep,' she told him in a low tone.

'No way. I intend to stay right here and keep an eye on mother and daughter for the rest of the night. Just in case there are any more Xenara crazies running around.' He opened the door and peered into the corridor. 'At least the foot traffic's down for the — '

The loudspeaker by the nurses' desk at the end of the CD unit overrode his voice. 'Code E. All personnel, Code E.'

'What the hell's that mean?' he asked, turning to look at Helena.

'It's a major emergency,' she said, shifting her shoulders uneasily. 'Usually it means the arrival of a lot of multiple trauma cases in the ER at the same time, so they need extra doctors and nurses.'

'Like from a pile-up on the freeway?'

'Could be.' She leaned over Laura. Her daughter was resting quietly, the IV running as ordered, her vital signs normal. God only knew what might be going on in the ER. The operator would be calling doctors at home but it would take time for them to get to the hospital. She was already there. She bit her lip and glanced at Mak.

'I know what's bugging you,' he said. 'Forget it. You don't have to rush to the ER — you're dead on your feet after all that's happened and there's Laura and — '

'I know.' She sighed. 'But if I go, my being there might make the difference between life and death for someone. Laura doesn't really nccd me hovering over her every second. You'll be here and the nurses will come in and check her every fifteen minutes if I tell them I'm leaving. I have to respond to that call for help, Mak. I couldn't live with myself if I didn't.'

Mak sighed. 'I suppose you'll be safe enough in the ER.'

20

In the ER, Helena skirted gurneys, avoided hurrying personnel, and dodged uniformed policemen while she looked for the nurse wearing the red triage triangle indicating the person who would decide who would be treated first.

When she found the man wearing the red triangle vest, he was bending over a child on a gurney. The child had a facial laceration and a splinted leg.

'I'm Dr. Moore,' she told him. 'What happened? Where do you want me?'

He glanced up at her. 'Freeway pile-up. Cubicle 3's next. She's unconscious — brain trauma — and pregnant with vaginal bleeding.'

Helena hurried to the cubicle where an LVN was taking the woman's blood pressure. 'Ninety over sixty,' she said. 'Dropping steadily.'

Helena reached under the woman's dress and felt her abdomen. Rigid. It didn't feel like a labor contraction. Quite possibly the trauma of the accident had caused the placenta to break away from its uterine attachment, flooding the uterus with blood.

'Do you have a name, age, anything on her?' she asked.

'Nothing.'

'She needs blood and a C-section stat,' Helena said. 'We can't delay. I'm going to wheel her up to maternity and get her into the section room. Any lab people available?'

'They were called.'

'Okay, I'll draw blood for a typing and cross-match, you run it to the lab and tell them to get four pints of matching blood to maternity for Jane Doe stat.'

To Helena's great relief, when she arrived on maternity one of the OB attending men, Nick Dow, was just finishing a delivery. While he examined Jane Doe, she told him what little she knew.

'You made the right diagnosis,' he said when he finished. 'Let's get her set up. I'll call my partner, but we can't wait — you'll have to scrub in until he gets here.'

Nick's partner, Dr. Linnett, reached the hospital in record time and Helena found herself monitoring the patient's vital signs at the head of the table in the anesthetist's spot instead of assisting with the section. She was relieved of that task when one of the anesthesiologists, summoned by the night nurse, hurried in. So she wound up with the pediatrician's job of taking the baby — premature, limp, blue, and not breathing.

The nursery nurse handed her an endotracheal tube and she inserted it. No sooner had she gotten it in the baby than Nick called, 'Here's Baby Number Two.'

Twins!

The nursery nurse brought over the second tiny premature newborn, easing her next to her sibling in the isolette, the incubator for preemies. This second one, though smaller than her twin brother, was reddish-pink and gave little mewing gasps. Helena and the nursery nurse worked over them both until finally the baby girl wailed thinly.

The boy never breathed on his own and eventually, faced with a flat heartline, Helena gave him up. By then the two obstetricians, standing in blood, were removing the woman's uterus. Helena gave them the bad news.

'There were two placentas,' Nick told her. 'The boy's was ripped loose from the trauma of the accident but the girl's was still attached — probably why she survived. The mother could use another pint of blood — she's damn near bled out.'

'I imagine the lab's still rushed; I'll go get one,' Helena offered, feeling it was safe to leave the girl twin with the nursery nurse.

Carrying the type and cross-match tags, she left the section room. As she passed the maternity nurses' station the night charge slammed down the phone.

'What's wrong with him?' she asked. 'Why doesn't he answer?'

'Who?' Helena asked while she waited for the elevator.

'The pharmacist. I know he's there because I talked to him forty-five minutes ago and he promised to get the ampicillin I need up here stat.'

'I'm going to the lab — I'll take a look in the pharmacy on my way,' Helena told her. 'If he's there I'll pick up the ampicillin — if it's ready.'

'Thanks, doctor. Things are really hectic tonight or I'd go myself. Why does disaster always strike on weekends?'

The elevator arrived and Helena got on.

The pharmacy, on the first floor, was down a short corridor from the lab and, after collecting the pint of blood, Helena hurried there. The counter was closed but the door was ajar and the lights were on inside. She pushed the door open wider and stepped into the room. Something crunched under her foot and she looked down.

Pills were strewn over the floor. Had something gone wrong? She saw no one.

'Hello?' she called. 'Is anyone here?'

There was no answer.

Alarmed by the combination of the spilled medicine and the unlocked door with nobody in the room — it was a cardinal rule always to keep the pharmacy locked — she advanced cautiously, stepping on more pills as she glanced down the shelved aisles. At the third aisle, she stopped abruptly.

'Oh my God,' she muttered, hurrying to where Reed Addison sprawled face down on the floor — the same way she found her sister! For a long moment she couldn't move, then she pulled herself together. Kneeling beside him, she immediately discovered that he wasn't breathing. Her stethoscope showed her he had no heartbeat. She thought of CPR and shook her head.

Reed was dead and she had no idea how long it had been since his heart stopped. By the time she called for help and then started CPR, if there was any result at all, the prolonged lack of oxygen to the brain would make Reed a vegetable.

She got to her feet, clutching the container of blood in her hand. Reminded how desperately the woman in the section room needed the blood, Helena hurried to the door, ran for the elevator, got off on maternity, thrust the blood at a passing nurse, and ordered her to take it to the section room.

Taking a deep breath, Helena grabbed for the phone and punched in the ER number. She got a response on the fourth ring.

'Dr. Moore,' she said. 'Are the police still around?'

'One's drinking coffee right here by the desk.'

'Let me talk to him.'

After she'd arranged to meet Sergeant Leonard at the pharmacy, Helena wondered if she'd done the right thing by contacting the police first. Should she have notified Dr. Rand, the chief of staff? She decided she'd better call him before she returned to the pharmacy.

It was after four in the morning before she got back to Laura's room. Relieved that her daughter's condition hadn't changed and that she was continuing to do well, Helena collapsed onto a chair near the window.

'You'll never believe what's happened,' she said to Mak. 'It started when I got to the ER. There'd been a two-car, one-van accident on the freeway — a bad one — and we got the survivors, every one of them with multiple trauma.' She went on to tell him about the C-section and how she'd gone to the pharmacy and found Reed dead.

After he listened to all she had to say, he shook his head. 'I have a hunch Addison's death isn't from anything so simple as a heart attack. There's this gut feeling that tells me his death is connected to our nine cases. How much are you willing to bet the post shows no cause of death other than cardiac arrest?'

Helena stared at him, realizing his words were no surprise. From the moment she'd seen Reed sprawled on the pill-strewn floor, she'd had an uncomfortable suspicion his death was neither natural nor a suicide.

'Fran's death wasn't natural either,' she said as much to herself as to Mak.

'I haven't forgotten your sister,' Mak assured her. 'If I'm right, we're faced with a killer who's murdered eleven times. I mean to nail him before he kills again.'

She nodded, still upset because of the baby boy she hadn't been able to save. And the pharmacist's death had brought back all the horror of finding Fran dead in the shower. She longed to have Mak wrap his arms around her and hold her — just hold her.

'Do you mind if I go talk to the cops and see if they've come up with anything?' Mak asked.

She knew he had to go, had to uncover anything he could that might lead to the killer, but she sighed inwardly, hating to give up her chance to be comforted. Concealing her distress, she waved a hand, saying, 'I'm okay. Go ahead.'

After he left, she moved to Laura's bed, rested her arms on the side rail, laid her head on her arms, and closed her eyes. Though she was mortally tired, the bloody C-section and Reed's sprawled body were so vividly fresh in her mind that she didn't really expect to fall asleep.

Helena floated, disoriented, in profound darkness. At first she thought she was alone but soon the hair on her nape prickled with the awareness that something else shared the darkness. Her apprehension mounted when she realized it wasn't another human but something alien.

In desperation, she tried to flee but found herself unable to move. Terror overwhelmed her when she understood that the alien creature was actually inside her. Slowly, slowly it coiled itself snake-like around her most vulnerable organ — her heart — and began to tighten its coils until her heart, trapped and squeezed, faltered, unable to beat. Paralyzed, she could do nothing but wait for the inevitable. Panic beat in her throat as the chill breath of death touched her . . .

Helena woke, moaning, and found herself

draped over Laura's side rail. Her head whirred dizzily and, with the dim realization she was about to faint, she pushed away from the rail, dropped into a chair and bent her head until it was down between her knees. What was the matter with her? She found her radial pulse and counted the beats. Fifty-six! Good God, her heart rate had never fallen that low. The snake squeezed my heart, she thought hazily. That's what's wrong.

No, that didn't make sense. What snake? Whatever was wrong, though, she needed a stimulant. Caffeine would do. She looked around but Mak wasn't in the room and she vaguely recalled him leaving. Knowing there'd be coffee in the nurses' lounge on Three North, she pulled herself to her feet, holding to the side rail until her lightheadedness eased enough to make it safe to move.

Laura's eyes opened briefly, focused on her, and closed again. All her daughter's vital signs registered normal. It was safe to leave her long enough to bring back a cup of coffee.

Helena walked slowly to the door and into the corridor, feeling if she tried to hurry, she'd collapse. Unnerved by her abnormal physiological reactions, she looked neither right nor left, focusing on making it to the lounge and getting the coffee. After she passed through the red doors onto peds, something flicked past to her left but she didn't turn her head — it took too much effort.

Reaching the lounge, she diluted the hot coffee with cold water so she could gulp down half a cup in a hurry. Refilling the cup, she started back to Laura's room. By the time she pushed through the red doors to CD, she was beginning to feel more like herself. It was then, without warning, that the snake dream uncoiled in her mind. She stopped abruptly.

She'd dreamed of a snake squeezing her heart — like the snakes Vada had seen coiling around and killing the nine babies. What could it mean? Did the dream have a meaning or was she overreacting?

Was it a coincidence that her heart rate had slowed alarmingly? God knows she'd been drinking enough coffee in the past ten hours to float a battleship. Her caffeine intake must be at an all-time high, yet as a result of the dream her heart had beat slower, not faster. Why? Just thinking about it disoriented her.

Could Vada help her?

She reached in her pocket and retrieved Vada's card. Glancing along the corridor, she saw the nurses' desk was deserted. Hurrying to the phone, she punched Vada's number, keeping an eye on Laura's door while sipping her coffee. Through the window beside the desk, she saw the grayness of early-morning mist.

'This is Vada,' a low, husky voice said. Before Helena could identify herself, Vada gasped. 'I see snakes twining around my phone,' she cried. 'Who are you?'

More shaken than ever, Helena gave her name.

'Be careful,' Vada warned. 'I sensed danger when I was at the hospital with you and now I feel an icy chill around me.'

Helena told her about the snake dream. 'What could it mean?'

'I can't tell you because I don't know the meaning of your dreams. Only you know. You might ask yourself what snakes mean to a doctor.'

Helena could come up with no answer to that question. The caduceus, the symbol of healing, was twined with snakes — but the snake she'd dreamed of was anything but healing.

'Be very careful,' Vada repeated before ending the call.

As Helena started to pull open Laura's door, she saw Jeff arrive on the CD unit. He hailed her and she waited for him.

'I bumped into George in the ER during the code call,' Jeff said, 'and he told me about your daughter. First I'd heard. Why didn't you call me. I'd have come immediately. George said Zel and Ty removed all the tumor — how's Laura doing?'

'Come in and see for yourself,' Helena said, preceding Jeff into the room.

'Oh my God!' she cried, staring in shocked disbelief at Laura's bed. The IV container, tubing, and equipment remained but Laura was gone. The green alligator stared down on an empty bed.

How could she be gone, Helena asked herself. I watched the door all the time I was on the phone with Vada and no one went in or out of the room — or of any room on CD.

But she hadn't been on CD all the time she was gone. There'd been those few minutes she was on peds, fetching coffee. Someone could have slipped in then — must have. Helena wrapped her arms around herself, shivering. No doctor or hospital employee would be taking Laura anywhere for a legitimate reason — not before seven in the morning and not without bringing the IV along. She couldn't believe her daughter had suddenly roused, climbed over the side rails, and disappeared. What had happened to Laura? Where was she?

Jeff pushed past her to look in the

bathroom. 'She's not there,' he said. Returning to the bed, he examined the IV tubing. 'It doesn't look like she left on her own — no kid wrenched this off. Whoever removed it knew exactly what they were doing.'

'Somebody's taken her!' Helena's voice shook. 'Vada warned me.'

'Vada! What's she have to do with it?'

Helena was too distraught to explain. 'Find Mak and tell him,' she begged. 'I think he's in the ER. Hurry!'

Without waiting to see what he did, she rushed from the room, ran down the corridor, looking in every room on the CD unit. She didn't find Laura. Bursting through the red doors onto peds, she saw Idalia getting off the elevator.

'Idalia,' she cried, 'Laura's missing! I can't find her.'

'Oh, Lord, no.' Idalia's voice rose, taking on the shrillness of hysteria. 'You never should have brought her here, not to Harper Hills. Didn't I say not to? Dear Lord, why didn't you listen?'

'What's going on?' George demanded, hurrying along the corridor. 'Idalia, stop that screaming!'

Idalia began to keen wordlessly. George shook her without stopping the high, piercing wail. Releasing her, he slapped her hard across the face, then yanked her against him, holding her close as she sobbed on his shoulder. He looked at Helena, eyebrows raised.

'Laura's not in her bed. Someone's taken her.' Helena spoke flatly. Much as she felt like screaming and crying, for her daughter's sake she had to stay calm.

'We'll search the hospital,' George said. 'Starting here.'

Vada's words came back to Helena. *An icy chill*. How could that pertain to Laura? She refused to believe it meant death. Laura was alive, she had to be!

While George alerted security, Helena began a methodical room-to-room search of Three North. As she passed the nurses' station, she heard Idalia, her composure restored, speaking to George in a low, urgent tone.

' . . . do something . . . ' was all she caught.

As they came to the reluctant conclusion Laura was nowhere on peds, Mak arrived with Jeff on his heels. Taking Helena's arm, Mak led her back to Laura's room.

'Tell me how it happened,' he said, listening to her explanation as he looked around the room and examined the bed.

'I should never have left her,' she moaned.

'It's as much my fault as yours,' he insisted.

423

'I should have stayed with you. But guilt trips won't help us find Laura. You've no idea who might have taken her? Or why?'

'Isn't it the — the killer?' she faltered. 'The one who killed the other children?'

'But why kidnap Laura? It doesn't fit the — ' He stopped abruptly, his eyes narrowing. 'Because of you, that's why. You'd be back too soon, you're a doctor and you'd see something was wrong with Laura and try to save her. Didn't you notice *anyone* on your trip to the nurses' lounge?'

She closed her eyes and tried to remember but nothing came to her. 'I guess I was concentrating too hard on just being able to get there.'

'You really felt that bad?' After she nodded, he asked, 'What kind of drug could cause your symptoms?'

Helena forced her mind to focus on Mak's question. 'There are several medications that slow the heart, if that's what you mean. But I didn't take any of them.'

'I don't know exactly what I mean — I'm searching for some kind of link. If the killer has Laura, it wouldn't make sense for him to try to leave with her — she must be somewhere in the hospital. Searching every room's too time-consuming, though we'll keep at it. Think, Helena, where's the most likely spot in Harper Hills to hide a child?'

It was Monday, she remembered, so all departments would be on normal schedules. Where would there be few or no people?

Jeff pushed the door open. 'Mak, Sergeant Leonard's on the phone.'

Helena followed Mak into the corridor, Jeff walking beside her.

'I'm going up to search the surgical units now,' he said. 'I'll keep you posted.'

She nodded, only half-hearing him, still trying to come up with an answer. Vada had warned her about snakes and cold. Snakes had no place in Harper Hills — how about cold?

Helena stopped, staring at the elevator doors that had just closed behind Jeff, horrorstruck by what had occurred to her. The morgue with its cold-storage vaults!

I've got to get there before it's too late, she thought frantically, rushing to the fire stairs rather than taking the time to wait for an elevator. Down one flight, two, three. Ground floor. Then the basement level.

She shoved open the heavy fire door and hurried along the underground corridor without meeting a single person. Not unusual, she realized, since none of the departments down here would open until eight or nine. But the loneliness of the empty corridor with its closed doors made her skin prickle, the more-so when she recalled the man who'd attacked her in the medical records room. That man had been captured, no need to fear him. But he wasn't the one who'd taken Laura!

Her steps faltered. Was the killer waiting behind one of the doors? Maybe she ought to retreat, call Mak, and wait for him to join her. The fear that Laura's life might depend on reaching her immediately drove Helena on.

Confronted at last by the morgue door, her heart sank when she realized it might be locked. She grabbed the knob but when it turned, she hesitated. If the killer *was* waiting, this is where he'd be. But that meant Laura would be here, too. She *had* to go in and protect her daughter.

Helena opened the door and flicked on the lights as she stepped into the room, finding herself in the morgue office. She walked through to the larger room beyond, her searching gaze probing every corner. She saw no one. The autopsy tables were empty. Pulses pounding, she hurried toward the cold-storage units.

There were six. The first one she pulled out was empty. The second rack held an adult male. The third was empty, as was the fourth. In the fifth she found what looked like a teenaged girl. She opened the sixth and last and saw a bandaged head. A child's head. Laura! She released her pent-up breath as she yanked the rack as far open as it would go.

Please let her be alive, Helena prayed as she reached for her daughter.

Finding Laura's skin cold to her touch, for a moment Helena despaired — but then she felt the faint throb of her daughter's carotid pulse under her fingers and knew her prayers had been answered. When she lifted her from the rack, Laura whimpered.

'You're safe with Mama,' Helena crooned, cuddling Laura in her arms. 'Mama's here, you're all right, everything's all right.'

But she was far from being sure what she said was true. She needed to examine her daughter thoroughly to make certain — not here, though, anywhere but here. She turned from the vaults and walked through the autopsy room. Before she reached the office, she heard the click of the doorknob turning. She froze as the door slowly swung open.

Shrinking back, her arms wrapping protectively around Laura, Helena first saw a pink jacket. A volunteer? Or was it a trick to fool her? Then she recognized Carin Wittenburg and all but collapsed in relief.

'My God,' she began, 'I thought you were — ' Helena's words trailed off as she noticed Carin's fixed smile and the odd glint in her light brown eyes. Come to think of it, what was Carin doing in the morgue?

A memory flicked through her mind with the speed of light — the flash of pink off to the left as she stumbled to the nurses' lounge on Three North for the coffee, leaving Laura alone.

Pink. Pink for volunteers. Carin? But hadn't George taken her home? No, George had answered the Code E; he hadn't gone home — so Carin would have been in the hospital when Laura was suddenly missing.

But why would Carin want to hurt Laura? What possible reason did she have? Though she couldn't come up with any motive, the false smile on Carin's face chilled her — something was terribly wrong.

'I'll take Laura,' Carin said, advancing, one arm outstretched, the other in the pocket of her pink jacket.

'No,' Helena whispered, backing away, glancing around frantically. She'd never give Laura to Carin.

Carin was between her and the door, making escape impossible. Burdened as she was, it was hopeless to try to overwhelm Carin but if she could lay Laura on one of the steel tables, she might be able to fight off the woman.

Without warning, Carin flung herself at them. Trying to hold Laura away so Carin couldn't grab her, Helena saw the large syringe and needle in Carin's hand. Too late. Before she could free one hand to shove Carin's arm away, Helena felt the needle pierce through her skirt into her thigh, felt the burn of injected fluid.

She kicked Carin and the needle pulled from her thigh, the syringe flying up and onto the floor. Quickly, Helena stomped on it, crushing the plastic barrel under her shoe. What in hell had Carin shot into her?

'You won't last long,' Carin told her. 'Fran didn't.'

Oh, God, what would happen to Laura, Helena thought desperately. She had to get away, had to find help. Her only hope was that Carin hadn't managed to get the full dose into her so she could stay on her feet long enough to escape with Laura.

Take Carin by surprise and shove her aside to reach the door? Her only chance. Helena edged to one side, hoping to trick Carin into believing she meant to retreat farther into the room, then she suddenly rushed toward the door.

Carin stepped in front of her and, as Helena's shoulder rammed the other woman, a wave of dizziness hit. Helena staggered, going down on her knees, losing her hold on Laura.

Carin scooped Laura up and backed away toward the door. 'No one can stop me,' she said. 'God protects me because I do His will. He doesn't want Laura to live — she'll die next!'

'No!' Helena cried, hearing her own voice only faintly. Her vision blurred but she heard the door slam shut with hideous finality.

She was alone in the morgue. Was she dying? She seemed to see a dark writhing in the fog that clouded her vision. Snakes, crawling toward her, toward her heart. Serpents to squeeze the life from her. Serpents. The word echoed in her mind.

Serpents to slow the heart. Reserpine! Rauwolfia serpentina. A drug given to lower blood pressure, among other things. An overdose would kill — and leave no trace.

She had to let Mak know. He'd search for her. Find her. She knew he would. But blackness already licked at the edge of her mind as the drug slowed her heart. If the dose was massive enough, soon she'd be in fibrillation. Then she'd die. Mak would be too late.

She must do something to tell him — but what? She lay on her side, unable to move, the shards of the broken syringe jabbing into her arm. Where was the needle? With tremendous effort she moved her hand, feeling for the needle. She didn't find it but her fingers clutched a sharp bit of plastic.

With what little strength she could muster, she jabbed the pointed end into her arm. When she felt blood dribble from the puncture, she smeared her finger in it and struggled to write, 'reserpine' on her white coat. Before she finished, the darkness coalesced and claimed her.

21

On Three North, Mak put down the phone and looked around for Helena. He didn't see her. Off to one side of the nurses' station, Idalia clutched George Wittenburg's arm, speaking in a low but urgent tone.

'Go after her!' she urged. 'It has to be her — who else can it be? I've kept quiet because I wasn't sure and because of you.'

The desperation in Idalia's voice alerted Mak. He'd lay odds this wasn't private; this had to do with Laura's abduction. He faced the pair. 'Who do you mean?' he demanded to know.

'I don't — ' George began.

Mak grabbed him by the lapels of his white coat. 'Laura's missing, damn it! Tell me! Or do you want her death on your hands?'

George glared at him.

'He's right,' Idalia told George. 'It's too late to keep it a secret. If you don't tell him, I will.'

'Let go of me!' George shouted, clenching his fists.

Mak obliged, scowling.

Smoothing his lapels, George muttered.

'My wife is — well, she's been acting a bit odd lately.'

'She took Laura and you know it!' Idalia cried. 'And she was on the unit when those other babies died.'

Mak was jolted. Carin Wittenburg?

'Where's your wife now?' he asked George.

'She's in the hospital somewhere. I hadn't even gotten out of here last night when the Code E call came. I went to the ER to help. Carin said she'd wait in my office on Three West.'

'She always does that when he's called to Harper Hills at night,' Idalia put in. 'She wears that damn pink volunteer jacket so nobody takes any notice of what she does 'cause they think she belongs here.'

'What the hell are you waiting for?' Mak demanded of George. 'Go find your wife!'

After glancing around dazedly, George headed for the elevator.

'Where's Helena?' Mak asked Idalia.

'I caught a glimpse of her opening the door to the fire stairs. Haven't seen her since.'

Mak's brows drew together. The fire stairs? Why the hell wouldn't she use the elevator?

The phone rang and Idalia answered it. 'It's Jeff,' she said.

'Mak?' Jeff said. 'Laura's not on the surgical units.'

'When did you last see Helena?'

'She walked to the elevator with me when I went up to — '

'You went up?'

'Yeah, the surgical — '

'Meet me in the lobby right away,' Mak said.

If Jeff took the elevator up, Mak reasoned as he hurried to the fire stairs, then Helena used the stairs to go down because she didn't want to wait for the elevator. Now the question was — where was she going? And why was she in such a hurry she hadn't stopped by the nurses' station to let him know what was up?

She remembered something, he told himself as he ran down the stairs. He tried to recall all she'd told him during the last few hours. There was the pharmacist's death and that crazy business with the snakes. She'd called Vada Rogers. What was it Vada had told her? The snakes, yes, but Vada had said something more.

He dashed into the lobby just as the elevator doors opened. Jeff hurried toward him.

'Icy coldness!' Mak exclaimed, remembering. 'What the hell does that suggest to you? Here in the hospital, I mean.'

Jeff stared at him. 'Refrigeration.'

'Where?'

'The kitchen, I suppose. And the morgue.'

Mak went rigid with fear, thinking of what might have happened to Helena. 'The morgue's in the basement, right?'

Jeff nodded, his eyes widening as he caught on. Rather than waiting for the elevator, Mak grabbcd Jeff's arm and shoved him toward the fire stairs. They plunged downward and burst through the door into the basement corridor. There were two people straight ahead.

'I found her, I tell you!' a woman's voice cried shrilly. 'Why should I give her to you?'

Seeing the pink coat, Mak knew it must be Carin. He pounded up to them just as George wrenched Laura from his wife's arms.

Mak grabbed Carin by the shoulders. 'Where's Helena?'

Her smile chilled him. 'Beyond your reach,' she told him. 'Beyond anyone's reach, forever and ever. Amen.'

'Carin!' George's voice was anguished.

'Let me take Laura,' Jeff said. George blinked at him, then handed the child over without comment.

'Laura's alive,' Jeff said.

Mak was glad to hear it but it didn't get them any closer to finding Helena. He shook Carin. 'Damn it, you're going to tell me where she is.'

Carin began to laugh, high and shrill. Mak had heard that kind of mindless laughter before and let go of her, knowing his attempts were useless. He ran down the corridor toward the morgue, his guts in a knot, terrified of what he might find when he got there.

She can't be dead, he told himself. Not Helena. Not the only woman I'll ever love.

He pushed through the morgue door, sped through the office, and halted abruptly. Helena lay sprawled at his feet, unmoving, blood smeared on her white coat. He dropped to his knees, hardly noticing as sharp plastic fragments stabbed through the cloth of his pants. Was she breathing? He couldn't tell. With shaking hands he tried in vain to find a neck pulse.

'Jeff!' he shouted. 'Jeff!'

Moments later Jeff appeared, thrust Laura at Mak, and crouched beside Helena, feeling her neck. 'We need to get her to the ER, stat,' he said.

'She's alive?' Mak didn't breathe as he waited for an answer.

'Barely.' Jeff started to lift Helena.

'No!' Mak cried. 'I'll carry her. You take Laura.'

He cradled Helena in his arms, realizing how tiny and fragile she was. As he hurried along the corridor to the elevator, he whispered to her.

'Live, Helena. For me. For us. You're a tough lady, you can make it. I need you, oh, God how I need you. Don't leave me. Fight!'

Her eyes remained closed, her dark lashes emphasizing the paleness of her skin. Too pale, almost bloodless. He noticed the fingers of her right hand were blood-stained but there'd been no blood on the floor. If she was bleeding, it must be mostly internal.

It wasn't until he eased her onto an ER gurney that he realized the smears of blood on her coat formed letters.

'Jeff, look at this,' he ordered. 'Here's an 'R' and an 'E' and this looks like an 'S'. Res. What's it mean?'

Jeff shook his head. 'Nothing comes to me but I did see a broken syringe and a needle on the floor beside her.'

'That means Carin shot something into her. Think, man! Before she passed out, Helena scrawled this on her coat with her own blood. She wanted us to find it. R-E-S. She was trying to tell us what Carin jabbed her with. What could it be?'

'R-E-S,' Jeff repeated, frowning.

A sudden inspiration hit Mak. 'Snakes! Do the letters have anything to do with snakes? Or with the heart slowing?'

Jeff's brow smoothed. 'Reserpine! *Rauwolfia serpentina.*'

'Resperine's what Carin must have injected into Helena. Can you counteract it?'

'We'll damn well try. Now that we've got some idea what we're dealing with, she's got a chance.'

In the CCU, the cardiac care unit, Mak stood aside while Jeff and other doctors and nurses hooked Helena up to equipment to monitor her heart and blood pressure, a breathing machine to force oxygen into her lungs, and connected IV tubing to a vein in her arm. He watched and waited, refusing to leave or to let her out of his sight.

When they finished working over her and gave up arguing with him about leaving, he pulled up a stool and sat beside her, his fingers gently covering hers.

'I'm here,' he told her softly over the beeps of the machines. 'And I'll be here when you wake up. Because you're going to wake up.'

Later, Jeff came back to the CCU cubicle to tell him Laura was doing well — she hadn't been in the refrigerated vault long enough to cause any adverse effects. And there was no sign of her having been given reserpine.

'Helena must have gotten the dose intended for Laura,' Mak said.

'You're probably right. Though I don't think she got the full dose Carin intended — or she wouldn't be with us.'

Mak shuddered but all he said was, 'Make sure Laura has her stuffed alligator.'

⋆ ⋆ ⋆

Alligator. The word drifted into the darkness surrounding Helena. She didn't know what it meant, she didn't know where she was. Alligator. Green. With white teeth.

Someone whispered to her, a man's voice, soft and warm. She knew the voice, knew the man, but it was too much of an effort to think of his name. He was the one who'd told her she had to fight. To come back. Come back to him.

She didn't know how long she continued to float in the blackness, hearing words she recognized but that meant nothing. Drifting was easier than trying to think or to move but something worried her, pulling at the fringes of her awareness, something of vital importance she'd left undone. A name circled closer and closer, finally reaching her.

Laura.

Laura! Helena opened her eyes, frightened, struggling to rise.

'Take it easy, you're all right.' Mak's voice.

439

She tried to focus on him.

'Relax,' he said. 'Laura's all right, too. You saved her life.'

She tried to smile. Mak was with her — she was safe. And so was Laura. Her eyes closed again.

The next time she woke, her mind was clear but her memory was still fuzzy. She looked at Mak, sitting beside the bed. A hospital bed, with monitors, oxygen, IV's.

'Mak?' she asked. 'What happened to me?'

He told her and, as he spoke, she remembered with horror exactly what had brought her to this cardiac unit. Before she got around to asking more questions, Jeff entered and removed the IV, stopped the oxygen, and disconnected the monitors.

'We're transferring you to Laura's room on peds,' he said, grinning. 'CCD can't take any more of Mak.'

By evening she was sitting up in a chair eating the salad Mak had brought her. Laura, who'd been awake earlier, was sleeping.

'You owe me some answers,' Helena told Mak. 'What's happened to Carin?'

'She's in the psych unit. I talked to George earlier and he told me he never once suspected Carin was killing the babies. Idalia apparently had her suspicions but couldn't bring herself to believe Carin would actually commit murder.'

'I'm sure Carin's derangement is connected with the Wittenburg's retarded son, the one in Anaheim.'

Mak nodded. 'George put him there, out of her reach because she tried to drown the little boy in the bathtub in what George called 'a fit of depression'. He thought she'd gotten over it. Instead — ' Mak shrugged.

'Carin told me God wanted her to rid the world of defective children. I realize I got in her way and that's why she tried to kill me. But why Fran? And Reed? She must have killed them, too.'

'My guess is Fran saw her in the nursery the night that baby died. After Fran got fired, she must have finally confronted Carin, maybe even accusing her of the baby's death. We'll never know for sure. Carin's no longer rational. As for the pharmacist, he was an old friend of hers. She probably visited him often, picking up the rescrpine while she was there, without his knowledge. I suspect he eventually caught her at it and she killed him.'

'So my sister and Reed died because they threatened to expose her,' Helena went on with a grimace. 'It's no wonder the pathologist couldn't find what killed them and the babies when he did the posts.

Reserpine's absorbed quickly.'

'I should have caught on to Carin sooner,' he said.

'How? She seemed perfectly normal except for her refusal to admit she ever had a retarded son. I never once suspected she was the killer, even though I knew she insisted on coming to the hospital with George at night.' She sighed. 'Carin really does need psychiatric care. Permanently. How's George taking this?'

'He blames himself for not realizing how sick she was or what she was doing.'

'Men are often blind to what their wives are up to — especially if the man is having an affair on the side. But I do feel sorry for George. Who could have guessed about Carin?'

'Those who did guess didn't last long,' Mak pointed out. He smiled one-sidedly. 'You're the only survivor.'

'I wasn't sure I would be.'

'I was. Tough ladies never give up.'

'Hey, you told me I couldn't. I remember hearing you.'

He pushed the table aside and drew her to her feet. 'For once, at least, you listened to me,' he murmured, bending to kiss her.

Helena went home the next day and after a short hassle about who was going to live where, Mak moved into the apartment. They brought Laura home a week later, the day before Helena was due back at work.

'Don't worry about Laura,' Mak told her. 'She and I will get along just fine.'

'You can't possibly hang around the place day after day taking care of her,' Helena protested.

'Who said we were going to? Laura's well enough to ride in the car and sit on the beach. As she improves we'll have fun seeing the sights, the two of us.'

'But — your work?'

'I've solved this case — ' he paused and grinned at her — ' or rather, we did, you and I. And maybe Vada. I need a vacation before I start the next one. Laura trusts me — didn't she smile at me this morning? Didn't she call me Alligator? It'll work out. When she's completely recovered we'll look into finding the right kind of caretaker.'

Helena glanced at him. 'Good ones cost a fortune.'

'Laura's my responsibility, too. Do you think I'd let you bear the entire cost?'

'But — '

'Laura and I understand one another. She trusts me — it's like she's my own little girl. I don't care how dismal the prognosis is — the kid's better than I've ever seen her. More alert. When she looks at me, she really sees me. Who's to say the brain tumor didn't contribute to her autistic symptoms? Who's to say she won't eventually be a normal kid — or close to it?'

Helena, who'd noticed Laura's improvement but was afraid it was her own wishful thinking, threw her arms around him. 'How am I ever going to stand living with such a blatant optimist?'

'You ain't seen nothing yet,' he informed her, hugging her to him. 'Wait till you *really* get to know me.' He swung her around and deposited her on the couch.

She didn't know it yet, Mak reflected, grinning down at her, but she was going to be living with him for a long, long time. Forever, if he had his way. So he'd sworn never to marry again, so what? This was the woman for him — for all time.

They'd stay in El Doblez until she finished her year of peds residency at Harper Hills — he could handle his investigation business from here. He might even consider taking in a partner to make it easier.

After that he hoped she'd want to practice in the LA area so they could live in his house in Portuguese Bend but that was in the future. Whatever their mutual decision, they'd be together and where didn't really matter.

But he'd let all this, marriage included, kind of creep up on her

He sat next to her on the couch and put his arm around her, cuddling her next to him. With Laura napping in her bedroom and apt to wake at any moment, lovemaking would have to wait until tonight. Before Helena, he'd never realized how pleasurable it could be just to hold a woman. All the same, holding her did arouse him. He'd better bring up something controversial to distract him.

'I'm still not sure I should have let Garcia persuade me to keep my distance from the Silver Shrink,' he said, scowling.

'The lieutenant didn't want to run you in for assault and battery. Anyway, with the state medical society investigating Peter's link to Xenara, he'll wind up being barred from practicing in any hospital in the state and, since the Xenara scandal's getting nationwide publicity, will probably have his license revoked, too. Plus the strong possibility some of his disillusioned patients are likely to sue him. That's punishment of a sort.'

'Not enough.'

'He lost Quinn.'

Mak shook his head. 'That cold-blooded bastard lost Quinn a long time ago. I'd say about the time he drove his wife to kill herself. I wasn't taken in by the smarmy tale he made up for you — he wanted to rid himself of the woman and he deliberately set up her suicide scenario. Quinn sensed the truth — he admitted as much to us.'

Helena sighed. 'I hate to think you're right — but I do. Vada's well rid of him.'

After a moment Mak asked, 'What would you say to Vada helping to treat Laura?' He braced himself for Helena's reaction.

There was a long silence. 'I don't know,' she said finally. 'Jeff tells me Randy, the cancer patient from San Diego, has improved remarkably since Vada began her sessions with him.' She sighed. 'Poor George. He can't bear to believe Vada isn't dangerous. Jeff had to move Randy to the neuro service so Vada could continue.'

'I thought you'd blast my head off for even bringing up the subject,' Mak confessed.

'I may be stubborn but I'm not a fool. Vada's visions, or whatever they are, helped to save Laura's life. Now that she's divorced herself from Xenara, I might even come to trust her.'

'As well as admit there's something to this business of spiritual healing?'

She made a face. 'That's pushing it but I'll agree I've opened my mind a tiny bit. God only knows what weird stuff's going to leak in through that crack but I'll just have to put up with the inconvenience. How do you feel about it?'

Mak shrugged. 'One thing being a cop taught me — whatever works, give it a try. Vada's got something — why not take a chance? I think you'll agree she can't hurt Laura.'

'Let me think about it. I sure as hell don't want Vada around when I'm not.' She fixed him with a stern gaze.

'Jealous?'

'You bet.'

Mak laughed, pulled her closer and kissed her. 'Beautiful blond psychics aren't my type,' he murmured against her lips. 'I prefer stubborn, sexy brunettes. Especially if they're doctors.'

Who'd ever think I'd prefer this Abe Lincoln ex-cop to any other man in the world, Helena asked herself as she savored his kiss, reluctant to have it end. Though it was almost as good just to have him hold her.

She'd never expected to find such a wonderful lover. But Mak was so much more. He was her proof that not all men were as uncaring as her ex-husband, nor cold, conscienceless egotists like Peter. Knowing Mak had made her open her heart to love again. He'd persuaded her to open her mind as well — maybe even enough to listen to her

mother's ideas without automatically reject-
ing them.

She'd have to come to terms with what
she'd experienced herself — the dream vision
of snakes. Maybe it wasn't precognition; she
hoped not, but it wasn't beyond the realm of
possibility she'd inherited a few weird genes
from her mother. If so, she'd have to learn to
live with abilities she didn't want.

Helena smiled wryly. She might even have
to admit her mother wasn't as skewed as
she'd always thought, might be forced to ask
her help in understanding psi abilities. If so,
perhaps at long last they'd come to know
each other better.

'I never connected the two — Xenara and
babies dying at Harper Hills,' she said,
snuggling closer to Mak. 'Yet, in a way, they
were related — through Vada. I wonder what
might have happened if Peter Herron had
never corrupted Vada's ideals. Do you think
Vada might have helped heal Carin if Xenara
had never been built? And, of course, if
George hadn't been so unreasonable about
faith-healers.'

'Hey, listen to who's talking about
unreasonable.'

She nipped his ear lobe. 'I'm no more
unreasonable than a certain ex-cop I know.'

Although she didn't intend to spring it on

him immediately — it was better if he thought it was his idea — she planned to marry him. Why not? She'd never want anyone but Mak for as long as she lived.

Fran, she said silently, wherever you are, I'm sorry I couldn't save you. But, senseless though your death was, it brought Mak and me together. Good came from evil. Rest in peace.

Suddenly Helena breathed in the fragrance of honeysuckle. Startled, she pulled away from Mak and sat up, glancing around. There was nothing to see and when she sniffed, trying to find the scent again, it was gone.

It's a coincidence, she assured herself. No matter how well you aired the apartment, a bit of Fran's honeysuckle scent must have remained.

'What's wrong?' Mak asked.

About to say that nothing was wrong, she changed her mind. After the terrible events of the last week, she ought to have learned rationalization wasn't always the best or the right choice. It was time to be honest. Her sister wasn't completely gone — some fragment still remained.

'I just got a message from Fran,' Helena said, smiling at Mak though tears filled her eyes. 'Wherever she is, she wishes us well.'

We do hope that you have enjoyed reading this large print book.

Did you know that all of our titles are available for purchase?

We publish a wide range of high quality large print books including:
**Romances, Mysteries, Classics
General Fiction
Non Fiction and Westerns**

Special interest titles available in large print are:
**The Little Oxford Dictionary
Music Book
Song Book
Hymn Book
Service Book**

Also available from us courtesy of Oxford University Press:
**Young Readers' Dictionary
(large print edition)
Young Readers' Thesaurus
(large print edition)**

For further information or a free brochure, please contact us at:
**Ulverscroft Large Print Books Ltd.,
The Green, Bradgate Road, Anstey,
Leicester, LE7 7FU, England.
Tel:** (00 44) **0116 236 4325
Fax:** (00 44) **0116 234 0205**

This book may be returned to any Wiltshire
library. To renew this book phone your library
or visit the website: www.wiltshire.gov.uk

Wiltshire Council
Where everybody matters